Dark Coast Press

3645 Greenwood Ave N.
Seattle, WA 98103 U.S.A.
www.darkcoastpress.com
info@darkcoastpress.com

ISBN-13: 978-0985035501
Library of Congress Control Number (LCCN): 2012930507
First Edition

Cover and text design by Charles Brock, Faceout Studio
Original illustrations by Peter Reed
Edited by Jared W. Bowers and Jarret Middleton
Distributed by Ingram Publisher Services
Manufactured in the United States of America

LEAGUE of SOMEBODIES

SAMUEL SATTIN

DARK COAST PRESS

INDEPENDENT LITERARY HOUSE | SEATTLE, WASHINGTON

TABLE OF CONTENTS

PART ONE:

SAVAGE RISING

PART TWO:

ON ATOMIC BOMBS,
SOMEWHERE, WITHOUT REASON

P A R T   T H R E E :

SUBMISSIVE MEMORY

PART ONE

SAVAGE RISING

CHAPTER ONE

THE FIRST TRIAL OF MANHOOD

As a dying man, Lenard Sikophsky would often look back upon the night when he was a child, and his father, Fearghas Murdoch Sikophsky—the first generation of Scottish/Jewish/Polish (with a lower case 'p') émigrés pilgrimming into America by briny way of the Massachusetts coast—stuffed a sponge soaked with chloroform between his lips, wrapped a sash around his eyes, and got ready to introduce him to a concept he called manhood by way of a speeding train.

"Look up at me, boy," Lenard remembered his father saying, after permission to lift the blindfold was given. It was late December in 1967, around dinnertime, when the twelve-year-old found himself crouching on the train tracks below the bridge at West Fourth Street, just outside Dorchester.

"Look up at me."

His father stood, beard forked, above Lenard on the bridge platform's center. Below him, in stone relief, a porpoise-like creature begirded the bodies of four grinning cherubs holding swords. He walked over them in blasphemous bursts, slapping against the stone with his Old-World brogues, while his mohair suit, slithering with pinstripes, struggled to keep up the pace. His beard and muttonchops twinkled with silver. The purple dollop of his boyhood yarmulke bit into his head as if it were a small, angry animal, and he had a look in his eyes, something bacchanal, conveying to his son the simple, sinister phrase:

It is time.

"I thought I couldn't look up," said twelve-year-old Lenard, the words whimpering from his massive mouth. The enormous size of that mouth, and head that held it, earned him nicknames from children around his home of Milton, Massachusetts, like *queer globe* and *pregnant face.* "No matter what. Like you said back at home."

"I never said that," growled Fearghas.

"But I heard you."

"The words I say are not really words," he continued, scratching the fabric over his ass with vigor. "Remember that I, unlike you, am a daredevil of language. A regular Evel Knievel on the subject of tongues. You want to see *through* my syllables, earn the ability to understand the space in between them—soar over them on your own goddamn motorbike! But you can't just wake up into greatness, see? The history of such happenings is impossible."

Lenard, with a twitch at his left eye, nodded.

"It's like asking a horse why it's a horse," Fearghas carried on. "Urging me to recount what I previously said. Don't resign yourself to a life of constant puzzlement, Son. There are far better routes to embark upon. Like tonight, for example." He grinned. "Tonight is both the beginning and end of your once-stupid life. It is tonight that I will tell you: prepare to run, wee fucker." He bared his teeth. "It is tonight that I will tell you: prepare to fight."

Earlier Fearghas had forced Lenard to wear the blindfold while giving what he called an explanation for this mayhem. It began with the child's Bar Mitzvah lessons one-month prior at the tucked-away synagogue of Rodef Shalom. Rodef was a granite building, shaped like a nipple, that attendants believed unknown to the goyim. The presiding Rabbi was more than a century old, and when he spoke it was rumored that paint flaked from the doors of the Ark. The congregation was comprised of no more than fifty Old-Worlders—crestfallen Europeans and scholars from Algeria—and their chipper, American-born children, who had the tendency to sneak out of services to smoke pot.

It was at this tiny synagogue that Lenard began squeaking out his communally task mastered Haphtarah. It was also there that his father prepared his unusual destiny. Under the eyes of theologians with copper-rimmed spectacles, Lenard chiseled away at his people's text without a single inkling of his fate. He never remembered the names of the ones who watched over him, but remembered the way they smiled, like the vowel-less letters themselves. How sometimes, even if he'd thought he'd pronounced them well, they'd pinch him on the shoulder and scold, "Nu, do it again. These things you say 'ist mistake!" or "These America-boys—brain is rotten. Intellect for penny candy and Superman."

At the time, Lenard supposed they griped for his perfection, as well as for the perfection of every child of American soil, because his country would never resemble the land where they were born. How could he have anticipated anything else? He saw how they constantly kvetched of how nothing was as good here as it was at home. The citizens themselves, they'd say, were spoiled, and the neighborhoods, crowded; the American Dream, they'd say, was far too implausible, almost in the way of a myth. They never mentioned anything about the dark and scaly windmill of Lenard's future, and so never gave him reason to worry. Actually, the more they belayed him with their daily grumbles, the more the boy began to forget about his studies and feel sorry for them. It was easy to see that Rodef Shalom of Milton, Massachusetts, was not something they were used to. It was most certainly not Har Zion of Itchki, Poland (a wondrous shtetl of winding brooks, silver flowers, and traditional ideas) where Fearghas, many years ago, had been lined up for greatness by his father, Apollonius Sikophsky. On the fateful day of his own Bar Mitzvah, the feral youth had been ushered from the pews wearing a Tallis adorned with Yemenite gold. Approaching what was rumored to be the most important ceremony of a Jewish boy's life, rather than being mesmerized by *The Twilight Zone* or *Hogan's Heroes,* in the manner of his son, he learned of a sacred tome passed down through his family for generations. A book considered more sacred to the male Sikophskies than their very own people's Torah. In Lenard's twelfth year, while he studied away, thinking nothing of his life was any more extraordinary than it was for any child his age, he was secretly being prepared to assume a position of a most dangerous persuasion. For it was in his father's fathers' book that his life would take its stake. He wouldn't learn about the book until after tonight, until after he was stolen from his room and thrown in the back of his family's Cutlass and told to stay quiet until otherwise notified.

The Manful Exercises of Aesop Mac'Cool, it was called. Or, as it was deemed to those familiar: *The Manaton.*

"The rule tonight is you don't look up, unless I tell you to look up," Fearghas said now, glowering down at his son. "So, if I tell you to look up, then. . . ."

"I look up," Lenard completed tentatively.

From behind Fearghas's back came a cane, black as an oil stick, and he used it to murder the ground.

"Ready?" the Scotsman growled, baring a canine.

"Yes Sir," lied Lenard.

"Then look up."

"No, Sir."

"Why? What are you waiting for?"

"I'm scared, Sir."

"Why are you scared?"

"I've never seen you like this before."

Lenard watched his father smile. He wondered how he could do so, considering where they were. With the Scotsman looming on the bridge above him, there seemed to be no escape. Two concrete walls grown over with ivy rose above Lenard on his left and right side, and behind him, just like in front, tracks carried on with no end. Adolescent graffiti was scrawled amongst the vines, curse-words and drawings of body parts whose meaning he could not fathom, but about which, even under the circumstances, he still wanted to learn. Every few seconds he thought he felt something nipping at his shoes, but tried not to think about it. There was already enough to be frightened of as far as he was concerned.

"Come on, Son," his father said, sweetly and softly, as has been typical before tonight. "There's nothing to be afraid of.

Just meet me eye to eye, as men are meant to do."

Lenard chanced a gaze at his father. Slow and careful. His eyes were still sticky from the blindfold.

"Bad decision," Fearghas muttered, and from his fist a small kettle potato flew straight at Lenard's head.

"Idiot!" he yelled. "Never look in me eyes when you're on the tracks of life."

He might have gotten out all his words before the potato beamed Lenard on the left temple.

"*Ow*," he yelped–though it hadn't hurt that much at all, only left him confused at being assaulted with what usually became dinner.

"*Ow*," Fearghas sniggered, hands up in mock-alarm. "Halt your yapping. There'll be plenty of pain to deal with later in life, you hear? Plenty of ouches. You haven't seen nothing yet. No you haven't, *Bar Mitzvah boy*. Here's an idea for you—these tracks," his hand scoured over the entire expanse of railway. "Think of them like life, from beginning to end. And you never let your guard down on life's tracks. Do you?" He dipped his ear forward for a response. After hearing nothing from his son, who was still a bit stunned, he answered himself with, "No. Not for a second."

Lenard, just as clinically passive as he was terrified, said, "Sorry, I won't do it again, Dad." He'd never seen his father full of such animus before, and witnessing it felt surreal and, strangely, exciting.

"Damned right you won't," said Fearghas in response. "And don't ever say you're sorry. And don't call me Dad, either. Tonight, you will refer to me as Fearghas. *Fearghas*, hear?"

"Okay. Fearghas."

"I'm trying to protect you."

"Yes, Sir."

"I don't want They to stand a chance."

"Who's They?" asked Lenard.

"What?" asked Fearghas.

"What?" asked Lenard.

"I love you, boy." Fearghas made himself stand proudly. All the wild hair below his yarmulke yawned in a mane down his cheeks. "Oh," he mused, "I do. And it's for love and only love that I've brought you here tonight. Whatever happens, and though you might be angry, know you'll thank me for it all one day. When you pass it on to your own wee ones, and to their own wee ones after that. And to their own wee ones, the weeest, weeest of ones. And the weeest of the weeest of wee ones they end up having."

Fearghas had crouched closer to the ground with each and every enunciated "wee," and their eventual superlatives, which were spoken in a loud voice as he sat into a squat.

"You catch?" he asked, leaving Lenard to guess as to whether or not his father knew the appropriate way to use Scottish adjectives (or if anybody did, for that manner).

"Love," said Lenard. He said just that one word. Stated it. It got caught in his mouth for a second, but then simply fell out. He thought of how he would never have been able, in his wildest imagination, to throw any of his "weeest ones" onto the railway tracks outside of Dorchester, or any Chester for that matter, or to launch potatoes at them, all out of the desire to see them, well. . .what was it they were doing?

"Love," said Lenard again, as if it were a conclusion. Some argument he'd stopped with a gunshot. "Yes. I do understand that."

"I'm glad you do," said Fearghas. "For it is my biological responsibility as your father to drag you, screaming, into the hungry sea of enlightenment. Now, wee fucker." He wiped his hands, placed them on his cane, and wiggled his Hungarian-styled moustache. "Let's try this again. Look up at me."

"Nu-uh," said Lenard, as he tightened his fists. "Not this time. I learned my lesson."

Another potato whizzed out and struck him on the head.

"Always expect the unexpected when walking the tracks of life," laughed Fearghas. He shouldered up a green burlap sack filled with golden, red, and white spuds—one he wore sprightly in the manner of a purse. "Here, the approaching train isn't your only enemy. No." His eyes scooped the air. "Here, there are many other villains of whom you should keep constantly aware."

"Like flying potatoes?" asked Lenard, rubbing his head. He was impressed at his own first attempt at sarcasm, but couldn't ignore the meekness it accompanied.

"Yes, like potatoes." Fearghas paused. He postured one of his fingers against his chin in demonstration of how easy it was for a male Sikophsky to actively, if not visually, become stupider. "Or, as I like to put it, in more adult terms: distractions. Distractions, with a capital 'D.' Like They, for example, that's a distraction. Or women. . .oh yes." He paused. "And what sorcery flows from *their* vulvas."

"What's a vulva?" asked Lenard, for some reason visualizing a whale-like creature in his mind.

"Quiet, sparrow droppings," yelled Fearghas, raising his cane.

"Sorry."

"Prepare yourself!"

A bell tolled in the distance and Lenard stayed silent, touching at his product-hardened hair. He looked so out of place upon the tracks. He'd become well known around town for the naivety he demonstrated towards American fashion as it warp-sped through time. For him, the word "clueless" would have been an insult to the entire body of human decorum. As a way to bond with his father and the obsession the man had with Rudolph Valentino, Lenard sloped back his hair back with globs of pomade, making him easily spotted from land, air, or sea like a dollop of mobile tar. His clothes were too big. His shoes were too small, and he moved in the manner of a hiccup.

"Prepare yourself," Fearghas screamed again. "Your world is already at its end!"

Lenard felt the ground rumble. He heard the windbag of his father's voice inflate into the fog. Though he couldn't see it, he knew the train was somewhere in the distance. He didn't want to face it yet, but knew eventually he would have to. The redbrick walls were high and narrow. Yards before him a stream of smoke hissed out a manhole below a grate.

"Wee fucker," commanded Fearghas, glowering down from the bridge. "Listen to me good. This is only the beginning of your many endeavors to come. Only the start. So now, on this night two months before your Bar Mitzvah, you must be strong, fast, and outrun the train. Tonight's overarching theme: life always gives you a way out. Understand? Cause if you don't," he said, as if he hadn't realized the following fact himself, tongue against his cheek, "You'll get your gut box ripped out."

Lenard took a deep breath. He thought squeamishly about his only (difficult to imagine) "gut box," and turned around. Even as he wondered if this entire scheme had been concocted in spite of something he'd done wrong during his studies, if he was being punished for singing off pitch, or not being enthusiastic enough about his Torah portion. He would do this for his father, just this once.

"Prepare yourself!" Fearghas yelled again. He brought Lenard into the present by drumming his cane against the ground. "Prepare yourself for the test of a lifetime. There's no turning back now. The train approaches."

"I don't see any train, Sir," said Lenard, watching the lightless tracks carry on into the distance.

"But you feel it?" Fearghas smiled.

It was true, Lenard did feel it. He'd felt it since he set foot on the rail.

Fearghas licked his lips and looked down the ends of the tracks where, finally, a tiny light appeared. "Fear is what makes us unlock the impossible," he said, as it extended its range. "Can't you see? *You,* boy, are going to live an extraordinary life. And you must not allow fear to suppress your future. Look into the distance. Prepare to fight. Make those eeny weeny testes of yours beat for survival in the face of your zeitgeist—or, what I like to call. . .your *Kraken!*"

Kraken. Just saying that name, slurring it from thick, sloppy lips, set a dark bedtime story into motion.

"Dad," Lenard pleaded, looking over his shoulder. "I'm scared."

"Scared?" said Fearghas, crossing his arms and laughing. "Consider yourself lucky you're scared. There'd be no civilization without fear."

"No civilization without fear?"

"No fear without the breath of life."

"No fear without the breath of life?"

"The crap in our pants is what guides us."

"The crap in our pants is what guides—"

"Shut it, boy, and watch for the train."

Fearghas had chosen *20,000 Leagues Under the Sea,* Jules Verne's epic of underwater adventure, to read to the boy every night, over and over, in order to secretly spark, as his own father had failed to spark in him, a potential for heroism and greatness. Though cruel, whatever Fearghas did to Lenard he believed was done in the name of an ancestral duty the boy couldn't possibly have known about. The fact that fear was necessary to encourage strength was a terrifying prospect, but something Fearghas believed this special, chosen child would have to learn. He often embellished on the novel itself, making the beast's tentacles blacker, slimier, more resilient to defeat. After years of inundation, the Kraken was set so deep into Lenard's psyche that he would never escape his fear of it, no matter how old or wise he became, for the two of them, human and beast, had formed an inky, cellular relationship. When he was a child, the mighty squid, in one fell swoop, conquered the proscenium of his dreams. Lenard was defeated before he was strong enough to fight, and so defeated for the rest of his life. Such thrashings nurtured violent existences in heroes introduced to their nightmares early. Noble, maybe, but nonetheless violent. Something Fearghas acknowledged with glee.

"Look to the yonder," the Scotsman screamed, arms wiggling like the Kraken's tentacles themselves. "It approaches."

Lenard did look yonder now, not that yonder, for the train was closer than yonder, and gaining quickly. A storm was coming with it. Clouds swelled in the sky. A bit of thunder boomed in the distance.

"Run," screamed Fearghas. His eyes were spotted and round like quail eggs as he stomped one brogue against the ground. The brass buckle that overlay the heel went *click, click, click*, and lightning dissevered the clouds. "Run, you wee, daffy fucker. Run for your stupid wee, daffy fucking life!"

Lenard froze. He looked at the train as it phantomed forward in a rage of light. It was mesmerizing. It looked alive. The wheels barked. The front grill, shoveling downwards, seemed capable of unearthing steel.

Lenard wiped the sweat from his eyes and noticed his father above him. He laughed as if he was crying. "Fly from the cold 'fuck you' of fear!"

Skreeeee, came the voice of the train, and Lenard began to run from it as fast as he could. He ran somewhere straight ahead where there seemed to be nowhere. Away from whatever this crazy test of jungle manhood had become. His feet knocked up pebbles as he thumped across the rails. He noticed a small gap in the wall beside an empty oil drum.

"There you go, Son," screamed Fearghas, his voice barely etching over the roar of the train. "Now you get it. You run or you die. You escape or you die! Can you hear the Almighty, now? Can you hear him when he speaks?"

Fearghas was throwing his tiny potatoes. They rained down in a bizarre, tuberosum meleé. One struck Lenard on the shoulder, but he didn't care. When the next one came, he swerved from it. *Skreeeeeshhhhhhhtp,* he heard, and, with a leap that took his shoe, slung himself inside the gap in the wall, barely big enough for his body. His shoulders smacked the concrete and his eyes saw color. Half his body fell to the rails. The hell he'd endured in getting to this point, gone. The hours he'd sat blind and hungry, listening to words about destiny, duty, a mysterious entity called They; whatever happened to have micturated from his father's mouth, evaporated.

"Do you accept?" Fearghas had asked him, before removing the blindfold and guiding his shoulders atop the tracks. "Or," he smiled, "do you sip at the teat of mediocrity, like the rest of this abominable planet?"

Now, as Lenard's face was scrunched half-conscious against the concrete, pressing out his left cheek for air, he wished he'd changed his answer.

The wind blew at his back.

Just the sound of it was cold.

He thought he heard something like, "All right, Son," though distant.

"All right, Son, time to go home. But don't think you've won half this war."

Lenard was astonished at the clarity of his father's voice and, for a moment, forgot where he was. He couldn't hear the train anymore. Maybe a patter of rain.

Then, Fearghas finally screamed. "Come! Boy! Home! Now!" Which Lenard heard pristinely. "It's time for dinner."

As he found his footing he emerged onto the tracks. The train, which he now realized was only the front locomotive, remained still. He walked towards it with fingers outstretched, waiting, with increasing self-doubt, for the point when he'd fall through the light from a trick mirror and fumble to his face. But no, it was real. Real and grim as an occupied coffin.

"You've done a good job." Fearghas wiped his brow and fastened on two leather gloves far up his wrists. "Not a great job. But a good job. It's time to go home."

"What are you talking about?" yelled Lenard, exasperated. He looked around at the night, his father, as if they'd become trick mirrors too. "*What?* What job did I do?

"Don't raise your voice, boy. You sound a fool."

From within the train's cabin window suddenly protruded the body of a shocked-looking man in what seemed like his fifties, no, his eighties (his hundreds?), wearing once-white pajamas turned orange. In the crook above his left cheek, he had a bulging eye that was obviously made of glass, and as he took off his hat, a wheel of fluffy hair wiped out towards the sky.

"Thank you, Argyll," said Fearghas, waving one hand without turning to address the man. He adjusted the collar of his mohair jacket and began marching towards a set of spiral stairs.

"No problem at all, Fergie." Argyll saluted Lenard's father with his glass eye cocked out. Nearly all of his teeth had turned brown. "I'll see you down at the Men's Club."

"I still don't see what the hell's going on," said Lenard. His arms were limp at his sides. His face was limp, too, dripping with sweat as he questioned whether he knew his father at all. This man who stole trains, or had others do so for him. This man who used to make pancakes on the weekends, or sing the *Highland Fairy Lullaby* to help his son fall asleep.

"Don't you dare use that language with me," yelled Fearghas now, spinning on his heels. "Or I'll scour your mouth with painting oil."

"Sorry," squeaked Lenard. He hadn't even known he'd cursed. The shock of facing death, or the shock of not facing death but thinking he had, scrambled his mind. Something he wondered if his father had noticed. "I just can't believe. . .the train. It was never going to hit me?"

"Well, of course it wasn't going to hit you," said Fearghas, seeming in genuine shock as he tapped down the stairs. "Do you think I'm a G*u*d damned sociopath?"

Lenard shook his head at his father's *u* substitute, making God sound more like *goot* when naming their people's chosen deity. His legs shook as well, though he didn't stop to realize it. He thought, for a quick moment he probably wouldn't remember years from now, that maybe, as the Scotsman had claimed, he truly wasn't a sociopath. That maybe, upon sparing Lenard actual pain, he'd been trying to teach him a lesson. Something to hope for on this dreary Boston night that came, of all places, from the unscrubbed depths of Fearghas Murdoch Sikophsky's sphinx-like heart.

Though at the moment, such sentiments seemed laughable.

"Now, pick up those potatoes and bring them back for dinner, or your mother will have my hide. And Argyll," Fearghas commanded his co-hort as he set foot on the tracks. "Make sure and return that train to the museum before midnight! Hear?"

"Yep, Fergie." The chalk-haired man made an effortful little bow. He jittered with something in his pockets. As he got up for a moment to search the train's cab, Lenard noticed that he wasn't wearing pants. "Sure do."

Lenard received a needed cooling as the rain continued to fall. His eyes centered on the dying train before him, the itinerant-looking man inside its iron cabin who smiled and waved one hand. His father was pushing ahead of the scene towards a door he hadn't noticed in the tunnel.

As Lenard watched the storm puddle below his feet, an impulse to cry fell upon him. Lenard Sikophsky didn't cry, though. No. He didn't. Because brave boys didn't cry. Weak boys cried. Weak boys were injured. But brave boys, they just kept on running, and fighting, and Lenard was a brave boy. Or at least he thought he was—something, in retrospect, that probably kept him sane, especially after his father revealed that he'd been sneaking what could be considered poison into his food to alter his mortal constitution.

A hand fell over Lenard's shoulder. It was the very same hand that, moments ago, had been throwing potatoes; but this time, it squeezed him tenderly.

"Come on, my little hero," Fearghas said. They heard the warning bell announcing another train. The Scotsman's voice had suddenly changed, laced with a sweetness Lenard was used to. "You've done well for today. Very well."

Lenard looked up at him, less afraid now, and nodded, pretending he'd expected those words. He held the potatoes tight in his half-soaked shirt. A smile shadowed through Fearghas's silver beard and the great hawk-ish eyes looked down.

"Why don't you give me a couple of those potatoes, now," he said, picking them from Lenard's shirt and stuffing them back in the sack. The small boy's stomach filled with a love so lurid, so damn sharp, he thought it would cut through his kidneys.

"Your mother." Fearghas smiled with all his rotting teeth. "She's making a mighty fine stew."

CHAPTER TWO

THE MANATON

"You've been working very hard lately," Fearghas said.

Only two weeks after his son's first test, he moseyed into Lenard's room and was stunned by what childhood still happened to remain under his watch. It made him wistful. Reverent. A near-forgotten modesty pushed his hands behind his back as if automatically. As rainwater dribbled down the shingles above the window, he imagined the time when his son's youth would fade, and as he did so, a nostalgic little smile spread across his face. He admired an abused-looking beanbag they'd filched from the dump that had been sprayed with at least three rounds of buckshot, and the row of action figures on the windowsill behind it, arranged to look militant and fierce.

"Interesting," he growled, hiking up his pants by their belt-loops before coming in for a closer look. "This culture of youth. Surrounding itself with images of strength while real muscles stay scrawny and useless."

The Scotsman had just cleaned himself and his body smelled of the same bar of soap they all used. A sticky brick by the name of Remus. It came from a package that looked like cornhusk, and smelled of old man's shoe polish mixed with some sort of embalming fluid. Inhaling it made Lenard feel nauseous so he often avoided the bath. He wasn't worried about salvaging his social status, anyway, which had been torpedoed long ago.

"When I was growing up," Fearghas said, pinching the mobile plastic arm of a stiff-jawed American soldier. "I had a wooden horse for a toy, and all I could do was look at it." He sighed and let go. "Those were different times."

Lenard, eyes bleary from studying Torah, now fiddled with the spokes of a model '58 Bonneville he'd been given from a boy who'd felt sorry for him at school. He cuddled a tube of superglue, squinting before his desk-lamp. In his room, Lenard was always hard at work on maintaining what someone else, most anyone else, would have considered trash.

"What are you up to in here, huh?" Fearghas asked, stooping down to the Bonneville to examine it. Lenard's lips trembled as he did so. Having so little of actual value, he was afraid to snap off even the tiniest bit of plastic. He'd portioned all the pieces side by side over yesterday's newspaper, its headline reading: *The Boston Strangler Sentenced to Life.*

"Shameful hobby to have. . .this model-building," dismissed Fearghas. "Recreation of the real. Hopefully not taking the place of your studies?"

"No," Lenard lied. "No. It hasn't been."

Fearghas smiled, forgot what he'd been saying, as was wont to happen, and stretched his arms to the ceiling.

"It's getting late, my boy." He yawned. "Time for sleep."

"Dad?" Lenard asked, as he climbed over his covers. He was already dressed in his yellow flannel pajamas. He had a fizzling aftertaste in his mouth from dinner that, though he didn't know it then, was not the result of his mother's cooking, but of something sinister and brilliant his father had been sneaking into his food since he was barely six years old. "Why must we listen to the words of Aesop Mac'Cool? Sometimes. . .I think. . .Well? The kids at school don't even know about *The Manaton.*"

"And you don't enlighten them?" Fearghas asked in a way that wasn't quite a question.

"No, Sir, I don't."

"That's good, Son. Keep it up."

"But why must we—"

Fearghas goaded Lenard into bed and shuffled the covers up to his Adam's apple. The boy put his cheek to a pillow that had butter-colored moons sewn on both sides, and took a deep breath. It smelled musty.

"Our family, we are. . .special," Fearghas said, twirling his moustache. "At least we men are. Years ago, you see, Aesop Mac'Cool discovered a way of living that would protect us. A way of living that, when handled correctly, unveiled a method of achieving societal success and *divine* fulfillment. A way to improve upon our bitter world and, dare I say, help it survive."

He raised his hands slowly to the ceiling as if introducing the first act of a circus, but instead highlighted the rundown roof beams of their home.

"Now, there is nothing in *The Manaton* that can't be found in the world around us," Fearghas continued. "Like most great works of philosophy, it's. . .an entryway into clarity. And it's our responsibility that entryway doesn't fall into the wrong hands, as it has in the past. Maybe we can look at Chapter One to illustrate my point?"

"Awww, do we have to?" asked Lenard. Youth, for him, felt like endless catchecism, never standing free of his pupil's desk.

"It outlines our kind's central beliefs."

"Our kind? Like Jews?"

Fearghas laughed, low and sad as he often did, and shook his mighty head.

"Are we ready to begin?"

Lenard nodded, noticing how far away he was from his drying wheel and axle, and knowing that he'd probably have to put glue on them yet again, and wait. Wait for solidity, as he often waited for in himself, even as a child, a wild thing.

Fearghas reached in his vest pocket. The book that came out was about the size of a Siddur from their synagogue. He drifted his fingertips over the scaled leather binding, the letters, Cyrillic gold and purple and blue and even deeper blue. The A on Aesop had begun to chip away towards the top. But that was okay.

The point had most certainly been made.

Chapter 1

THE GREAT CHAIN OF BEING ACCORDING TO THE GLORIUS MAN-PONDERINGS OF

Aesop Mac'Cool

Or, *as it has been previously referred:*

MANOVOLOPOLIS

I, am Man.

Man. Morphus. Manicus. Phallus. Testes. Prostate.

MAN.

I am Man.

My other name is Aesop, only a mask. For the purpose of this text, Aesop Mac'Cool. And this, good reader, is The Manaton, of which you are only half-welcome.

The word Man, itself, comes from Mannaz, or Man-Person, or arguably, in Old Norse, maor, but more efficaciously, Man refers to phallus, testes, hair, the need, and the right, to conquer.

The word Manaton is a combination of Mannaz and Mastadon. Or Mannaz and Decammeron. Amongst others.

My real name, however, you will never know, and God damn you, and your offspring, for asking.

But with my wisdom, and the wisdom of my colleague, the fine gentleman I know as Beamish, we shall proceed. For we are the gracious ones. Here to serve. Please, light your pipe, and enjoy.

By either manifestation of the flesh, Adam will remain the subject of my Manbook's symphony. Not the creature called woman. No, here, and only here, within these pages, we are Man. Cheer now:

Maningdom. Manaticus. Manu.

Now please, light your pipe, lay back, enjoy, unless you are a woman, in which you should light yourself on fire, offer yourself to wild beasts, or the dregs of some vicious ravine. This is a Man's book. A work of great testicle. No others may pass without permission.

"Dad?" said Lenard, turning from the book, and his father's bassy voice as he thundered line by line. "I'm getting sleepy. And this is the fourth time we've read this since Tuesday. Is there any way we can start again to-morrow?"

"Tomorrow," said Fearghas, tongue sizzling from the text. "Is the solicitous whore of today. And I, wee fucker, don't run a brothel."

Lenard rubbed his eyes, hoping that when he stopped his father would be gone.

When he wasn't, he murmured, "Okay," smelling whiskey some-where in the air.

"*Echem*," his father began:

The heavenly orbs were not created by God, but Man, as you may not necessarily know. However, due to Didacus Valedes, a Franciscan Minister in the 16th century, and his platforms of spiritual descent, beginning with the divine right of kings, we have been blinded by ignorance. This philosopher Didacus believed that there was an order, a set way, underlying God and his angels, with the creator above, on the top rung, and man right below him, followed by the flora and fauna of all sorts and series. This model of society, we have learned to accept.

I wish, however, to defecate upon these outdated ideologies. No, let us not be so harsh. I wish to shite only lightly upon The Great Chain of Being, its philosophies and theories, by exercising the sublime nature of my own mighty man parts. Cheer now:

Manuptus. Manarar. Mantasm. Manilite. Manascus. Manighteous. Manu.

Now consider, if I am to explain the true, and secret, order of the universe, than it must be inhabited by a specific type of Man. The creature I speak of in this chapter, to be sure, is The Savage that once existed in Eden. The Savage is what culled humanity from primordial stew, and withheld, or protected it, from the ennui our aristocrats have lived out in Europe.

———————————————

"The Savage?" asked Lenard, sitting up a little in the bedsheets. For his short lifespan, he'd been interested in the history of man, and the words captured his drifting cotton tuft of attention.

"None other than the purest of pure," said Fearghas. "A man deemed primitive by nothing other than truly primitive minds. Manascus. Maniscus. Manu."

"Minascus," repeated Lenard.

"Manascus," corrected Fearghas.

"Manascus."

"Feel the power."

"Maniscus.

"Manascus."

"Manu."

In the forests of The New World, the plains of the Yucatan, I have glimpsed this man called Savage, glimpsed him tear about the undergrowth while he flees the hand of what, I still call, New Spain. He makes fire, or whips it into being. He flints tools, lances spears, defecates under the sky and its clouds and, above all, reigns supreme over the kingdom God has given him. This man is a tool of the orbs, an original Adam. He is nobler than most, and, disregarding modern civilization, ignores the allure of overpopulated cities. We should, therefore, look to the Savage for knowledge of Man's first people. We should look to him as an old spider to our historical web.

Now this part's important," Fearghas said, finger slipping under the next page, just to lift it a little. "For life is a bastard," he growled, "that makes no discernment of where he squats."

On this page (Fig 18), we have a model of our European tradition's Great Chain of Being according to Didacus Valedes:

(Fig. 18)

Now, as it would be ignorant of me, as Man, not to credit Didacus with the discovery of a basic form of Heavenly government,
one that baptized early Man's divine right of rule, applying it to
Sir Thomas Aquinas's philosophical researches, lions at the center
of the animal kingdom, females as the conduits for our progeny,
and so forth, it would also be worthwhile discussing The Savage,
this 'Purest' Man, and the way in which his very existence recre-
ates this order, for the purpose of my argument.

On the next page (Fig. 19), I have remonstrated my point by
a careful self-redrawing of the celestial strata. A new hierarchy,
influenced by my own glorious Man-ponderings.

Cheer now:

MANTUS. MANIPUS. MANU.

(Fig. 19)

MAN

LIONS

SEA MONSTERS

GOD

EVERYTHING ELSE

"Now, Son?" asked Fearghas, closing the book and dropping it back in his pocket. There was an uncharacteristic hum of patience in his voice. "How did that make you feel?"

"Confused," responded Lenard quickly, sitting up in bed and attempting to focus all his hate upon the pages, and not his father, as he might have been inclined to do. He'd never felt so frustrated, so intimidated by *The Manaton*, as he had tonight. Perhaps it had something to do with his recent run from the train, or perhaps it was something far scarier. For recently he'd noticed that, in contrast to the rest of his rapidly burgeoning body, his legs seemed to have slowed their growth. Every day the condition worsened, becoming more and more noticeable. It was as if his maturity had gotten caught in a tug-o-war that he was already well on the way to losing. If his father had plans for his future, then he was blind to them; being lambasted at all angles by theories and tasks he had no true way of firmly grasping.

"Aesop Mac'Cool is harder than Hebrew," he said, rubbing his tiny thighs beneath the sheets. He could almost wrap his hands around the lower half close to the knees.

"That may be true," said Fearghas, looking out the window into the moonlight.

"I remember the first time my father read to me from these pages. Yes. Your grandfather. Before he was. . . . " Fearghas widened his nostrils as if to sneeze. "I was barely your age. Young and God-ugly. He read me this chapter whenever I was allowed a break from my Torah portion. He read to me by lantern light while the winter storms in Edinburgh hammered down on our cottage's roof on Lochend Road. Shortly before my Bar Mitzvah. Shortly before puberty. Shortly before he stole my dear pet turtle, Francis, and shipped him off to be held for ransom in the Philippines." After he said this, they both went silent for a moment.

"The Philippines?" asked Lenard. The tropical country, for him, was as tangible as Teotihuacán, but it took his focus away from his maladjusted legs, which usually consumed his thoughts before sleep.

"It's a long story," said Fearghas, shaking his head. "Just know that

I, too, found *The Manaton* to be a struggle when I was young. I didn't want to study. No! I wanted to run the streets of my father's city of foreigners, my city, under the cold stone of Edinburgh castle on the hill, down the smoky paths leading to the Forth Bridge, past the new synagogue we'd begun to attend, B'nai Israel, where the other shiftless Polish boys and that strange, dark-eyed ruffian from Algiers—the one with the diseased cat he called Broccoli—gambled for marbles in the street. Even if there was a war on. Even if we were scrounging for fallen shrapnel in exchange for chocolate." He sighed in reminiscence, chin to the ground. "Instead of enjoying all that simple thrill, I studied. I remained in the city, in the house, trapped as my father's prodigal student, a constant servant to the book, against government's recommendation that we kids be evacuated to the country after what happened in London. I sacrificed everything, Lenard. I risked my life. Just as my father did for me."

"For *The Manaton*?" Lenard asked, crawling back under his covers and staring past his father at the ceiling. "That's what you sacrificed everything for?"

He visualized, in the empty white space, a place to escape to, but instead, in every world he entered and left, there were speeding trains to run from, nightmares chasing his pajama-lidded bottom, nipping at his ankles and knees. Then, he suppressed a violent sort of glee and, oddly, worried about letting his father down. About not being able to prove that he could, in fact, become a man like this legendary Aesop Mac'Cool. Even if he didn't know why, or how, a creature such as he could have existed, as his mind became quiet, and true fatigue settled in, he found that there was some kind of nobility in the battling of one's fear. But maybe he felt that because he was settling into sleep, the time when fears could become their worst.

"That's what I thought at the time," Fearghas said, patting down the blanket around his son's waist, comforting him. He bent down to kiss his forehead. "But no. Not for *The Manaton*. For something greater than that."

"Something greater?" asked Lenard. His eyes were already lids.

Dreams were on their way. Demons to conquer. Angels to alight. "What could be greater than Aesop Mac'Cool?"

Fearghas pointed to his son's nose, right between the nostrils, and pressed down until his finger left a small, doughy crater.

"So They won't even stand a chance," he smiled, before taking that finger to the light.

CHAPTER THREE

COSMONAUTS

In high school, in the same year Apollo 11 came to berth in the Pacific, when boys and girls first dreamed of becoming rocketeers of Western discovery, of steering space bound shuttles over dust glaciers braided by hydrogen and plasma, Lenard, save for the world of the dead, stood closer to the Earth's surface than anyone he knew. He had a long torso that didn't align with his legs. They were, quite tragically, the most Martian things about him. Covered with thin deposits of fur on the muscle less sides of his calves, his adolescent body had tried to fight against atrophy by forcing his feet to turn pigeon-toed. Nothing had changed in Lenard's disposition since he was a child. If anything, it had grown worse. Neil Armstrong may have shook his head in pity upon glimpsing his state, while Collins and Aldrin, in their journey home, would have turned tail and returned to orbit. For Lenard didn't walk, he bobbed, a goose stacked with some Mastodon's chest, something misplaced from the Pliocene, it seemed, as he studied the cover of *Weird Tales of the Macabre*. Since his hands often cramped, most books and magazines he read by pinioning them between his heroically beefy biceps. He liked to flex them sometimes, and smile while he did so. They were the only things that made him feel normal.

Normal. This was a word Lenard thought about often. Normal was something everybody searched for, but some found easier than others. It was a lie the whole world tried to hide behind. Strange, however; strange was a staple. Everybody understood strange, and went through limitless measures to disguise it. Thus, even while the adolescent was clearly strong, his strength was more of a deterrent to his social life than a grace. His appearance seemed to scare off even the most tyrannical school bullies. A surprise, since most Jewish kids—perplexingly small, allergenic, and often reclusive—got pushed down on the playground and called Christ-killer by Irish toughs wielding their motherland's stamina. Scaring off bullies, however, would have been for fine for Lenard, if he didn't also seem to scare off everyone else. He felt like the carnival that rolled through Milton and set up shop annually. The attraction best observed from yards away.

Along with losing the hope of becoming what people called normal, as if to add his many devolutions, he'd become less tolerant of food. Unlike the past, and due to circumstances he'd soon become aware of, every morsel to meet his tongue reeked of such acidity he wondered if his mother was cooking up rocket fuel in the kitchen. He'd learned to dread dinner, and often avoided eating. Under his father's eyes, however, he was forced to consume at least four full-sized meals every day, and only at home.

Never out.

One morning he saw Fearghas receive a package from Argyll at the front door. He'd meant to be studying, but stood at the scuffed banister landing, peeking through the fluted rails. Lenard winced as his father stole away the package into the cellar. He caught the imprint on the box's side, however, before he disappeared down into that eerie, padlocked damp.

After the Bar Mitzvah four years ago (which he had succeeded in completing but quickly repressed) the emerging adolescent found that his entire body was rebelling against him. He began to feel literally squeezed of energy, than occasionally overcome with bouts of sexual ambition that were nearly impossible to fulfill. He'd discovered soft pornography, was driven wild by the allure of flesh-toned swimsuits. Girls, however, avoided him with purpose and sometimes were even known to scream. As a by-product of the failed shuttle launch he'd learned to call adolescence, Lenard found himself considering that not sex, not sex at all, but a long road of crippled, earth-bound masturbation might have been the only pleasure left in store. In his dreams he tried to escape his fate. He inhabited an altogether separate reality, where he was not himself, not even human, but a creature of pure intellect, who could materialize itself in backstreets and corridors, on top of Himalayan peaks or amongst the stars of Andromeda; thus were the yearnings of poor, tired children, withheld from the luxury of being young.

Lenard's pediatrician, Dean Fezzeliski, still claimed confusion as to why his patient's body was so abnormal from the waist down. He'd been saying so since his thirteenth birthday.

"It's like he's growing in some places, but in others, he's just not. For example," the doctor said one Saturday morning, as he chewed a cigar. The Macanudo in his lips—seemingly the same one he'd been smoking since the fifties when that sort of behavior at work was acceptable—made him sound tougher than he was. It was stubbed out, but its damp tobacco smell still rotted in the room's every corner, which, as far as rooms go, was small and organized as a doctor's should have been. "His biceps are like carburetors. His neck, an ox's yoke. His hands, absolutely mammoth. But his legs. . . ." The doctor ran his palm down the bonsai limb that was Lenard's right thigh and calf. The flesh was pygmied, as if he was a child who'd grown into adolescence only from the waist up.

"Abominated."

"And what about his member?" asked Fearghas, dressed in surgical greens. He looked worried as he stood behind the doctor—for him, a fairly unusual emotion. A paper-shower cap held up a few fat segments of his hair, yarmulke, and overgrown sideburn. He seemed as if he hadn't slept in weeks.

"Dad, please?" pleaded Lenard, embarrassed as he lay, face down, on the examination table, surrounded by clown-themed wallpaper. He was naked from the waist down below a heavy cotton sheet as the doctor examined him with a flashlight. Though he thought the doctor would have been horrified at that question, the drab-cheeked bald man asked Lenard politely to turn over, so he could answer Fearghas's question with certainty. His eyes grew large, and then frightened, as he stared down. Lenard seethed at the fact that his father had brought up his "member" to begin with, and felt like saying, "examine your own."

"It's doing. . .just fine," Fezzeliski said, clicking the flashlight off and lowering the sheet. He turned towards Fearghas and looked at him in disbelief—as most people did, and for different reasons. "More than fine. Huge. Frightfully huge. It's as if all the growth from his legs culminated in his," he nodded, fingers on his chin, deciding whether or not to open up his mouth. "Organ. Which is preposterous."

"As expected," said Fearghas, a response both Lenard and the doctor were confused by, but allowed to pass.

The Scotsman crossed his arms to hide some sort of secret relief that he was betraying naturally with a smirk. His paper hospital cap only blurred the purple vengeance of his yarmulke. Standing beside his son normally, he would probably be just as tall, even with Lenard's legs; he was definitely the type of small man that, when he wished, could seem very large.

He lifted up his right foot and slipper to scratch his left knee. Directly below his scrubs the kilt socks he'd stolen last month from Argyll made his legs look like poorly groomed poodles.

"We all believe in the existence of giants," he said.

Doctor Fezzeliski, a man of rounder proportions, with a slightly high look in his gaze, bit the side of his cheek in contemplation. As he did so Lenard thought of what had been baffling him in the mornings as he tried to rise from bed with a thirteen-inch erection. Talk of his manhood had been the hot topic in the household, his parents arguing back and forth about how he should be kept inside to avoid breaking the law.

"What do you think the boy's going do with that damned creature of his?" Fearghas said at the dinner table a few nights previous, while re-murdering a slab of roast beef he'd picked specially for himself from the middle. "Make a lady feel at home? No. He'll impale her on his mammoth baby-snake and bus us all out to the penitentiary." His eyes were wide, filled with tears and the stupor of six whiskey-drams. "Eh? What think you, female?"

Lenard's mother, Floris, also mostly drunk, especially since the time long ago that Fearghas began to refer to her as "female," slammed her hand against the chair arm, looked at Lenard, whose mouth was dumbfounded with steak, and blurted, "I say he stays in the house." It was what she usually said in times of decision, though she wasn't given many opportunities.

As he watched his father and the doctor speak, Lenard's imagination lingered on the hearth of his family's dining room. The shadow of his mother. The all-too-opaque grimace of his father. The images itself caused him to become both hungry and prickly beneath the blanket.

"Fearghas?" Doctor Fezzeliski asked, though without too much concern. "Why are you wearing surgical greens?"

"That's Doctor Fearghas," Fearghas said, doting on himself while smoothing out his own uniform in mimicry of the real doctor. He then flicked his crotch forward with a thrust as if to showcase whatever treasures lay beneath.

"You're not a doctor."

"But I can sure act like one. Isn't that right, boy?"

"Yes, Sir," said Lenard, remembering what his father had taught him last week from Chapter Seven of *The Manaton*, *On Taking Deserved Credit from Others*, which mostly discussed ways to usurp fame and fortune. "Yes, you can."

Doctor Fezzeliski was familiar with the bizarre nature of Fearghas's demeanor, so instead of challenging, he merely drew his stethoscope around his neck, sighed, and placed it on one of the small, useful-looking platforms in his office. He placed it next to a metal container, cracked open to reveal a sparkling bounty of doctor's tools.

"Needless to say, Lenard's sexual organ is the last thing you should be worried about."

Fearghas beamed with pride.

"But," he continued, "you should worry about the rest of him."

Lenard cringed as the doctor put on a pair of spectacles and wiped his forehead of what seemed like perpetual sweat.

"Are you sure your boy hasn't experienced recent trauma?" he asked, rummaging through the container, not referring to Lenard at all, as if he could have been a faulty carburetor.

"No," said Fearghas, rubbing his thumbs together. "Can't think of any trauma."

"Been exposed to lab chemicals?"

"Of course not."

"What about radiation?"

His hand was deep in the box now.

"Would there be any chance he came in contact with a teletherapy device? A power plant, perhaps—though," he mused to himself, "that probably wouldn't have done it, not unless he'd thrown himself right into the reactor. Hey, you're not experimenting with any of those voodoo medical tonics, are you? From the abnormalities in his growth, the sickly color of his skin, it seems like he's being fed Radithor."

Fearghas laughed off-key. The doctor was referring to the medical quackery of William J. A. Bailey, who, long ago, purported that tiny doses of radium combined with triple distilled water was capable of inducing a mood of perpetual sunshine. Even if, in truth, the product it sold was lymphoma. There hadn't been many sightings of it in the last twenty years, but there were still some peddlers of snake oil strewn about. Cure-alls for the perpetually desperate and depressed. Unfortunately, due to the circles he ran with, the doctor dealt with it more than he'd have liked.

"I thought that stuff was outlawed in the twenties," Fearghas said.

"Me, too," said Fezzeliski, squinting with suspicion.

"We brought the boy in here to have sores examined on his arse," Fearghas said. "That's all. Nothing to do with power plants, electromagnetism, or some other toxic brew, only an evil God and his neglect."

"Umhm," the doctor ignored, pulling something from the metal chest. "I wish I had a Geiger counter. Well, I'll just have to settle for a blood sample instead." The smoothness in which he spoke could have been mistaken for pillow talk as he brandished a pearly syringe. "Just to be safe."

"No," said Fearghas, seeming confused at his own response.

"Why not?" asked the doctor.

"Just. . .no."

"He could have radiation poisoning. He's exhibiting symptoms."

"I don't give a shiny shite."

"Dad?" crooned Lenard, wishing he could tell the doctor to just do his job, even if he knew he never got a say when it came to his own medical treatment. Maybe it was a generational thing, but his father had told him that he could find his own physician when he was man enough to stock womb/s (plural $\geq$ better) with babies. All this at the age of twelve.

"Quiet, boy," said Fearghas, corroborating that rule. "Just give us a cream, Fezzeliski, and we'll be off!"

"Dad," said Lenard. The words *radiation poisoning* still rattled in his head. "He might be on to something."

"Lies," he growled. "Lies. Lies. Lies. He's probably working for They."

"Who's They?" asked the doctor.

"Who *is* They?" Lenard wondered. He still didn't know. He felt something dark grow inside him as he thought of them, though. Another addition to the fear already dredged forth by Dr. Fezzeliski, the only man in the room, so it seemed, struggling to come to his aid.

Eventually, however, and even though it appeared to cause him anguish, the doctor set down whatever invisible arms he'd been dueling with. He paced the room, pretending not to think about the ethics at stake. Some patients were like this, he knew, especially Fearghas—who usually contrived absurdities to conceal a foulness he'd committed, some disease he hoped would go away if he just ignored it long enough. An iota of guilty conscience would push him into a panic, and then, here he'd be, ranting on about some imaginary rash. The doctor was a working professional, a husband (six times), a father himself, and had a way of sensing these things. Now the boy was being punished for something he had no way of controlling. Whatever the Scotsman had gone and done this time, he'd obviously gone too far, and, as the doctor gazed over the boy's deformities, piteous, preventable things, he wondered if he should alert the authorities.

"This is ridiculous," he said, waving the syringe above his head. "In all my years of practice. . . ." But then, as if shocked into sense by something in the air, he calmed down and loosened his grip. There was that time years ago, when the Scotsman helped him get a hold of opium for recreational purposes. Then there was that other time just last week when he'd done the exact same thing. Actually, the doctor had been receiving opium shipments from Fearghas since 1962, bimonthly, and had an addiction that landed him in often-dark places on what were supposed to bright Sunday mornings, not to mention the divorce of his fourth wife. And fifth. Opium tasted sweet on his tongue. So sweet he felt more kindred with his Mongolian pipe than his family. Therefore, whatever battle the doctor waged would have to be done right here in the office. No matter how much he cared about Lenard's well-being, he wouldn't take the chance of putting his primary dealer in prison. If anything, he'd have to try and trick him.

"Alright, Fearghas," Fezzeliski said. "I'll give you some unguent. It should fix everything just fine."

"Well, finally," said Fearghas.

Lenard nodded his head abstractly in accordance, wishing he'd just given the drug-addled doctor a little of his blood. He couldn't wait for the day he'd be old enough to make his own decisions. Something (other than his personality as ether) he also dreamed about.

"Now, I'm going to write you a prescription, and, on a piece of paper, I'll give it to you. Why don't you jot down a brief signature of consent for treatment, being you don't have insurance due to our agreement? Yes, just like that." The doctor nodded. "There you go. That part's not important. No need for your glasses."

Fearghas, dropping the doctor a vicious look, then read the disclaimer aloud. "By signing this, I consent to whatever treatment you recommend."

"For the records?" the doctor offered, his flagging smile seeming to realize just how poor its head's plan had been.

Fearghas crumpled the paper into his pocket.

"You know, Dean?" He began saying, combing his stray sideburn up into his paper hat. "I once heard this story about a woman in Chile back in the fifties. She was at this zoo in Santiago, one of those old fashioned European gardens for animals, where the fences are too low to keep the humans out." He puffed out his chest to take a breath, the type that sounded very necessary. "And, you do know, zoos are different in different countries. In Santiago, for example, they try to feed the animals, like they do in Australia. They feed them whatever they can, just to see if they'll do flips, roar, or claw each other to shreds. But this woman." He grinned. "Do you know what she did? I think she was a tourist, from The Netherlands, around the age of thirty-seven with gigantic, unfairly gigantic, teats? During feeding time, as opposed to throwing heads of lettuce, she jumped right into a lion's den. And then, in a split second, was torn apart. Some people think she was touched, but I don't give a damn what she was. Insane, depressed, drunk. Who cares? The only important thing to know was the lions were waiting. Waiting to tear her right in half like she'd never been whole in the first place."

Lenard closed his eyes in exhaustion. This was the sixth time he'd heard this story since yesterday, when his father heard about it from Argyll, who also informed him that he could probably fly if he concentrated hard enough. Which he definitely couldn't.

"Pleasant," said the doctor.

"No," said Fearghas. "Truth."

"Come on, old pal," he said, cupping one hand on Fearghas's shoulder. He shuffled closer, tried to look him in the eye. "Let me help."

"Since when did you grow a heart, *old pal*?" Fearghas spat.

The two men paused.

"Times have changed."

"Times are always changing, Dean."

"And we're friends," he smiled.

"There are no friends in this forgone, fucked-up canary of a world."

Lenard pulled his pants up, not caring anymore about whether or not he was supposed to be finished.

"You're guilty about something," said the doctor. "I don't know what it is, but I have a feeling it has something to do with that book you were ranting about last Thursday at the tracks."

"Well maybe your senses have been retarded by a certain narcotic I know of," Fearghas began to yell as he threw open the door. "Let's see if I can remember what it's called."

As he tried to wrangle into his jeans, Lenard's enormous manhood startled a passing female nurse carrying a tray of medications in ketchup cups, causing the two of them to turn many shades of red.

"You'll conceal God's marvels from the world no longer," Fearghas yelled down the hallway, a constricted passage without windows that led into a small waiting room. His message seemed to be directed towards the universe, however, and not at Lenard or the doctor as it should have been. "That's right," he continued, snarling as he snagged Lenard by the collar of his shirt. "I'm as close to heaven as you're going to get, boy. These medical men, they don't know a damn thing. Playing God in their holy pools of iodine. There's as much wrong with you as there is with the original Adam and you're going to be the strongest bastard on earth, I swear to you!" And then he really began to scream. "Manossus, Manatica, Manu!"

"What the hell are you talking about?" asked Lenard, swiftly wondering why he'd even bothered to ask.

"Stop cursing, boy," Fearghas screamed, as Dr. Fezzeliski slammed the door to his office. "It's not what a gentleman does!"

Lenard finally adjusted his belt in his father's 1967 Cutlass, a car that would always remain the color of a candied apple.

His pants squelched against the leather, dribbled back and forth a couple times for comfort. He felt too tired for a sunny afternoon. The fact that since the beginning of his appointment he knew he hadn't actually had a rash filled him with shame. Fearghas, according to Fezzeliski's suspicions, told Lenard there was something he wanted the doctor to see, or, rather, appraise in his deformed body, like a sport horse before his first race. But he also told Lenard they couldn't say what that thing was, and they'd be entering under the guise of an arse pathogen. As usual, all the questions he hoped would have been answered about his makeup were left to nothing but a ubiquitous argument. Fearghas now looked proud of that as he drove, on the verge of being happy with whatever decisions he'd made, but not quite, which to Lenard was a small victory. Though he was often afraid to speak up for himself, there was a certain comfort he took in not contesting his father's convictions. It was a reward for being meek, of being able to sense injustice, and then letting that injustice reveal itself.

Looking into the rearview mirror at his congealed puck of hair— he'd begun using an expired can of Brylcreem to replace the labor-intensive styling tools of his past—Lenard did wonder, however, what possessing his father's vindication would have felt like. For the adolescent didn't believe in himself at all. He had nothing inside him save for a bleak hope that one day he would transcend his current state. His unexplainable growth defect had become little more than a slight annoyance compared to more contemporary ailments: virginity, specifically speaking, and his surfeit of. It had been so long since he'd known normal legs that he'd truly begun to forget they existed as anything but obstacles to keep him from playing sports. But sex, that was a three-dimensional, nine-toed beast of a problem capable of destroying any single-minded adolescent, and it reminded him of his freakish nature more than the deformities themselves. It wasn't like he was Bob Dylan, being torn from performance for a year (*a single year?*) by a motorcycle accident (*a motorcycle?*). The folkster would have been awaited by every female body with breath in its lungs to fuck his gypsy way back across the United States. All while Lenard struggled, plowed through the ardor of everyday life to do the little things most children grew into naturally: walk, run, even jump sometimes, when his bones allowed it, though not more than an inch from the ground. The possibility of female interaction, thus, became a near impossibility. And sex—as remote as Siberia. To make it worse, his father, the mighty, the manful Fearghas, played down his problems to a fault. He promised the boy a pay-off of Roman proportions: banquets of sex, food, and kingly adoration. He reminded him that only through toil greatness was achieved, and that one day he'd understand his sacrifice. That when fate allowed him the final chapter of *The Manaton*, his crippled life would swiftly be rebuilt.

"I was thinking about asking a girl to the prom," Lenard said to Fearghas, who was turning up a radio that always blared the bagpipes. They both tried to forget about the doctor's office, but had a hard time doing so. For Lenard was too tired of his father's secrets.

"Oh you are, are you?" Fearghas laughed uncomfortably, slapping the dashboard to the backdrop of the drums. His eyes had seemed to reach a level of excitement that bordered mania. "And how are you going to slow dance a *bint*, with, well, look at the state of you?"

Lenard sighed, wondering why his father had never noticed that he, too, could enchant the floor with his toes. That he could do an addled Waltz, on request, or whirl around the room in semblance of the Boogie-Woogie.

"Well," Lenard said. "I was thinking—"

"Boy, I have something I need to tell you."

Lenard rolled his eyes. "Boy, I have something I need to tell you." He'd been hearing that exact phrase for years. The adolescent took a deep breath, inured himself to what he knew would become another lengthy monologue. Usually, when the Scotsman had something he felt important to say, it remained on his mind for months, even years, in the form of violent pride, until he couldn't bear it anymore. Lenard remembered the time, not long ago, when he prattled on for a full afternoon about the rise and fall of the Third Reich, which then led into a lecture on the wiles of females, the annual production of the half-German Brigadoon and its importance in Edinburgh's cultural revival, and finally ended the next day in a tutorial on how to brew Scottish whisky properly according to scholar David Daiches under the growing monopolization of the peat moss market in the Highlands. Apparently, all of that information had been pertinent to Lenard's growth. As had been the kilts Fearghas occasionally forced him to wear to school during the warmer, and more socially condemning, summer months.

Not to mention the mantra he'd been forced to recite thirteen times daily: *I am the great claw of destiny.*

Now, as the Scotsman frowned and licked his lips, his stomach, as if attacking him, snarled. There were scores of Stinking Willies unfurling along the roadside. Seasonal rebirths always soured Fearghas, and, as if stirred by the warm Massachusetts earth, he began to stutter, "Uh, um." This time, as he prepared to speak, he sounded afraid. And that, Lenard noticed, was a first.

"Are you okay, Dad?"

The Scotsman's body shook.

"Dad?" repeated Lenard, beginning to wonder if he should be afraid. "What's wrong?"

"I'VE BEEN PUTTING A SPOONFUL OF PLUTONIUM IN YOUR BREAKFAST, LUNCH, AND DINNER SINCE YOU WERE FIVE AND A HALF."

Now, Lenard had heard many insanities rappel from Fearghas's maw, but this one in particular, this one, if true, would run the rhetorical gamut. The pipes on the radio blared loud and sincere, however, even as he tried to ignore them.

"Sorry?" he managed to ask, even if he wasn't sure how.

"I've been putting one full teaspoon of crushed plutonium—we'll call it—compound, in your breakfast oatmeal, stew, soup, whatever it happened to be, daily, ever since you were a parasite," he reiterated. "There, I've said it. Are you happy?"

Lenard tried to respond. Tried to repeat, *Happy?* He immediately both thought about and felt his sad, shrunken legs riddle beneath him. They were the answer to Fearghas's question, and yet seemed to shiver without reason in the pee-warm car, unable to speak for themselves, unable to stand up and fight. Could it have been that his father, the man he'd respected as an authority, an avid and respectful reader of *The Manaton* with undying stake in the success of his son, was actually trying to kill that son, and with little to no remorse?

"You *should* be happy," Fearghas said.

"I should?" Lenard ended up asking, biting his lip. He watched the gap between his teeth in the rearview. He thought about what all those tainted meals must have done to him. How they'd insulted his taste buds, and then his entire body. He felt like giving up on the relationship he'd been forcing himself to build with his father, and instead rising up to show him that he could barely even stand. If he'd have been brave enough, he thought, he'd have struck him a couple of times. He'd have torn out his own hair, leapt from the car like the creature he felt undulating beneath himself, and wreaked havoc upon their city streets. His life was a madhouse he needed to burn down. Just a matchbook, some kerosene, and a steady, determined hand would be needed. Instead, however, he repeated, "Why?" So meek that he hated himself.

"Well, you bastard," said Fearghas, most carelessly. He turned the volume down on the pipes. Amber sun spread through the Norwegian maple trees to the tarmac in preparation for spring.

"The truth is," Fearghas said. "I've been preparing you for a non-stop life. One full of danger and triumph."

Lenard sat still as a bird swooped down—something from the sea—and shat upon their windshield.

"I've been altering your once-stupid future."

The pipes wheezed.

"I'm making you into the next *Gud*-Damned Superman, for the sake of all sakes."

The clouds came lower. There was a superfluity of shared breath in the car.

"But, why would I want to be the next Superman?" Lenard asked. "I'm failing all my classes. I'm terrible at sports. I don't even read comics. I guess I like Superman, but don't know much about him save for the fact that he can fly."

"It is because I recommend it so," said Fearghas.

Lenard sniffled.

"Because soon, my boy," he said, his face betraying a purple, bloated color, as he realized his explanation to be inadequate. "You're going to have so much power, you'll have no other choice."

"I won't?" Lenard asked. Now that his father's deeds had been revealed, it seemed as if he hadn't much choice to begin with.

"You, Lenard, are a good boy," said Fearghas, half his lips folding into a frown. "Better than I ever was. . .you could never be a villain, no matter how hard you try."

"A villain," Lenard repeated in a whisper. The word itself seemed to house so much profit. And yet, since his father had been the one to inform him, it felt meaningless. The body he possessed was definitely not capable of carrying out mighty feats of strength. He felt weaker and more incapable than ever.

"Unless you try real, real hard," Fearghas said. "Then you could become a villain, alright."

"But—"

"And then, I want you to be ready."

"Ready for what?"

"For whatever I want you to be ready for."

"I'm going to die," Lenard decided. The gap in his teeth seemed larger. "I'm going to fucking die." The non-existent chin, existent. The Cutlass with its interior subsumed by the malcontent odors of man. There was the stench of a passed cigarette—probably Argyll's. The swoon of old aftershave to cover up a cryptic funk.

"Oh, you're not going to die," said Fearghas, dismissing his fears with one flick of his hand. "Not even if you want to, unfortunately. The plutonium compound, when combined with *The Manaton*'s code. . .nothing, Lenard, will be able to stop you. Oh," he shook a finger. "And stop cursing."

"Dad," said Lenard, feeling himself on the verge of some alternate reality, where the other half of him, the real half, was supposed to reside. ". . .I don't understand why you would do something like this. I mean, look Dad, my legs."

Fearghas stopped the car, took out the keys, glared at his son, and concentrated. His amber irises pinwheeled. The sky outside seemed lower than normal, and the temperature, a little bit higher. In a rush, in that flaming stare, the man who was Lenard's father seemed to expose a multitude of seasons. The adolescent had seen this look before: the equivalent—nay, reinvention—of an evil eye. The reflection of a sprinkler sprayed its majesty, imprinted from a western lawn in his father's left pupil, and it took on the qualities of meteor dust railing through small cosmic spheres. The space they shared in the car seemed prophetic, and Lenard imagined Fearghas without his noble flourish of hair. When he was bald, naked, bare, and then, finally, geriatric, a sensation befell him of relief. This creature of bones and pale skin. This creature lurching towards a pit. Lenard looked at it, across a void, and a bridge between the two of them slowly assembled, clicking together, brick by brick. A bridge, Lenard understood in that moment of loud, yet ineffable, manhood. Above them both, in a cradle of brumes, a cobalt figure, ambiguously human, with wry, halogen eyes and a shadowy simper, gathered together stitches of darkness, and allocated them, two by two, to be positioned as joists below the suspension. From its cuneate back, six wings unfurled, shoulder to torso to buttock, and, in evil silence, stretched up towards the heavens. Its mouth opened. No sound came forth. Only a seditious tongue of light.

The adolescent was not inspired by this vision, but merely enthralled, like the mindfuck he'd received from the Jefferson Airplane concert he'd somehow been allowed to attend last month. As he'd thought then, he wondered if he should open his mouth or sway side to side, but neither of these seemed like good options.

"Let's go find you a prom date," Fearghas then said after a long pause. He turned back to the dashboard to re-ignite the pipes. Lenard stared back at the bird shit thoughtfully, and then, the road. "That's what you wanted, right?"

Lenard gave up and nodded, noting the starkness of his surroundings. He wasn't sure if he had any other choice.

"She lives a mile and a half due west," Fearghas said, beating his hands to the rhythm of the lap snares on the radio. It was a station zapped to being in 1964 from a remote AM frequency, called Moray Firth, broad-casting out of some octogenarian's apartment, somewhere, in the state of Connecticut.

"And oops—" he looked to his wristwatch. "She should just be get-ting out of the shower."

Laura Moskowitz was just getting out of the shower—Lenard quickly fig-ured out—as he and Fearghas lurked into a cluster of her family's treasured mountain laurel. His armpit was right in Lenard's nose, shoved upwards at a crooked angle. Now, with the secret off his shoulders, he seemed giddy and overly relieved. The mullions waffled Laura's body through her bath-room window, and Lenard became embarrassed for the both of them more quickly than he'd have liked.

The boy struggled to watch her in the southern end of her household. The part where she preened herself was fanned out into a curved fenestra-tion with the lace curtains generously parted. The adolescent Laura had ashen hair, ashen to the point it seemed sad. But, in that sadness, it was strangely emboldened. It reminded Lenard of a book his father owned, *The Road to Victory*, or something like that, which, more than a novel of tri-umph, seemed to catalogue, in dreary black and white, the bare minimum of what hadn't been lost during Hitler's Reich. Laura's body, like something beautiful that survived Europe's wreckage, would look striking beside the treads of a tank. She made it seem as if all women, by genus, and unlike their male counterparts, had come to hold the secret of survival.

As Lenard's pupils slopped over her body, he wondered if that se-cret was annoyingly disguised by the flesh he knew of, from a distance, as breasts. Laura's, in particular, were worthy of college dissertations, with areolas like circular space ports, and the ability—he suspected with envy—to travel into the future with without even gleaning a wrinkle. He thought of Apollo 14 when he saw her. Of Alan Shepard broadcasting in Vidicon color from the moon.

There is a tree in Paradise
The Pilgrims call it "The Tree Of Life"

All my trials, Lord, soon be over.

She sang out "All My Trials" from Peter, Paul, and Mary, while twining herself in a towel. She dashed a perfect smile against the mirror and, soon following, cleared the shower-fog by swinging the wind around her hips. The girl, beyond her immediate beauty, also had a non-immediate, human look to her. Something receivable of harm. Lenard found himself staring at her with the greatest sensation of want, knowing she was something he needed, not only to possess, but to be.

"Feast your eyes," Fearghas then said. His stomach grumbled. Twigs snapping through his beard made him take on the appearance of a forest monster. "On the girl you will one day marry."

"I don't even know her," Lenard whispered. His eyes maintained careful focus.

"Not yet you don't," said Fearghas.

"So, I'm going to meet her?"

"Something like that."

"Have you already met her?"

"Er. . .yes."

"When?"

"Last year."

"Last year?"

"Ay, wee fucker."

"But, why?"

"I had to make sure she wasn't one of them."

"One of who?"

"None of your business."

"When can I meet her?"

"When you can walk properly—hey, don't feast too much. She'll catch on."

Fearghas and Lenard were visibly hanging out of the bush. Fearghas was actually standing more beside it than inside, with his high-support socks kicking out sideways. Lenard, like a body attached to Fearghas's stomach, was staring off through the window, wondering what his father had meant by

SAMUEL SATTIN

the word "properly."

The morning sun frosted Laura's hips. She picked up a brush fit with boar bristle and ran it through her hair. She noticed Lenard's broken smile, his broad chest, his legs stowed somewhere in the shrub. Her teeth sparkled whiter than the boy had ever seen before on teeth, and it was then, he'd remember, for the very first time, he knew he could want something bad enough to hurt himself.

Laura looked at Lenard and, he couldn't believe it, was smiling, while covering herself halfway by the window drapes. Then she looked beside him.

At Fearghas.

"*Eeeeeeeeeeeeeeeeeeeee!*"

"We've been compromised," he yelled, tugging Lenard by the pants. "Abort! Abort!"

"Dad—Jesus!"

Fearghas dragged Lenard away from the house and canned him inside the car. The pipes keened on with the windows open, while their tires burned Band-Aids on the street.

"Did you like her, Son?" yelled Fearghas. He was smiling as the wind ripped through his hair.

"I, I think so."

"Well, you either think or you know."

"Okay, then," Lenard said, struggling to yell. "I know."

"Louder."

"I know!"

"Good," Fearghas said. He rattled his head to the pipes. "You know— you better know. A fine female creature she is. Big doe eyes. Body like a praying mantis of *sex*. Not too stupid, either, which might have to be dealt with in the future. It took me a while, boy, yes, but after her brother was murdered, and a nominal—let's call it—fee was negotiated, her parents were more than willing to entrust her to me as your future bride."

"Brother?" asked Lenard, speaking the word fondly. "Murder? Bride? But we haven't even met yet."

"Yet is an anticipatory term," said Fearghas. "You'd be surprised what terrible things people are willing to do to and for their children. All for a little—*haggis*."

"Haggis?"

"*Shhhhhhhh.*"

"*Shhhhhhhh?*"

"Shut your yap!"

The Scotsman slowed and went silent as they came to a crosswalk. He made a show of turning down the pipes. Slugs dangled from the Norwegian maple trees, flirting together in rows on both sides of Polypherm Road, the avenue where Laura's family lived. They crawled down through the lower branches, occasionally plopping to the street. Lenard noticed that he and Fearghas were stopped at a crosswalk where a group of children was walking home from school. As they did so the slugs were occasionally squished beneath their tennis treads, without any notice at all. One person among them, however, was cool and calculated, wearing a bright yellow vest as he stepped out into the street. He was goading the students along the crosswalk with a stop sign raised to traffic. He wore a beaten-down conductor's cap, Madras plaid pants and green argyle socks. He had a twinkle of dementia in his left eye, where the substance of his pupil was made of glass.

"You've got to be kidding me," Lenard said to his father, grappling with the seatbelt over his waist that seemed to trap him now more than ever. The undercover Argyll dressed as a crossing guard squinted his right eye and nodded slowly, obviously, at Fearghas, who adjusted his yarmulke and nodded, with that exact slowness, back.

Fearghas then turned to address Lenard's question.

"I would cut my own face off before I ever told a joke. And," he nodded. "I would cut yours off, too."

Later that night, Lenard had been made privy to the source of his 'fuel,' as Fearghas would come to call it. He saw the gangly Scotsman retreat into the cellar, and retrieve a box of the sort he'd seen delivered by Argyll that one chilly night, a few months ago. Starched stiff, and bluer than linseed flowers, the cardboard bore, on each side, the same symbol he'd seen before.

Lenard watched Fearghas savage open the lid, and mull through some Styrofoam peanuts as if with disdain. He then pulled a glistening aluminum bottle, set vertically, from inside, and set it carefully on the kitchen counter. It was shaped like a missile, slim at the bottom and slimmer at the top, and had a screw off lid, in the manner of a canteen. Fearghas opened it carefully, and, with safety goggles slapped around his eyes, let a dash of the clear, mucilaginous liquid knead its way into the meatloaf batter he'd been preparing. As he watched him do it, Lenard couldn't believe that the syrup hadn't been more offensive to his insides. The smell itself, freshly minted, was no less toxiferous than gasoline.

When Fearghas replaced the lid on the bottle, Lenard noticed it had a symbol on it as well, engraved towards the top, right below the lid. Though this carving was different than the one on the box.

"What's it mean, Dad?" asked Lenard, quietly, from his seat at the table, where he sat breezing through an illustrated book about pterodactyls. "The circular shape on the bottle?"

Fearghas looked visibly peeved at his son even opening his mouth, not wishing to be bothered as he put together dinner to the best of his terrible ability.

"What does it mean?" he tossed down a wooden stir spoon and pretended to examine it closely, squinting his eyes narrow for a half of second. "Nothing, wee fucker. That's what it means. The symbol on the box," he flung his finger towards the busted open package as he returned to the meal. "If you look closely, is what men call an atom. A basic unit of earthly matter. So I assume what's on the bottle is that same symbol, rubbed off during its travels."

"But it seems permanent," said Lenard, stretching his neck for a closer look.

"You know, like a coin. Engraved."

"The only thing that's permanent in this world is your testicles," Fearghas laughed. "That and the God-forgiven will to hold them together under stress—which you will experience, lord help me. So cup your rotten skein and fetch me a glass of Scotch."

"Yes, Sir."

"And make sure it burns."

After dinner, Lenard returned to his room with fiery content in his belly. He began to assemble a 1970 Chevelle SS 454, ammonia-blue, with his pudgy, cramped fingers over the desk. He glued the left front wheel onto the sheet-plastic axel. In their broken down two story home that didn't belong in green and wealthy Milton, he heard the neighbor's dog, a black lab Fearghas called "God's fuck-up" but whose true name was Tucker, run back and forth on a cable stretching between two trees. Lenard paused from his model to look down at the poor creature, now being taunted by a couple of twelve-year-olds passing down the block.

"Stupid mutt," they snarled, as they lunged at him with maple sticks.

"Hey," Lenard shouted from the window. "Fuck off!"

The kids looked up at Lenard and, due to the absurdity of his broad chest, stole away in a frightened snicker, whispering, "it's the retarded bomb-target. The Queer Globe." In the warm light of his room, and from the waist up, the adolescent did look global. Universal, even. He sighed, however, knowing the history of his life. How much he wished to change what he'd become.

Angry, old Tucker barked at the children as they ran away, took full responsibility for Lenard's bravery, and dashed to the edge of the cable. Like a brainless muscle he choked himself forward just to assert a little dominion. Lenard felt an odd moment of identification then. He looked down Central Avenue, the street where they lived, and smelled the last of the fudge being baked by their neighborhood Chocolatier—a sarcastic, yet unfunnily-so man named Eddy Fontanello, who beat his daughter and might have killed his wife—as he closed down shop. He then looked less down at his legs, and then again to "God's fuck up," growling into the night from his finite kingdom. He growled because the night had somehow become offensive, and yet remained off limits. Manipulated by the fairly normal forces that tied mutts to ten-yard suspensions.

It was barely eight-thirty when Fearghas summoned him again. Lenard pined at having to leave what was becoming a comforting summer evening spent within his own four walls, but the door creaked open and Fearghas stepped through it. He had no other choice. Lenard tried to identify the taste of plutonium on his tongue as his father came to his side, and, upon sensing nothing, wondered if he'd been inured to it. What had come out of that bottle was officious to the nose, the very notion of tastelessness seemed preposterous; he wondered if it became diluted soon after it left the container. If it lost its frills like a nudist lost his pants.

Speaking of pants, Fearghas was dressed in normal, human clothes again, in a black t-shirt with the words *Malibu Nights* scribbled in disco-yellow cursive. He had black jeans on, too, a bandana with skulls wrapping his silver hair, and, in a certain light, looked quite terrifying. In another more realistic light, he looked ready to perform bad theater in a seedy bar/restaurant downtown. Or rob a bank.

"Put your pants on," Fearghas said, incongruously throwing Lenard

57

a t-shirt. "We're going out."

"Where are we going?" Lenard asked. The tiny plastic wheel was still in his hand.

"To the cinema."

"To see what?"

"Does it matter?"

Lenard answered him with an obvious stare.

"Fiddler on the fucking Roof," he muttered.

Lenard made a sigh. "Do we have to?"

"Ay, we have to," he said, turning out the door. "It's either that or Mary Queen of *Scots!* Now clinch your crapper and get ready to enjoy the fruits of your great people's culture."

Lenard frowned and finished twisting the wheel on the Chevelle's axle. For him, though he didn't quite know it then, tonight would become more than a simple viewing of film. A simple understanding of culture. *The Manaton* would reveal its secrets like a pony spraying its sex upon the earth. When Fearghas sprinkled Lenard's vittles with the first teaspoon of pluto-nium years ago (mixed with a clandestine equation of chemicals engineered by Argyll's associate, Matthias Moon, a scientist given the hook from the Manhattan project for malfeasance), he'd watered his own dark garden into bloom.

The moon was wide, but not full. A line of distant trees speared it into the sky as Fearghas and Lenard crawled back into the Cutlass. Lenard could see his mother, Floris, in the kitchen window. She was framed before a body-length mirror, trying on different shades of lipstick, running them over her top and bottom lip and pausing to make little Os. She briefly looked down at Lenard, like an alien from an observation deck, and smiled, with dim interest. He realized, upon smiling back, that they barely knew each other. The Sikophsky household was run on a schedule of men with men and women with women. Since Floris was the only woman in the house, it was no surprise she took to the night to find company, leaving him, and Fearghas, snorting and spitting, to scavenge the planet on their own.

Lenard's smile turned to a frown as he realized how far she was away from him, how much of an empty vessel she was, oared in and out of their home. The road ahead of Lenard, much like their relationship, was empty, and the only human orbiting his lonesome existence was the milquetoast man to his right.

"Excited, are you?" Fearghas asked, as he stared at the road with deep-set eyes. His tone was enthusiastic in the way an auditor's might have been on the way to foreclosing a home. He sat back in a slouch, the skull and crossbones on his bandana glowing with an aura of the moon. He drew one hand across his mustachio, sharpened it at the ends. He seemed not to care that his wife would be leaving the house, probably soon, to frequent the local singles clubs, to let her skirt rise up her thigh in places with names like Dickles, La Donna, or Jack Sweeney O'Firth's.

"Are you?" he asked again.

Lenard nodded his answer and looked out the window. He spotted the occasional silhouette of a pub or Chinese restaurant with its cantilevered sign and its drainpipes corroded. A huddle of forgotten colonials rested quietly in the distance, shrouded in elm trees. Their branches created a dome, something to protect against change. In passing, it was easy for Lenard to understand that, just like these Colonials left in their stasis, if he stayed at home with his father, if he remained for much longer, he would be sure to become trapped as well.

A clinking sound came from the backseat. Something like bottles being packed into a trash bag. Lenard was afraid to look, not knowing if this cruel and abandoned outside world had slinked into his father's car and come, at last, to suck him into service. Fearghas leaned back into his chair, took one hand from the wheel, and stretched it up towards the roof.

"Argyll?" He said over his shoulder.

"Ay Fergie," came a voice from the backseat. Lenard repressed a scream as he looked back and saw the white-hair rise from its hiding place, wherever that had been. The old demented man was still dressed like a crossing guard, soaked through with sweat. "What you be needing?"

"Did you get those barbiturates from my *bastard* cousin out of Christchurch, New Zealand?" asked Fearghas.

Argyll gave an unintelligible answer.

"All right then." He snapped on the right blinker. "Let's get started."

The Cutlass pulled over to the side of the road and shut off its lights. Lenard looked to his father, saw a faint corona of silver taste his bifocals, the ones he claimed to wear only when he drove. The Scotsman breathed heavily, and Lenard knew that behind those dusty shards, his eyes were dissecting this moment, wondering, hoping, that whatever was about to happen, was about to happen correctly. Morality aside, Fearghas was a creature that demanded fluidity. If the world wasn't working in his favor, he squeezed its rind until it did.

"Dad?" asked Lenard, pleading for his father's eyes. He felt a slithering in his arms and legs that made him recall the true taste of plutonium—nice and chewy, a little bit hot, latently sharking through his breakfast porridge. "What are we—"

Argyll was already around his neck.

His grubby hands grappled. Lenard smelled the old man's breath (had he eaten beef stew?) as he whipped his body to get loose. In the rearview, a flash of light the needle—dripping with barbiturate like dew off the beak of a hummingbird—quivered towards his neck. Lenard breathed heavily, yielding under Argyll's palm as it pushed his chin against the chair.

"Hurry up, Argyll," said Fearghas calmly, checking his watch, an old military timepiece given to him by his Polish father, Apollonius Sikophsky, after the Great War. "We're behind schedule."

The needle came cleanly out of Lenard's neck.

"*Fiddler on the Roof?*" the adolescent asked. It was as if he were already sitting before the movie screen in a stupor, rationing off popcorn for later.

"Sorry, wee fucker," Fearghas said as Lenard's world faded. The pipes came on again in alluvial descent, with the smell of a freshly lit cigarette. "The only fiddle being played tonight is your own."

CHAPTER FOUR

BARBITURATES

Lenard awoke to the sound of Laura gagging on a pillowcase. He knew it was she immediately, before his eyes even focused on the sky, the stars, the blare of six stadium-style halogen lights soaking the whole night in pink torpor. The ground was hard and, when he sat up, seemed to be stolen from Utah.

A deodar cedar was hunched over him. It branches stenciled shadows across his stomach. Its leaves were dying and the air smelled like sweat and healthy, grain-fed feces. Around him boulders swam in a lagoon of red gravel, and around them were tall concrete walls. They reversed Lenard's vertigo in the way any traditionally inescapable pit of death would. The adolescent felt, upon the first deep breath he took, that he was breathing, in fact, something else's air. Something like carbon, hot and acrid. Something that reeked of old meat.

Tied to the opposite side of the deodar tree, he saw Laura's hands and feet struggling beneath ropes. They were wrapped snugly around her waist. Her eyes were blinded by a cowboy handkerchief of the Hopalong Cassidy variety, and below she was wearing an evening gown. It was see-through, but nudity was withheld by her undergarments, a thick pink brassiere and white floral panties that, although disconsonantly matched, made Lenard's hands knuckle with want.

Lenard knew he was somewhere his father had left him. This was it, he thought: the second test of manhood. This was it, he thought, his body's danger sensors had most certainly blown a fuse. But his body's love sensors. He paused. They were as pert and determined as ever, zeroing in on Laura with depraved determination, both hating and worshipping Fearghas for allowing him to wake up beside her. It wasn't exactly how he'd planned to meet his life-long love. He'd planned on asking her for coffee one day.

He'd planned on bringing her an iris.

The night howled over the edge of the pit. There was a feeling of danger worsened by Laura's warble. *Where the hell were they?* Lenard wondered. He watched her body tremble, then wobbled to his feet over a sloping rock into a small valley below the tree. No more than a few feet down, there were four living creatures, yellow, brown, and breathing in the sand. One let its muzzle flop out, and snorted.

"Oh, shit," Lenard said, looking upon the bodies of four sleeping lions.

Laura turned her head to Lenard's voice and squealed.

Lenard had known it was Laura when her voice first cried through her gag. The mew of her fear could have only originated from such beautiful, pink and healthy lungs. She was the exemplification of woman that his father didn't grasp, that seemed to forgive every single sin of her species' supposed decrepitude with the fragrance of skin, the offerings of lips. Lenard knew it was she when he first opened his eyes. She was a person he felt like he'd known forever the very first time he saw her. And also, of course, he'd known it was her because he'd seen Argyll near her house earlier that day dressed as an elementary school crossing guard.

Lenard stopped before the figures on the ground. They snarled, curled fatly in their sleep. He gazed over their bodies, and then tiptoed backwards. He had to think quick.

"Aww. . .would you look at him Fergie," whispered a voice from above, nurturing and soft. "Just like his good old Dad."

"Shut your ugly hole, Argyll," came the response. "This is his test, not ours."

"*This is fucking ridiculous,*" whispered Lenard, looking up at his father and Argyll. They peeked over the edge of the pit like a couple of evil Muppets, so much so that the teenager wondered if they had each other's fists up their asses. In a belated attempt to elude discovery, Fearghas tried to duck away, pulling Argyll with him, but upon seeing he'd failed, whispered back, "Stop cursing!"

The lions, with their paws nestled around their heads, were much larger than Lenard would have taken from picture books, or crude sketches in *The Manaton*, where every animal seemed more like his tiny model Chevelles and Mustangs than actual living infrastructures. These creatures, they were siege engines of sublimity. They were as old as the earth. Just lying on the ground they seemed to bend it to their will, forcing divots in the sand with their bellies. Lenard imagined how one would look standing on all fours and *peeped* an ashamed sound of horror.

"Argyll," whispered Fearghas from above. "Why aren't they moving?"

"Don't know, Feargie," Argyll whispered back. "Maybe they're just sleepy."

"Sleepy?" Fearghas growled. "They look dead."

"Ay."

"Ay, what?"

"Ay, nothing, Fergie." Argyll interlaced his fingers behind his head. "I'm, I'm just saying, I didn't know the exact dosage to give them."

"So how much *did* you give them?"

"Well, I shot each feller with a few darts of curare—"

"Curare? A few darts? You were supposed to use pancuronium. And just a fucking dash!"

"There was none, so I improvised. Jeez Fergie, no need to be so abrasive. I can't control what comes out of Christchurch. You know that better than anyone."

"Just shut it," Fearghas said. He crossed his arms over his chest and let his chin hang over the pit. He watched the comatose lions and willed them to move with his mind, just a little bit. They were supposed to have been slowed to give Lenard a fighting chance, but not drugged-dumb as they were now. The smallest one looked close to dead. "Oh, for Christ's sake,

Argyll," he said leaning backwards. "You probably killed the poor bastards. *The Manaton* forbids. . .aw, never mind."

"Well, if I did, Feargie, then let me give my sorries prematurely. Sometimes these things, these things just can't be avoided."

"Giving your *sorries* won't make my son a man."

"Ay, that's true." He scratched some dry skin from his scalp and grinned. "Want to go grab a popcorn, then? All will be forgiven, eventually."

GRRRARRRRRRRRGHHHH-HHHHHHHAAAAHHHHH!!!!!!!!!

A roar blasted through the pit. Fearghas, Argyll, Laura, and especially Lenard, heard it, taking a few seconds to dissipate. Argyll and Fearghas looked at each other with stupidly inert eyes.

"What was that?" asked Argyll. Fearghas stooped over the pit to observe. He watched a dark shadow stalk through the already dark shadows, two yellow eyes like slimy larvae.

"Oh, no," said Fearghas. "I thought you said there were only four?"

"There were only four," said Argyll. "This one must be a transfer."

"A transfer? From where?"

"Do you want me to tranquilize it?"

"No, you might hit Lenard." His face pruned with thought. "Or the female."

"What do we do then?" asked Argyll, fumbling the blowgun in his hands.

"Quiet down," Lenard said. He attempted to untie Laura's ropes, but found little success. He instead turned to a sharp rock to file the fibers until they eventually snapped away.

"Don't use that tone with me," Fearghas whispered back.

"*Shhhhhh!*"

"You *shhhhhhh!*"

Lenard heard a snarl coming from behind him, but ignored it, as Laura fell, for the very first time, into his grateful arms.

His body braced her bulk, which was not much of a bulk at all, but pillowed, rather, with the smell of flesh and yogurt, like she herself was uncultured youth. She had a human feel to her that was unlike any of the humans Lenard had ever touched before, something that made him want to shield her from harm. Was this what his father was trying to teach him, he wondered? As he watched the swanly nape of her neck. To love out of a need to protect? Or, he wondered, was he teaching him to love out of a need to obsess? Or was it as *The Manaton* taught in Chapter 22 concerning the evil qualities of ancient female sex magic; how it forced all men to serve the matronly appetites, no matter what the cost? Or was it simply him, and the tendency he had—

"WATCH OUT FOR THE LION, WEE FUCKER!"

Fearghas screamed as a full-grown Panthera Leo with ochraceous fur rippling its mane, weighing in close to 550 pounds, scrambled up the rocks towards Lenard and Laura. Its jaw drawled open in a display of gums and hunger.

"RUN!!!" screamed Fearghas.

The lion pounced and Lenard, deciding he wouldn't drop Laura no matter what happened, kicked out his legs to the best of their meager ability and ducked to the right. He crashed down the hill into the pit where the other four lions slept, protecting Laura with his massive back, while his assailant careened into the tree, splintering something in the process, It barely took a moment to spin to its legs again and leap down into the pit. Lenard remembered what *The Manaton* had suggested on the proper way, the only way, to fight a lion.

Something involving bare hands.

"Son," yelled Fearghas, watching Lenard cripple into defense as Laura gibbered through her gag. The lion stalked them in a circle. "You must now rise to your *feet*. For it is time. Time to realize your potential." He slammed his fists against the concrete until they opened up and bled.

"Your legs are not anchors, they are rockets—NOW STARE DOWN THE DARK PIT OF DEATH AND FIGHT!"

The lion crackled through rubble in the trench and into Lenard's face and the boy caught its snapping teeth with his hands. He pulled them open, muzzle towards the sky and chin to the ground. Laura whimpered at the popping of bone. Fearghas and Argyll whooped from above. "AHHHH!" screamed Lenard, forcing the jaw until it began to rip. His face ratcheted with veins, skeletal definition, pure rage that tore and split and fissured the animal's maniac-complex of muscle. A sound like pain ushered from its throat; Lenard felt its limbs fall loose, and then, just stop. Flicker. He saw the creature's eyes, how earth-bound they were. Felt it clinging so desperately to life. This gigantic, Paleolithic creature, nobler than Lenard would ever be, one life, one spirit, one nebula of experience. Under the threat of Lenard's own doom, he wished it no harm. In fact, he was the invader in this lion's domain. And wouldn't he have preyed upon someone traipsing through the center of his own kitchen, or reordering his model cars while he slept?

Lenard relinquished his grip, let the great feline, clearly injured, whimper and hobble away. Death was too black, too beautiful a thing for him to deal out. Or at least he felt too scared of the power.

He took Laura into his arms instead and brushed down the nose of her blindfold. She looked at him for the first time, pupils shrunken by the reappearance of light. She looked straight through the gap in his teeth to his tongue, and smelled the acrid oils of his moustache.

Then, as he untied the gag, she asked, "Who are you?"

"My name is Lenard Sikophsky," he said. "And I am your hero."

Fearghas cooed and exhaled.

Lenard watched Laura's lips, a fevered shade of scarlet. He bent in to give her a kiss. He felt her close her eyes as he closed his, and then, with the blowing of an astral wind, felt her young body slip into unconsciousness.

"Oh, damn," Lenard said, as Laura's limbs went limp, arms swinging over his elbows. "Wha—what do I do?"

"Nothing at all, Son," called Fearghas from above, wiping his tearful eyes with a handkerchief. Lenard had almost forgotten he was there. "You've done well tonight considering the circumstances. You are now truly ready to become a man."

"You mean I haven't become one yet?" Lenard asked.

"Manhood is battle, boy," said Fearghas. "Manustus. Manuciple. Manu. You can't expect to earn your pass by fighting *a* lion. I once fought and bested *five* lions in six minutes. And I was only thirteen."

"Six lions," Argyll added.

"Six! Six lions."

"And a lioness," said Argyll.

"Not the same thing."

"Fuck."

"But I'm not you, Dad!" yelled Lenard, silencing them both. "I can't keep on doing this forever." He held Laura's head up with his elbow, caught her thigh in his palm. "*Manaton* or not, I'm not your experiment. I am a human being, you hear? HUMAN. I can't believe that you'd make me—that you'd make me fight lions. That you'd kidnap a poor girl against her will."

"That's not exactly accurate," said Fearghas. "The 'poor' part."

"Sometimes I think that all this is *fake*," said Lenard. "That you're just a pathetic, old—" he choked, and mustered his strength. It was almost as difficult as cracking the lion's jaw. "I mean, when did this madness begin? You were good once. You were my father. But now. . .I don't know what you are. Or," he frowned, "what you've made me into."

"Lenard," Fearghas smiled, as if anticipating his son's words. He pointed into the pit where the wind had ceased to blow. "Why don't you look down?"

Lenard did look down, angry at first, for Fearghas had clearly glazed over everything he just said. But then his mouth, almost warring the emotion off, brimmed into something beyond a smile. His legs were hard, pulsing, crammed full of red-veined muscle and filled out like a real human's should be—*more* than a real human's should be. His body was proportionate, and formed. Power, physical power—for the first time he felt it. He suddenly got a taste of how people could betray their brothers, how armies turned coats.

Withhold something long enough, and then deliver it in the biggest, most terrifying dose imaginable, and the body yawed so selfishly it was impossible to fault it for doing so. Lenard began to chuckle, then cackle. Laura woke up and cackled, too, though gingerly.

"Where am I?" she croaked. "Who are. . . ."

But Lenard, in the way he would for the rest of their lives in times of great excitement, ignored her. He was too busy kicking out his feet, then jumping, plying his capable toes. Fearghas measured his son's composure while he carried on, dealing out bits of praise, happiness, but then revoking a few, playing a shrewd game of red rover with the amount of accomplishment he'd allot. Argyll smiled and shed a tear from his right eye, enveloped within a fold with one wart. Fearghas stood up and wiped the blood and dust from his hands.

"Argyll," he said, finished with the evening. He nodded towards the injured lion that hid its muzzle behind two paws in the corner. The sky swirled up through the neon like a rotten swirl of peaches and cream.

"How much room do you think we have in the back of the Cutlass?"

CHAPTER FIVE

AN EMPTY BOX

On Lenard's seventeenth birthday in early September, only days after his night at the zoo, Fearghas entered his room in the hours before dawn. A thin glow settled over his bed from the light in the hallway. Fearghas's hands cupped a tiny box fit for an engagement ring. He settled down next to his son's sleeping side, defying the rigor mortis of the box spring, and nudged him awake with his elbow.

"Progeny," he whispered sweetly. Lenard's eyes unscrewed. "Progeny. Wake up. It's your birthday."

"Oh?" Lenard crooned. He knew it was his birthday, but he didn't know why he was waking up. He stretched his shoulders, coughed a couple times from the insistent cold of midnight. He saw his father sprawled over him like a hoary condor, hair engraved by the glow of the moon.

"Well, of course," he said. "Don't you even know when your own birthday is?" Fearghas rolled his eyes and picked up a model car from the table—an unpainted Plymouth GTX that was still airing from last night's glue. He bit it softly upon the bumper and gave it an affirming grunt. "Solid," he said, smacking his lips. "Good."

Lenard looked at the box in his father's hand. Purple, unextraordinary. Lit by one slit of moon lizarding in from outside. He'd warmed up to Fearghas a little since his legs had taken shape. The very first battlement of trust the two of them ever forged. He remembered one of the recent chapters of *The Manaton*, 16, in which Aesop instructed men on the proper ways to grow and cultivate their body hair, and how to compare it in contest. He waited for the lid to open as he pondered this, patting his chest for nascent fur.

When it didn't open, he quietly asked, "What is it?"

"It's a box, my boy," Fearghas said. "A box like no other."

Lenard blurred his eyes. Almost immediately, a large sphere of nothingness seemed to unfold from the inside, fanning out in procession with Fearghas's rising hand. The two of them seemed captured inside it.

"It's empty," Lenard finally said.

"That's one way to look at it."

Fearghas placed the box in his son's hand and closed his own palm over it.

"I see it as waiting to be filled. You can put whatever it is you want inside," he said, letting it down to the bed. They each scooted away to give it room. "It is a box for your hopes and your dreams. Your tiny histories and your even tinier mistakes. Don't think of this box as empty, think of it as waiting to be filled. Filled with anything you want. The chip of a star. A waning dream."

"An engagement ring?" Lenard asked, head turned. He thought of Laura and her almost translucent skin, the way he longed for it, without respite. The box seemed, though, through all of Fearghas's sermon, to still look so ordinary. So plain and undeniably empty.

"Sure, a ring if you'd like," said Fearghas, lifting his eyebrows. "Or, the key to time travel. A mermaid's scale. Whatever your mind can envision."

"Thanks, Dad," Lenard said, looking at the emptiness inside the box, noticing how that emptiness was more vast than any other object or substance he could describe. It took over the room, ran over all its boyish artifacts. Made them all just a little more worthless, or intimidated by higher ideas. It made his father seem empty. It made him *feel* empty. From the moment he saw it open, a void spread into his life.

"Anytime, Son," Fearghas said, squeaking up from the box spring, slapping his hands together as if to wipe them clean of another recent ca-lamity. "We'll be lighting your candles around noon." He doubled back. "If candles are something you'll still be wanting. Turning seventeen means you're fucked enough to make your own decisions."

"All right, then," Lenard said, smiling at his empty box. "I mean, yes, I do. I want candles." He ran his hands over it again and again. "Sir."

Fearghas nodded. He left his room. Lenard's smile lingered for a mo-ment. Then the hall light clicked off, the moon went dim behind a cloud, and that smile turned to a frown. From the basement he heard their new pet roar (or what they now called their pet), probably in a confused holler for breakfast. He felt like roaring back, but snuggled deeper into to sleep instead, mustering up a fading meow.

CHAPTER SIX

TRAUMATISM

At eighteen years old, apart from hearing back sad words from local colleges and universities (Fearghas told him he'd have to stay close to home in order to protect their family's fragile connect after his wife's untimely death, and Lenard had really never been that smart), Lenard regularly jackknifed into the proverbial ocean of his destiny by destroying falling cinderblocks. They were lobbed at him from the top of an abandoned construction site twenty minutes north from their Milton home.

"Fruit of my loins," Fearghas yelled. He clicked three meshed loads of debris onto a hook. His eyes had lost a shade of their opulence—the unabashed animus found in them before withered to a dull, koala-like curiosity. His face was a mess of wrinkles. He was perched atop the highest iron construction beam more than fifty feet up, wrapped in a trench coat of fog. He steered the shaft of a crane made from pvc pipes and stolen harbor rope. "Make sure to only use your feet," he said. His voice seemed older than before. He drew a knot loose from the crane's sheave and let it slack. "Feet," he covered his mouth and sneezed—he'd been a bit ill lately, a little gray— "are the key to not using our hands. For where are our hands always to be?"

"Out of the pudding!" shouted Lenard from below, quoting *The Manaton*, Chapter 2, on staging necessary betrayals, poisonings, and successfully faking one's death. To his father's elation, and partly to his own since the development of his legs, his studies had recently taken off, though he often felt ambivalent about them.

"Right you are," said Fearghas. "Now," he breathed deep. That sad, wicked grin of his eating through his beard. "Make sure you hit every God damned one."

Fearghas tipped the mesh bags and let loose a rumbling of flagstone, cinderblock, and glass. Lenard inhaled and leapt from the ground. He used his arms as buoys to lower him slow into the moist Massachusetts air. He was dressed in a tracksuit that matched the evening fog so intimately that his body resembled some sort of thermal disturbance. Lifting his legs, the cracking of objects began—the cracking didn't even sound like cracking, more like the crumbling of gingerbread—until the result settled to the ground through the fog. The aftermath hissed. Fearghas's forearms prickled with goosepimples, and he sputtered his lips in a sigh.

"You asunder me, Son," he said, hiking up the waist of his kilt. His lower lip began to tremble.

"Oh, Dad," said Lenard. "Please don't cry."

"Can't help it," said Fearghas, now lapsing into sobs. His head, topped with a burgundy fedora, looked like a strap of old rawhide. The last year alone had revealed the downfall of his mental empire. Lenard could see it in his forehead, which looked battered by years of war. His skin was getting older than he was. He was smellier than he'd ever been. Ever since Steve killed Fearghas's wife, Floris, before the Purim carnival in March, the Scotsman just hadn't been the same.

Steve, of course, was what they'd renamed the lion Fearghas dragged home, loaded with tranquilizers, from the zoo during Lenard's epic of plutonium-inspired strength. Before the Purim Carnival, while Floris assembled her costume—she was dressed, quite convincingly, as what she'd referred to as Gandhi's mistress, sewn from the Kantha quilts bequeathed by Fearghas's world-travelling grandfather, Filicjan—Steve, not being able to withstand the small room where he'd been caged, burst up the basement stairs chasing a rat. He shivered the padlock he'd been trapped behind and made Floris leap out the second-story kitchen window. She landed in the garden, supine.

Slap. Deepening the soil where dying marigolds grew. She landed in the territory of 'God's fuck-up,' who looked skyward quizzically and began to yalp as the brand-new sprinklers chimed on.

"I could have warned her about Steve's distaste for rats," said Fearghas, now. His face in his hands as he yowled atop the building. "Then she wouldn't have been so afraid." He knocked his fists against the side-beam, vibrating, along with his body, the corduroy ridges of his jacket. Lenard wondered if he would have to catch him as his feet clicked closer to the edge. "Angry, sure. Confused, maybe. But dead. . .I never thought this would be so hard."

The whimpering resumed.

"She wouldn't have understood," cooed Lenard from below, thinking that his mother would have understood, or at least tolerated. She'd found a way to endure insanity, or pretend it didn't exist over the last thirty years. Or maybe she'd become insane herself. A logical practicum for one married to dementia's flagship. When living with the mad, you became mad. That was what Lenard had learned, now knowledgeable of the fact that he'd spent the last three years in training to become an actual superhero.

"You did the right thing, Dad," he said, willing to sacrifice honesty, which had never gone far with Fearghas anyway, to sandbag his emotional monsoon. "Don't be so hard on yourself."

Tear's scuttled down Fearghas's face while he cried and whined like a tortured scallop. It was loud enough that Lenard became afraid the two of them might attract law enforcement.

"Hard," Fearghas strained before his rattling pulley. It ebbed the rope up and down the wheel. "Hard, is the body you have, Son. The body that I have given you. My body, however," he sniffed, appraising his tattered petticoat from the feet up. "Is flimsier than chapel glass, and, though only half effective as yours, is three times, no, four times more beautiful."

"Yes, Sir," Lenard shook his head.

"I've left you a motherless mongrel!" the Scotsman screamed. "You've got nothing left but testicles and Steve."

"It's okay, Dad," said Lenard. "I'm going to be fine. I promise."

"Nobody can promise they'll be okay."

"I can, Dad," said Lenard, just trying to quiet him down. "Really, I can."

Lenard said what he did because his mother's death hadn't really been much of a surprise to him. She'd been displaying unusual moods in the last couple of years. Risking late hours into the evening, providing a fantasia of excuses. Pageanting herself before her commode in a frazzled Kitty Foyle dress or in lingerie. Or nude. Lenard suspected an affair, or multiple affairs. It wouldn't have surprised him since according to the rantings of his father, Fearghas and Floris hadn't actually touched each other since 1961 due to some horror neither would speak of. In the last few years the members of his family, like a deserted cluster of unbalanced planets, had begun to near collision. Lenard had somehow been kept safe. He was a small moon with minimal traces of water, ciliatic threads of bacteria teeming beneath its regolith, which had been bull-wrangled into close orbit by the blazing sun of Fearghas to encourage growth. Floris, however, had zipped off into a different solar system. She'd found a more auspicious rock cluster and merged with it kindly for a brief while until the chaos of space and filial circumstance prepared to xenon her into oblivion. Neither Fearghas nor Lenard had been home to witness her plummet to death, but when she was discovered there was a peace at the sides of her mouth, a smile. Or maybe it was recently satisfied hunger. Whatever it was, it made Lenard feel like she had beaten something. A small, true licking.

This final victory made the funeral pass much more quickly. It made Lenard's mother's death close to bearable. And the so-called "apotheosis" that Fearghas had following: (disappearing to Peru for three months and six days; participating in a cleansing ritual with a desultory coven of Amazonian shamans selling questionable spirituality on the limestone streets of Cusco; taking ayahuasca (a hefty psychotropic) and getting swallowed by a hallucinatory dragon with the eyes of his mother; dancing with a circle of cave frogs inside its belly; breaking free of that circle; eating the dragon himself; throwing it up for hours onto a phosphorescent flower patch; recovering slowly the next day; hobbling back to America; having his plane crash en route; and then being wrenched from the wreckage by Argyll, who had

75

been surreptitiously following him the entire time in disguise as a swarthy Chalan with a tattered blue and red Jipajapa) not seem so excessive.

Fearghas climbed into his scaffolding box and lowered himself to the ground, each squeak on the pulley whining its little traumatism. The platform scraped against the gravel and he stepped out towards Lenard with vampiric intent.

"Gravitas," he said.

A wind fell down upon him. His jaw looked sharper, defter, in the shape of a hairy ball-peen. A rattle of rain sprayed over the tops of the construction site, where, at its bottom, both Lenard and Fearghas tipped foot to foot. Lenard gulped as Fearghas took on a shiver of his irate self again. The tears temporarily ceased.

"What?" he asked.

"Gravitas," Fearghas said again.

"I don't know what that means," said Lenard, half-curious and half-bored.

"Iustitia, Pietas, Dignitas, Gravitas," Fearghas warbled, over-syllabically, looking deep into Lenard's eyes. "*Manaton*, Chapter 19, the four virtues that ancient Roman society expected all noble men to possess, according to Aesop Mac'Cool. Gravitas: the dignity, the duty, the seriousness of existence, not to be confused with gravity—though there are subtle linkages between the two. I want you to remember this word. I want you to recite it yourself while you walk the streets during the day and before you sleep at night. It will be your new prayer. Your murmur. Your war drum. Your substitute for sex. . .when needed. Gravitas: duty. Gravitas: momentum. Gravitas: dignity. Gravitas: man. You will find it, my boy, at the bedrock of your strength. You will remember it for your remaining days."

"What do the other words mean?" asked Lenard, deciding he was interested as he ducked under a set of roof beams to avoid the rain. "I-ew-Stew-tia?"

"Ah, fuck the other tenants. Never got anyone anywhere. Except for They, maybe. And God wish them death."

"But?" said Lenard, still unsure of who They was save for the scape-goat for Fearghas's angst.

"Ektasis," Fearghas said, turning his chin to the rain. A thundercloud boomed. "Now that's another important one to know. The ancient Greeks termed Ektasis 'mystical possession.' Convening with something greater than you. Great Rabbi Akiva was said to once embrace its concept with Judaic awe. The final chapter of *The Manaton* says of it, well. . .you're not quite ready for the final chapter of *The Manaton*. But I can tell you that when a boy comes of age as you are now, without your beautiful mother and her once-wrinkled teats, he must wean himself off his egg of origin and confer with the all-knowing spirit of man." He smiled a wide, dangerous grin. "What do you think about that?"

"I have to meet Laura in a half an hour," Lenard said, brushing up his sweatshirt to check his watch. A Mickey Mouse club timepiece he'd had since he was thirteen with a missing minute hand clicked towards an ambiguous seven. "But I will meditate upon what you have told me."

"Ay, procreation," Fearghas said, staring into the clouds as if they were plotting his demise. "The necessary payoff of this gigantic joke called life."

"Agreed, Father," said Lenard, feeling sorry for the man. Recently his faculties seemed so endangered Lenard worried he would lose his earthly tread and bugaboo off into the stars. But then Fearghas would lower his eyes and put his hands on top of Lenard's—as he did now, warming them only slightly—and say something like, "Son, you are truly the apple of my eye. No matter what anyone ever says, know that you are the strongest—the most heartful boy in the world. I believe in you." He placed his palm on Lenard's shoulder. His words were slow and sincere. His breath smelled familiar in its motliness, each immobile stench maintaining a personality in his throat. "Just as I believe you can do anything you set your mind to."

"Thanks, Dad," said Lenard. He felt his skin swell. There were times when Fearghas seemed like the most kingly creature on the planet. A self-proclaimed God on their planetoid. But, careful not to mistake paternalism for opportunity, Lenard asked, "Can I borrow five bucks?"

Fearghas rummaged through his pocket and withdrew seven and a half dollars, wrapping the bills over the coins in Lenard's hand.

"Anything for my little savage," he said, patting him on the forehead. "Anything at all."

Lenard smiled and stuffed the money deep inside his sweatpants. He didn't understand why his father called him "Savage," a word *The Manaton* revered, or why he didn't care to be concerned. Charles Manson had recently been sent to prison, and now, as summer began to burn at its peak, he wondered if new homicidal maniacs were being weaned in their cribs, sucking too tough, and long, at the nipple. As he tried to remember the shape of his own mother's areola, and how hard he'd suckled and with what intent, he felt the money sashay through his pocket. He thought about the way his mother had died. How little he had felt in comparison to how much he probably should have. Then, the money, ecstatic, ready. The madness of how quick it would be spent. Obtaining it could be a lot like the suckling of teats, especially when it came to Fearghas Sikophsky.

"If you spend it all, I'll kill you," the Scotsman followed up, tapping his toe against the ground.

Lenard nodded. "Clear as day." Though there was no telling if he'd really understood.

For a long time, almost twenty years, the Sikophskies had been living off generous disability checks Floris had been receiving from the government. For a disability that she, Fearghas, Dr. Fezzeliski, and Argyll, had fabricated as a means to collect welfare. A few times a year, Floris rolled around in a wheelchair under observance for ALS disease, acting the part of a paraplegic for those who remained in doubt. The payoff had been more than substantial for all involved parties, save for Argyll, who received nothing, of course, but orders. When she died, Fezzeliski infiltrated the morgue and rewrote the coroner's report, demonstrating, through the speedy reception of her life insurance, that some good things could come from a mother's death. Especially now that the checks had increased, and to Lenard's sad and embarrassed elation, he was bestowed with more and more pocket money.

Under her front porch's pergola, Laura awaited Lenard in faded blue jeans and a yellow blouse. The street-facing side of her family's compound (different from Lenard's house, which looked more like a condemned mine shaft) was actually the back, one colossal hexagon sliced down the middle and stuck into the ground. He hadn't got a chance to look at it, legally at least, until after his fight with the lions. But when he did finally, he felt it necessary to stare.

From Lenard's school days, the home reminded him of an inheritance trip he took with his class to see the Harlow Fort (a once-house, now museum) in Cape Cod. The old cabin was a model of 17th century settler life on the east coast, torn down in war by King Phillip, and restored two hundred years later by the Antiquarian Society with the intention of keeping history alive. Laura's home at 1210 Polypherm Road reminded Lenard of that trip, and the feelings of inferiority it once conjured. Except much unlike its historical elder, it was not to be held as litmus for the historically folksy or quaint.

At night it was collaged with windows at varying levels, unrevealing of the number, or concept, of floors. Hand-sawed blue cross boards sagged in color and bled, from left to right, into chalkier pastels. Within the jack pine hearth, there were stairs spinning into various directions, rooms stacked like answers to an Escher sketch. It was a disjointed labyrinth that could only be pleasing from the outside. A cool verdure to the garden suggested able economic upkeep, and this made the whole thing innocuous. From far away, it could be construed as a typical sight south of Boston. Something, more or less acceptably, touched by money, thus ignoring the insanity inside.

On the front porch, water brimmed over the gutters and created a screen over the Moskowitz's door. It was made of Pacific cherry, and, from the doorknob down, had been carved into raised panel-narratives depicting Indians on spotted horses. Lenard stared at the green curtain of rain a moment as he snuck, yet again, into the Moskowitz's mountain laurel. The green came from a wheat-colored light, coming through the beveled glass above the door's lintel. Behind, Lenard was sure, Mindy Moskowitz, Laura's mother, was probably holding one of her bimonthly Socialist Matriarchs of America meetings. Under her prized lime-tinted chandelier she'd brought back from vacation in Mexico, she advocated the abandonment of capitalist piggery.

"Then those SOB's down at the Oval Office will be forced to take us seriously," someone cried loudly from inside.

The others hushed him, before someone else yelled, "You never know who's listening."

Lenard knew that Mindy had been selling bank loans and buying up real estate since she was at least twenty-five, and had a vast empire of money and property that made his wide, plebian mouth water. But he also knew it was taboo to speak of any of it—as did everyone else. The subject was at the height of off limits, and enforced by Mindy's verbal gavel. Money was the evil subject that took up the bulk of every SMOA meeting. Whenever she hosted, she beleaguered their nation's system of unbridled economic expansion, evoking Lenin; snarling Marx; quoting, with a spiritual earnestness, Robert Owen; touting a Marcusian agenda, but always keeping her own system of earnings quiet. Someone had to host meetings, after all. Someone had to purchase the whitefish.

"You scared me, Corn Cob," said Laura, as Lenard crept on her from the side of her porch. He weeded his arms around her shoulders and kissed her neck from behind.

"They say terror is a mean aphrodisiac," he smiled, possibly at himself. "I thought I would set tonight's mood."

She assumed, then, they were still on for the movie as he leaned in to finish his hello. *Purification*, it was called, a newly popular film about a little girl from a wealthy family in Connecticut being possessed by a demon. Laura giggled when Lenard licked his tongue inside her mouth to answer her. She warbled "all right already" and pushed his face away. "The pinkos will hear."

"Maybe they should hear," Lenard said, groping her body indiscriminately as Chapter 7 of *The Manaton* had instructed (in which all men were advised 'to mark their allotted females like sextants searching for Atlantis'). "Might make them grow a pair of real, steel, American balls."

Laura cocked her right eyebrow.

"Likeyouknowwhatitmeanstohaveanyparticularnationalityofballs."

"You wanna see what it means?" Lenard said, mock-flailing the belt above his blue jeans with his left hand. "I'm sure I have at least one to spare. You can issue it a visa. Stripes and stars, Tush. Cracker jacks."

"I'll pass."

"Aw, come on, you can take' em to a Sox game."

From inside Mindy laughed, startling Lenard from the porch. As he dropped into the grass, he briefly wondered if she was a magical creature, some duplicitous hare, or maybe sloth, that he remembered existing in storybooks. He thought this way because, as he saw it, Mindy was merely concerned with the pitch and timber of her own voice. More so, anyway, than the words it carried. She was certainly more concerned with giving proclamations that toasted the downfall of evil empires than engaging in any action to change them. Lenard saw her only very rarely, an elusive, fat white stag, but could sense her tarp of loquacious bullshit from afar. It was a side effect of dating her daughter, he thought. Or, of being able to sense bullshit—something, he had to admit, he'd learned early on from Fearghas.

Now, as a rare occurrence, he glimpsed the prow of Mindy's shadow, the impression of a snowstormed Yeti, and wondered if it had been real. It expanded as it made the sermon of the evening, while glossy-eyed Jewish faces, a couple of them clearly Soviet, wondered if they could get away with nodding her praises while stealing to the table for whitefish. Lenard wondered what compelled them continuously to attend, under this wide hand that wrung out their honesty, as well as the honesty of socialism. Perhaps whitefish contained measured amounts of morphine. He never would, and never did, know.

"Let's get the hell out of here," Laura said. Just hearing the sound of her mother's voice could launch her into action. She bounced from the porch and into the rain. "Up, up, and away, Corn Cob. Before they turn their collective, commie heads."

Lenard mumbled a response not worth enunciating. He watched the water reveal parts of Laura's body beneath her puffy yellow blouse. He'd never before observed her in a downpour. And now that he did so, it frightened him.

"Come on," she whispered, motioning with her hand. "Come on, before they find us. We have to go."

But Lenard couldn't do anything but stare. In the past few months she'd become so slim. It could be said she had a waifness to her now, one that she tried to hide with baggier clothes as people did when putting on weight after a disease. She, however, could keep her secret well. Nature itself, the rain, was the only thing capable of revealing her sunken thighs—bony like a church saint's, narrow like said saint's vision—and over-swollen breasts under the guise of Massachusetts' rainfall. She was terrifically beautiful when wet, this much was true. She was enflamed when wet. She was youthful, but Lenard knew that with that youth there was also something undernourished about her. Some worm inside, snacking and swimming. Lenard saw it and it made him fear her, yet burn for her equally well. There was something inside their fragile relationship that diminished their love. Some fading halo in the space they inhabited that was, simply, too thin to see.

"You're the boss, Tush," he said, shaking his face from the red it betrayed, slipping through the grass as he tried to catch up to her. His navy umbrella glistened open.

"I'm your empress, Corn Cob," she yelled in response. "Note the difference between the two."

Thankfully, after his feat against the lions, Lenard's member had deflated, as if punctured, to about six and a half solid inches, which Laura still thought was too large. Sex, however, was had, and the frequency, nothing less than inspiring. Between training sessions with Fearghas, Lenard, like a mindless cage fighter, forewent his studies to be with Laura in bushes and the backseat of his father's car; Laura, like a caged bookkeeper, studied while Lenard mad-dogged his body into something similar to iridium. Her father, Jay Moskowitz, kept her in a scholastic isolation appropriate to any girl who was expected to obtain unobtainable success. He was an ornery old bastard who just looked like he kept secrets. He was also a dentist and an egomaniac. Listening to him talk about tooth surgery was like getting sodomized by a monocled ivory hunter in a tuxedo. So eloquent. Unnecessarily informative. Indulgent, histrionic, inappropriate, and everybody knew it. When he wasn't sputtering about innovations in dentistry, he was constantly aloft on stentorian rants of modern topographical muck-ups, vast historical plateaus, dated, and improper, research on the Inuit wolf-hunting practices in which, one day, he hoped to correct. Still, in the long run, as far as Milton went, he was respected. Even Fearghas, who hated most people, in some of his weaker moments admitted he was in awe of the man's prowess, or at least, persistence, of speech. And Lenard liked him for his ability to fix things. He had a trait that could actually make people better. Even if, as a father, he carried out his wife's orders in a bored, violent manner. It was rumored that his hand could be as convicted as his words, but again, that was rumor, word of mouth. A very quiet mouth that rarely opened.

Drawing his hood over his head, Lenard turned to Laura in the Cutlass, his fingers curled into claws. He loomed above her, inching towards her neck.

"Are you ready to be Purified, Tu*sssssshhh*?" he hissed, wiggling his fingers. "Are you ready to feel the ultimate—*Oomph*—"

Laura grabbed Lenard's jaw and yanked it toward the middle of the car.

"You've been doing it again," she shrilled, eyeballing his teeth. Lenard's sinister smile went limp along with the rest of his body. "Come on, Corn Cob. What did I say about grinding?"

Lenard rolled his eyes to the upper left of his head as if the answer were lurking there. Thoughtfully, he answered, "That it will make me go bald."

"Exactly," Laura said. "So you better start putting your mouth guard in at night. No man wants to lose their dignity before twenty. And look," she pushed up his damp black hair, the pale skin of his scalp where, beneath, his youthful hairline was already on the retreat. "You're well on your way to disgrace."

Lenard frowned and apologized, knowing he was far too young to be losing his mane. Especially if he was somehow encouraging its loss by unconsciously grinding his teeth. If true, that would surely mean he'd been responsible for aggravating the physical deterioration his father's plutonium may have started. And he'd made a promise to himself since that day of discovery at Dr. Fizzeliski's office: he'd have nothing to do with his own downfall.

"Nobody wants a *bald* superhero, sweetie," Laura said, teasing her vinyl hair back in a ponytail. "Imagine Superman with a comb over," she laughed. "Fucking A."

Lenard's chin sunk to his chest.

"Oh, honey," she frowned, noticing she's hurt him. "I was just joking. You'll be a great superhero, bald or not."

"Really?" Lenard pouted.

"Really."

Laura knew she was much smarter than Lenard, and, though she tried not to wield it against him often, had told him recently that grinding his teeth would one day make him go bald. She'd inherited from her father, like other, more terrifying things that would one day be revealed, an unwanted mania for healthy mouths. She honestly cared more about mouths than Lenard's foredoomed hairline, not to mention his body weight, malicious odors, potential unemployment, or disease. She thought it was a good idea to lie, however, to keep him on his toes. Even though Laura knew Lenard took his hygiene seriously, she also knew the simple logic of dental maintenance might not mix into the lazy butter churn of his mind. She wasn't even sure he owned a toothbrush. And in their relationship, anyway, he was the engine, and she, simply, was the brain that controlled that engine. *Fin.* That was why they'd been brought together by their parents to begin with. After the death of Laura's little brother (by a serial murderer pushing a converted ice cream rickshaw who'd been brought to court, but not to justice), her father and mother, as remote and sermonic as they were, found little moral opposition in searching out Fearghas and his nefarious crime-fighting plan, known of at the time only by a select few Scotsmen and prominent synagogue hush-mouths. Both Lenard and Laura had remained uninformed while all the arrangements were made, however. Right until after the lions, when the truth gushed forth like a septic leak.

"I haven't seen your father lately. Did you dump his body somewhere in the Charles?" Lenard joked, now hiding his hairline with his palm.

"Do you see pumpkins turning into carriages?" Laura asked. "Do you see a magic gentile rising from the ashtray? Then I'd say he's probably still a dentist. Alive and well. Forever unchallenged and tyrannical."

"Don't you mean genie?" Lenard asked.

"Same damn thing."

"I'm not sure if you'll get three wishes out of a Catholic, Tush," Lenard said, arm around her neck.

"Doesn't have to be a Catholic," Laura said.

Lenard pulled her over the center of the car, slowed down the acceleration, and kissed her on the forehead. "You take life so. . ." he shook his head, "seriously."

"You just can't fathom the degree to which I loathe the man," Laura whispered.

"I guess I can't see it," Lenard laughed uncomfortably, looking out the window. "All I know," he said, pointing at the dashboard every other syllable as he spoke. "Is that you live in a castle. A fucked up fun house of a castle, but a castle."

"I'd trade it for your house any day."

"My house," said Lenard, "Man. My house isn't even a house. It's almost falling off the foundations."

"Still better than what I've got."

"Nothing ever changes about you, does it?" Lenard asked. "No matter what anyone says, you're the same as ever."

"That's not exactly true." Laura looked out the window. She drew herself from under Lenard's elbow. "The degree to which I hate him. That changes. I certainly hate him more this month than I did last month. And I hated him more last month than the month before that. I just hate him, and my passive excuse for a mother, and my house, more and more and more every month. Like months means up. Like this." She started her finger low against her thigh and then ascended it slow on an invisible ramp, trying to trace what she felt inside, that boiling in her blood she couldn't cool. "My hate's like. . ." she paused, watching her pupils in the rearview, "something manufacturable for me. Like a Manhattan skyscraper, or a soufflé in the oven. If you put in the effort, or the heat, it just keeps rising and rising. . . ."

Her finger trailed up toward the roof of the car, and then through a crack in the window where its tip became wet with cold rain and she made a *popping* sound with her mouth. She then giggled. "Just like that."

"Well, you've definitely learned how to talk from your mother," Lenard said, making a poor joke to cover up whether or not he'd understood a word of what she'd said. "Soon you'll be a regular SOMA matriarch. I mean Jesus, Tush. Your mom, okay. But your dad? He's a bit of a ball-buster but he's not all that bad."

"He *is* that bad."

"I know the guy. He fixes teeth."

"He turns people towards suicide."

"He keeps a roof over your head."

"You know what the problem is?" She smiled wide, overly wide, so that each and every one of her perfectly straight teeth sparkled her father's acme of dental perfection. "You're easy. Too easy. Something sent here just to show all the rest of us how fucked up we are." She stroked two of her fingers down his face, down his nose. "Don't you ever get angry, you know, at my father—at your father, for what they did to us? He threw you into a lion pit, remember?"

Lenard nodded. His face sunk lower and lower into his neck. "I remember," he frowned. "And you should too. Your parents arranged your kidnapping."

"Oh, I do remember," she yelled. In the only way she could. A perfunctory rise in the volume of her voice that echoed the ethics of her household. So many times she'd had her thoughts flattened by hand or howl; the result of her parents' labors to keep life quiet. Now she practiced that quietness with Lenard. She practiced that quietness with everyone. "That's the problem," she finished, in her quiet voice.

To her satisfaction the words quieted Lenard, too. He started the car and they rode in silence until he flipped on the radio, tuned in directly to Fearghas's reeling pipes. He changed the channel, heard a man lowing his sympathies for Jim Morrison, whose death was being celebrated in endless encomium across the nation. They passed into a tunnel, under tiny dome-shaped lights that whizzed over them predictably in twos.

"Corn Cob?" she said, placing her hand on Lenard's knee. One more question. "Do you love him?"

"Love who?"

"Come on." With her right hand she removed a bag of butter mints from her purse, took out a bright blue one, and sucked on it along with the tip of her index finger.

Lenard heard the pipes on the radio, but didn't track their melody. He knew whom it was she spoke of.

"I don't know," he said, steering the Cutlass onto the highway. It lurched like a horse as he put it into third. He remembered the seven and a half dollars in his pocket, taken, in the end, from his mother. He stretched out Fearghas's gift, his legs, buzzing just a little bit with the amatol of twin V2 rockets. He felt his heart beat that quantum boom he'd come to know, louder, stronger, more punctilious than moon cycles. He remembered *The Manaton*'s methodology, Chapter 33, on domesticating a rhinoceros for combat. "But," he said, flat and slow, while he visualized a galloping valley of white horns, and then a man, a monstrous man, falling from the sky upon those white horns, to wrestle them under his chest, "I do respect him."

Laura *humphed* and cracked open the window. The wind passed over their heads.

"I think it's the opposite for me," she said, clamping the mint against her cheek with her tongue. She sighed and reached out to change the station.

"But then again, I'm not as easy as you."

Purification was exactly what Lenard had hoped it would be: terrifying. He held Laura tight through the previews in anticipation of ghouls before they even materialized, often groping her salaciously within view of an older, more disapproving-of-everything couple sitting in the chairs to their left. They, in particular, were fleshy, pink, like a couple of pigs in poor disguise as they hid from the butcher. They squished into their seats with their belted stomachs bulging above the cup-holders, hating Lenard and Laura before the movie started, the adolescents could tell, just upon their entrance into the theatre—their smell of new and evolving youth filled their nostrils with the poison gas of nostalgia.

Behind, Laura noticed, was the couple's equally unsavory opposite. A long, lanky man, all skin and ribs, wearing a misapplied ski mask. His eyes reflected the screen like two sleepy nickels, and his mouth hung open through a hole in the cloth in a way that made Laura briefly wonder if he had died during the film's last showing. He seemed to have been sitting there before anyone else, anyway, and smelled like the bottom of a tugboat.

For the first half of the film Lenard was sucked into a beaker of cinematic mist. His tongue lolled out of his mouth. He withheld the urge to pass gas. The consequences of a nervous Jew like him watching a film like *Purification* was that, afterwards, he'd have to consider the question: but what if the Christians are right? Hell, Satan, demonic possession, holy water, head-spinning; these were all notions cherished by the goyim, but utterly enigmatic to a Jew. If this movie scared hardworking salt of the earth crusaders of Christ, then it scared the living bowels out of awkward Hebrews who'd been searching out their own demons their entire lives. Christians had an entire universe of the macabre to work with. Jews, they had mother-complexes. Honestly, Lenard found the former more favorable, even if for him, though his particular complex involved a raving, burly Scotsman. Maybe it had been the part of him educated by Fearghas and *The Manaton*, or maybe for some reason pure evil just put all one's ducks in a row. Who needed to create something to be afraid of when Hell and all its demons could be found on thirteen-hundred-year old wall frescos in Florence? When good and bad were so epically segregated, life could be solved with a calculator.

"This is fucking terrifying," Lenard whispered. He was basically on top of Laura, squishing her with his pregnant thighs as he slowly, and with all his weight, took a lean.

"I have never seen anything scarier," Laura smirked, maneuvering his shoulder and face to crunch down on a handful of popcorn.

Lenard ignored her as the little maledicted girl, once named Maria Rosaria Santa Cristo D'Angelo but now referred to as simply "the possessed," spun her scarred, purple face from front to back on the screen. This was while a man who looked like a priest, even without his collar would look like a priest, named father Coglione, battled her down from her acid spittings, contortions, and ice-breathing, into the soiled creases of her brass-framed bed while screaming *Bitch of Bethlehem!*

Lenard lashed out in genuine horror as the little girl's head spun round on its neck. He sent a spray of popcorn into the empty seat in front of him. Laura tried to catch some as the fat couple scowled.

"How do they do that?" he whimpered, infant in his fascination of the screen.

"They cut off a pig's head and swab it over the doorsteps of synagogues," Laura snickered. "Awakening the dark lord himself." She slapped his cheek lightly. "Come on, you dope. It's Hollywood."

The power of Christ repels you. The power of Christ repels you! Priest Coglione continued to chant from the screen. He doled out holy water, twirled rosaries, yelled out twenty-one badly pronounced Hebrew and Aramaic names for God. The demon imposter inside the girl screamed, *God is the bitch, Coglione! God is the bitch!*

The couple beside Lenard ate their movie snacks, which involved home-brought commodities like a Tupperware full of sloppy-looking spaghetti and a slab of marbled cake. The spindly man behind them seemed to suddenly wake up upon hearing mouths smacking. He began fiddling through his sole belonging; a leather jacket torn through at the left pocket. Coolly, Priest Coglione said something to the demon about God clearly possessing male genitalia, which started a long argument between the two of them on celestial anatomy.

The man behind Lenard rose from his seat.

He stuck a cold pistol between the sweaty, top-most rolls in the fat man's neck. Stray noodles flopped from his lips to the floor, fine saucy driblets on his shoes.

"All of your cash," he said, nudging the barrel. "Metals, too. Jewelries."

The priest lifted his cross into the air.

"Mandy, your purse," said the fat man, whispering.

"Wallet, fucko," said the ski mask, as the gun swept to Lenard's perked ear.

As the gunman had been preparing his stick-up, Lenard was busy gripping Laura's arm, wrenching it, while her prim, blockish face, bored behind the fat-rimmed glasses she only used for the megaplex, waited for the whole damned miserable thing to just end. When Laura watched a film, especially a horror film, she watched it with intention of rooting out all the miracles of cinema, the would-be-convincing moments of tragedy and terror, just to show herself that it was possible to see through it. She waited with cool anticipation for the moments when the screen screamed FEAR. She then chuckled in her lungs, rejoiced in her ability to remain independent of the herd, to soar above the pheromones and terror. Laura didn't care for stories, fictions, or distractions that disguised themselves with louder words like creativity and serendipity. Meaning. As far as she was concerned, film, fiction in general, was a masturbatory impulse, and there was far more paucity in the act of masturbation then actually engaging the flesh. She, for one, liked to roll in the muck of dirty, filthy, life. To know what she touched was real. She hated watching the faces blur across the family television and, in her constricting navy pantsuit, making regular appearances at the Boston Opera House. She hated having her nose in a book all day, because since a young age, since her first of what would become many attempts to snuff out her own life, it had been clear that she knew how to read one too well.

"Did you hear what I said, Gaston?" growled the ski mask, green teeth gnashing through the cloth.

Lenard's pupils shrank as the film's horror escalated. As the priest, somewhat, but not completely in surprise, tore his clothes off and screamed. Lenard's body stretched further from the Megaplex chair, transfixed by Christian battle. The fat man sitting next to him, more or less indistinguishable from his contumacious snail of a wife, with spaghetti still dribbling from her lips as well, knuckled him firmly on the shoulder.

"Don't be a hero, kid," he said.

Laura had been aware of the gun since it first emerged from its weathered pocket. She watched it flicker back and forth between the two men's heads, leaving the women on the periphery of a peculiar boy's game being reasoned out with pistols and popcorn. Laura almost felt like she wanted to be included, wanted to shout "pick me, I'm shootable." Like 'shootable' was 'approachable,' or 'touchable' or 'screwable,' and all of those better than 'negligible.' She scooted herself around in the chair and whipped her hair in a cue around her neck, opting to draw the pistol closer.

"Don't think you're getting off the hook, Ms. Proper," the gunman said, saying proper like *plopa* as he leaned over her shoulder. "Look at those fresh thighs of yours." His lips were wet. "Like I could take a bite."

Laura's mouth peaked as the voice came towards her. It followed an uneducated lisp. Bits of orange hair tetched out from under the mask, sweaty and streaked with dark blotches as he shoved the pistol right behind her ear. He came close to her neck, breathed on her skin. She thought for a moment he'd kissed her.

"I'd like to lick a little a danger into you," he said. His tongue slurped out towards the screen and the gun barrel swelled against her temple. "You wanna lick some properness into me?"

A shot went off in the theatre as Lenard, screaming, erupted from his seat. The bullet zipped a small slit through the priest's shoulder, leaving a tiny anus to flap in the vinyl.

"Calm down, Lenny," said Laura, exasperated. She tried to appease the frightened moviegoers by seagulling her arms, saying, "He gets worked up real easy—damnit Corn Cob, put the bad man down." She pulled Lenard by his waist and tried to cram his legs back in the chair.

"You don't think my female is dangerous?" he screamed. "You were wrong, pal. You were wrong!"

"Corn Cob, calm down!"

"Get the fucker," yelled the fat man next to them, rolling his fists. "Break his fucking legs."

"Somebody get the police," someone said.

"I AM THE POLICE!" Lenard yelled.

"*GodNJoseph*," the ski mask cried. "Please put me down."

"My female IS danger!" Lenard screamed. "You touch her, you touch me. You touch her, YOU TOUCH ME!"

"Eat his ballsack!" yelled the fat man, engorged like a steaming beet.

"Let me eat his ballsack!"

Lenard hurled the man in the ski mask through the movie screen, right through its middle, collapsing *Purification* into a carnival of light. The skin of the vinyl billowed like a mast under cannon-fire. Bright red curtains wandered loose from atop the stage. The flickering face of the demon continued to snarl, rippling its hell across the wall. Laura yelled, "Let's get out of here," and Lenard nodded his general approval.

As they stole away, the fat man stumbled up to them, snagging Lenard's arm.

"You're phenomenal, kid. Where did you get that strength of yours?"

"From my father," Lenard said, as Laura dragged him, with her entire body, down the aisle. He put his hands on his hips and stopped. His eyes glistened with melodrama. "As every man does."

The demon continued to spit the words of a dying Beelzebub. father Coglione lashed out Catholic wisdom, his wavering cross only sensible on the theatre walls by the oleo tinge of its wood. Cameras told lies, Laura thought as they ducked out the exit doors, elbowing their path through the mob. Artists told lies. Made people believe in the impossible. The only way to truly portray reality was not to portray it at all, but to just participate, she thought. Just like the only real way to kill a man was to stab him in the face with a knife. Or toss him through a megaplex viewing screen, she added, silently, as they spilled out into the parking lot.

She would have to admit, however, days from now, that spaded tongue that spit and licked, those grim incantations, those Christian thrusts of repressed and dark imagination she'd witnessed on that screen, must have worked its way into her mind somehow. Even if she didn't let it affect her on the surface, her typically empty dreams would be plagued by the howls of Maria Rosaria Santa Cristo D'Angelo for weeks.

"Now, that's life," said Laura, as Lenard scrambled for his keys. She was so happy, and sure that the stars, though she couldn't see them, were bright.

"No, Tush. That's work," Lenard said sternly, thinking of his father, and how proud he would be, as they buckled into the Cutlass and were confronted by a silence.

"Call it what you will, Corn Cob, but even if it didn't say so," she whispered, "the world knows you just saved the day."

Laura smiled. She smiled because Lenard, in all his stupidity and sock stench, was just so damn beautiful. Such a brute, unalphabetizable animal. Yet, so basic. When she thought about him in terms of how she thought about a lot of things (*e.g.* her high school biology textbooks), he seemed perfectly, stupidly congealed. It almost made her forget about the conditions of their relationship. As if they'd met on the winds of destiny.

As she pondered this, she grabbed the back of his head. Tickled his hair. Brought her hand down into his shirt as he keyed the ignition. She envied how people became like him: just present in life. He'd never understand her, but that was okay. He'd learn to provide other things she needed. He'd fight every one of her battles. He'd allow her the space to deconstruct her surroundings, her body, and eventually herself, as she continued on her long, almost meaningless jaunt through existence towards a quick, and, as she saw it, meaningless death.

"Let's have sex," Lenard said. "Right here. Right now."

Laura whisked off her shirt and said, "Anything for a hero."

She thought of the subject of high school biology. She thought of her and Lenard as a ganglion of cells that were lost and predictable, sealed inside a troubled sphere of air and rain. Mitochondria splitting and replicating and dying. The neurons incited when Lenard kissed her lips, when her parent's caused her pain, when a convict held a gun to her neck. When he pushed it slightly forward, making death come so close, so close she wanted to kiss it.

Though Laura didn't know it now, she'd be immured in these passing daydreams for the rest of her days. She'd reinvent her own way of touching and seeing. Or what her ways of touching and seeing could manifest as creations, scientific innovations. But for now she knew, by seeing more than touching, nothing was better than dating a Jewish boy with a dead mother. For, if anything else, it was Laura who'd become the replacement. The power, in a way she truly hated, was almost flattering. It was a responsibility girls like her were supposed to dream for. Passed down by mothers for generations. Passed down by generations to therapists. Passed down even if she didn't want to be a girl like her, a girl who appreciated power, not because power was bad, but because it was something to appreciate. Something away from home. She was sure Lenard replaced something for her as well—as he reached under his skirt, swiped up her knee to her thigh, up up inside—but was reluctant to admit exactly what. Whatever it was, though, she wasn't sure if she was ready for it.

"You are loved," she moued, and kissed his hairy lips. If not by her, then by someone. She shimmied on top of his lap. She was repulsed by his wide-gapped teeth as he breathed, so she clicked his jaw closed with her fingers by pushing on his chin. "You will always be loved."

And they continued caressing as the police cars rolled by, and their uniforms rushed the panicked theatre.

Later that night, after Lenard drove Laura home, after he was lectured at the door by her mother Mindy—who relayed to him the importance of encouraging universal healthcare in the Nixon privatization era of essential human rights that she didn't necessarily care about, but was too purposeless to ignore—he came back to his house, crept past the snoring cavern where wifeless Fearghas now slept alone (one eye open, with his arm around Steve), into his childhood room, and immediately fell asleep.

A clock, shaped like a lunar rocket with the numbers still stuck to 12, 3, and 6, ticked out the seconds into morning. It was surrounded by tiny metal axles and shiny hoods drying on dull plastic car beds. Behind a jar full of nickels, a glass-framed map of the Yucatan took on the color of the moon. Lenard nodded in and out of sleep. His dreams were inked with splotches of blood on white linen. His mother with bloated veins between her toes. Crosses. Christs. Limbless Lauras with red-laser eyes abandoning him. Betrayals. Stabbings. Seedy underworlds sultry, and other manifestations of his childhood monster, the Kraken. His eyes edged open, and from the foot of his bed, a faint limning of silver weeded all his trash, toys, and models like runes on a Celtic gravestone. He saw, at the purple pit of that light, the spreading of wings, more than two of them, like crumpled para-chutes, and the opening of two dull white eyes. Glitter vermiculated over the walls and stray locks of hair leaned down over the bed.

"Ektasis," he heard, in a voice that blew tardy, like wind lowing over an icefield. Lenard's skin felt aroused. He was erect and filled with hot breath.

"Ektasis," he heard, writhing and moaning. He'd never before felt such pleasure.

"Gravitas. Iustutia. Ektasis," he heard. "Gravitas. Iustutia. Ektasis."

Chapter 12

ON CONQUERING FEMALES

Or,

*on utilizing manful Spermatozoon to subvert
the inferior gamete,*

ACCORDING TO *Aesop Mac'Cool*

Upon taking an afternoon stroll with my friend and partner in
Man-things, Beamish, who is a philosopher of sorts, a skilled
owl taxidermist, and has been known to hurl boulders into harbor ships as a way to demonstrate procreative prowess, I realized
that my Man-bible had yet to describe its rituals on capturing
a female. Now, I do know that female, or femella, femina, is a

grotesque substructure of earth's glorious species of bipedal male habilis—Manu! She is a medusa of sorts, capable of enchanting men into servitude (see chapter 9, Female Sex Magic and How to Protect against by Defecating in Concentric Circles) through their motley vulvas and the poisonous tunes they play. But, as Beamish and I concurred, after a long conversation examining the aftermath of a flatulence contest we conducted under a tunnel arch just east of my home, the vagina (just to say that word makes my Manheart sink) must be accessed to give unto the earth more Man.

Oh misery.

Therefore, in the tradition of those who have come before me, Plutarch, Shakespeare, Yeats, de Sade, I will enliven the secret cabal of Love, that hideous, mendacious word, by outlining a series of simple steps. Beamish-approved, these steps are the work of two Manful minds. Two minds of Man. Two Man minds that, when combined, are more than two Man minds, but four Man minds multiplied, or the mighty mind of ultimate Man, or maybe just two minds. Or one.

STEP UN

ADORNING THE CHEST REGION WITH MODERATE PUBIC CONSISTENCY

Though I am fairly unblessed with a pelt of fur necessary to convince arctic wolves that they are my kindred in the winter, Beamish, being of higher selective altitude, is a beast of perpetual man-forest. Laden with more than 14 centimeters of androgenic fuzz at selected points during the year, he is what I like to call, the anti-female, or the antipodal opposite of anything carrying traces of vulva. Manaticus! That beast, in particular, I still refer to as Gorgon, after the three monstrous Libyan sisters with wiry beards and razor-tusks, and I practice warding myself daily from their licentious methods by adorning my front door with animal skulls.

Beamish stands at four meters tall, has a cranium the size of our southern Queen's mutton-fed arse, and likes to eat grass sometimes, as he pretends he is a grazing Holarctic Caribou, while contemplating the heavenly spheres. He is what every Man hopes to be, or what every Man truly is, within his tinier, more unfortunate body. Sometimes I smell the brute, when he isn't looking, of course, and inhale his salts and musks as if they are ether from Apollo. Frequently, I wish to bottle those intoxicants and distribute them for profit around the emerging new world. I could become rich this way. Beamish, of course, would have to be disposed of (please refer to chapter 17, on Man-Marketing).

However, when it comes to procreating, Beamish's mythological nature frightens even the most feeble sort of female (if such a thing can even be scored). Those with warts, or syphilitic brains, have been known to flee his presence, often soiling their already-dirty skivvies with even daintier, disguised forms of filth. And all this presents a problem to my colleague, for, under these otherwise favorable circumstances, the anti-female has no son to wean, no creature to trek up into the mountains and reveal the miracles of flatulence, no wee, stupid youth to curse at God with, or take into the forest to wrestle bears.

Beamish's testicular gusto began to wane as his dreams of procreation became unrealized. Often he sat by the fire, which we tried to always keep burning in the hearth of my cellar in frequent case we needed to roast hocks of wrestled seal meat, and stared, watching, what I thought to be, his own soul crackle into smoke. It was upon one of those nights, when Beamish began to defecate on the floor because he felt a toilet was no longer useful for a man without a son, that I found a possible reason for his evolutionary lack of copulative success.

Here, as I saw it, was a mighty bastard, an unfellable tree, like Itone, the whorish daughter of Lyªius, except, needless to mention, more Male. Much like that mythical vegetation, which grows too many leaves in the summer to allow the sun to set foot on the soil, Beamish's body hair gives him the appearance of something non-human (which I believe him to be). Something resembling, in his most favorable light, a Cro-Magnon curiosity. Thus, upon realizing this, a hint of genius played its familiar note across my Manful mind. Upon examining my own body, which has engaged in filthy exercises of coitus in order to brew my foredoomed future a son, I found that it had only terse mappings of noble fur, like island archipelagos, barely grazing my shallow water's skirt.

The following is a self-illustrated portrait of Beamish:

(Fig. 47)

As one may notice, the baby he carries is not his own, but stolen, in essence, to supplant his own inability to perform coitus. In effort to attempt and barber the creature, or at least hem down his truly magnificent MAN-shrubbery, I tried to outline a more selective diagram of acceptable chest patterns to induce mating. I also returned the stolen child to its owners under threat of enforced penal law.

Using myself as a model, thus, I attempted, over a series of months, to artfully recompose my body's natural endowments. The figure on the next page is the result of said experiment.

(Fig. 47a)

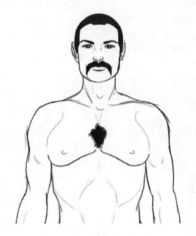

the milkless teat

Cicero

Goldilocks

GRAR!

Now, to my laboratorial elation, and somewhat disgust, each of the four separate designs attracted different specimens of female. While what I like to call 'the milkless teat,' positioned on the upper left of the diagram, drew a daintier beastie, thin, with hooked features, knobby, if not clubbed, toes, and a general attitude of regality, the drawing on the lower right, which I refer to, simply, as GRAR! attracted a buxom succubus of foreign order (possibly Portuguese), who wore nearly suffocating abdominal attire to accentuate her mammaries, was dumber than bread, and excelled, above all, in activities of fellatio. The hedging in the upper right, which Beamish termed Cicero, brought forth creatures of, what I would call, a psychotic sexual nature. Amongst the slew of heinous acts they asked me to commit under the candle of coitus, most of which I will not mention, I remember, at my darkest moment, being made to wear my mother's retired marital garb at musket point.

The figure in the left hand corner, which I have named, somewhat ironically, Goldilocks, has retained the most normative results. For the most part, the animals driven to bed by its wiles have tended to be fairly standard in their requests, escorted themselves from my premises promptly following, and spoke nothing of the size of, what I think is, my sizeable Manhood, even if other women have tended to disagree.

"Hmmmm."

Argyll placed *The Manaton* in his pocket, right before approaching *Step Duex, Constructing the Proper Net,* which involved the making of an actual Gravattian fishing device to snag unsuspecting women from kitchens and convents as an alternative means to paying dowry. The rain above Milton turned to snow. November snow: New England's first storm. It came and went like gout through the night, but around 3 a.m., as Lenard twisted in his bed, the sky outside Blue Hills Reservation on the skirt of Randolph turned nearly black as a coal burn. It was swinishly dark in the air Argyll glimpsed beyond the downpour, with ash clouds circling in a coven of three. Trees looked defiant in the new winter white.

Argyll came strolling from the mouth of a cavern. It was a bestial gash in the side of a hill where a train route skimmed the other side. His dirty scarf whipped around his shoulders, along with his hair and the swinging railroad lantern at his belt, casting a sickish light. Wiping his brow, he came to the edge of a drop-off, where below he could see Boston glow. In the distance, it seemed sad, the dream of a foreigner that had raised a civilization just below his standards, then let fail. Let suffer over the reality of an ancient land. The Charles River looked so beatific that it seemed possible to wipe it like mortar. The lonely buoys left no ripples in the surface.

Argyll belched and spit off the cliff side, watched the spit fall until it became nothing more than a sound. Its death was stolen by the near whine of a train chugging round the Blue Hills. He took from his pocket a messy collection of forged passports he'd be selling soon to a high-bidding party. Belarus, Bolivia, Japan, Tunisia; each wallet looked so shiny. His toes puttered on the ground to keep him warm, crunching down soft in the snow.

"Is it time?" came a voice from behind him, followed by a roar.

Argyll stuffed the passports into his ragged pocket with *The Manaton* and turned around to face his colleague, Fearghas. The Scotsman was wrapped in a fluffy Turkish bathrobe, and seemed to be wearing nothing beneath but a pair of unsocked tennis shoes. He looked freshly bathed, though, and more freshly annoyed. His fingers itched with zeal at his hips.

"Fergie?" Argyll squinted at his colleague. "Where did you come from?"

"That's not your concern," he said, looking down slightly. From the thicket, Steve emerged. The lion stalked the old man in a slow, close circle, looking especially dangerous in the snow.

"Ay," Argyll said. "So it's not." He began to turn in circles as well.

"They is getting closer," Fearghas said. "It's possible that last night They found our location."

"Jesus," said Argyll. "Is He with them?"

Fearghas looked to the ground.

"I assume so. Being He *is* their new leader."

"I thought *He* was dead."

"*He* should be."

"And does He know where you are?"

"Not yet He doesn't. And I plan to keep it that way. Do you have the passports at hand?"

"Always."

"What's my new name?"

"Uranus Zatkin."

"Good," said Fearghas. "And Lenard's?"

"Lantana Zatkin."

"Also good. And what about the plane tickets?"

"Two nights from now. Stopover in Guam."

"And the machine?" Fearghas asked.

He paced in close so that his breath misted up Argyll's glass eye. His shoulders ruffled his robe, puffed out and like he was an owl emerging from its roost. Steve came to his side and Fearghas offered him an ox tail from his pocket.

"Warp speed," said Argyll, handing Fearghas back *The Manaton*. Fearghas thumbed through the pages to make sure they were intact.

"Warp what?" he snarled.

Argyll took something from behind his back, something resembling an aluminum shoebox, snapped together by a few snags of duct tape. It had an array of multicolored buttons and dials on one side and a pair of rabbit ear antennas on the other.

"Sure as my virginal birth," he said, turning a bright yellow dial.

S K R E E E E E E E E E E E E E E E E E E E E E E E E E E E E E E C H H H H ! ! ! ! !

Fearghas stumbled into the snow.

The sound roiled from inside the cavern, crumbling stone and shale from the mouth. Argyll smiled and slobbered. Steve even seemed frightened, letting the half-devoured ox-tail drop from his mouth.

Argyll brandished the box in his hand.

"Very ready," he said, giggling.

"And what about the situation with **NORDEK** labs? The pig carcasses?"

"All taken care of weeks ago."

"Go find the boy, then," Fearghas commanded.

Argyll launched himself down the slope.

"And be quick!"

The Scotsman stepped towards the precipice, his work boots, recycled from textiles during WWII like most of his wardrobe, digging dents in the snow. He, too, began watching Boston, not his home, but his resident city, as it chilled in its icebox below the horizon. It was the place where he knew he would die. He was getting too old for anything else, and for some reason, this contented him. His days were closing in quick, days as a salesman's bargain. Something to keep paying for, even as each passing sun and its roll around the earth murdered an unrealized dream.

"The Great 'Fuck You' has arrived," he said, running his tongue across his fat wintered lips. The city opened up to him like one wide coffin, beckoning for him to find rest. "And tomorrow," he smiled, "we will welcome it."

CHAPTER SEVEN

THEY

They came as a masquerade of murderers gestating plague between their
fingers; they had masks with bolts on the chin and cheeks, cockroach-black
tuxedoes and weedy red ties. White shoes. Guns were held behind their
backs in the way of planning a terrible joke. The one with the walleye, who
they called Agamemnon, rang the doorbell with the back of his revolver. A
dragon being chased could be smelled inside, so the smallest boy, Peccadillo,
took out his knife for skinning, thinking this would be easy. A leader of this
tribe of teenagers, a tall, handsome man approaching his fifties with a furry
Ushanka on his head, read with interest the front welcome mat. *Doctor's
In,* he read aloud, and he stepped in front of them, holding his hand in a
halt. Wrapping fingers around a cold Sig Sauer, he smiled for the first time
in years. For people like them, invitations were frowned upon. They were
content when the world barred them in.

Dean Fezzeliski opened the door, a bit of startled smoke between his
lips. As he began to speak Peccadillo elbowed his gut, and they were upon
him. The door closed, and inside silence became disturbed by bursts of insanity. These men enjoyed the vision of a cleaner world. There were no wishing wells or magic north stars, and silence was not the end of a gun, but a
finger, pleasuring trigger after trigger, the bullets, and their pleasure, in turn.
The leader was tired, watching through the window into the streetlamp,

examining erosion in the yard. He left the dirtier work to the others as a reward for their toils. And they were enthralled to do so—especially Agamemnon, who may have had an erection as he snapped the old man's kneecap with the butt of his M-14. He had aspirations to become a small business owner, but for now, breaking limbs made him feel alive. A thumb was severed. An eye gouged out. Something emerged as the stomach was gutted, about a boy of remarkable deformity who'd grown into unrivaled strength, a boy whose father was an aging Scotsman, someone by the last name of Sikophsky. An address was given in Milton and the leader took off his shoes—a custom of his—softly padding towards the doctor. Lifting a revolver, the old man's lips trembled.

"I know who you are," he said, bowing in the last of his blood.

The handsome man in the Ushanka laughed a little bit, cocking the shaft. The look in his eyes was weary.

"No," he whispered, before pulling the trigger, and an orange fire blazed with unholy intent. "You don't."

CHAPTER EIGHT

DEATH AND DANCING

Lenard was cold all day. Sweating and sour. Last night's dreams had resulted in a bed sheet soaked with his secretions and slimes. He felt like he'd caught, battled, and passed on a flu; like he'd scaled a mountain in the shape of sex; like he'd played the part of some shadow overfucked by a heft of light, that sex became more of a pathology, or injury, rather than urge. But, upon finding Laura in his arms again, making love, or something similar to making love—him making love to her while she wondered if they were making love, or while she counted the weakening chemical reactions in his body as they rose together towards an awkward teenage orgasm that was almost painful—he realized that nothing was too difficult to forget, or forgo. Especially when he wasn't sure, concerning the previous night's. . .vision, he'd call it, as to whether or not he was losing his mind.

He'd taken his dose of combinatory plutonium base that morning (in green pill form now to better the taste of food, courtesy of Argyll) before shirking all things academic to end up in the Cutlass again, beneath the patter of Massachusetts' rainfall, beneath the thighs of Laura, her Stooges Fun House t-shirt with its libidinous montage of Iggy Pop covering the upper half of her body like a provocative Pan. It grazed down Lenard's sides—up and down, down—while voices on the radio coolly prattled on about the My Lai massacre.

"Cold," she grunted.

"What?" asked Lenard.

There was a moment of gunning rain before Laura let her body go. The radio sizzled. *Women and children.* Laura's legs were moist and Lenard felt her sharp, fatlacking femurs dig into his abdomen. Her body rose, crowned through the shadows as if it were stuffed inside a car-shaped aquarium. Her scalp dipped through a skirt of gray light. Her eyelids seemed marine. Lenard felt Laura's rhythm, and remembered the two of them dancing, how she taught him to do something besides lift his shoulders up and down as if he were shrugging off music itself. She taught him how to do the Monkey, the Watusi, the Blue Beat. She taught him how to let his head go with the guitar when Hendrix wailed out anything at all, but particularly "3rd Stone from the Sun." This girl he'd become connected to out of parental obligation, coaxing residual trauma from his legs, drawing him into her now, kneading him now, extolling his wealth in gentle bursts.

When Lenard was younger, and abnormal, and undergrown, he remembered positioning himself atop the bleachers at middle school, watching the pretty girls walk by like transoceanic pompadours, immortal mahatmas in halter necks with lives so rich and wonderful they'd seemed off limits to anyone who couldn't purchase a country west of Tunisia. But Laura, she helped Lenard's insignificant self become conscious of its worth, or at least of its ability to perceive worth. She took him to shows to watch dark, dangerous music, haggard hands at the drums or guitar. She taught him how to look like a human at early versions of what became discos and punk-rock clubs, and by doing so became more human herself. She preened him before mirrors, made him turn his feet forward when he walked; she hadn't even known about his legs. Lenard felt, however, that when he was with her he was accepted amongst the living. Within the voodoo of Laura's bony waist, he became a real member of humanity, released from the sheltered whimsy of his youth.

"I'm ready," she whispered, grasping the neck of his shirt. "I'm ready."

Lenard expelled the last of anything he had, a little bit of powder or dust, as someone on the radio voiced, *Calley's only the beginning,* and his eyes opened shrewdly as if Laura were a bicycle, purchased second-hand, and she fell on top of him and spaghettied her dewed black hair down his chest until her forehead found itself lodged in his armpit. She inhaled him: saline, pond rock, the bottom of pond rock, and remembered the time when he'd saved her from making a drastic decision; not a bad decision, but a hasty one. When, soon after her brother's serial murder, soon after some man last named Turney, first named Bill or Gordon—she didn't give half a hell to remember—at the Boston Globe, stupidly blocked **Ice-Cream Vendor Sells Snowcone of Death** in sensationalized gothic letters on Sunday's front page, she'd almost taken enough quaaludes to euthanize a bear.

She remembered how Lenard stayed her hand halfway through her bottle, or at least showed up before she could take the rest of it. How he brought her to Dean Fezzeliski, around midnight, in an ice storm, in her soiled French cut underwear, and had her stomach pumped in secret under a ceaseless cloud of opium. The quaaludes had been the residue from her first real boyfriend, a college boy nicknamed Squid, who still inked about with fourteen year-olds to this day. Four years ago, however, he was busy snatching Laura's vulnerability and self-alienating intelligence and weaving it into a dependency on narcotics.

The night of her attempted suicide, Laura wasn't as troubled by the newspaper as she was about finding out that her mother had actually sold her, by contract, to a man named Fearghas, in exchange for darker deeds. Laura objected, of course. Asked what century it was. Mindy told her that matchmaking was common amongst their people, and that her daughter should not think of it as a property exchange, but as a reflection of her good judgment and love. Did she know this man? Laura had asked her. Very well, answered Mindy, but it's his son you'll be interested in. A strong boy. A strange boy, but a strong boy, with faculties. A boy who's going somewhere. I'm sure.

Always a smart and vengeful girl, Laura reacted violently. She slapped Mindy's jaw slack and went for her neck. Mindy, who could be even more vengeful, however, slapped her back, again, and again, threw her to the bed, searched her room and finally found a thimble's worth of marijuana. A scapegoat for her behavior. And, though Lenard never knew it (she'd made up something that involved the building of a bird house) had her husband launch her bony teenage body into a forty-pound fireplace grate, not for the first time, and as a warning for those under their flat, seditious roof who spoke up against their duties. The Moskowitz's, anyway, were pretty, smart people, who were capable of unpretty, unsmart things.

Black and blue in her bedroom later that night, brain a little loose in the head, Laura read from her mother's yellow-faced college copy of *Hippolytus*, which she'd stolen months before. She was sealed inside with a padlock made of lead, bending below her desk lamp, turning the pages as if they were empty, or hefting them often from the bind. She fell in love with himations, firbulaes, shame and hubris, and, after the nurse's betrayal and Phaedra's epic dishonoring by Hippolytus as he denounced the female sex for pages and pages on end, sat up, and touched blood back into to her cold, naked toes. She put the book down in her lap and looked out the window. Her neighborhood was quiet and clean. The sky was orderly and the clouds were combed. It reminded her of father's dental office, the tone of his voice, the simplicity of his swift, mastering hand, and her mother's words, full of unrealized ennui, which fed her long scoldings and monologues. It was like the times she pretended not to see the bruises on her chest, and so unlike her brain, with its incus storms and seas. How could her parents exchange her, like currency?

It wasn't matchmaking when murder was involved.

Mindy would tell people, years from now, after her daughter's actual death and her belated return from a thirty two year Baja reclusion in Mexico, that something in the girl changed after that night. The drugs, they'd all tinkered with her brain's chemistry, ruined a simple girl. But not her, she'd say, not Mindy Moskowitz. She'd sent her daughter up higher paths. As did Jay, and his seemingly amnesial fist. Giving her to Fearghas, that was an extreme act of prudence brought about by their son's death. People could agree to crazy things after they'd been touched by crazy people. That, even she admitted.

Yes, the Scotsman found the killer for them—the man could track a hawk through a storm of whirling feces. The Scotsman found him and dragged him into the forest and he was loaded full of slugs under a sophist moon by an old hunting rifle with Jay at the trigger. A body in the dirt. Spit on and buried. Dirt on more dirt. Urination on the dirt. Revenge was de-troughed. Murder for murder. And with such great delight. On a Saturday.

Following her parent's decision, and particularly after she'd been kid-napped and thrown before the lions, Laura plotted her revenge every day. It became ceaseless. A game against herself. Mindy had offered her up for the schemes of a madman in exchange for a world without the ghost of her son peeking over her shoulder, and, by doing so, in her selfishness and lies, cre-ated a new sort of ghost. A self-loathing Dybbuk; an old, wandering spirit that after a few months time lodged itself deep in the cartilage of her daugh-ter's shallow lungs. Laura remembered something outside of herself made the first attempt against her life. She remembered some smiling human with its face in the moon, and not Mindy, nor Lenard, her father, or Fearghas, but some Greek-faced dead thing, like the Hipploytus she'd imagined, flawed and hissing *"the steam of hecatombs ascends,"* while his icy hand and bit-down fingernails gripped for her throat through the clouds.

Lenard had come over while Laura's parents were at a Marcusian anarchist function being held in the foyer of the Hilton. This recent stranger, this contractual component, seeking her out in the night. Not hearing from her for three days because of what her mother and father called punishment, he'd resolved to climb through her bedroom window and try to entertain her—he'd recently been learning how to juggle carburetors. Instead, how-ever, he found her in a pile of vomit. He cupped her face, forced open her eyes. Laura still remembered why she decided to hold on that day. When she saw Lenard alive, in the bone, alive, standing over her. His body, that brute force, that stupid, unwarranted loyalty unstoppable, needed her and wanted her like that was the only human thing to do. It was as if suddenly human life could be made meaningful by one honest look of protection, and that was enough to justify their fate.

"Where were you just then?" Laura asked Lenard now, missing just for one second that exact same look while he stared into the back of the front seat instead of her. Her hair, like a colonial doll's, was round and uncompelled.

"I had a nightmare last night," he said.

"Must have been *some* thing." She pulled out a cigarette, a habit Lenard admired at arm's length, lit it, and threw herself against the upholstery. The two fingers, thinning red polish, held it over her knee. "Never seen you so beat before. What kind of nightmare?"

"Can't remember," he lied. "But it was bad."

"Well, you know what they say about the ones you can't remember?" Laura said. Lenard turned to look at her, watching the smoke camber over her knees. They were curled up below her chin like she was some perfect machine able to simply adjust her limbs anywhere now, anytime. Able to operate on set laissez-faire, even if truly requiring constant restraint. "If you can't talk about your nightmare the morning after you had it, then you'll probably have it again."

"God forbid," he said.

"Forbid God."

She exhaled a yarny ball of smoke.

Lenard lifted himself onto his elbows, wrapped his body around Laura's and kissed her left shoulder. Her sagging t-shirt revealed the drooping aubergine strap of her brassiere, the defiant imperfections and deformities of her skin that, when exposed, looked like insults. They sat in silence for a moment. The two of them looked at each other and thought about the downbeats dictating their very first dance steps; then they thought about their families. They thought about how no one else would survive this world but the two of them. If that.

"Lenard," Laura said. She waved smoke from his face. Her shoes were untied and shoved between the armrest and the gearshift. She took a moment to think about the possibility that, although they had been matchmade, although they'd never chosen each other free of their parents' diabolism, that she'd begun truly to care for him. And that scared her a little. The fact that she wanted to go places, see things, clear her misty brain, and that he wanted to do little to nothing but flex his superior muscles around town, bust up vagrants and streetfights on the weekends, and make love to her more than she could stand. Without her in his life, Lenard would be as useful as an empty matchbook. Just the fact that she'd become comfortable with him at all scared her. According to her parent's contract, she was his actual property.

"I think there's something I should tell you," she said.

Lenard looked at her. Even if his father had organized their union, he cared for her more than she could know.

"It's about my acceptance into Boulder."

Laura tensely watched his face.

"What about Boulder?" he asked her, not angrily, but with a bit of boredom, and ignorance.

"Lenard," Laura heard, as she prepared to answer.

"Lenard!" Argyll yelled through the glass. "Lenard! Lenard!" He slammed his fist against the window. "Lenard, please open up."

The old man's great glass eye was fat and slimy as usual, a snail lodged in the corner of an attic. He stepped back for a moment and treated the air suspiciously. "Please? Open the door?"

"Hold on a second, Tush," Lenard said, covering his exposed nethers with a leg of his sweatpants. Laura was already fully clothed and miraculously preening her hair in the mirror.

Lenard clicked open the back door just enough to allow Argyll's massive head, fit with its renegade Petri-culture of hair, to waggle in. It brought a stench into the car none of them would have welcomed under more domestic circumstances, including Argyll himself, who sniffed his upper lip with disdain.

"What do you want?"

"I'm sorry to bother you," he said, grinning, "and your female, but duty calls." He stared at Laura as she gave a final suck on her cigarette and stubbed it into the ashtray.

"What are you looking at?" she snapped.

"Lenard," Argyll said, shifting his gaze. His face was unusually sweaty, even for him. "Your father requests an audience."

"Now?" Lenard asked, noting the darkness outside.

"Ay."

"Why?" asked Laura.

"Not a clue."

"Come on, Argyll. No games."

He allowed himself into the front seat, settling with a sigh. He lifted one of Laura's shoes to his nose, a faded gray Converse, and gave it a prolonged sniff.

"He's fallen ill."

"Ill?" asked Lenard, snatching her shoe from Argyll, which he gave up without a struggle.

"Fatally so, I'm afraid."

"But I just saw him this morning," Lenard said. "He was whistling old platoon songs and grilling shanks of lamb."

"Ay," said Argyll, staring at the motionless trees as they flectioned over the hood. "But now, he's not fine. The great 'fuck you' comes upon him. Yea, I've said it. Snuck right through the old man's barricades and shat all over his face. He probably won't make it through the night."

"The great 'fuck you?'" Lenard asked, chewing on one knuckle. Laura bulleted her eyes at Argyll in the rearview. She could sense the buzz of some foul deed. Everything, with Argyll, was some foul deed.

"It is the end that comes to all great men," said Argyll, looking out the window into the sky, a cerement of altocumulus clouds, towards a constellation that he had specifically chosen, arranged, and marked off with imaginary stars. His glass eye was dank and full of dusk as he watched it.

"Please be there as soon as you can," he said, before opening the car door to leave. "I am only a messenger. Manu."

A couple of minutes passed in silence after Argyll left, even if his ghastly smell didn't.

"He's dying?" Lenard was asking himself.

Laura wrapped her arms around his shoulders. No matter how much she hated how her boyfriend bought whatever Fearghas and his cohort sold, she maintained her respect, realizing how powerless she felt before these massive moguls, these staggering gatekeepers of masculinity. She said, "maybe Argyll's over-exaggerating."

"What if he's not?"

"Now, now," Laura puttered. She caressed Lenard's head. "Haven't you learned not to confide so quickly in men like Argyll."

"It can't be over yet. Not now."

"What can I do to help?"

Lenard began to cry, or tried to cry. Laura said, *good, just like that,* as he did so. Tears themselves were relatively unknown to his body and, as he felt them come, his throat gurgled in protest. He leaned forward and hit the seat with his forehead and before Laura could hand him her last balled-up Kleenex, sputtered, in dry, absent bursts, like a baby geyser.

"Well, it's just that. . ." he choked, "the tests, my manhood. We can't be finished yet. There's still so much left to learn."

"Is there really, though?" Laura asked.

"Well, of course there is," Lenard sniffled peevishly. "I thought you understood. Without my lessons, I can never become a man."

"No, silly, I *understand,*" Laura laughed, albeit with restraint. "I just thought, you know, you didn't take them all so seriously." She shook her head, thinking of all the times Lenard called his father's trials a standing 'act of idiocy,' and then, afterwards, how he reverted allegiance, felt guilty for everything he'd said. How he paid sorries to no one and everyone at the same time, often to the point of annoyance.

"I know," he said, wiping the corners of his eyes. "But I thought that he'd always be there? That we'd always have more time. . . ."

Laura sat into Lenard's lap and stroked his moustache, which was now stemming off into a fuzzy, teenage Fu Manchu. She was unsure of how something called the great "fuck you" could wound anybody outside of a drunken cursing contest. She was unsure of why she felt such love for the boy before her, this piece of meat tenderized by measured fists of madness. Maybe because he was just as much of pawn as she was. Pawns in the same rigged game.

It was then she decided to spit out her big news. Spit it out straight from her gut. She decided upon envisioning a future with Fearghas and Lenard, under the command of some dreamed-up phallic creed—something like undergoing a quest to sabotage a Russian research station for the government. She imagined the father and son duo in the future, twenty years from now, undertaking a mission to test their aging strength, dressed in tights and capes, hiking out across the Arctic. She imagined herself treading behind them with deer pelts and a tent strapped across her back, with pink-mouthed children wailing from her arms while she screamed into the icefields for help.

No. She couldn't live life like that, she thought. She had to stage some sort of intervention. Nobody ever talked about the wife of a superhero. The tribulations she went through while her hubby prevented the collapse of planet Earth.

"I just got accepted into CU's five-year biochemistry program," she spurted. A natural reaction to her thoughts.

"There it is. That wasn't so hard. Aren't you happy for me?"

Lenard was silent.

"I was selected from a gigantic pool of applicants. Monolithic. Right? Amazing?

Right? It goes without saying I have housing. . .a generous stipend. More than enough. So, if Fearghas takes a turn for the worst, then I could take care of you." She scanned him head to toe, caressed his muscled hock of cheek, and wondered why she was saying what she was. "All of you."

Though Lenard felt uncomfortable being provided for by anyone, including himself, he asked after a moment, "Take care of me?"

"Every inch of you."

"Dress my wounds?"

"And lick them clean."

"Hide my identity?"

"And burn away its roots."

"Raise my kids?"

"And make them serve you."

"I don't know," Lenard said. He fiddled with his hands.

"I've still got to finish school."

"You're flunking all your classes."

"You promised your parents you'd stay in Boston."

"They won't care if I'm gone."

"But we can't do anything without him. . . ."

"Yes we can."

"And I'm not sure if I'm ready to leave."

Laura looked upon Lenard, surprised at how much she was willing to do for him.

Every time he realized something new about himself she thought her brain grew lighter in her skull.

"Wait," Lenard yelled, as if just realizing something important. "What if it's They? What if," he put his palms to his cheeks, "what if They's responsible for this entire mess?"

"Who are They?" asked Laura.

"*Is* They," corrected Lenard.

"*Is* They?"

"Just They."

"What?"

"What?"

"I don't know."

Lenard sat back. He also didn't know. He hadn't built up gall to ask Fearghas about They, either, out of fear of unearthing more secrets that would give way to more secrets, and then *more* secrets. But for some reason, he was terrified of that word. Just the name itself, probably due to the countless times and ways in which Fearghas had uttered it, was enough to inspire the very same nightmares he'd experienced as a young child.

"Honey. . .death is a terrible thing, but you do *know* it happens," Laura continued, feeling so much pity for him and finding so much unexpected wisdom in herself. He and she really were two vastly different sides to the same rail run coin. Both being inducted into destinies they'd not asked for, all for the ambitions of others. "It happens every day, far more than life happens, and it just keeps on going and going. Happening and happening.

With the end of it all only being the world's end."

"You're all lollipops and sugarplums today," Lenard said.

"All I'm saying is that, if your father is to die—though that would be terrible—you can't do anything about it but move on. Accept the possibility of future. Change it. Dedicate it to something true." She gazed at him without wavering. "Something honest. Something you've never had the chance to really make: a decision."

"What's that supposed to mean?"

She sat on her knees.

"It means, no more tests. No more *Manaton*. No more listening to the *rules*. It means you and I can be free to live our lives. We can start a family. Superheroics aside, I can give birth to a squawking little baby, you know? Chubby cheeks and diapers. You can work a job. Normal jobs. We both can. Try to be happy."

"But how will we, you know. . . ."

"Fight crime?" Laura asked, with the distant intent to humor Lenard, "without him?"

"When we're ready?"

Laura sat back into the seat, took Lenard with her, sucked on his lips until eventually she got them to open and suck hers back. They shared a nebulous combination of breath. And as far as Lenard's question, Laura, despite her reticence, had actually begun working on a project in her parent's basement. She wasn't sure what to call it, but knew that one day it could be big. More so, anyway, than digging the great Kola Borehole or sending more Apollos to the moon. It was far beyond what anyone she knew would care to comprehend, and after all the time she'd spent with Lenard, staring into those dumb yet charitable eyes, she'd began to wonder if becoming a vigilante, if fighting crime, could solve her problems, help her patent foul-weather lights bright enough to navigate life's darker seas. The incentive of becoming a hero, an actual super-anomaly, seemed to have worked for Lenard, who in the face of such a demented call to duty was as high and translucent as Samsara. Could she become a hero, too, or would she simply remain a secretary to greatness?

"You just leave that to me," she said.

"I can't leave it to you," said Lenard, wiping his lips. He had trouble finishing his thoughts. "We need him. He needs us. And, well, let's face it. You're a woman."

"And what does that have to do with anything?"

"I shouldn't have brought it up."

"Look," Laura said. She was getting angry now. The fact that he'd referred to her gender was just as infuriating to her as it was charming, and for a reason she couldn't decide, which made her even angrier. She took a deep breath. "It's okay to say how much you hate him," stroking and preening, thinking of Fearghas, her mother, her father, and then bashfully, of Lenard himself. "It's okay to say he's better off six feet under. All this great 'fuck you' business. Lions and plutonium. *The Manaton* and manhood and. . .it's okay to want him dead. I mean, crimefighting, heroism, *that* I understand. But all this other nonsense. He deserves what he has coming. Just like a lot of parents do."

Lenard, after a moment of deliberation, reached out slowly to touch the dashboard. He then took his hand and, reaching over Laura, opened her door.

"I think you should go home," he said. His muscled arm lay across her to nudge the metal on its hinges. "I'll see you tomorrow. You look tired."

"You must want this insanity in your life."

"No."

"It's a circus you're involved in, you know?

"I've never thought of my life as a circus."

"You patronize me everyday, and I stand by. I nod. All because I love you, Lenard. Not because I have to be here. Even if I do. Even if—because I want you to succeed. No. Because I *admire* you. Because I'm jealous of your gumption. But these theatrics you abide by, these mad men who rule your life . . .you're becoming a freak for their entertainment. You have such potential. Why can't you use it for something that matters? Do you think Fearghas will help you feel right with yourself? Do you think he really wants to change the world? Do you think there's really something called the great 'fuck you?'"

"Well," Lenard said, feeling her left thumb dig into his knee. "No. Yes. I don't know."

"Because to the outsider you look like a clown."

"Then what are you?" he asked. "Huh? If I'm such a clown?"

She smiled, took a drag of her cigarette.

"I'm a contortionist."

"Look, Tush. It's been a long day."

"You know what happens to circus acts, Corn Cob?"

"I have to get home."

"They roll through town, once a year. They get everybody real excited."

"Please, stop."

"All the kiddies tug their Mommy's coats until someone finally gives in. Then they go to the carnival. They watch the lion tamer. The trapeze artist and the wolf man. They goggle their stupid little eyes. And then? They go home 'til next year, when the entire circus has changed, all the acts left or quit, and there's room—so much room—for new faces."

"I'm done with this conversation," said Lenard, tightening the drawstring of his sweatpants. "I have to see my father."

"You think the world only needs one tightrope walker?" Laura asked, taking his hand into hers. "You're like a wolf without teeth. I never thought about what it would mean, having a real hero come to life. But now, the more I see that dream come true, it becomes a nightmare, and not the type you can forget. I'm not going to be hated with you, though. I'm too smart for that."

"At least my Dad didn't *sell* me," Lenard snarled. "Yea, okay, he's a lot of things, but he'd never put a price on my head. I was prepared for greatness, but you were sold *to* greatness. You were nothing more than an afterthought."

"Fuck you."

"Get out of my car."

"Gladly."

The engine's rumble lowered its pitch. Laura dipped out of the driver's seat. The weather rained sideways, coming and going. Not really sure of its pitch.

"Just know that if I go to Colorado alone—and I *am* going to Colorado," she said, leaning against the Cutlass's hefty door. The wind blew around her and lifted the sex-rumpled pleats of her maxi skirt, nostalgic of all the floors they'd danced upon, all the mattresses and car seats they'd squeaked in mutual, aggrandizing, content, through the cerement of their teenage years. "That I go alone forever. Remember that I'm hungry, Corn Cob." She seemed a little tired as she spoke. Her body, for a hungry person, still seemed undernourished. But the words came flying forth, "I've got a wicked big appetite for life. And if you want to walk the tight rope alone, or even if you join the Flying Wellendas, then you're going to plummet without me. I swear to you. No matter what."

Lenard looked at her, saw how much he couldn't understand in her face. The couple feet she stood away from him was already so much more than uncomfortable. The pain of leaving shortly after making love made more than his heart pull with despair. His actual loins themselves became fearful, wondering if this had been their last chance. But still, he held the door, his mind elsewhere now.

"I know," he said, furious with himself as he watched her go, as he watched the wind leave her body to travel its own trajectory, away from him, into the letting rain. He wondered if mistakes were made by life itself, and not the people who made them.

CHAPTER NINE

SAVAGE RISING

When Lenard came home, Fearghas was sitting on a chaise recliner in a pair of tiger-print underpants, eating a hamburger the size of half his face. His body, when exposed, was bony, but mallowed around the middle, slightly puffy and dolloped with rose-colored ketchup. Upon examination he was actually lying down more than sitting, with his toes and legs dangling off the edge. The Celtics game was on, a bilious sound on the television as John Havlicek stole the ball and ran it up the court against the 76ers. Screams of victory piled into the living room, where lambskin loveseats were entombed in hard plastic, 16-inch walls kept the outside out, and a rug Argyll gifted them (made from the fur of about six different endangered animals strewn together by crude leather string) stretched underneath a tangerine coffee table that was scratched up by knives, cigarette burns, and Steve.

"Ah, Son," said Fearghas, stopping the hamburger—which only looked chipped at—about an inch from his lips. "It's good to see you."

Steve rummaged through the kitchen as he spoke, breaking. . .something. The shadow of him was ominous at least; the clacking of teeth, the animal huffing and the smell of a passed fecal movement now stewing in an aluminum sauté pan that Fearghas had dashed with kitty litter. Lenard leaned through the kitchen door and saw the lion's rump whip back and forth. His tail snapped while the rest of him tore a hole through the kitchen floor.

"That damned creature," said Fearghas, scowling. A broken floor-board snap-landed somewhere in the hallway. "So damned spoilt. Won't stop searching for food—there's no food in there, you hairy disaster," he yelled. "Like he doesn't know what I'm saying."

"Did you feed him already?" Lenard asked.

"Of course I did. Five times today. Big, fat, ferocious irrelevance will eat me out of house and home," his head sunk. "If I even have a home by morning."

"Dad," Lenard asked, watching his father's hamburger as if it was a stage prop. "Argyll told me you were ill."

"Ay, ay," Fearghas spit. "It's true. I'm dying. The great 'fuck you' has come for me at last as the final chapter of *The Manaton* predicted. The one you *cannot* read until you have come of proper maturation," he shouted, wagging a finger. "See, this is what I was trying to hide from you. The ultimate end to each male Sikophsky. Ordained by no one else but. . .well, you'll see."

Steve came stalking out of the kitchen. His lungs hefted his ribcage and his eyes were dim with the same tired veins they usually teemed with. Passing by Fearghas, he took the old man's hamburger into his mouth and padded across the living room.

"Steve just stole my hamburger," Fearghas announced, as if no one had seen it happen. His hands fell to his knees. "What more could possibly go wrong?"

"What *is* the great 'fuck you,' Dad?" Lenard asked, sitting down on the plastic loveseat with a, even considering the situation, thoroughly satisfying squelch. He still felt the cord of abandonment stretch from his heart to his pelvic region, the longing that came from wondering whether or not he'd ever see Laura again. "I have the right to know."

"It's the end that comes to all great men," Fearghas said, licking his lips.

Steve kittened apart Fearghas's hamburger in the corner, slashing through it with delicate swipes from his claws. The shutters were all drawn and a small fire roiled in the hearth. Its flames toasted a cardboard box marked ~~Confidential~~ HERPES. Fearghas took a heaping slog of amber liquid from a green glass bottle and let it trickle down his chin. It ran down his chest and into his crotch.

Lenard watched his father, thought of the little ways in which he knew him. For the most part, the old man had always been the same. Completely capable of carrying out his terrifying promises. Even if before the trials he was gentler. After the madness of his cause took hold, there was danger, derangement, and action, all wrapped together inside a foul-looking coffer. But then he gave Lenard his legs. And his Laura. Gifts to make his son great. Now, in that boy's eyes, that boy becoming a man, he became royal, even if decrepitly so, like Alexander the Great in a mental asylum, a seething Nobunaga in diapers, letting his gaze rattle between the fire and the television as if they were illusions lain out by the heavens.

Finishing his hamburger, Steve coiled up next to Fearghas, under his armpit, and nuzzled the bristle of his beard tenderly. The two of them growled together, licking their own sated chops, and watched Lenard like a next meal.

"Are you really dying, Dad?" Lenard asked, kneeling at his father's side. Steve turned away with a coy swishing of his bum and sat recumbent onto his haunches.

"I'm afraid I am, Son," Fearghas said, petting Steve's mane. "You see, the great 'fuck you' operates on a heavenly calendar of impossible comprehension. I was chosen to die now, and therefore will be hammered by the hoof of God this evening, under the stars. Just as your bastard grandfather was, and his bastard grandfather before him." He levered another slug off his bottle and took on a grim, philosophical look.

"Like Abraham, I shall have to climb a mountain and offer sacrifice tonight. And like said sacrifice, I will offer myself, as my own son," he paused, confused, "to the heavens. You see, progeny, I received *this* this morning," he threw Lenard a piece of rolled-up parchment with a broken wax seal. "The message of my timely demise, as mentioned in the ending pages of *The Manaton*."

Before he read, Lenard looked at his father for more.

"Don't worry," Fearghas said, crossing his legs. "One day, you, too, will understand."

He unrolled the scroll.

Dear Fearghas,

You are hereby chosen by the hierarchal mandate of the great fuck you to climb on top of a mountain and die.

Angrily yours,

God

"I think by mountain he means hill," Fearghas said.

Lenard folded the parchment and frowned.

"Found it on my doorstep this morning," Fearghas said. "With the paper. I knew it would happen, but I never knew when. *The Manaton*, it never says when."

"So you're not actually *sick*?" Lenard asked, part angry and part afraid.

"I'd call being ordered to end yourself by God as being sick."

"But you don't have a virus? Cancer? A house cold, even?"

Fearghas was silent.

"Oh, dear."

Lenard gave his father back the scroll. Was it possible Fearghas told the truth? He wouldn't have put it past God. But he also wouldn't have put it past Fearghas's more-or-less malfunctioned theme park of an imagination to throw the two of them (and anyone close by) into the uber-dilated oculus of madness. Lenard had probably already lost Laura—not that she would care much, or that, according to her contract, he could—and even if Fearghas had ulterior motives, he could probably do a decent job of accidentally killing himself before that motive was unearthed. Lenard felt the empty box in his pocket, cool, and beckoning to be filled. He ran his eyes over Fearghas's orgiastic sprawl, this pitiful, finished trundle of bones who probably still belonged in prison.

"I'm coming with you, then," Lenard said.

"I wouldn't advise that. It might get ugly."

"I'm your son. I'm coming with you."

Fearghas swigged down the dregs from his bottle.

"I guess you really are becoming a man."

"Are you chewing tobacco?" Lenard asked.

"Something like that."

He licked his yellow teeth.

"When did you—"

"You turned out all right, boy," Fearghas clapped his hands. "Just like your old man."

"I did?" Lenard blushed.

"Of course you did," he yelled. He pushed Lenard's head so hard that he tipped over backwards and fell into the lamp stand, sending a fragile Egyptian statue of Isis they'd found at the dump just last week to the ground. Violet wings crumbled across the rug.

"Now let's go get me *dead!*"

"Off you go to get dead, Fergie!" Lenard heard Argyll cry from the toilet, which he promptly flushed behind a closed door in the hallway.

"Shut your diseased yap, Argyll," Fearghas said. He motioned, "and make sure you wash your hands."

The troupe of them hurried up a hill sponged with yellow grass into a patch of woods behind the abandoned construction site where Lenard once battled cinderblocks. Fearghas wore a satin robe, faux-gold, stitched with a hood he'd draped over his eyes. The tie was undone and flapping through the chill December wind, exposing his rawboned legs and tiger-print underwear. His soccer cleats spiked up the mud as he set the pace, faster and faster, sending Argyll and Lenard in a dead sprint up the incline. As he ran he recited the following:

Below the thunders of the upper deep;
Far, far beneath in the abysmal sea,
His ancient, dreamless, uninvaded sleep
The Kraken sleepeth: faintest sunlights flee
About his shadow sides: above him swell
Huge sponges of millennial growth and height;
And far away into the sickly light,
From many a wondrous grot and secret cell
Unnumber'd and enormous polypi
Winnow with giant arms the slumbering green.
There hath he lain for ages and will lie
Battening upon huge seaworms in his sleep,
Until the latter fire shall heat the deep;
Then once by man and angels to be seen,
In roaring he shall rise and on the surface die.

Steve ran circles around them, diving down right before Argyll so he tripped and smacked nose-down in the mud.

"Fergie," he screamed, stretching out one hand. "Wait!"

"No time," yelled Fearghas.

"Dad?" said Lenard, stealing a glance back. "We can't just leave him there."

"He's not the one God's coming for," said Fearghas. "Here, take this." He tossed Lenard a freezing metal canteen with liquid chortling somewhere inside. His chin canted the way up the hill. "Drink some water."

"God's not coming for me either," Lenard said. He unscrewed the top and glugged while running. He coughed. "This tastes terrible!"

"Oh, does it now?" Fearghas averted his eyes. "Probably should have washed the bottle better. So sorry."

Lenard screwed the top on the canteen, spit the rancid taste from his mouth, and kept on running. He wondered, *Since when did his father say sorry?* and, along that same bizarre vein, *since when did his father drink from a canteen?*

An hour later they were still running. Lenard huffed and trudged forward, hating the leaky shoes that numbed his feet, the washed-up old Reeboks with dirty pink toe boxes and a long-forgotten need for repair. For some reason, each step he took seemed more and more negligible, less like a step and more an idea of step. Fearghas, a mischievous Puck, a Dionysian hoax, slipped in and out of the trajectory of scarlet maples. Lenard dodged what he had to as well, occasionally reaching out with his arms to schism a tougher web of branches latched to the trunk of a poplar. He could hear Steve roaring somewhere in the distance—far in the distance. The sky became thicker, and darker, and the forest, it began to move. Lenard looked down at his body as he ran, watched his legs. . .*grow* below him, or seem to grow, raise him, stretch him, higher and higher. They cranked his pelvis upward in a display that, he assumed, was scientifically wrong.

"The hell?" he asked aloud.

"*HAHAHA!*" he heard somewhere in the forest.

He halted. He was in a suffocating thicket. The trees shed their ice around him. He felt, in that shivering of burden, that they revealed a shade of what they actually were. Then the thicket became more open and he saw a little bit of moonlight etching through the snow and the canopy.

"Come on, progeny," he heard Fearghas's voice say.

He whispered from some place above, even though, when he looked, the old man stood right before him, the ground as white as the sky.

"I'll carry you safe."

Lenard grabbed his father's calloused hand and he found himself stable, walking slow and quiet for a time until they both stood alone in a valley bright with stars where the snow fell lighter than before.

HEATHEN, the stars said, spelled out in deep space. Above Lenard, a hill, a skinny membrane of land, pallid and cragged as the moon's terrae, somehow stuck off into the sky. It was long, with a buttress of stone whiter than the hill, and so seeming invisible. There was no sound where they were. No sound at all. Larger snowflakes dropping intermittent and tiresome like origami pygmies from a paper cloud.

"Welcome, Son," said Fearghas.

He seemed taller than usual. He was miraculously dressed in a loin-cloth now as if spun through a superhero's phone booth. It was brown bear fur, with the actual skinned head of the bear covering his scalp and fore-head. His arms were across his chest and he reeked of something terrible.

"What's happening to us, Dad?" asked Lenard, unsticking his mouth as he tried to speak.

He felt so damn funny.

"You've taken a strong dosage of the South American hallucinogen, ayahuasca," Fearghas said. "Only way to enter the Kingdom of Heaven."

"Kingdom of Heaven?" Lenard said, thinking that other than the rancid canteen liquid and Fearghas's voyage to Peru, his father's statement made sense. His senses were elongating everything, stretching the forest and sky into tapestral patterns that could have risen from the southern hemisphere itself. But still managing to play along, he asked, "Is it up there?" pointing to the top of the hill, all alone in the night.

"Something like that," said Fearghas.

"I want to go to Heaven," Lenard said, grabbing two of his fingers with his right hand. The more he thought about it, if heaven was at the top of the hill, then he'd prefer to be there over any place on earth. He began to walk towards it, but Fearghas stopped him.

"No you don't, boy."

"I think I would like it there."

"That's why you're stupid."

From the ground behind his loincloth the Scotsman drew a stop sign, an actual stop sign, though a little smaller than normal, and tried to bang Lenard over the head with it.

"S. T. O. P." he enunciated as he missed. "Strength. Terror. Oppres-sion. Perfection. Heaven is a place filled with fat cats and dust." The bear on his head seemed like it was chewing his scalp. "Earth, my boy, is where you belong. Either that or in hell. Your two fierce feet on the ground. Gravitas, remember? Gravitas!"

He then began to puke.

Lenard looked up into the stars through the snow, which could have been mistaken for more stars. An extragalactic nebulae revealed itself, The Milky Way, intimate as projections on a planetarium's dome. The lesser twinkles changed their spelling of the word HEATHEN to a striking NOTHING. And then again to just THING. Lenard put his hand in his mouth, chewed on his fingers, and felt his eyes—his pupils—grow big. "*Woooowwwww*," he said. And then he too began to puke.

Fearghas looked like a figure from a cave painting, geometric, earth-toned, the color of cowpie. His beard was smashed against his face as he wiped the vomit from his chin. Lenard thought of Laura and she came into his head as some old woman, mummified-old, and left alone on an armchair squeaking in an attic without reason. When he thought about himself, as those on hallucinogens were wont to do, life became much more complicated. After he felt the last of the bile leave him, he tried to express that complication in words:

"I don't feel like a man. I feel like a fist. Like I deserve to die here tonight."

His hands looked like boxing gloves, the red mittens he'd been wearing swollen to the size of balloons.

"And I only feel like that because you," he pointed at Fearghas, crouching in his bearskin. "YOU, put plutonium in my fucking food every morning as a child." He looked himself up and down. "I could have been anyone. I could have been anything."

"You could have been nothing, too," Fearghas snorted.

"I am nothing!"

"You are *everything!* Rock eater. Conqueror. Death bringer."

"You talk and talk."

"And always with good reason."

"If only that were true."

"You are a protector, Lenard," Fearghas said. "A protector of the human race. Don't doubt the gifts you've been given. Don't ever forget where you came from."

"You made me who I am. I had no choice."

"Everyone is made by someone," he said.

"Then why are we here tonight?"

"For a sacrifice." Fearghas wobbled. Using his arms for balance, he kept on his feet. "Whoa, this stuff is *strong*."

"A sacrifice," Lenard said. "A sacrifice?"

But as he spoke, the previous questions he'd asked were stifled by the antiseptic glare of the moon. It was so bright. And *large*. Hanging on a thread from the sky.

"I get it," Lenard said. "I finally get it."

"You do?" Fearghas pulled his beard and stuck his tongue out, which seemed, in Lenard's eyes, to come out very far.

"We're all sacrifices," Lenard whispered.

"Yes."

"In the clouds."

"Yes. What?"

"The clouds are sacrifices and I am God. I just wanna eat them. All up." Lenard began biting the air.

"Yea, yea eat those clouds," cheered Fearghas.

"I can *taste* how good they are."

"Soooooo good."

"There was a man from Belarus who unpacked a box of bubblegum," Lenard sang. They both began hopping up and down.

"I love that song," Fearghas said.

"Just made it up."

"I love that song I love that song keep singing."

"He blew bubblegum up to the roof and killed his whole family when it popped and that's what happened!"

"You are so smart!"

Lenard truly felt smart. No, he felt something different than smart, the opposite of smart, which, when he thought about it properly, probably meant he was *really* smart. No. It meant something different. It meant he was a dancing yahoo, one of a pair, leaping up and down through a universe only they, as men, could see. He stopped, waving a finger at Fearghas's head.

"You're dressed up like a BEAR. Did you *know* that?"

"Oh?" said Fearghas, rubbing down his fur in a way that was almost inappropriate. "I guess I am. Whoa. . . ."

"That's *weird*."

"I KNOW, it *is* weird. Where did I even get this thing?"

"Argyll?"

"He likes to smell woman's shoes."

"I love you, Dad. Please, don't kill yourself."

They started to laugh uncontrollably.

"Who said anything about killing myself," Fearghas said, still guffawing. "I just have to die."

"How?" Lenard asked. Fearghas was talking so fast and Lenard was nodding so fast that one looked like he was eating the other's words. "How you gonna die?"

"Don't know yet. Waiting for God."

"Did God tell you to take drugs?"

"God tells me to do a lot of things."

"Did God tell you to give me drugs?"

"Ummmmm."

"Oh, Dad, I love you so much." He gave his father a hug. "You son of a bitch!"

"I love you too, Son. That's why I have to put you through this last test tonight. I just need you to hold on."

"I am strong. I can hold on."

"Strength can be paid for. I need your heart."

Lenard nodded.

"If you're going to fight for America you're going to have to hate everything America stands for," Fearghas said. His lips moved with the wet floppiness of a fish, indignant, and somewhat absent of anything else but a slippery, elusive instinct. "You're going to have to be the ax the deliberator the scales the time traveler the heathen the gallows the thief the recluse the bastard the bitch the father the mother the echoes that drive you the beast of law the hero the darkness the code the love the justice the who? the what? the sex the fist the dog the cat the animal that uses his past to prevail over a dark human dream AMEN."

There was a moment of silence.

"What?!" Lenard quacked.

SKREEEEEEEEEEEEEEEEEEEETCCHEEEEEEEEEEE EEEEEEEEEEEEEEEEEEEEEEEEEEEEECH!

Lenard and Fearghas looked to the top of the hill into the porcine light of the moon. The two of them were on par with its height, but far away, and watched a mess of gangly tentacles snap their way over the ledge. They were black with silver suction cups, attached in eight places to an obsidian mantle. A translucent forehead in the center revealed the workings of a type of mind: colliding opal blobs of liquid in an enclosed bubble. Directly below that bubble, that luminous alien eye, was stamped a symbol Lenard recognized from the aluminum bottle pulled, one dark day, from his father's box.

Why it was there, he couldn't begin to reason. For a moment he wondered if it were actually there at all. But it did frighten him; that he did know. As if he'd bitten off a chunk of evil destiny and ingested it into his system. It tasted rotten.

Whatever vocals the beast could make lowed throughout the valley. Its chromatophores gave its body a metallic sheen. Lenard looked down at his own body and realized that, for some reason, he had gotten himself mostly naked, save for his ass-torn underpants. Not knowing how that had happened, he wondered for a moment if he was really anywhere at all, or what difference it made anymore, head swimming with the snow, the aya-huasca, the last eighteen years of his life. The creature snatched a piece of the hilltop and crunched it into its slithers.

"Oh, whoa boy, it's time," said Fearghas, squinting his eyes at the creature before them. "Guess this is what God chose for my meeting of the great 'fuck you.'"

"The Kraken," said Lenard.

"I suppose," Fearghas mused. "That does seem to be the odiferous bastard. Strange how all those stories you get read as a child putrefy your mind."

"No," said Lenard. "No. No. No. God help us."

"God is here to destroy me," Fearghas pleaded. "Damn it boy, don't pray to him. Look at that bastard he's sent, crunching earth's bone."

"I don't want to die," said Lenard.

"And you're not going to," Fearghas said, laughing. He placed his hand on Lenard's shoulder. "Why do you think we came here in the first place? I'm going to die. Remember?"

Lenard and the aging Scotsman exchanged a brief look of hallucina-tory understanding and love. Lenard watched Fearghas's face turn into the face of someone else, someone he knew, whispered something that sounded like praise for a life well led thus far. And that, precisely, was when Lenard stole Fearghas's stop sign, held it high, and clocked his father across the face.

The aluminum sound zoomed through the psychotropic sky. "No," Lenard said, and Fearghas seemed to float to the ground, swaying, like an angry feather, into unconsciousness. "That over there is my monster. My God!" He pointed at his chest again and again, screaming at no one in particular, the air, the Kraken. "I earned it. See? I earned it."

Tears were in his eyes.

"I lived it."

Lenard took off towards the Kraken as it beat its appendages in Kong-like succession against its head and the hill. He lifted off the ground, feet still running. His fists were aiming ahead. He was actually floating, running, flying above the earth. Flying! Was he actually flying? Was he hallucinating that he was flying? Was he watching a video of himself flying from above? Was he falling? Shit, he was actually flying in a straight-ish line, kooky Ayahuasca or not. His body tunneled quicker towards the Kraken's crystal eye—gleaming and focusing its liquids into something of a pupil. He looked up briefly to the sky at a barreling speed where the stars asked brightly WHO ARE YOU? He aimed himself, left fist forward, hair and ratty Fu Manchu whipping around his left shoulder as his underwear revealed a pallid patch of his right ass cheek and his clenched teeth gleamed into the night. His hands took on a pale, yellow glow. He gasped and traveled back through time and opened his eyes to an ancient expanse of biblical desert. Men labored on a ziggurat the color of Mediterranean water with cold stone tools in the ford below. Click clack click. The sound was soothing. It sounded like a time when life was youthful and still excited upon seeing the primordial indigestions of plasmids and parasites, not trying to catalogue their defeat. Lenard's forehead burned beneath the ancient sun and his heart beat faster. He watched himself turn into a white long-horned ibex, digging up the ground with its hooves. He was older, stronger, than anything that had lived before; he was a prophet, then an urge. Then a scavenger. Gyps fulvous with red, bandit's eyes. His desert froze over with ice and ashen caves and carried him further backwards in time—the late Pliocene, glacial and bristling with mountains and black, geodic pools.

He watched his body change again. It took less than a passing whisper. Then, he was a moaning Megatherium, head swinging like a hoary acolyte with strong legs that splintered up the ice. Muscles from the Arctic could go on for days and possibly weeks without any sign of debilitation. He was a battering ram and a wrecking ball; a pitch of hot sand through cold, Antarctic wind. Hunching over, his massive body crawled into the imperfect stature of a man again. An early man. Cobbling together animal skin into a tent with hands that were dirty and gray. His face was Mousterian. His nose was broad. He took a spear and went off to war. A man's flesh was splayed open, white as agate. He screamed to the okra-green sun. He told stories before the flames of a fire, shadowed by the murmuring tongues of his ancestors. Then, with a rush, he became an American again. A soldier with a bloodletting bayonet and a green, webbed helmet. The ground was fertile and smelled of rain and bodies rotting in an open ditch. The smell was far worse than putrid. The world had a taste to it of poison and the feeling that death was falling from the sky into a pit that would never be filled. That soldier roiled. As a luger bullet whizzed through his head, he rushed past his death and became another man. A man splattered in tanning oil reading the paper on his back porch, tearing a kosher hot dog apart with his teeth. A man plugged with eight crumpled metal fillings, his belly button pooling with sweat. Juices streamed down his quadrified chin. The flag of his country was on an open parasol covering his body in two yards of shade; it was brightened by the sun, so blue like blue fire.

"Who am I?" Lenard asked, as he returned to the valley, zooming in a blur below the stars. The Kraken and its arms jerked out before him as if in welcome.

"Who am I?" he asked. "Tell me, up there. I need to know."

SAVAGE

The stars spelled out, each one in its deliberate tracing.

SAVAGE

Lenard nodded.

He splattered through the Kraken's head, tearing through its outer shell like he'd cracked the surface of a massive cobbler, white ooze sifting through his fists as he battered the way to its brain. The smell was sour like paper mache. The way through seemed endless. Finally as he dug deeper he unearthed a heap of sludge filled with inorganic scaffolding, and found a hard piece of. . .wood? He scraped it clear of goo—found it was a door. A trap door. And he stared at it confused for a moment while the morphic walls seemed to collapse around him. He heard another roar, a roar like Steve's. He looked over at the Kraken's bubbling eye and punched through its outer shell. The surface felt like semi-hard plastic fit for a kiddy pool as he fisted through to the mordant slop inside. The white globs turtled out— he smelled his fingers—oil lit white by a lantern in a metal holster swaying above. He could see more clearly now, the hallucinogen was sputtering off its apex and, looking below, he flung open a copper latch and fell through the trapdoor, into a dry room made of unfinished pinewood, with a small console of buttons and levers where a man, an Argyll, the Argyll, was visibly going into a berserker rage of work. He was sitting in a control room. There was a circular glass window above the console where the valley was visible outside. Steve was playing with a potato sack in the corner and looked somewhat gangly and old, claws distended as he pried apart the weave.

"Argyll?" Lenard asked, hitting himself open-palmed in the head to see how alive the ayahuasca still was. "Steve? What are you doing here?"

"Shit," said Argyll. He pedaled a standing bicycle whose gears went like roots below the floor. There was a red flashing light bulb over his head. A row of beaconing buttons and a remote control in his hand. In anxiety he pressed it and they all heard, SKRRREEEEETCH!!!!!!!

He leaned into a large microphone mounted like a periscope from the ceiling and announced, "Fergie, I think we have a problem, here. You'd better come up quick."

Steve flopped to Lenard's feet and looked at him as if he'd been deeply responsible for everything that had just happened.

"Fergie," Argyll repeated into the microphone. "Fergie, where are you? Code fucking five. Fergie!"

Lenard's head grew hot with rage.

"FERGGGGIIIIIEEEEE!!!!"

CHAPTER TEN

THE FOOLS-GOLDEN RULE

"The thing about manhood," Fearghas proclaimed, lifting a cup of coffee to his head, not mouth, bandaged over his right eye with a strip of ragged cotton, "is that it can't be forced out of you. You have to rub it out, like a stain."

"Ay, Fergie," Argyll said. He sipped at a strawberry malt while inhaling the fumes from a demented Pall Mall in his right hand. His good eye was wide and red from his quotidian guzzling of morning stimulants. "I mean, if you hadn't made me try and establish my own kingdom in Connecticut, I don't where I'd be today."

"And you almost succeeded," said Fearghas.

"Ay. Fucking Feds. Won't let you create your own currency."

"Bastards. I liked the idea of the 500 billion Argyll peso. And reinstating *droit de cuissage*? Genius."

"Who didn't think so, Fergie?" said Argyll, shaking his head as he bent down to feed upon his curdled malt. "Who didn't?"

"Will you two shut up," said Lenard.

He was wrapped in red flannel blankets, sitting outside with the two of them in front of a small mom and pop café, minus the mom since last year, called DiMaggio's. The patio had laced metal chairs rumbling to passing cars and busses. The inside, seen through shiny bay windows, had been drawn together like a baseball card collector's autoerotic emporium. Worn maple, the walls themselves drowned in bats and gloves like flotsam from a stadium-bound Nautilus, and photographs of dark eyed, golden-aged drunkards, swung, or leaned, or clung, to that wreckage, attempting to survive another epoch of fame.

"Just stop talking."

"Well, would you look at him," said Argyll, pointing a thumb.

"Sometimes I feel like I didn't even raise the boy," said Fearghas.

Lenard's face was pink, bubblegum pink, with his droopy, post-hallucinogenic eyes flat behind their lids. His mouth was blistered with bruises. His feet and fingers, frost bitten. He had cuts all over his arms and legs from his descent through "The Kraken," (those quotation marks indicated dire sarcasm), and he donned a cast over his shattered right leg. It would heal in less than a week, Fearghas said, due to his radioactive makeup. But it still hurt like a broken leg should.

"Fuck you," he said.

"Oh, come on, Son—"

"Fuck you."

"But—"

"Fuck. You."

"Fortunately he's allowed to say that now," Fearghas said, shifting uncomfortably in his chair. "Because he's come into manhood."

"Whoopdee doo!" Lenard yelled, throwing his stir spoon in the air. It landed on the flagstone and rattled itself into a crack.

"He'll come around," whispered Argyll.

"I will not come around," said Lenard, hammering the table with his fist so that everything they'd ordered—croissants, cherry danishes, a Byzantine metal fruit bowl filled with peaches and green grapes—all skittered upward in chorus. "You almost killed me last night! I mean, what's wrong with you? Feeding me drugs? Putting me on an invisible wire and convincing me I could fly? Building a two-ton fucking machine to resemble my childhood nightmare? Are you insane? Are you beyond insane? I know I'm not that smart, I know I'm not, but please, just tell me, the great 'fuck you'—what was that about? Couldn't you have just dragged me out into the forest and forced me to take drugs? Did you really need to try and convince me that you were offering yourself to God? I trusted you, for fuck's sake. What's stopping me, right now, from using my super strength to bury you? What's stopping me, huh? You've got to have a reason. What could possibly be stopping me? You've ruined everything, you know? My body, my love, my life. . . ."

Fearghas looked at Lenard as if he were crazy. The family nutcase allowed out for a stroll. He smiled nervously at the only other person outside, a man in a cashmere trench coat buttoned to the bottom of his chin who pretended to refasten the lid of his coffee cup. Fearghas smiled as if saying, in a way most commiserable, 'don't worry, happens all the time.'

"I already explained to you," he said, lowering his hand with each word to keep the raving protégé at bay. "Everything we did, was done to convince you that what you were seeing was real. If not, you would not have realized your identity. You wouldn't have tried to save me. We needed to make everything look as authentic as we could. The great 'fuck you' is what we, our kind, like to call a serious kind of joke. Now, if you would just stay calm—"

"I'm calm."

"It doesn't look like it."

"Oh, I'm calm, Dad. I'm fucking calm. Calm as a bowl of jelly. Can't you see?"

"I don't think he's very calm, Fergie," said Argyll.

"Shut the fuck up," Fearghas and Lenard said in unison.

"The one thing I really don't understand," continued Lenard, if only because he saw an opportunity. "Is why, in the name of all that is sacred, did you stamp that fucking weird symbol on that mechanical thing's head? Was that necessary? Hmm?" He gave the two of them a pause. "Was it just to freak me out?"

"Look, wee fucker," said Fearghas, for a moment looking genuinely confused. "I don't have a cock's idea of what you're talking about, but I can assure I know nothing of symbols, anti-symbols, or pictograms in general.

Argyll?" He turned to the one-eyed maleficent. "Did you have a filthy hand in this?"

"I might have Fergie," said Argyll, finger to his chin. "And then again, I might not have. Sometimes I do things, and I just don't know why, or where, for that matter, I do them. Who knows the motives behind men's actions? It is truly a miracle we are here at all. . . ."

"You rotten piece of idiocy," Fearghas growled. "I'll get to you later. Look, Lenard," Fearghas said, shaking the conversation into a direction he found more fitting. He got up from the table and put his hands on his hips, inhaling the cold. It was fairly clear in Boston, with sun on the shinier aspects of their banquet. Fearghas picked a champagne glass poured from a bottle of Grand Siècle he'd recently stolen from Laura's father, smelling the bubbles as they fizzled up his nostrils, into those dark, tangled weeds. His yarmulke was too vibrant for Lenard to look at. Fearghas took a belabored sip from the glass and murmured a glib sound of happiness.

"I did all of this because I wanted you to know what you were capable of," he said, returning the glass to its table. "You see, now that you're sitting here with us, post-manhood-attainment, there are no more differences to be had. We're all equals here. We're all men. And you, well, you're more than a man. You're a hero. Now you can ask anything you want and get an honest answer. We—we can talk about something other than *The Manaton*. Like the latest trends in music, for instance—have you heard of Konzerthanusorchester Berlin Orchestra? Now that you know what I know, there is nothing that we cannot share. My father," he gulped down those words, lowering his glass. "My father—I hated him too for a while after he had me stowed off to Eastern Europe in a cargo hold. Or, after he stabbed my first girlfriend. And my second," he sighed. "But afterwards, I learned to respect him. Oh, how I regretted the day that he was killed."

"I'm going to go to the Jacks," Argyll said, not seeming capable of seeing Fearghas so emotional.

"This has to stop, Dad," said Lenard, not caring about the volume of his voice, but looking straight at Fearghas as the old man teetered on the verge of tears. "I mean, I appreciate the. . .gesture, and I'm really, really glad that you didn't kill my girlfriend, but these tests, they're madness. They have to stop. No more. This is not how a superhero is created. What you've done, it's monstrous."

"It has stopped, Son," said Fearghas, stepping out onto the curb. He inhaled another gust of air and car horn beeped to warn him away from the street. "Last night. I tried to do what my father couldn't. I tried to create a hero without destroying him. You say that superheroes are not brought about from darkness, but I would completely disagree. Heroes, of all sorts and series, are the children of darkness. Which is why they long so deeply for the light. See, my beloved boy, what I've done is kept you safe."

"Safe?"

"From They."

"Who is They!"

Fearghas sighed. His fingers cracked open the insides of a cherry walnut scone. He came back to the table, sat down, and made a dribbling mess.

"Testosterone Heightened Enforcement of Y."

Lenard cocked his head. "You've got to be joking."

"I wish I wasn't, boy."

Argyll stumbled back to the table, partly falling into his chair.

"Did I here you two talking about T.H.E.Y.?" he asked.

"Quiet Argyll," said Fearghas. "You never know who's watching."

"Right, Fergie."

Fearghas leered at Argyll, drawing a deep gulp of his coffee, emptying the mug.

"I think it's time."

Argyll raised the skin over his glass eye.

"Are you sure?"

"If he doesn't see the final chapter now, he'll never understand."

"What's going on?" asked Lenard.

"You're about to find out, boy."

From the Scotsman's pocket, emerged Lenard's Gordian Knot, *The Manaton*.

As he looked at it his blood felt heavy in his veins. He began thinking that, as long as he'd been alive, books had been a source of infinite terror. From his childhood Kraken to Aesop Mac'Cool, he'd been driven towards heroism and insanity by words, manipulated by images, these inarticulate signs of human expression. Funny, how this little bound block of paper, and leather, could now make him shiver with fear.

"It is time," said Fearghas, cracking open the cover.

"Time for what?" asked Lenard.

Fearghas gulped, lifting the silk red ribbon. "For you to understand your strange and unusual destiny."

Chapter 35

ON EXTIRPATING DREAMS AND ENLIVENING NIGHTMARES

Or,

ON *raising a Manatonian according to the greater-still man-ponderings of*

Aesop Mac'Cool

Or,

REALMS OF MANTASIA: THE VERDICT

Or,

THE FINAL INSANITY

144

URGENT NOTE:

READ NO FURTHER UNLESS, IN A WAY ACHIEVED OTHER THAN MURDER OR HOMOSEXUALITY, YOU HAVE ASCENDED THE OFFICIAL TITLE OF MANATONIAN.

Manivity. Manastodon. Manu.

It must be said that, as a species, but more notably coven of aging, nay, ancient, and forever-virile MAN-things and their lesser derivatives, we must arrive at a point in our ever-fucked lives where we perceive the growing gaps twixt myth and reality. Though shorn from the bones of historical fact, legend, as if spun off a minstrel's tune, enchants us to believe that beasties such as Tarasques, Grendles, blood-suckling Strigoi and their evolutioned Vampyre brethren, are to be given sincere consideration as actual entities when, in fact, to make such claims as anything but storybook wonder would be absurd.It is Man's responsibility, therefore, to balance this fine line between truth and legend, and, to use a provincial American verb, keep from 'retarding' our future youth—Manu!

As the father of history Herodotus prophetically wrote, humans "trust their ears less than their eyes," and, although, it should be added, would do better trusting both, I agree: we must see a legend in action in order to truly believe it. Though Beamish (who is now what I call my foe after attempting, many, many unsuccessful times, mutiny on my philosophical armada) would argue that this method should be used to achieve regional power and political control, I will still assert that The Manaton and it roots are in 'moral' purpose and truth, with intention, as the Gods of Euripides once shared with our sex, to ensure protection of and over our world.

Argyll hollered, "Manitucus. Manasterous. Manu."

"Shut the fuck up, Argyll," yelled Fearghas, flapping his arms. "Dumber than a piece of bread."

We begin with recounting the story of the Children's Crusade at the crawl of the 13th century as a point to make my argument. Nearst the year 1212, a boy from either what is now the savage border-lands of France or Germany began preaching that he'd spoken to that inferior Bastard of a creature we refer to as God, and was instructed to enlist over 30, 000 teat-suckling tykes to be brought against the Mussalman in Jerusalem. By tale of ear throughout Europe, these children spent the fag end of their lives under the blade, and were aught slaughtered at first clash. 30, 000 perished before the golden temple under the countenances of work for old Christ.

But alas, this long-told and long-believed story is false. A wives' tale, as wives are meant to tell—which is why I do not have a wife. A pandering to lesser minds, it has existed in earnest to divert us from truth, while, in actuality, the Western European boy who's desire it was to drive children to their doom by way of The Crusades was, in historical fact, a Man and, much like his followers, not young of age, but poor of money and ragged of clothes. And it was a fact that when these beggars arrived at the foot of the Mediterranean Sea, without a boat and on the prom-ise this teenager had made them, (one of viewing miracles in the East), they expected the waters to part as they had once had for the Gypsy-rapist Moses. When the waters did not part, how-ever, they hissed at the prophecy and returned to their poor and miserable lives. Most of them died early deaths due to poverty in Europe, but they were not children who died. Not a one. There-fore, the mythic tale itself was told in utter mendacity. If not to instruct, than to be used as a means to stoke fear in the masses.

"Why is Moses a gypsy-rapist?" asked Lenard.

"A better question," said Fearghas. "Why is Moses not a gypsy-rapist?"

"That's stupid."

"So you can't answer the question?"

"I can try."

"And you will fail."

It is in the space between myth and reality, where The Mana-tonian humbly resides—Manu! He is an unquestioning servant to, not only what is found in this book, but all of Man, and his guardianship of earth. He must flourish of hair, testicle, and stench. He must frighten trees from budding and curdle milk to cheese. Or, he must produce curdled cheese directly from his person, and make that cheese tasty, and soft.

To attain Manatonian stature, therefore, I dictate three rules :

RULE ONE: *Creating a Nightmare*

With the birth of the first son, there is always a fear that he will be lost to the relative comforts of his sex: fattish women, food and drink, and all the other ubiquities held by the peasantry to keep the fear of death at bay. However, as a Manatonian, you must prepare your child for a vastly elevated caliber of existence, where reality, in its simplest form, no longer retains relevance.

The sole way to do this: Create a Nightmare.

A nightmare, by essence, should be a false representation of imaginary fears. However, during the early stages of the child's development, it is better to introduce that fear with sufficient gravitas, provoking the possibility of its existence. There are many different nightmares to choose from in this world. Whether Hell and its demons, Wyrms, Silkies, the plague, Pocks, or engorged vulvas, but regardless of your selection its reinforcement must be considered seriously. No other stories but ones of aforementioned darkness should be told. The child should be secluded, cut off from the world and its pleasures, until he finds himself convinced of the polemic in his mind, and the only way out: to wage war against it. If a future Manatonian is to combat evil, its brain should know evil from a young age. I even suggest beginning while the child is still in the womb, by screaming loudly at, or inside, it.

RULE TWO:
In Which to Combat Said Nightmare

Next, after the nightmare is chosen, there must be found a way to combat said nightmare. This, of course, is to encourage the development of appropriate Manatonian testicles, or what I like to call, Mesticles, which Beamish would claim full rights to naming because he is nothing but a mendacious curd. However, in order to form proper Mesticles, it is imperative for the child to eat, drink, and sleep survival before the nightmare's potential existence. For, throughout his future, the nightmare itself will be the object of combat, and not the combat itself.

"Mesticles?" asked Lenard. "Really?"

Argyll grabbed his crotch. "Only got one left."

"Quiet," said Fearghas. "We're getting to the best part."

RULE THREE:
The Staging of Great Illusions to Convince the Extraordinary is Still Ordinary

It is here we discuss the importance of creating great illusions, and not with the intention of turning fantasy to reality, but to convince the disciple of extreme situations, and the imagination needed to foil them—Manu! The reason why historical heroes usually fail at their goals is because most of them are swayed by selfish circumstance. Politics, amongst other pursuits of wealth and religion, deter dreams into the wallow of reality. A Manatonian, however, must become Odysseus, Perseus, Achilles, the Cyclops, Poseidon, Jupiter, and Mercury. A manifestation of the mind and body, for the first time completely entwined. In order to create a hero of such all-encompassing heights, it is imperative to make those heights ascendable, so that a form of spiritual self-commitment, or Ekstasis, can occur.

SETUP AND APPLICATION, AS PRACTICED
by Aesop Mac'Cool:

With my son, Apollonius Ingenious Methuselah Mac'Cool, the following three illusions were based on the book I read to him as a child: *Dracula.*

ILLUSION ONE:

After placing Apollonius inside a coffin, and inducing a coma of whiskey, I buried his body in three full meters of hard-packed soil in a cemetery during a thunderstorm. I would have pulled him to the surface should he have begun to go blue; however, on the verge of suffocation, he clawed free.

ILLUSION TWO:

After telling Apollonius that his mother (who he'd never met for she was dead!) was waiting for him across the Irish Sea in Dublin, I smuggled him aboard a ship set for Eastern Europe with nothing but a wooden stake, crosses made of corn kernels, and a small note ordering the capture of three lesbians. I secretly followed him for two months. In the end two lesbians were caught, and restrained.

"Twisted," said Lenard, his body trembling. "What a horrifying thing to happen."

"Ay," said Fearghas. "You don't want to know what happened to the lesbians."

"What did happen to the lesbians?" Argyll asked.

"Shut the fuck up happened," said Fearghas.

"What was that like?" asked Argyll.

"Fantastic."

"I believe that the original word for lesbian in English was Two Forks."

ILLUSION THREE:

Dressing up Beamish (when his loyalty was bare) in a wardrobe likening himself to Count Dracula himself, he forced Apollonius to capture a virgin, who was then later made into his bride. Soon after, she produced many children, most of which died, and Apollonius went on to procure Manatonian status. Unfortunately, soon after, he went completely mad (the illusion of Dracula had become too real) and stabbed his wife with a stake through the heart for refusing to cook with garlic. As opposed to becoming a protector of the human race, he spent time recovering from his disease-pit of a brain, and attempting to make a better rendering than him of a world-saving Manatonian in his first son, the one in which, to this very day, we place all our hope.

"Is that you?" asked Lenard, looking at his father across the table. "Are you the son of Apollonius Mac'Cool, who stabbed his wife in the heart with a stake because she wouldn't cook with garlic?"

Fearghas hung his head, tapped the page with a dirty finger.

"I don't believe this," Lenard said, slamming closed the book in his father's hand. "I don't believe a damn word."

"Look, my beloved man-thing," Fearghas said. "You can choose to pursue whatever creed you wish from here on out. You are of age. Just remember that there is a reason why I did what I did. I wanted you to be kept safe. And now, safe you are."

"Safe?" Lenard asked. "Safe from whom?"

"T.H.E.Y., of course?"

"But who is T.H.E.Y.? I still don't understand."

"The Beamites," said Fearghas. "Descendents of Aesop Mac'Cool's comrade turned-enemy, Beamish. Horrible, dangerous men, they are. If *The Manaton's* secrets fall into their hands, they could be responsible for the creation of some of the world's most reprehensible villains, worse than Stalin, Lenin, Hirohito, the works, maybe not Hitler, but you get the idea. These guys are looking to organize. They have the first thirteen chapters, but not the remaining twelve. And that is why we, as Manatonians, must preserve our secret."

"But what is the secret?"

"It's the secret," said Fearghas.

"The secret?"

"Like any secret, we have it, and they don't, so they want it, to see what it is."

"What?"

"To us, the secret isn't a secret, it's just a practice, but to them, it's sacred. And forbidden."

"But what is the secret?"

"It's very special," said Argyll.

"A special secret," said Fearghas, "that only we know."

"And which is?"

"Something you'll be ready for when you're older."

"So why not share it with them?" Lenard asked, and as he asked this both Fearghas and Argyll seemed to have been electrocuted by their seats. "Wouldn't that fix everything?"

"Share it with them?" Fearghas asked. He looked at Argyll. "Share it with them? Them, being Beamites?"

"Share *The Manaton*," said Argyll. "With a descendent of a Beamish?"

"A descendent," said Fearghas, "of Beamish. A descendent of the one, the man, who, ha, who tried to, ha, ha, bwa—hahahahaha," they fell into riotous laughter, grasping their stomachs, heaving.

"That ones funny," cried Fearghas, actual tears at his eyes.

"I'm glad I could make you laugh," said Lenard.

"Lenard," Argyll guffawed. "T.H.E.Y., the Beamites, they're our enemies. They'd kill you the second you held out your hand."

"But what if we just tried?"

"They'd tear you limb from limb," said Fearghas. "We're not at war because we want to be. We're at war because we have to be. Some books, Lenard, some books are just powerful for reasons we can't understand. There's nothing more ridiculous found in the pages of *The Manaton* that you wouldn't find in any biblical text. But since it has been written, lives have been changed, achievements have been made. *The Manaton* has officially influenced two revolutions along the Soviet belt, and attributed to the philosophies of both Karl Marx and Mao Zedong—the latter of which we didn't intend. But it reinforces the fact words can change people. And that makes us careful. The Beamites, you see, want more than the book. They want revenge. They feel they're entitled to what they're not. They have their definition of history, and we have ours."

"Okay," said Lenard. "I don't understand. But even if I did, why wouldn't T.H.E.Y. be open to change? I mean, are they even alive anymore? Are you sure they didn't disperse sometime at the end of the 19th century?"

"The sins of the father," sighed Argyll, shaking his head.

"You remember how I told you I did some time back in the day," said Fearghas. "Well, I lied."

"Shocking," said Lenard.

"See, I was really on the run, hiding out in Cairo, New Delhi, Israel, Uruguay. That's why my papers were so mucked up when I came into this country."

"Because you didn't have any papers," said Lenard.

"Because," Fearghas said, taking *The Manaton*, folding its cover and placing the bind in Lenard's hands. "I have the one thing they want."

He nodded towards the book.

"And now I'm passing that want onto you."

"Oh, no," yelled Lenard, removing his fingers. "So now what? I wait for T.H.E.Y. to come to my door and try to get it back? Why don't you take it? How the hell is this book going to save me from, what you claim to be, a bunch of uncompromising psychopaths? And who cares if they get their hands on it, anyway? What do you think they'd be capable of taking from it besides tips for stylizing their pubis?"

Fearghas shook his head as Argyll turned away. He then looked at Lenard's legs, and touched one.

"Wars have been started for much, much less," he said, betraying the most serious gaze he had thus far. "But since you will be strong, you will preserve what is rightfully ours. *The Manaton* does not belong to T.H.E.Y."

"Oh, that's right," Lenard snorted. "It belongs to the world re-nowned, yet unheard of cult of The Manatonians."

Fearghas tapped the table with his pinky. He looked at Argyll, who, Lenard didn't notice, nodded in the secret, nervous way, and turned his neck.

"We're supposed to be celebrating today," Fearghas resumed with twice as much cheer. He placed a hand on Lenard's shoulder. "You are strong enough now, Lenard. You are the first successful rendering of *The Manaton*. The first. The other," he brooded, "was a terrible mistake and had to be. . .abandoned."

"Poor creature," said Argyll.

"Evil creature," corrected Fearghas.

"Poor, evil creature," said Argyll. "Wonder where he is now?"

"See, though you didn't turn out exactly as we expected," Fearghas continued, "using the Superhero as a model for your formation worked quite well. Who knew that comic books held so much wisdom between their pages, too? Someday, someone will use them to justify both beautiful and terrible acts."

"Beautiful and terrible acts," said Argyll.

"Shut the fuck up," Fearghas continued. "Now Lenard, if we just plot the next few years of your life successfully, you won't be in danger at all. And, finally, when T.H.E.Y. is a thing of the past, this book can be used as initially intended."

"And what way would that be?"

Argyll piped up, "To make normal boys like you into the world's first Supermen!"

To which Fearghas reared about and slapped him.

"Unfortunately, the idiot is correct," said Fearghas as Argyll rubbed the soreness from his cheek. "You must restore order to this God forsaken country and the dream it has so sorely failed to entertain. It is our tradition. To protect and serve the good of all mankind. We are what the stonemasons should have been. We are the guardians of earth. You, as one of us, have this burden on your shoulder. You must swear yourself to utter secrecy."

A garbage truck clattered by.

"Which is why you'll be departing with me this evening on a one-way plane to Nepal."

Lenard blinked.

"Oh, no I'm not!"

"It's either that or death."

"Then I choose death," Lenard said. "I'm not leaving, Dad. I'm not leaving Laura. I. . ." he gulped, "I love her. And I can't lose her, even if I might have already."

"Who ever said anything about leaving Laura," Fearghas said.

"What are you talking about?"

"Someone has to bear your progeny."

"Her passport alias is Lily Zatkin," said Argyll.

"And yours is Lantana Zatkin," said Fearghas, impressed with himself. "Myself being Uranus."

"I like the sound of that," said Argyll. "Lenard and Lily Zatkin."

The traffic picked up behind Fearghas's back. Exhaust in the lungs. Lenard thought of his mother, who he'd never been close to, and then Laura again, who was the only woman he'd ever been close to. Then he thought of Superman. Face-locked chin, indistinguishably brawny. Cobalt haircurl never, ever atremble. The iron will to rewrite America. Could he really become a person like that? Like Superman? The last son of Krypton? The alien that could never be human, and thus, he guessed, because of that ignorance, actually save the earth? Was his father correct about *The Manaton*? The fact that all books, if written well enough, and with a sufficient amount of zeal, could influence both the most vicious and honorable human beings?

"Are you in, or out?" Fearghas asked.

Thinking of Laura, thinking of nothing but Laura, swooping her into his arms, and tired of talking, and even more so of thinking, Lenard nodded. His life no longer felt like his own. It felt like it belonged to those who had created him—a notion, he suspected, that was typical for a superhero, who were caged by their duty to mankind.

"Splendid," Fearghas said, shooting a glance of intent at Argyll, before hopping up and down. Argyll nodded back slowly and rose from his seat. In the distance, something was coming they both seemed to recognize, but they didn't let Lenard see what it was. Instead, in a display flamboyantly executed to distract his son, Fearghas spun himself into a toe click and flew from the curb.

"Dad!" Lenard screamed, as he watched Fearghas launch himself into a leap of unconscious misdirection.

Bright. White. Bus. Red wheels.

As the bus changed lanes, everything slowed down, everything slowed down. There appeared to be a chance for the driver to catch the twirling Scotsman out of the corner of his eye, but he revved the rage of his motor. Or at least so Lenard thought as he sat immobile in his chair. For a boy who was supposed to become the world's first superman, there was so little he could do to prevent the smallest of accidents. He closed his eyes. An awful sound, like that of a frightened pig, was heard. Death became a profound splat. So profound it barely made a noise. For a second Lenard jumped from his seat, but then fell back (as if pushed back?) ineffectual and scared. Here was an absence of blood, a faint hum of joy leftover in the air. Here was nothing but a lack of something else, and silver shapes, like falling birds, trying to make a fractured little circle below the sun. Lenard couldn't think of anything at all. A vague notion crossed his mind, something like failure, but also like freedom; something that made him feel immensely strong, even if he was glued to his seat in shock.

The bus driver stood up and looked out a window that wasn't rolled down enough for his head. Through the scratched glass he seemed to have a grimace on his face. A perfectly square chin and a walleye. Argyll clasped Lenard's hand and said, "Quick boy! The book," dragging him through DiMaggio's café, smashing tables and spinning out the back door. The bus driver stepped down the steps and clicked his tongue. He lurched off in the direction of Argyll's trail through the cracked glass and wood, and the Boston street left was ugly and silent with the death of Fearghas Murdoch Sikophsky.

AN EXCERPT FROM THE IMMATERIAL JOURNAL OF MALACH DENNY

Year, date, time, unknown.
There is a moon above.

It's true, I've only been at this, this being flying, fleeting, seagulling, for a little while, but I think I'm starting to understand what it means to keep my feet on the ground (when there is ground) and, when I want to, pretend it doesn't exist and float above—the world I inhabit is swelling in form, always has been—and maintaining six wings isn't as easy as it looks. In fact, it's fucking undimensional. I can't remember whether I was born or not (not that a lot of things can). But I also can't remember yesterday, or last week, or a week as a nominal for time, like a year, or century, or scattering of seconds; units I can't comprehend. Time, in my opinion, was made to keep schedules. But I'm not a farmer. And I definitely don't care about being late. Some, including myself, might even say that I don't exist, but if that is true, then I am not unlike most things. I think, I dream (viscidly), I act on autonomous impulse, and if I was spit from ether rather than the womb, than so be it.

The womb is hot.

I have a name: Denny. It's my only name. But it's not the best way to describe who I am, not that a lot of names draw the proper horizon their heritors deserve. But I understand that some creatures grow into their names, and, if that is the case, than I am truly an anomaly. Denny is a name for truckers out of Toledo, not an immaterial Malach, and I don't think I'll ever feel like it represents even a shard of my soul. But all things considered, I suppose I am lucky, for if humans can claim, "I think therefore I am," all I can say is, "Someone thought, therefore I was." Funny, yes? A fair enough deal? Denny. Me. The immortal Malach. Who ever gave a damn about surnames?

Now who actually titled me? Some things are lodged in the memory like tumors, and, like tumors, incur amnesia. I'm kind of a question's question, like literature, art, maybe even death, except unlike all those things I can respond to commands with infinite patience. I can advise. I can cry. I can also fuck, believe it or not. I'm very lonely, so I must exist in some way. Nothing can't exist that feels lonely.

I think.

But enough blabbing about my abstractions, my wearies and woes. It is in this letter I will recount the recent watch I took of Lenard Sikophsky: my maker. Whatever orbs birthed me, birthed me for him. Remember, I do not know if I exist, which is probably why I am journaling so, just to make sure, when I decide to, I can read it. Sometimes I feel strong and secure in who I am, and other times I think I am turning so invisible that even translucence will abandon my property. But Lenard, he began as real, and then, as he was reared, turned into a figment. His father made sure that the world he inhabited would always fly just far enough away from his grasp to dissipate before they touched. He had poor inner vision. An even poorer brain. In some ways is more obscure than I.

But alas, by Lenard I was dragged forth. I think his father had something to do with my summoning. I wanted to know more, so I lingered, and listened, but the human planet is so quiet and dull of ideas that I could have no way of understanding my origins. Following Lenard through his trials was not enough for me to understand him. I am Malach, anyway, and that means I am jealous of earth, all on earth, especially since I must watch events occur that, for me, are only passing thoughts. Whether they are Lenard's thoughts or mine, I can't be sure. But they are thoughts, this I know. Long, undigested thoughts.

Since I wanted to understand myself better, as well as my

origins, as you or any self-contemplative élan might understand, one night, while the boy was asleep, and though it seemed dangerous, I swooped down from my celestial pediment and came before his bed. I stroked his penis into erection, I pulled his dreams forth, loved him for hours until I was made into his image. Now, that's something you might have a hard time understanding, being made into another's image. But know that I had to—every Malach needs a face to emulate, and I hadn't yet found a God with hands strong enough to mold me.

Anyway, I remember the boy had strange elements in his blood. Unnatural sours in his semen. It was toxic (my maker, toxic?), and unbeneficial, but still, fucking him helped me convince myself that I was alive, that if I could touch, if he could cum, than he could see me, if only through the thickest of veils. His eyes were like drugged buttercups as they glimpsed my silver locks. His fingers thumbed them. We touched.

We, as Malach, are shackled to a place between somewhere like Heaven and Earth, you see, and therefore must remain between the two. The closest way to describe the paths we walk is imagining the creaking walls between dreams. Again, it is possible that I do not exist at all. I could be the lilt of a storybook. A fiction reticulated by a very clever boy who has great hope and pain deep inside him. But still, the philosophical implication of our union was nothing short of tantamount. If a creator can be urged into orgasm by his creation, then existence can be turned on its top.

As I began my exploration of my maker's life, however, Laura was the one I became most worried about. For whatever happens to her also happens to Lenard, and also, needless to say, affects me. I saw that she was recently possessed by a Dybbuk, a vicious, nasty example of the species. And oh yes, he exists, and unlike me, knows it. This one in particular sports a beard, wears some sort of cape, and has wide, ice-storm eyes. Something suggests he is definitely Goyim. Maybe the strength in his hands. Anyway, this Dybbuk possessed Laura in her weakest moment, and drove her to make an attempt against her life, which she would never have done otherwise. This is clearly speculation, but who the hell would even contemplate suicide? Life is space between voids. The strange thing about this Dybbuk in particular, however, is that he came in tandem with a woman, some ghost inseparable from his. She seemed to have died young and afraid, yet attached to him, and watched as he carried out his mordacity towards Laura. Unfortunately, though I do have power, I could not do anything to stop him from driving the pills down her throat. This made me sad, but our realms are different. The ghosts of Earth's ancestors are dead, you see, and I am, or at least I think I am, alive.

This Dybbuk, let's call him H, liked to beat his counterpart, we'll call her P, as if prescribed on a schedule. He could become jealous very easy, and liked to use his feet and his hands. One day it seemed that P took a liking to Lenard, and her spirit longed for him so that it attempted to stretch itself from H's reach. The sight was miraculous, like watching an earthworm tear itself to pieces. And do you know what H did when he saw her do so? In death he nearly killed her. He beat her spirit so bad that I thought new rules would be broken, new planes of existence enflamed. I thought that the universe would wangle up its own anus and make death into utter ubiquity. But instead they returned, side by side. P closed her eyes and cried. I found it strange that even the dead were angered by breaches in monogamy, but what could I argue, my name is Denny, and I'm not sure I exist.

Now let's talk about the Great Fuck You, for it is a subject in which all of my maker's life was recently dismantled. And contrary to what his father may have attempted to make his son believe, the letter, ordered by something called God (who I'd like to meet), was written by Fearghas in a dire attempt to frighten him into accomplishing supposed holy tasks. These tasks, however ludicrous, were satisfied with amazing candor. Lenard, under the enchantment of the hallucinogen, ayahuasca, was able to read messages drawn out by me (and others?) in the stars, messages I'd been sending to him my entire life but he'd never had the ability to read. I have to admit that I enjoyed the Scotsman's game. And since I can see into all men's souls, I knew what he tried to do he did out of love. But I also saw, as the test came to its height with that mechanized beastie upon the hilltop, that his actions evolved into something so fantastic, so munificent and exaggerated, that they began to affect the very heavens. I saw odd patterns coagulate, cancer in my skies. My wings ruptured, and I almost fell to my doom. The beast from the hilltop invaded the skytops. It was a terrifying time, and disturbed.

But then, afterwards, the tests, they ended, and so did what I perceived as turmoil. My maker was boiling with an awful sort of anger, but I couldn't say I didn't understand. This band of ruffians with bolted masks and sharpened appetites were coming to try and steal that filthy book of manhood (and its owners) away, and engorge themselves on whatever was left. Maybe they'd found, as I had recently witnessed, its words could be used to alter heaven. But these men, unlike my maker and his father, and even that diseased hobo Argyll, were dangerous. Though there is no evil that exists in any world, they were too close to death, to pain. I was afraid they, like me, were other Malachs, but who had learned to be earthbound, to walk in human feet and kill with human hands, who had opened a new evolutionary door in existence, and, in turn, would close many others. So it was here that I did my duty to save my maker for the first time. I kept him in his chair with an invisible grip. I kept him from dying with the bus—which he would have had he leaped free. He thinks he is responsible for what happened that day, but I can assure you, what he really is, is alive.

One thing I should add: the moment Fearghas Murdoch Sikophsky died, something beyond me, beyond Lenard, beyond his realm and mine, and all the others stretching beyond into nothing beyond nothing beyond nothing, a spark was lit, a kindling of substance, and though on earth it was invisible, high in my realm I could glimpse the dying shards of a miracle. They looked like origami birds, swans, pelicans, but alive, and, lo and behold, they were bleeding. Tortured as they circled from above my eyes to below my feet. I caught one in my hands and it chirped one word for me.

"Manu."

Confused, I dropped the tortured critter from my hands, it was no bigger than a human thumb, and joined its fellows in their descent into earth. The shape of their formation looked like this:

But remember, I'm not sure I exist. My words are relevant, like alchemy.

PART TWO

ON ATOMIC BOMBS, SOMEWHERE, WITHOUT REASON

CHAPTER ELEVEN

TRADITION

For Nemo the trials of manhood began when he was barely twelve. Twelve, unlike other twelves for other boys, was for male Sikophskies (and now Zatkins) a time of trial not only for the son, but the father. In the case of today this father was Lantana Zatkin; Lantana, a name, much in the tradition of its bearer, had been borrowed and twisted during its travels, to the point where it resembled a child's play on nomenclatures, a cross between Lancaster and Santana, perhaps, if any thought had gone into it at all. The unforgettable dream of Massachusetts had been banished to a similarly make-believe province of the past; much time had elapsed, yet not been forgotten. Now it was 2006, post-millennial, value-systems away from Fearghas and his tests. The Zatkins were removed—perhaps too removed. Safe, they thought, from ancient threats and the conflicts that perpetuated them. The world they now inhabited was still America; some would have said 'real' America. All this depended on your coast of origin and one's personal definition of 'heartland.' On this fateful winter day, in the Midwest—Colorado, to be more specific (a little more west than Midwest; Colorado was a little more west, less Nebraska than Nevada)—stood an unlikely victim, Nemo Zatkin, a brilliant and capacious young mind. When he woke up that morning and traced the ice-prickles on the outer glass of his bedroom window with a warm finger, he never suspected that soon after breakfast he'd be carted into the Rocky Mountains under orders to wrestle a bear. But that was how the ouroboros of family functioned; self-consumption was not prescribed, it was regimented.

"Look up at me," was, if not the first thing, at least the most prominent he remembered his father saying that day. "Look up at me."

For hours they'd trekked into the misery of Silver Lake, almost 11,000 feet above the ocean. By nightfall they were forty miles from Denver, and if the clouds were sparse enough, the surface would be eclipsed by the constellate biceps and shoulders of Hercules. Here, the air was dry. A globe filled with stillness. For those in transit respiration was earned until they reached an open vale within the trees. As to why they were here today, that was a more difficult question. Lantana tried to answer it once at his son's request and ended up proclaiming, "Because everyone is like someone in the end."

Whipping snow salted Lantana's chin as he came to stand, hands at the hip, in lee of a magnificent boulder. His good eye was closed to a squint, and the other one, slapped shut with a leather eye patch, remained a tiny pall through the snow.

"Look up at me," he said again, licking his lips. The patch had an S printed on it in chartreuse. Over his jeans he wore a toga, below his jeans he wore Spandex, and everywhere he seemed to be grinning.

"But I am looking up at you," Nemo said.

"Excuse me?" asked Lantana.

"I'm looking up at you," said Nemo, pulling his cap, a deerstalker, over his forehead.

"Actually, I'm looking straight at you, because we're standing right across from each other, and I'm a little bit higher on this incline. . . ."

Lantana chewed his lip in thought at the boy's logic, and then, in his creaking hardwood webs, crunched across the snow.

"You think you're smarter than me?" he asked.

"No," said Nemo.

"Cause I'm not even as smart as me," spit Lantana. "And that means something.

Don't it?"

Nemo coughed.

"Then, look up at me."

The boy craned his neck up until his mouth was flush with the sky, which, Lantana soon noticed, was worse than before.

"Alright," he said, shaking his head. "Just close your eyes."

Nemo, thin and unremarkable, obeyed. As he did so, he heard his father scurrying through his camping pack.

"Where did I put those freaking chicken livers?" he whispered, slinging the pack to the ground. "Ah, fuckit. Open your eyes."

Nemo obeyed again and prised his pupils to a turgid sky. His feet were simmering over the frozen remains of pickerelweed as they neared the lake. The forest around them, with its sobering labyrinth of lodge-pole pine, seemed to trap anything chancing its way through the Rockies, where nothing, not even death, seemed to care where its mazy jaws could shut. Here, the boy noticed, as opposed to at home, was nothing but light. Here was comfort in its natural form. And majesty.

Beneath his deerstalker he had his yarmulke on, something he'd become accustomed to this year on the verge of his Bar Mitzvah. His parents thought it was unnecessary, but he didn't care much for what they thought. For him, it was only an experiment. If God was really watching every Jew under Earth's sky, and if Jews needed to be recognized by the respect they demonstrated by wearing a hat on their heads, then God was everywhere, and Nemo, he was nowhere, in a vast, centerless center. Right? He hoped so. According to him, there would never be one place he could stand in twice. But by spraying forth his person in every direction, by repositioning himself in a million different pinpointable locations into space as day spindled on into night, he'd be able to ascertain as to where exactly above actually was, by his own, wacked out process of reduction.

Lantana took out *The Manaton* from his bag and flipped through a few pages, mumbling. "So what happens if. . .ah, okay—so, little bastard, tonight is the moment of your discontent, bla bla bla," he read with one finger. "Here it is. Today, one year before your Bar Mitzvah, you must be swift, strong, and fight for the lasting vigor of your life. The theme: man always triumphs!" he rocked his fist without looking from the page. "Somewhere in that thicket, just down there," he pointed to a crumple of wood and snow to the western shore of Silver Lake, "is what I like to call your *zeitgeist*. Gaze now upon your greatest fear. Mwa-ha-ha," he said, pronouncing the *Mwa*s and, has like self-important people said, *bla bla bla*. "Your Kraken!"

Kraken. Just saying that word, slurring it through wet lips, or sending it through the valley with the treatment of an avalanche, stirred nothing, absolutely nothing, in little Nemo Zatkin at all. Yes, Lantana had tried to frighten the boy with daily readings from *Twenty Thousand Leagues Under the Sea*, but its effect had been wearisome specifically since it remained now a fact that, off the coast of Japan, squids large enough to be considered mythical had been discovered, making them little more than another species worthy of global conservation by biologists who, even in their drab love-letters, possessed the emotional muscularity of the tone-deaf. No, by the age of seven Nemo had graduated to far more complex texts than anything Verne could have dribbled out, and by ten had already breezed through half of *The Collected Works of Anton Chekhov* (boy, did he hate anything by Ayn Rand) and had developed an affinity for creatures of non-human make, whether as dangerous as a tiger snake or timid like the fawn. Were he to actually encounter something resembling a Kraken, he probably would have attempted to stroke its silver suction cups rather than storm its eye with a bomb lance. Though he wasn't surprised that his father didn't know these things about him, and that lack of knowledge hurt him, he didn't think it ever would have been too late to ask.

"Now that you're consumed with terror," tittered Lantana. "You must hurry down into the pit of all madness and face the great demon your-self!" He launched his fists in the air even higher, waiting for something to occur. When it didn't, he repeated, "The great demon yourself!" Hearing nothing again, he cursed, and using his webs to bother the snow, screamed,

"THE GREAT GODDAMN DEMON YOURSELF!"
"Oh—uh,. . .BOOGA-BOOGA-WOOGA!!!"

"Goddamnit," Lantana whispered, shutting his good eye with menace. As he saw Nemo examining him, he said, "Well, what are you waiting for? Get down there and face your destiny, or whatever."

Nemo shrugged along at his father's apathy, and, taking nothing but himself, the snug little plaid-printed peacoat and deerstalker cap he wore in the manner of a tiny Sherlock Holmes, trotted down into the thicket. On his way down, he looked into the center of Silver Lake, which, he thought, was quite beautifully deco. Mounds of ice rippled in a circle on the frozen acreage. In the air was the legato of glaciated earth, the smell away from school buses and their gasoline-sleet. Nemo was raised a child of winter, without much of a presence whenever weather turned hot; he preferred layers, for the most part hated beaches. He was so unlike his father, a man vexed by clothes, who, in purple Spandex wound up to the rim of his navel as if eonianally imprisoned there, had an idea that the proper way for a man to live involved drawing as much attention as possible to the existence, daresay size, of his testicles.

Nemo tugged his cap over his forehead and spent a good few minutes sidestepping some snow-buried timber. Unlike his father, he had no heroes, no one he considered supreme or holy, and was still trying to understand whether or not he believed in God as anything beyond an ineffable blather of molecules. Lantana, on the other hand, embarked on a weeklong bender involving alcohol and Disneyland after he received his first periodical in what happened to be *Golden*, Colorado's least popular village newspaper. In all honesty, Nemo wasn't sure how intelligent his father was, and often wondered how he, a premature bloom, had been forthed from such desiccate soil.

The snowshoes burned his feet as he trekked the terrain. Every rawhide lace crinkled with rime and his steps felt a little like stumbling. As he went further into the forest, he became afraid that he wouldn't be able to work his way back, and took a fortune cookie he'd preserved in his pocket from dinner last night to leave a trail. The message inside read *You will inherit a diamond mine in Africa*, and on the back was the Chinese word for *loin of yak*.

"HAHAHA!" he heard his father laugh in the distance. "Fly from the cold fuck you of fach—" he began coughing.

Nemo cringed, more embarrassed than afraid. His father was the source of all his social angst. How could he have explained to any of his friends at school (not that he had any), who were now at home on a Saturday afternoon reading books, playing games, sports, simulated sports, or plashing their childhood dreams onto paper, that he was out in the middle of nowhere getting ready to fight a wild bear with nothing but his fists, feet, and wits?

As he brooded he heard a shuffle in a patch of trees to his left. He stopped and turned to them—shadows, the canopy of snow. Everything glued together. The current crawed at his feet and he smelled something foul.

"Okay," Nemo said to himself. "Stay calm. It's just one of Dad's tricks."

But as he whispered, something snapped its bulk through the branches making a sound like,

"GROWLLLARGGGHARAR!"

"Eeeeeeeeeeee!"

"That's right!" he heard his father roar in the distance. Nemo wasn't sure how far he away he was. "You run or you die! You run or you die! Can you hear the almighty, now? Can you hear him when he speaks?"

Daring to glance back, Nemo saw that he wasn't being chased by a bear at all, but from head to toe the quiddity was green and covered in what looked like scales. With dumb eyes and a silver loll of tongue it crashed through the trees. Its gait was, in all fairness, retarded.

Trying to think quick, the boy swung himself around a tree and found himself flopping in the opposite direction of the creature on his webs. He swooped his arm down and picked up a stick.

"Take that," he said, snapping it over its leg.

"GROWLLLARGGGHH!" it roared, head back in rage. "BOOGA-WOOGA-RARR!"

With claws clipping out towards Nemo, it clasped his tiny shoulders in its grip. The eyes were pupilless, opaque, and its lizard's mouth hinged loose. Ridges or bones like that of a Stegosaurus flickered down its humped back and tail. The damned thing looked capable of besieging Tokyo.

"Put me down!" Nemo pleaded. "Please?"

The shaking continued, and the monster abstained from sinking its teeth into the boy's flesh. Instead, it took him into a chest hold and, making an urgh sound, began to squeeze. Nemo turned a little blue. He saw the jerking of branches in the canopy and smelled plastic, hard plastic, and coffee grounds. Down the hill came the heavy steps of his father.

"I said, put me down," Nemo rasped.

Lantana skidded to a stop.

"GRAGGLEPLARARRRPLA!" the monster roared. "BOOGA-WOO-GA-RAR!"

Nemo's peal for release rose to a squeal and from under his fingernails, his cuticles, what looked like lightning snaked into the air. The monster stopped its squeezing and cocked its head in curiosity before uttering a windless oof as he was boomed yards away into a tree. The thicket filled with light. Winter crackled from the limbs like ceiling dust. The Zatkins were choked with silence.

Lantana, with the stale mystification of a communion cracker, tapped his wooden foot against the snow.

"Ow. . ." the creature moaned. "What the fuck—what the fuck was that?" It clicked its talons around its skull and began, with a slight heave, to remove it, revealing an odd-looking man with epicanthic eyes and a frowzled rice bowl haircut. His face was red, wired bifocals steamed. His top hairs were stiff with static as the mask lifted off.

"I. . .I don't know," said Lantana. He continued to stare at his son, as if right through him. "I've never seen anything like it before." Running his tongue across his teeth he turned to the man in the costume, slumped in snow from the neck down.

"What the hell happened?"

"Sorry, Licious," the man said, slow as if stoned. "They were out of bear costumes."

"So you chose to dress as," he looked him over, "a dinosaur?"

"It was all they had left," he rubbed his head and moaned. "It feels like I stuck my dick in a wall socket."

"So now what, Carl?" Lantana said, throwing his arms to sky. "The book preaches consistency. How the hell is the kid supposed to learn the dogma of Manhood from dueling in the forest with dinosaurs?"

"That fear itself is never extinct?" Carl peeped, to which Lantana casually walked up and slapped him.

Nemo watched the two men squabble—Carl flapping his dinosaur limbs, his father fumbling his fists through the snow. He felt queasy. Whatever was happening to him began a few months ago, and for reasons he didn't know. Just after he was sick from school with sinusitis.

"Can we go home now?" he asked.

Lantana took a break from slapping his friend and, seeming genuinely confused, shrugged.

"I think I need the hospital," said Carl. "Peed on my leg."

Lantana growled.

"Pooped too."

Lantana turned his one eye to the sky and looked through a tunnel in the trees, into the wind and white, as if God, somehow, or some other deity, were challenging him to a war of tribute. And, being the anti-God he was, the one-eyed beast abandoned by his maker, he decided that challenge was a declaration of war. Taking a toothpick into his mouth, placing it on the inside of teeth, atop his tongue, so the tip could splinter out between the incisors, he steered his son away from Carl and Silver Lake.

"I'll see you down at the men's club, Licious," Carl said, waving his talons frantically.

And Nemo wondered if the terrifying bulk of his father would look at him askew as they made a failed return to society. But as their journey carried on, he extended his hand. Nemo gripped it as hard as he could.

CHAPTER TWELVE

AN EMPTIER BOX

In the middle of the night Nemo awoke to Lantana's fervent nose-breathing. He stood below the phosphor stars and moons glowing on the ceiling. On his body, baffled by muscles, was a choking pair of blue Spandex and flagrant red toga pinned over his shoulder, and on his toes, golden sandals were laced thick and tight. He carried a titanium club in his fist and twirled it ever so slightly. As if contemplating whether or not to wake his son, when he found the boy staring at him he shuffled backwards and pretended to look for something on the dresser. A DNA helix modeled from steel epoxy twittered a little. He reached out to stable it with a snort.

"Just searching for my wallet," he said.

This room was so different from his own growing up, and he couldn't help from taking that in. Unlike the verging tenement of partially soldered roof beams and fractured windowpanes in Milton, this tiny room, in this large and secure home, was so serene, so mature for its inhabitant. The walls were stickered by the stars, moons, and what looked like saturns Lily put up to impress her coddling arms upon Nemo while he grew through her grip. In the center of the ceiling they made deliberate shapes. One formation, around the lamp, looked like this:

There were books, countless flipped-through pages, what could have been a disdain for the ebullience of childhood. Rather than action figures and model cars, sketches in vine charcoal, puerile renderings of men and women with circular lips and cigarettes spanned the desk and walls. Nemo created life with his fingers, it seemed, rather than demanding it from those around him with his biceps. Lantana felt so empty as he stared at the images, never so formally useless.

"Are you going out on the beat, Dad?" the boy asked, vaguely interested as he sat up in his bed sheets. They were dark green, the fertile hue of shamrock, and his pillows were the same assuasive color.

The baldhead nodded. "Police scanner just picked up some activity in Five Points. Gun trade."

He picked up a sketch of a strong, muscled Greek of a man with an eye patch, which, he soon realized, was more like him than he would have enjoyed. Saying nothing, he let the picture back down.

"Sound's exciting, huh?"

Nemo shrugged and closed his eyes a little.

"I'm not sure," he yawned, sucking in a little bit of the bedsheet. "Maybe."

"What do you mean, maybe?" Lantana asked. "High adventure. Fame. That only maybe sounds exciting to you?"

"I'm not sure," Nemo repeated. "Maybe."

Lantana snorted at what he saw as a lack of him in his son. How could pen and ink drive a boy's life when there was a world of terror and beauty to be had at the mercy of fists? It just wasn't natural for a child to be so independent. In the end, everyone was like someone.

"What happened today," said Lantana, coming down to his son's bed and shyly cupping his cheek, "was unnatural. We won't tell mom about it, and you can let me know if it happens again."

Nemo nodded through his embarrassment.

"We'll forget about it," he reiterated.

The nodding continued.

"It was a freak occurrence, and you are a normal boy. A perfectly normal boy. Just like I was. And I'm going to make sure you know that. Here—"

From a pocket in his toga, he took a small purple box. The same one Fearghas passed onto him long ago. Lantana, through all his years, had never found an object worth occupying its borders and, though he thought about it often, the emptiness had thickened with time. When it opened the room seemed to ebb its darkness. There were only walls to take away, and not fill.

"What is it?" asked Nemo, sitting up to take the box and shake it a little.

Lantana took a deep breath. "It's the equivalent of stepping outside under a dark wide sky, and pointing to a star, one unnamed in our constellations, and saying, that star right there is my star." He took his finger to the glowing shapes, the handicapped solar system trickling over the ceiling, found a small, circular button of a planet that could have been the Moon, Mars, or Jupiter. "Nobody else's but mine. Even if you can't reach it. Understand?"

"But there's nothing in the box?" asked Nemo, creaking the hatch and running his pinky finger over the velvet interior.

"Of course there is."

"But. . .I can't see anything."

Lantana shook his head and, as if offended, drew the box back into his pocket.

"Never mind," he said. He creaked up from his son's bedside, wondering if he should have started the trials earlier, if, like his father, he should have begun feeding him plutonium when the boy was young, as opposed to what had become the alternative. Honestly, he wasn't sure what was happening with his family anymore; as a child, his life had been a well-oiled formula.

"Just be careful, Dad," said Nemo, gently turning over to fall back asleep. Whether or not he felt kindred with his father, he didn't feel safe when he wasn't around.

Nodding, Lantana said, "I will."

A noise like creaking was heard above them, maybe the warped ancient wood of the attic? Some dyspeptic creature digging its clawed toes down and, as if in boredom, giving a push. Lantana gave it his attention for a second, but then left the room ruffling the frippery of his costume. As he left, though he didn't know it, he was tracked by his son's eyes. There was a static in the air he could feel. The box filled with nothingness seemed so heavy in his pocket, but he kept it close to his flesh.

CHAPTER THIRTEEN

ABUNDANCE

Middle school was a botanical garden of nightmares far beyond anything Nemo's father could have dreamed. Wholly more manageable than predictable stories of Krakens, Laredo, a redbrick square upon six wild acres of wheat and yucca, was a sacrificial mound for children on the terminus of puberty. One by one, they lined up for the budding of new desires, new disdains, unready as life drove their small bodies to the brink of adolescence like horses being panicked off a cliff. Contradictory to his father, Nemo was a well-developed boy with an average skeleton for average muscles, but when he walked through campus he drew attention to himself by the deerstalker cap he donned too snugly. Hats were okay to wear at Laredo. Hats that didn't have words.

Usually Nemo over-compensated to make friends, either rendering himself clownish or egregiously cool. All his efforts were transparent, even to himself, and by the end of seventh grade a rumor had been spun of amazing dido to solidify his loosely reinforced reputation as an overcompensating social idiot (namely that, in the month of January, when he was sick from school one Monday with acute sinusitis, he returned to the halls of Laredo Middle School to find his classmates fabricating, with conviction he was sure they, too, found farcical, that he'd been caught by the dean stroking his prepubescent kosher salami in the boy's bathroom stall). Nemo, however, at eleven years old didn't know how to masturbate yet and denounced the rumor multiple times. But, as may have been predictable considering the age group, this only increased its severity. Before he knew it the tale had snowballed from being caught by the dean in the bathroom with his boyhood exposed, to the stall being banged upon while Nemo, in the voice of a dimestore criminal, screamed, "You'll never catch me, Dean Veltry!" while vigorously shaking his wiener in the face of his discoverer until the door was ripped open (some said blown open by plastic explosives) and he was restrained by armed police officers still unable to curb his hell-bent drive to whack off.

Since the rumors began, almost daily the boy checked himself into Marlene Wendell's office with the excuse of a sore belly. Some unpopular boys had at least one friend to speak for, but Nemo had none. Not one helping hand in the whole of Arapahoe County—a large expanse of stenciled suburbs and prairie land. It was true, he thought. He was not a normal boy. And he'd never be able to feel clear of responsibility for his own dirty bomb of social doom. Even if utterly unavoidable, he felt, just by being his father's son, he'd signed on for a life of estrangement.

"I've recommended you for counseling," Ms. Wendell said a few days after he returned home from Silver Lake.

Her office was a deserted room, a sad, sawdust-colored place, with two rubber benches attached by fat nails to each wall. Her own brittle desk was filled with files, and beside it, a Lexan-door cabinet where an alchemist's rack of tinctures glistened, both old and new. Marlene herself was dressed in a translucent white blouse above a shirt of the same lonely hue. Tall and uniform, devoid of curves, she was something aquatic, like a sperm whale.

"I've heard about the rumors," she said. Her voice was high pitched like a spermaceti's would have been. "I'm not impressed with the school's response."

Nemo had his hands over his stomach. "It's okay, Ms. Wendell. It's not so bad."

"I'd like to you talk to someone. Share your feelings."

Nodding attentively as he always tended to do, Nemo whispered, "I'd like someone to talk to."

Even if he sounded precocious, Ms. Wendell caressed his cheek—diffidence was admirable in young boys—and when she did so, felt an odd prickle.

"You know," she said, pulling her hand back and wondering. "If there's ever anything you want to tell me. . .anything about what's going on at home, you can," she looked into Nemo's eyes—the left one seemed a little lazy, and his left lip was drawn down with it. He was not a handsome boy, but he would become handsome one day. Some children had to be ugly for a while in penitence for prettier futures.

"I know I can, Ms. Wendell," he said. "Thank you."

"Anything at all."

A grumbling was heard from down the hall, and, with the sound of flip-flops unsticking themselves from linoleum, Lantana appeared, stalking around the corner. He elbowed his way through the Ms. Wendell's narrow doors, and in a Gold's Gym tank top, purple Spandex and eye-patch, held out his hand in something between greeting and attack.

"I'm here to spring my boy," he said. After 'boy' he let a demented smile swim over his face. Something that was probably supposed to be congenial. "What needs to be done?"

"Mr. Zatkin—"

"Lantana."

"Well, Lantana, you're son isn't in trouble. He doesn't need to be 'sprung.'"

"But I heard he wasn't in class," he said that last word like it had been taboo until just recently, possibly due to the enactment of a new law.

"He had a reason for that."

"Is it money you want?" asked Lantana, removing a massive sack of nickels from what seemed to be his back pocket but could have been his underwear. "My wife gave me thirteen dollars worth of change and I don't want a Goddamn thing to do with it."

"Mr. Zatkin," said Nurse Wendell, gently shoving the bag of nickels away from her chin. "Your son has been the target of awful canards around school."

"Nurse Wendell, please?" said Nemo, not nervous, but wary in the dealings of family. "It's no big deal."

"What the fuck is a canard?" asked Lantana.

"Mr. Zatkin?"

Lantana scratched his head. "Oh my God. . ." he whispered, eye reeling wide. "Is he dead?"

Nemo and the nurse cocked their chins.

"Dad. . .I'm right here."

"Doesn't mean anything," said Lantana.

"Yes it does," said the nurse. "It means he's alive."

"No it doesn't. No it fucking doesn't."

Urging the brute into a small plastic chair that, on first glance, seemed barely large enough to cup a medium sized house cat, Ms. Wendell proceeded to explain to Lantana, in her patient melody of voice, the meaning of canard, or rumor (Lantana, for reasons associated with his former existence, his unsolved life's purpose, had practically carried on much in the way of a rumor itself, and thus, in the tradition of most things whose existence had been called into question at one time or another, was unfamiliar with the actual meaning of the word, or whether that meaning, once explained, could hope to warrant reprobation). It was a longer conversation than she'd expected to have; not to mention demoralizing, considering the state of her counterpart. Lantana bull-snorted whenever he felt patronized and filled her with one-eyed ire. After the end of her lesson, he confirmed understanding with a slight tip of the chin. Nurse Wendell then imparted the reason for bringing up the subject in the first place: Nemo had been falsely assailed with the allegation of masturbating at school, gunning down his endangered social esteem. The incident, she proceeded to explain, had in turn spurned him from his studies, made him afraid of his own shadow, and caused him to seek out the solace of a sickbed. Lantana, as he listened, tried to remain stately looking in his chair, with one spray-tanned leg poised over the other's knee, though he more resembled a lion teetering atop a circus-stool, pining for his memories of the hunt. Surrounding him was wallpaper with slightly raised engravings of what might have been cinnamon fern, tip to tail. All of it was soaked in a thick wash of butterscotch paint. And Lantana hated the taste of butterscotch. It made him sick.

"So, he was accused of masturbating in the boy's room?" he finally asked, feigning comprehension.

"Yes."

"And it wasn't true?"

"No."

"Why not?"

Ms. Wendell caught her breath.

"I don't know how to answer that question."

"The first time I masturbated was at the age of. . ." he thought to himself. "Birth."

"I highly doubt that."

"I highly doubt you, Nurse."

"You have something against nurses?"

"And doctors. And surgeons."

"Dad, please?" pleaded Nemo. "It's impossible to masturbate at birth."

"Mr. Zatkin," said Ms. Wendell, placing her angular fingers into a triangle above her stomach as if opening a portal of mild calm for him to stare through. As his trembling eye relaxed, it seemed to work. "Your boy needs the attention of a therapist to help sort out his curricular issues. Problems like this can lead to the development of low self-esteem."

Lantana's eye burned. "Did you say therapy?" he asked, remembering, just by the suggestion itself, the time he'd spent in Doctor Fezzeliski's office with his ass exposed to the ceiling.

Ms. Wendell nodded. "It's something a lot of children do these days."

Creaking from the chair, Lantana and his Spandex smiled, "Of course." He canted his chin at Ms. Wendell, letting her see how large, how burgeoning full of archetypal male he was. "Of course, of course. Forgive my hostility." He smiled. "Long morning. I'll be excusing my son from school for the day. Believe he needs the fresh air. You don't mind?"

"Not at all," said the nurse, scribbling some info in the records. "I'll set up the appointment with a counselor if you'd like.

We can have Nemo in care by next week."

Lantana, winking, said, "Don't worry about that, Ms. Wendell. I'll make the call myself."

She clicked her pen closed and looked down at her desk. Lantana took his son's hand.

"A father's love is remedy for all," he said.

Lantana and Nemo emerged from Laredo middle school into the albumen Colorado morning. Ice coated the sidewalks and parking lot, and the sun did its best to melt it all, locked in battle with the wind chill. A few students took their recess on the basketball courts, dribbling bodies, unimpressive layups. One boy, a tall Caucasoid by the name of Jeffrey Westcott, stole around his defender to sink a sideline shot. He looked up at Nemo and, with his lowboned Midwestern jaw, smiled.

"Where are we going, Dad?" asked Nemo, a little flush as he tried to look away from Jeffrey, checking the ball with a stouter boy named Byron, or Burton, he couldn't remember, who saw him and hollered out, "There goes the Masturbation King!"

Holding the ball high above his head, a couple of the boys joined him in flouting, juddering their hands as if they were filled with imaginary ketchup bottles. "Masturbation King. Masturbation King." One sunk to his knees in tribute, fanning his arms above his head. "Oh, Masturbation King, teach us your ways!"

"See," said Lantana, clopping his son on the back. "They fucking worship you. Goddamn. And that nurse thinks you need therapy? What a load of crap."

Jeffrey Westcott, standing with the ball in his hand and a pair of long Kappa leggings, lowered his head at the chanting and walked away. As he did so, Nemo watched the back of his shoes, the way his low-cut Reeboks revealed the bottom of his socks. He had such tall femurs, and what seemed to be a personality much like them. Though he didn't really talk to Nemo, and though he was what was considered to be a popular boy, he was kind whenever they crossed. Sometimes Nemo thought he was being studying by him, as if he'd become a new species of basketball. Though slightly creepy, it was better than being mocked. Anything was better than the ketchup bottles.

"Let's just go home, Dad," said Nemo, pulling at his father's pocket. The kids returned to playing ball.

"Home?" asked Lantana, as if Nemo had said hooker. "We aren't going home at all. Today you will learn what I once had to learn."

"Oh?" asked Nemo. He was hiding behind his father, but not sure why.

Lantana smiled.

"Something to keep you out of the nurse's office."

Nemo was terrified when Lantana steered away from their golden Saturn, encrusted in mud, and led him across the parking lot and up the street to Smoky Hill Road where the high school was. It, like the road, went by the same name, and was a host for the thousands of infectious microbes some people referred to generously as teenagers. The pioneers of Smoky Hill had set up the school on what could be considered a fault line of wealth and poverty. The community itself was the result of a fiscal earthquake, a perfect mix of hoodlums and baccalaureate conservatives and gun-toting members of the Aurora gang, Asian Pride, who had, apart from hand-held Uzis, scores of Hondas that looked an awful lot like time machines. Even for Lantana and his superior strength, venturing onto the high school's turf of perpetually dying grass was dangerous, and Nemo trailed him at the lip of his Spandex, praying to a God he didn't know.

As they passed around the western side of the school, they found a patch of fourteen-or-so-year-old girls chattering with cigarettes on a hill. For the most part, they seemed just as young as Nemo, even younger, but they didn't have the inhibitions of his classmates. Already their bodies gave off maturity in drafts, once-child's limbs confused by adolescence. Nemo was terrified just looking at them. This entirely new species of female.

Lantana, halting about twenty feet away, bent down to him on one knee and said, "In ancient Japan, there existed a country of feudal lords, or shoguns, and their serfs, much like the dark ages of Europe. This period was called Sengoku Jidai, and was a time of great war."

Nemo looked up at his father.

"What?"

Lantana shook his head. "Just listen! Three emperors," he put up as many fingers and checked to see if they were being watched, "great men, were responsible for the unification of Japan. Their names were Oda Nobunaga, Toyotomi Hideyoshi, and Tokugawa Ieyasu."

"Eye-ee-ya-sue?"

Lantana nodded. "These three unifiers represented three unique qualities that made Japan's modern evolution so successful. Nobunaga was the sword, Hideyoshi, the unifier, and Ieyasu, posthumously, was referred to as the Light of the East, due to the establishment of his Shogunate."

"I think we should get out of here," said Nemo, looking over at the pack of young girls. They snickered at some clandestine affair. There was one in particular who could have been a boy with short-cropped black hair and a squarish face. She had black converses with rubbed-down stars. A Virginia Slim spined between her fingers.

"Ieyasu created an empire that would rule Japan peacefully for two hundred and fifty years until the West forced its borders open," Lantana continued. "But he couldn't have done it without his predecessors, their violence and treachery, their ability to make. . .unsavory decisions."

"Dad," said Nemo. "I'm really okay. If you don't want me to go to the nurse's office anymore, or therapy, I won't. I promise."

"We'll do more than that, son. See, over there, within that gaggle of post-pubescent females, is your key out of social doom."

"Oh?" asked Nemo, despite his scrutiny, a little interested. Middle school had soured most of his options. Instead of shrinking, he grew a little bolder. If there was one thing he could do well, it was being forced to listen.

"All you need to do," said Lantana. "Is practice the three tenants of the generals, and, voila! Years of undisturbed peace."

"I don't understand," said Nemo, almost resolved to giving up. "What do you want me to do?"

"First, choose the one you like the most."

"Like?"

"Yes. Like."

"But why?"

"Just choose and I'll tell you."

Nemo looked over the crowd. Smoke from cigarettes cambered over fingernails, ponytails and strawberry blond curls—there was a black girl with straightened locks, shiny silver lips and an iris in her hair. As he watched the crowd, afraid they'd notice him as he attempted to choose, he found that he didn't really 'like' any of them. Instead they made him shudder, as if he'd like to know them, but not kiss them, as if he'd like to understand them, but not walk hand in hand with them. Then, with unexplainable bigness, he imagined the face of Jeffrey Westcott and his sultry kindle of yellow hair. When he did he felt his heart pulse at his wrist, as well as a little like vomiting.

"Her," Nemo said, pointing at the girl with the crew cut. "I, I want her."

"Good," said Lantana, focusing his one eye. "Wait, who?"

"That one," said Nemo, tipping his head. "With the short hair."

"Huh," stated the bald man, stroking his chin. "Well, I can't argue with individual taste. You don't think she's a little, I don't know...hideous?"

Nemo looked at his father and shrugged.

"No matter," said Lantana, shaking his head. "Now that you've decided on the female of your choice, you must stop thinking of her as a person, and instead treat her as a goal. An accomplishment. A landmass, like Japan. Consider yourself an embodiment of the three wise emperors."

"I need think of her like a country?" Nemo asked.

"Exactly. A country you need to conquer. Thus, like Nobunaga, you must be quick with the fist. Like Hideyoshi, smooth with coercion. And in faith to Ieyasu, allow her heart to shatter in your honor. Attack, coerce, wait for the payoff. So is the passage to manhood."

Nemo closed his eyes. "Attack, coerce, wait for the payoff."

"Now you've got it."

"Attack, coerce, wait for the payoff."

"Let's say it together—"

"Attack, coerce, wait for the payoff."

"Now go," said Lantana, urging his back with his palm. "Make that female yours. Manu!"

Nemo, ignoring all the nagging voices that told him to turn back, marched into the thicket of freshman girls, fists at his sides. Behind him his father watched with an excited eye. Thinking of Jeffrey Westcott, he came before the girl with cropped hair, a shovel of a chin, who looked at him and said, "Yea?" Smoke in his eyes. Nemo peered up below the brim of his cap, wound up his fist and punched her in the face.

"Be my girlfriend," he said.

The other girls screamed.

"Oh shit," said Lantana. "That's not what I meant!"

His victim began to cry and Nemo, thinking of the second general, said, "Please be my girlfriend? I'll make it worth your while." He took a dollar from his pants and tried to hand it to her. "There's more where that came from."

"Someone get the police."

Nemo folded his arms across his chest.

"Now, I await your surrender in relative peace. Do you have an address? I will arrange passage to my house."

Lantana grabbed him by the arm.

"Run!"

Father and son scrambled across the parking lot being chased by security guards in navy livery; they kept panting something like, "get on the ground." Nemo thought they were close to done for when, from behind a parked Chevy emerged Carl in his red leather jacket, screaming, "For the rising sun!"

He dove for their knees and skittered the two of them across the parking lot.

"Lantanalicious," he yelled, bounding after them in a limp. "Wait!"

But Lantana threw his son into the car and they slithered away through the sleet.

"I didn't mean actually hit her," he yelled, checking the rearview over and over.

"That's a lawsuit, kid. I mean, you probably broke her nose."

"But the three generals. You said—"

"There is a difference between the literal and figurative," said Lantana, surprised at the fact that he actually knew that. "I was trying to teach you a lesson in female economics. Not spouse abuse."

"So it's not okay? What I just did?"

"NO. Jesus Christ. Are we being followed?"

Nemo looked back. Shook his head.

"This is not going well," said Lantana. "Not well at all."

"What's not going well?" asked Nemo, sprawled against the Connolly leather seats with his cap aslope.

"I'll have your mother prepare the injection," Lantana said. "Enough is enough."

Nemo looked ahead of them at the road, quickening as his father sliced through Arapahoe falls, the wide, negligible pie of suburbia where they lived. Around every corner he kept his one eye alert, scanning like a broken down satellite.

CHAPTER FOURTEEN

A FEW YEARS AGO

In the winter of 1979, Jay Moskowitz, a descendent of doctors of an East Coast Meditocracy, began dealing in experiments involving LSD out of the Milton dental office he shared with two brothers by the last name of Schuster. Harnessing his humble beginnings as an organic chemist at Ithaca College, he synthesized ergotarnine tartrate to cull the finest blotter from Brookline to Worcester. The previous years had unsuccessfully yielded little to nothing in Jay's search for greatness. His dreams of hunting with the Inuit of Nunavut were flushed, nay reschemed, when his wife left him for a Guatemalan Trotskyite and gentleman horse rider named Jose Guzman, spending a sizeable chunk of the family nest egg on a Dodge Explorer and a scrap of Mexican land on the Baja where they could make the natives build them a home of easily unmerited luxury.

Jay had always been a man who followed a wife's orders, and, with Mindy gone and his daughter Laura in the hands of a western wilderness that refused to accept his frequent phone calls (she seemed to have disappeared), he took to a lonely sort of wandering which, out of madness, led him into the obsessive reading of books, and eventual experimentation with pharmaceutical agents to reconstruct what was left of his reality. His patients began to notice changes in the dentist's demeanor, mostly the fact that his usually lithe, assured and steady hand, began to tremble just a little, and then a lot, as it approached the outer gums. Soon, he just started having conversations instead of conducting surgery or checkups, lapping up nitrous oxide into his nostrils while reminiscing on his equestrian childhood, days of schul, the ivy league education he squeezed to the pulp while avoiding any semblance of a social life. He told one patient, Mrs. Mickler, of the time he lost his virginity, and the oddness of it, the way his body had been less nervous than his brain but did nothing to slow the rate of ejaculate. Then he spoke of his tendency to be rough during sex. Even brutal. He started sobbing at the story of his wife leaving for the Guatemalan Guzman, and was comforted by Mrs. Mickler, a woman of her fifties with a degree in speech pathology, who, after huffing a little gas off his mask, proceeded to hump him violently in the dentistry chair until three o'clock that very afternoon. Mrs. Allan and Mrs. Saferi did the very same thing in the following weeks, except with considerably less energy.

It wasn't until later that the full blown-manufacturing of LSD began, however, after Jay received an odd invitation from a chemist by the name of Lily Zatkin, in Boulder, Colorado, to partake in a central trial for recreational drugs that required his specialized knowledge. Then, as if rekindling a lost interest he never remembered having, he began familiarizing himself with the craft, producing in full volumes as both seller and customer, black tar, cocaine, and mescaline. LSD, above all, became his cleanest creation. He sharpened candied constellations, pills, tabs, until, upon taking a relatively large dose of his product, he wandered as a stowaway into the belly of a fishing boat off the coast of Plymouth for reasons he'd never remember.

After riding a rainbow of cartoon realities and snapping crocodiles in a space the size of an oil drum for a series of days, he finally awoke on a moldy dock at twilight in the state of Virginia. The boat's name had been Geppetto. The town, he didn't remember. Upon calling home, he found the police had ransacked his entire Milton laboratory and the Shusters, two frugal, honest men from Rhode Island, had slapped him with twin restraining orders. As opposed to returning to Massachusetts to face thirty years in South Middlesex, however, he hitchhiked across five states to Colorado, until his hair grew long and lips, dry. He got a tattoo on his back in Missouri of a knife stabbing. When he finally got to the Boulder campus he was unharrassed, but eyeballed incessantly as he searched, mainly by voice, for the woman called Lily Zatkin. He was found by a young anthropology student with a weakness for pitiable types and she escorted him to the sciences facility. It was no mystery that Jay had wanted to have sex with the anthropology student, of whom he never knew her name, and before they left each other, he dropped her a couple tabs of Clearlight and she gave him a blowjob in the observatory next to a glass case of mineral rocks.

Soon after, they arrived at Lily's office, where she'd taken up residency for her PhD. When his mysterious invitee opened the door and saw the face of Jay, haggard, yet illuminated, and the young nymphet flushed to the gills beside him, she tipped the side of her mouth in a smile. The old man didn't seem to recognize her, unbruised and beautiful in her lab coat, huge eyes much like his wife's had been. But since he'd spent a long time forgetting about his wife's eyes, he said, "I'm here for the trial, Ms. Zatkin." He smelled of sex, but still looked handsome. Demented, but handsome. And he was respectful. Lily thanked the young anthropology student and sent her on her way, closing the door to her office. Jay had already fallen asleep on her chaise lounge she'd unfolded along the western wall by the time she'd clicked closed the lock. His beard whorled around his shoulder. She thought it would be better to start the procedure now, rather than later, so she injected his frail arm with Clopixal and slowed his breathe to a crawl. His face as he dozed was the most honest and absent she'd ever seen. The face of a boy who followed orders, but who was dangerous when he followed them. He was so diminished she almost felt sorry for what she was about to do, but with her hand she cupped her fingers round his nose and mouth; she found the process simple. She saw his right hand, wondering why it, and not his chin or cheek or eyes, she remembered so well. Then, without shedding a single tear, she felt the breath hiss from his body. She said, "Oh Dad, it's been so long," and cancelled her appointments for the afternoon.

CHAPTER FIFTEEN

FILLED WITH LIGHT

What the Zatkins called home was 24 Survival Drive, a name, Nemo knew, that encouraged neither safety nor ease. From outside, anyone could plainly see that it was the largest structure in all of Arapahoe Falls. Slavered with wide berths of flagstone and adjoined by twin porticos, it seemed to grip the ground like an angry mastodon who'd been tugged through a prehistoric timewarp. Other homes in the grid of 13 sub-neighborhoods—all named after various fir trees or repossessed Indian hunting grounds—were more or less grape-colored, lime, or orange evolutions of 20th century suburbia. They were so unlike the Zatkin household which, while sturdy, seemed to have been built on an architectural dare. The rest of the neighborhood was allotted out in concentric circles that went wider and wider by the mile, until those miles became a fringe of cold concrete on the edge of dying prairie. Supplanted in that prairie was the city of Aurora. And Aurora was a rangy mass of poverty.

In a four-car garage that had the westernmost carport sealed-up and locked down, Nemo's mother, sweating in her lab coat, was scrapping a '64 Pontiac Bonneville. Restored from bumper to bumper, the Pontiac's invaluable Morrokide vinyl seats were removed carefully and placed inside the empty, and antiseptically sterile third garage, which had been opened almost all the way. From the frost-stained concrete she hauled each piece inside, and set them beside each other with geometric precision. Against one of the columns of brick wall that acted as an interstice between the doors, she leaned the almost translucent-red flattop. Nemo assumed that it, too, would be brought inside soon, for purposes withheld from him. The car would be taken apart to its very last bolt as if desquamating the whole of a buffalo carcass.

On a basal level the entire operation seemed violent. Such completeness be broken down to its crude innards. Piece by piece, the Pontiac was removed and dragged into the third garage. In the far left corner of it, an innocuous, stainless steel door gleamed icily in the shade. After laying the fender to rest beside the chairs, Lily dredged a keyless entry pod from her lab coat pocket, and, flinging it around with a bit of frustration between her thumb and finger, pressed unlock. What could have been a game show buzz shocked the winter air. The stainless steel door swung open into a room of shadows of which Nemo had never been privy: the westernmost garage. He was forbidden from the coveted place; only his parents had that clearance. He watched his mother jostle back over to the Bonneville's upended hood, and wrench a carburetor from the camshaft. She disappeared inside for a moment, before coming out again, wiping her hands and grinning mischievously.

"What's happening here?" Lantana muttered, in a way that seemed to lack conviction, as they rumbled into the driveway.

Nemo observed the bewildered look in his father's eye. Had Lantana been aware of today's operation? He certainly looked ambushed in some way or another, in his gut, perhaps, where even events for which he'd been prepared still roiled his febrile intestines. Nemo wondered if whether nostalgia had been the culprit for this queasiness, the result of his father's many misadventures now creeping back to haunt him. Was it his childhood he was recalling—something Nemo knew little about? Or Las Vegas, perhaps, after Fearghas's demise, but prior to Nemo's birth, when Lantana ornamented his evenings with psychotropic drugs and spirits of all percentiles? Maybe, upon witnessing the cruel destruction of the Bonneville in the driveway, a gland of lysergide, still stored up in his barmy brain, brought him into a visceral state of agitation that made him pine for simpler days. Maybe he was remembering how—while prize-fighting at the club near the Strip in the mid-seventies; he still liked to boast about it often—he spent many nights in the hermaphroditical arms of a city that was so thoroughly perpetuated by death it seemed impossible to thrive without loss. Maybe he remembered how he'd gambled up his winnings night after night; how he felt he had, in fact—after swallowing a drug cocktail that tested the veritable limits of chemistry—actually once flown over all of Las Vegas in red silk underwear, holding a radio that played the collected works of Rod Stewart from 1969 to '75, before waking up in bed with two women (one of whom was missing a leg) that he hadn't recognized in the slightest. The Bonneville, which he'd driven back then, had been as capricious and robust as he wished he still remained. Now, it was as if he was watching his high school sweetheart—the only woman he'd ever truly felt something for beyond obligation, or sex—dismantle, along with it, the very foundation of his youth, re-appropriating it for something she considered more worthwhile instead. Perhaps she was trying to build a more stable future his past. Would that have been conceivable? And if so, was a boy of Nemo's age truly prepared to handle such complexity? Lantana did tell his son too many stories sometimes. The graphic details grated on him, impelling an odd mixture of repulsion and respect. Nemo had a feeling his father did so to keep himself from falling back into retired habits. From recalling a time of missed opportunity.

Crawling from the passenger seat, Nemo plodded up the driveway to his mother. As he did so, he thought she could see him even with her back turned—eyes in her lab coat, ankles or wrists. She was one of those people who looked a little out of touch when enmeshed in labor, like a lot of people, but unlike a lot of people she seemed to absorb everything around her with the natural qualities of a sea sponge, and then forget about it all. Maybe she never slept soundly because of this (Lily was known to embrace the early hours), and with shrewd, political eyes turned to him.

"You scared me, Kettle Corn," she said, returning to work, loosening bolts with a torque wrench.

"Dad pulled me out of class."

Lily, in her tousled allotment of hairpins and curls, grit her teeth as she turned the wrench and said, "I always hated school."

"What are you working on?" he asked, thinking his mother's statement couldn't have been true. She was the most intelligent person he knew, and intelligent people, whether they admitted it or not, were enamored with the concept of school.

"Something big," she said, and, sweating even in winter, began to pull off her lab coat. But then she stopped. She bit her lip and chewed on it. In Colorado, in the recent years, Lily had become comfortable only in layers. Beneath her coat now she wore two sweaters, a pair of long johns and jeans. She was like a Siberian baronet perpetually preparing to train Samoyas to withstand the colds of the Sakha, and remained like that throughout all four seasons.

Lantana walked up to her, cold and discontent. They whispered back and forth before Lily hung her head, groaned and retired to the house. Lantana, shoving his hands in the shallow pockets of his Spandex as he tried to ignore his goosepimples, said something about food, and they left the dismantled Pontiac in shambles.

Sour pasta salad was shared at the Beachwood table in their kitchen while Lily disappeared behind that forbidden door in the garage. On the stripped down kitchen walls were newspaper clippings featuring Lantana's exploits as The Savage—black and white mirages, or malculations of color, featuring this emerging American legend, in a toga, standing or squatting ingloriously on rooftops, cityscapes, even the Sears Tower. There were articles on crime busts. Terrorism. Torture. Some of them didn't mention his direct involvement, though he had most certainly participated. There hadn't yet been a villain of high enough caliber to set the papers athunder with the fictional thrill Doomsday might have mustered for Superman, or even someone laughable like Calendar Man in his blasé attempts to pander Gotham City into committing a slow, and boring, form of suicide. And so, for a long time, The Savage clung to occasional fifty word columns, op-eds and sidebars. They called him the tireless vigilante of the Rockies, or sometimes a freak of the plains, who could claim an occasional good deed but had accrued a whole boatload of failure in countenance.

It wasn't until the famed Battle for Kansas, in 2003, that he found a new reputation, one for acts of valor and heroism in 48% percent of public polls. Afterwards he watched his career take off in a way he couldn't have seen coming, incurring an article in *TIME*, an offer from Oprah, a front page headline in more than thirty states. He changed up his costume (Lantana pre-'02 was a sight for ridicule) to build up his heroic awe. He then took to knocking down cocaine circuits in Aurora, investigating hate crimes in Wyoming, and curbing the drought in Arizona. He received the key to Phoenix and then, shy of spotlights, spent some time laying low. Now he was picking and choosing his assignments like men of rising fame were wont to do.

The older articles were still tacked to the unpapered drywall by clumps of thumbtacks and scotch tape, however. For even with his new-found acclaim, whenever the front doors opened he wished for the entire chamber to come alive with the gestational glory of his history. Just looking at them, Nemo understood why children didn't like him at school. He was too self important without knowing it. When your father was the world's first genuine attempt at a superhero, and your father was still your father, it was hard to say anything without lying.

"Watch your food," said Lantana, eye devious as, at the sound of eating, Steve Two padded down the hallway, following a long stint lounging in the green house. "The gut approaches."

The tiny, self-made greenhouse from where the lion emerged had been raised in 1999. It was a remarkable achievement on Lily's behalf. At least objectively. Since no one was allowed access to it but the Zatkins, no one truly could appreciate its technological improvisation but them; and since the Zatkins were exposed to many anomalous events, they tended to demonstrate little, if any, wonder. Lily built it originally to encourage the bud of environmentalism and self-sustainability she'd fostered in college to grow. She'd hoped to route more sunlight into her dreary soul, encouraging some sort of inner-bloom. The structure itself, practically swinging off the rear patio into a subsection of yard, was comprised of steel, biodegradable polymers and glass. It took up the inner left quarter of the quadrangular backyard, behind twin apple trees that bore anemic fruit. The crystalline rooftop was hedged and concealed by a high-planked, immaculately staked fence. The verdant heat of Houttuynia, nearing maturity now, could be smelled on Steve Two's fur as she came into the kitchen. The bulky lioness was sick— fortunately from some sort of flu and not CDV as they'd feared when the she was found last week trembling and capsized in Lily's office-laboratory. In the last few days, she'd made swift recovery, but snot still slimed her saggy nose.

As she came into the kitchen Lantana caught her scruff and gave her a mighty wraparound, biceps tugging her neck. He kissed her muzzle. Nemo, also, as tender as he was towards the pawed creatures of earth, ran his fingers down her mane.

"Jesus Christ you've gotten fat," said Lantana.

"Dad, come on," said Nemo, also concerned for Steve Two's fatness, but refusing to injure her anymore than Lantana's insults already had. It wasn't anybody's fault but his fathers' the lioness didn't get out much. After the original Steve's death, Lantana had become especially, if not sadistically, protective.

Steve Two looked at the pasta salad and roared.

"Alright, you heathen," said Lantana, fixing her a heap on a plate. "Suck."

A more delicate creature than her usual litter, Steve Two was unconcerned with hunting, fighting, or any sort of dangerous activity, instead finding solace in the sphagnum moss Lily cultivated in the greenhouse; along with the tides of radicchio, Jerusalem artichokes, butter lettuce and leafy houttuynia. There she licked her golden fur while sprawled out in lavish decree, waiting for her masters to bring her platters of raw flesh (9-12 pounds a day) to replete her udder of a stomach. In this way, the lioness was different from her predecessor. The original Steve had been bellicose to the point of stupidity. Steve Two's being a she, however, was a separate subject, due not to birth, but the first Steve's previously unknown hermaphroditical nature. Steve One was born with both a penis and ovaries and the lioness, by chance, was gestated with a labia and a large, manly mane when cloned by Lily in '98. Because that's what happened.

Lantana said, "now go roll back to your lair if you can."

Lantana watched his son glare at him while he chewed.

"Everyone needs a little criticism." He held his fork above his shoulder, a tortured little fusilli between two prongs. "You know," he mumbled, a little self-satisfied. "Character."

Nemo pecked at his meal—more interested in watching the lioness than his vittles. But as he heard his mother coming back in from the garage, stepping through the laundry room, he pretended to be ravenous. Blowing past the articles in her lab coat, she half-held up a small syringe with a hydraulic pump. Inside the pump was a mercurial liquid sloshing round at the rim.

"Alright," she said, priming the tip in her husband's direction. "You really think he's ready?"

"No one's ever ready for anything" Lantana said.

Nemo, putting down his fork, said, "I thought we were waiting until my Bar Mitzvah?"

Steve Two broke from eating and growled.

"I changed my mind," Lantana said. "Your mother and I, we believe you're ready now."

"Ready boys are good boys," Lily said. "I suppose."

"It's for the best."

Lantana nodded towards his wife. Nemo backed away from the table, facing the two of them. Though he didn't know it, he was shaking his head.

"What's wrong, Kettle Corn?" Lily asked. "You knew this was going to happen."

"I know," Nemo said. "I guess I'm having second thoughts."

Lantana's eye trembled.

"Why? Second thoughts are stupid thoughts."

"I don't think I need the injection. I feel fine."

"Fine?" Lantana gave a little heh. "Feel? This is not a matter of what you feel. Or fine. Feelings are fine excuses for actions, but doing's what counts in the end."

"Good boys make good choices," said Lily, sounding unconvinced. "Don't you want to be a good boy?"

"Well," Nemo said, thinking that if his family had its own law, then maybe he could use it against them. Without much of a voice, he spoke, "I thought you said that men are meant to choose their destinies? Answer to no one? How is me being forced to do something against my will going to make me stronger?"

Lantana exhaled and Lily coughed. The house was silent save for the occasional rustle of paper from the wall. Steve Two's stomach was heard digesting.

"Gravitas," Lantana said.

"Gravitas?" asked Nemo.

"Iustitia, Pietas, Dignitas, Gravitas, the four—"

"Main virtues ancient warriors of Rome were meant to possess," said Nemo. "I read Chapter 19."

Lantana looked like he'd been disemboweled.

"Smart, are we?" he said. "Then you must know that every man must acquire a kill, or be acquired as kill before the age of 15, lest his father should exercise control of his training?"

"Only if," contradicted Nemo, "the man hasn't decided on the kill of his choice, as described in Chapter 33."

"Bullshit," said Lantana. "The clause in Chapter 33 is only referring to those of a disabled nature."

"Or," said Nemo, quoting Chapter 26, "those who have not yet been placed in a dangerous situation with a live animal."

"But up in the mountains—"

"Was Carl in a dinosaur suit."

"Who was in a dinosaur suit?" asked Lily.

"Never mind," growled Lantana. "Our family," he continued on, peevishly attempting to reinstate his authority, "is special for a fucking reason. And besides, this shot here is safer than anything I ever put in my body. Destiny is a lie, but so is circumstance, and I didn't even have the luxury of knowing what my father was doing to me until he decided to do it. Man. . .were those different times."

"I don't know, Corn Cob," Lily said. "Maybe we should hold off a while."

"Hold off for what? For the boy to grow into some sort of sissy? Some typical, unevolved, Mummy-dearest French queer? No way. My son is going to be great. The very best. Number one on the planet."

"I just thought," said Lily, beginning to whisper. "I just thought. . . ."

"Can't we wait?" asked Nemo. "Just a little longer."

"It's for the best."

"I don't want what's best!"

Lantana took his son's arm.

"Breathe deep," he said.

"Please?"

Lily took his other arm.

"The more you struggle the more it'll hurt," she whispered.

"No," said Nemo. "This is wrong."

"One."

The syringe came closer.

"Two."

Nemo's hair crackled from his skull, independent of the rest of his body.

"Three," Lantana said. The needle nipped his son's skin, and as it did, the room filled with light.

CHAPTER SIXTEEN

HALF

The smaller, the spurned Peccadillo, was allowed to open the door, lurching down with his thumb of a body to shine his gums in the eye of the hostage. Reaching out with his fingers he yanked the old man from the back seat of the Buick by the roots of his skull, spit, and cast him to the desert. The body was too old to be much of a body anymore, a sad excuse of existence, old bones in a sack, with one glass eye still agape to the sky and its cloudless sweep of blue warnings. The one with the wall-eye, he was still named Agamemnon—though that connoted more now than before since he'd launched a bar in Brooklyn called Mycenae—slipped his new golden cape around his back and widened his massive chest, exposing a t-shirt that read Not Your Hombre in green balloon letters.

After he opened up for business last year he fancied himself a new image, a royal image, that only true patrons could understand. Whenever he felt unable to stand the weight of his obligations, he took to the streets, long after midnight, in a satin robe and cleansing mud mask, flashing his penis and muscled chest at harried and often sad-looking girls. Peccadillo, however, looked the same as ever. Bolted mask. Red tie. White shoes. He'd taken up online chess with a man in Vietnam which, if he ever lost, he'd find and kill. The Sonoran Desert was a choice world for them. Under the sun their tracks would be fossilized. The sun was high. Villages veered in the distance. Here, these men were the living ghosts of ghost towns. They haunted their very own skin.

"The Book says we gotta make him hurt," said Peccadillo, unhinging his gutting knife.

"We don't do nothing till he gets here," said Agamemnon. He turned around and began to piss on some bur sage. "Book or no Book."

"You should show more respect to the creed," said Peccadillo, winding up and kicking the old man. He was already unconscious but blood burbled out his throat. "How you like that, betrayer?"

Agamemnon, piss still in stream, grabbed his tiny shoulder. "Book or no Book," he growled. Urine slickened the old man's hair. Peccadillo began to chuckle and Agamemnon tossed him to the side.

No roads. No signs. Cactuses sponged along the pavement rock and sand. Under the sun they seemed to move like chubby coral, bobbing in a fata morgana. T.H.E.Y. had become a tired trio, sometimes without masks and sometimes with, moving from country to country with a sense of purpose that, until now, especially with Mycenae, seemed a substitute for being alone. From a horizon without roads came a car, a Lancer in its juicy red rumble with twin tail fins and a smile of fender on the head. On its approach Peccadillo stood straight, zipped his grin and dusted his tuxedo.

Eventually the wheels rolled to a halt. Without much bravado, the handsome, now-older man stepped from the door. He circled the body and bent down in the sleepiest way, dark eyes opening. They were shadowed by a hirsute, tri-cornered hillock of an Ushanka.

"Yep," he said, turning his neck. "That's him."

The old man looked up.

"You?" he said. Not scared, but amazed. His lips were so dry they were green.

"Me."

"Which of you?"

"Aren't we all the same?"

"I don't know where it is." His glass eye was shining out from its socket. It was white as his skin, not white as his hair.

"I'm not going to carry on a conversation with you in the way you expect evil men to do," said the handsome man in the Ushanka. There was dust from the desert that misted over his toes and ankles.

"I thought you were murdered," said the old man, before laughing. "But I suppose where one Beamite dies, another sprouts to life? Like weeds."

Peccadillo kicked the glass-eyed man in the kidney, to which the man in the black Ushanka stood up, and, without much of a sound at all removed his boot, a shined Tony Lama, and began to bludgeon him repeatedly in the head.

"Fucking rat weasel!"

"Please? No."

"Piece of shit—get up—get up!"

Peccadillo skittered away with his bloody face while Agamemnon remained still.

"Tell me what I need," the handsome man said.

"You're just going to kill me," said the old man, closing the lid over his glass eye.

"I know."

"So what then? You're going to make it less painful? Fuck if I need to be killed with dignity. I was born wretched. I can die that way."

"That's fair," said the handsome man, removing his other boot, and then his socks, letting his toes, long-nailed talons, scrape the sand. "I've heard men say worse. But before you go, I want to ask you a question. Nothing I need. Nothing I want. Just something to satiate a curious bone I've got burning somewhere in my sex."

The glass-eyed man was silent.

"Any measurement can be halved infinitely, right?"

Blood beaded his lips.

"You halve a centimeter, you get half of a centimeter. Then you halve that half, and you get a half of that half. And then a half of that half of that half until the number gets fuzzy and imaginary. So my question is," with his thumb and forefinger he pried the glass eye from the old man's socket, sharp nails forcing knicks into his chest as he moaned in pain. "Can the last second of your life be experienced forever? Like this moment, right now? Is it inescapable?"

"He's strong, you know?" said the old man, good eye whirling. "He'll stop you before you get it."

The handsome man took out a knife and began to pry out the biological eye. It snailed down his chin into his palm as Peccadillo chuckled.

"Depends on what side of that old chicken riddle you take, Argyll," the handsome man said. "Old clucker gave birth to breakfast or vice a versa? But you'll have plenty of time to contemplate that. See this right here, what you're doing, isn't really dying." He drove the knife deeper. "This right here I consider to be the beginning of infinity. And that mean's my face, and that sun, and this knife, they might as well be your pearly gates. See, I'm giving you a gift right now. The gift, oh so foreign, of beauty."

CHAPTER SEVENTEEN

TOO CLUMSY TO CROSS

"Count me out," yelled Lantana. He cowered in the corner of the kitchen next to the refrigerator, slowly sinking to his ankles with the unemptied syringe in his hand. Above him the ceiling fan flapped.

"Abomination," he muttered. "Perversion."

"What happened?" asked Lily.

"You think I know?"

"Well, I don't know."

"I didn't say you did."

"And even if I did know." She put her hands on her hips. "I didn't."

"What's that supposed to mean?"

"The boy's got a problem."

"A brilliant assertion, Tush," Lantana sneered. "Let me correct you—the boy is a problem."

"I'm sure we can fix whatever—"

"He's shooting electricity from his hands!"

"I'm sorry," Nemo said. He began to cry. His fingers he held out before him, wishing they'd separate, piece by piece, from their palms. "I never meant to. . .I don't know why. . . ."

"Go to your room," Lily said, suddenly assuming more authority than usual. When she spoke she could have lifted from the ground.

"Your father and I need to talk."

Leaving Lantana crouched in the corner, muttering something about dead happy days, Nemo accepted his punishment. Trudging from the kitchen he heard whispering below.

Once upstairs he picked up his sketchbook and a pencil from the desk. The art pad's cover had an air balloon penciled over a hill of vibrant kelly. In that pad he drew the outline of a whale, and within that whale, incongruent ribs and, within those ribs, a sack of a stomach where a boy sat, fanning a fire. The drawing wasn't good. The lines were heavy; there was no good perspective or centrality of light. Sighing, he let the pencil to the paper, and held out his hand to the ceiling. He couldn't control what came from his fingers. And now his mind, he thought, as he could have sworn he heard a cold voice saying something like, "Attic door."

"Of course I had nothing to do with it," his mother blurted from downstairs. But the whispers returned twice as soft, mimicking the echo of dropped pebbles. Then he heard Steve Two nuzzling at his door with a wet nose and muzzle and let her in. She plopped down next to him and whipped her tail around his cheeks, purring like a speedboat motor. She exposed her milkless nipples, and Nemo rubbed his hand between them for comfort. The phone rang a few times. He didn't pick it up, not that anyone would have called for him. He began thinking that, just by being different from the ones he was supposed to love, he'd set himself up for failure. Steve Two, a creature also birthed from confusion, seemed to commiserate, and she gave him the wealth of her enormous belly to rub. It could have swallowed Nemo whole. He found a certain comfort in that.

Minutes later a knock came at the door. From the softness of it, Nemo knew it was his mother. He hung his head in anticipation of more shots and punishments. Instead, as he recoiled, she gently said, "There's a boy on the phone for you. An actual boy—Jeffrey, I believe. He sounds. . .polite."

Before Nemo even dared the receiver, he thought about possible pranks and disappointments, additional little punctures his bleeding self-esteem could no longer be expected to bare.

He hadn't received a phone call, never mind contact in any shape or form since the end of the sixth, no, fifth grade.

"Hello?" he honked, holding the phone more than an inch from his ear.

It was Jeffrey Westcott.

How did he get his number? Why did he get his number? Was he being impersonated by someone very clever? No. It was him. And when he began to speak his voice was louder than in person, and twice as slow. There was something in the receiver that made the conversation completely believable and concurrently a fuming lie. But after a few moments Nemo was lost in the miracle of speech with someone other than himself, and agreed, pending his parent's decision, to catch a movie tomorrow evening.

As soon as he hung up, Lily burst through the door.

"What happened?" She panted. "What did he say?"

Nemo was more than bemused by his mother's concern, his fingers still tingling with the mystery of it all.

"He said he wants to go to a movie."

"With you?"

"Yea mom."

"And him?"

"Yea mom."

"Are you going to go?"

"Am I grounded?"

"Anything but," Lily said. "We don't ground in this house. We don't restrain. I'm more concerned with your father than I am for you. Don't you know that?"

Nemo shook his head.

"Sometimes, I do."

"Sweetie, I know I'm not always as vocal as I should be, but," she began to whisper as if to hush her own strange point, "I'm always on your side."

"Mom," asked Nemo, holding up his hands. As he watched them, they seemed less like they belonged to him. "What's happening to me?"

"Are you scared?"

"A little."

She smiled. "If there is an explanation for who, or what you are, it's better that you don't know about it. Special people are fucked from the moment they're born." Her gaze glittered with some dim ribbon of sunlight outside. "But whatever's wrong with you, know that you're strong enough, you're grand enough, you're beautiful enough to do whatever it is you want to do. And now, that thing you should be doing is going to the movies, not worrying about fame and fighting. Be a little boy, regardless of what your father says. Have yourself a real live friend."

"The plutonium. The tests," Nemo said, looking up at her, feeling brave enough to speak. "It's just not me."

"Well," said Lily, seeming satisfied, or in agreement. When they were alone, and by alone meaning without Lantana, she was always wearier, but kinder, and this made him angry, as if he she saved all her protests for empty rooms. "Right now it looks like you might not have to. Especially if fireworks keep coming from your fingers. It's like a natural defense mechanism." She put her fingers to her chin and smiled to herself. "Absolutely fascinating. Everyone should be so lucky."

Nemo came to his feet and hugged his mother, and when he did so her hair rose in curls. He knew that his father was obsessed with fame in the way any self-loathing talent was. He searched for fame like it was a free pass from death—a man, unlike the woman in his arms, horribly afraid of the end.

"You're a normal boy, Nemo," Lily said. Her hands pressed too hard into his shoulders. "And even if you're not, don't worry, not a little, because whether or not you know it sometimes," she began to whisper what Nemo had heard many, many times. Though now, even as he predicated the rhythm, the order of each word, they felt even less convincing than usual. "I'm always on your side."

That night they stayed at home and observed the anniversary of a man Nemo never knew named Fearghas. Lantana said he was a 'fantastic bastard,' which Lily corrected with 'fanatic bastard,' and passed a matchstick over a yahrtzeit candle that burned before an opening in the kitchen window, and when he wasn't satisfied with the memorial prayers they chanted, not to mention Lily's lack of participation in the Kiddush, he demanded that father and son don their yarmulkes and they head, all of them, to an unfrozen fork in the crux of the Smoky Hill River.

There, the iceflow was disturbed by globs of garbage, beer cans and plastic bags, prophylactics, but they found a bank of trampled cattails where the water was crystal, was loud. They fashioned a small bilge from a dome of Tupperware and cupped the candle inside. They set it to the tide and let it coast on the water, its small flame flickering with defiance. Lily smiled so big Nemo thought he saw a different woman, a healthier woman in her gums. Lantana forgave Nemo for all of his oddities and shortcomings by taking him onto his shoulders, and they watched the mellifluous candle crackle like a lightning bug.

He said, "You see? How important it is to remember the dead? Without the candle the river would be lonely. Abandoned in the night. Just like humans without, well. . .we need to know where we're going one day." And when the candle got caught in a hump of sleet next to a concrete rampart where the river choked, Lily scrambled on the bank of the river to loosen it, hands out, palms down, and she looked like an astronaut in her winter jacket and wide, luminescent boots.

The moon frosted the field while Lantana cautioned her, but she broke off a stick of pine and, teetering on the edge of the creek, stuck out her tongue in avid concentration and jiggled the yahrzeit loose. It floated free for a few more yards to where the river opened up, but then became caught again, and again and again, and no matter how much Lily tried to jostle it the current was stern.

"Just let it stay there," said Lantana.

Nemo tersely agreed.

"The ice isn't hard, said Lantana."

"You'll fall in," said Nemo.

"Come back."

"It's just a candle."

"We'll light another!"

But Lily trudged down to the bank. It was a bank she'd come to before, with her husband. A bank with its secrets. Its graves.

She tested the water with her boot, slipped a little forward, tried again. She wanted to make that little candle move, if for no other reason than it was stuck. But by then the river was just too damned wide and her treads were too clumsy to cross.

When she fell in the first time, up to her knees, she still didn't stop trying on. When her full body went in, Lantana pulled her to the bank, into the car, and rushed her home, making Nemo remove her clothes while he blasted the heat. Nemo was abashed by his mother's nakedness, her starfish areolas and thin, upcurled pubis. She was shivering and quiet, her eyes closed tight, but her body, it seemed to glow. She warmed herself later by the redbrick fire with her feet in warm water, a fuzzy bathrobe and a look of disdain.

"I could have nudged that candle free," she said. "Just a little further. That's all."

In Lantana and Lily's bedroom there was a small television mounted in a chestnut entertainment center against the wall. Lily wrapped herself in the bedspread, restoring the last of herself to health, and clicked on the digital cable. On the television came the flickerings of an older film, recorded long ago, but not too long ago, with touches of color, exaggerated flares of orange, shadows darker than shadows would have been in any modern picture. Purification, came the title, and she smiled. It was late now. Nemo was in bed. She made small noises of surprise and suspense. The door to the bedroom opened, and without even looking she recognized the sounds of her husband.

"I remember this movie," he said, dressed fully as The Savage.

"You better remember," she smiled.

Lantana, transfixed by the screen, said, "Things get fuzzy sometimes."

"Depends on your body temperature."

"You're talking about the river?"

"No," she said. "I'm talking about your body temperature."

"You look different," said Lantana.

Lily smiled in the smallest way she could. "Oh?"

"Yea," said Lantana, coming towards her, crinkling his golden sandals. "You look. . .younger. What happened to your skin?"

Lily kept her eyes on the screen.

"I've been eating olives."

"Olives?"

"And figs."

"Figs."

"It's not because of river water, Corn Cob, if that's what you're thinking."

Lantana reached out to her. His raddled hand, snail shells for knuckles, gingerly bumped down the curve of her neck to her clavicle. He seemed scared as he did so. Her skin was so soft, and not only that, but her body, it had changed.

"How beautiful you've become," he said.

"Haven't I always been beautiful," said Lily.

Leaning forward, he chanced to kiss her, and was relieved when she kissed him back. He slumped them into the bed. Lily's lab coat was removed and her bony shoulders felt the frame beneath the mattress. Her body, breasts, and the bones of her ribs, the dug out scoop of her stomach, all expanded wingwise like a Lepidopteron. Lantana's Spandex fell. He wasn't wearing underwear. He was gentle at first. Then less so. Then she turned him over and rode him. Her head swiveled on her neck, arching upwards. The laced iron headboard gently rushed with her hips. Then, as her chin returned to her husband, Lantana wasn't there anymore, but a man with a beard and meltwater in his eyes, grinning. His gray hair bristled. He smelled of winter. He had scabs on his arms and chest as if he'd been tearing through a thorn field, and his fingers were yellowed at the nail. She stopped moving on top of him as he closed his eyes and came inside her.

She screamed.

"Lily," Lantana yelled. He saltated from the table and stumbled across the room. "What's wrong?"

Lily heaved, uncovered her eyes with her hands. She saw her husband again, naked and afraid.

"I thought I saw a spider," she said. "A big, motherfucking spider."

"Where?" he began to search the bedsheets. "Where did you see it?"

"Somewhere near you. In the bed."

"I can't find it."

"Well, I saw it."

"Here?"

"Maybe over there."

"How big was it?"

"Really fucking big. Like this."

Lantana looked at Lily's measurement.

"Are you sure?" he asked.

"Of course I'm sure."

"Cause that's a really big spider."

"That's what I saw."

Lantana pulled his spandex back on, his toga around his left shoulder. He was meticulous at the process of fastening his sandals, and breathed out before turning for the door.

"I'll call the exterminator tomorrow morning," he said, before leaving.

"That would be a good idea."

"There shouldn't be spiders in this house."

"Things happen," said Lily, pulling on a t-shirt. "Things always find a way in."

CHAPTER EIGHTEEN

SEAHORSES

Though there were those, such as Lantana, who would have disputed the official number of times his wife Lily Zatkin actually attempted suicide (his postulation was no more than two), the official count fell between six and seven, with the most recent being half-precise; one of those ambiguous flirtations people had with risk that either meant they were depressed or devious. This was before the Fluoxetine. Before her Zen meditation and psychiatry. This was when Lily pulled out of their Survival Drive home and ended up at the neighborhood food store called Broods in search of the one thrill she longed for, but for almost a year was too scared of entertaining. The white stuff made her crazy, anyway. Or crazy in the way youth made you crazy. It made her skin and mind the age of sixteen. Her desires a little bit greener.

Broods was the beacon at the center of Arapahoe Falls, and she couldn't remember whether it or the neighborhood had been built first, but she did know that it was where the boy would be—where he always was—behind his bazaar of condoms and cigarettes, lottery tickets and chipbags of gold foil, where teenagers were kept and nearly preserved in the trappings of minimum wage. She'd never had the audacity to speak to him, and as she proceeded not to speak her desires grew and grew. She found it funny how uneasy he made her, this creature barely past the age of sixteen—sixteen like she felt, but like she wasn't, at least on the outside—and after she pulled into

214

pump six, she locked the gas nozzle into her tank and pressed pay inside for an even two dollars.

Above her was a pergola made from local pine with chips in the ceiling. As the gas gurgled through the rubber hose, she looked over her shoulder to the car at pump three, or what she thought was a car, emboldened by the lack of clouds. But the first thing she realized was that this car was not a car, but more of a chariot, a wooden basket resting on a widened brass axel connecting two great wheels together with eight spokes a piece. The wheels were rimmed with the shiniest iron, and a pair of reins with studded ivory harnessed the withers of white and black horses snorting steam from their snouts to the asphalt. From the back of the chariot dismounted a man with haggard cheeks and sunken eyes, a beard of faded nobility that had sorely yellowed with the years; he was dressed in a *himation* sewn from soft linen and it moved like mercury at his shoulders and feet. Lifting his chin revealed eyes rife with cataracts, and he turned to allow a woman from the chariot—dark hair over her face, dressed also in a *himation*, but green and pinned by a whorled fibulae—who descended to the pump and turned her cheek to his shoulder. He looked at her. She looked at him. Then with his hand, he smiled, softly giggled, and began to hit her. She took it with somber determination but Lily screamed and, when she looked again, no one was there but a woman with tattoos pumping 89 into her green Civic.

Is everything all right, she asked her. Lily, nodding, fled across the parking lot, lab coat gathering wind, and sailed through the sliding doors of Broods. Without paying much attention she reached for something to buy, shoes, much like those of a nurse, nervous as they scuffled. She decided on a jar of Planters. She carried her future purchase to the Gatorade cooler where she untouseled her curls and streaked her hair over the sides of her chin. She put on lipstick, a little too much, while a man with blond hair and what normally accompanied blond hair, some sort of overpriced fleece and cargo pants, raised his eyebrows as he walked out the door, checking out her polycotton ass. But her interest ebbed from him as she found the boy reading some Manga pulp, some comic strip featuring girls with lace panties.

When he looked up at her, noticed her for the first time as something beyond a customer, Lily felt like she'd reached the shore of Valhalla and with gory desire just stared at him a moment. I pressed pay inside, she said, opening her purse, and the conversation following was lost to her. She remembered they might have exchanged their lucky numbers—she told him that hers was seven, like the atomic number of nitrogen, and his was four (she informed him of Aristotle's Efficient Cause), and was so because it was his sister's birthday. How old is she? Lily asked. She was nine, and had Down Syndrome, as well as bad bones, and all the while he spoke she watched his mouth, the gumminess of it, the youthful spit. He had kinky teeth, damaged by fluoride. The dearest, darkest skin. There was a mutilated Camel behind his ear and wide basketball shoes on his feet that were bright orange with webbed toesocks and fat laces. As he smiled, Lily felt embarrassed, briefly remembering the face of her husband and the evolution of his skin as it journeyed through middle age, the teeth that, after years, had turned the dirtied-pearl sheen of an abalone shell. She returned to the boy with thoughts of conquest—actually, she felt like knotting him in caution tape, casking his body inside a barrel and then hauling that barrel out to the sea—but instead she said in her politest voice, why don't you come for a ride, settling herself over his counter.

Her breasts beneath her labcoat seemed to glow, so much the boy went instantly erect, and they traveled outside to the four-door Saturn. Why don't you drive? She told him. It'll make things more fun. He was only fifteen and complained about a permit, but she said she was technically his guardian if he asked her to be. Then he complained about her age, and the fact that he was too young for her, asked if he was too young for her, that he was fifteen, and not sixteen as she thought, and she told him that she was sixteen too, only one year older than him, and that she'd always be sixteen, for that was the age she wanted to stay for the rest of her life and she'd actually learned how to make that possible. If he wanted to, she told him, she could make him young forever as well, but he didn't seem to understand her and instead insisted that they get on the road before it got late and his boss returned.

Driving away from the great wheel of Arapahoe Falls onto interstate I-25, Lily took a deep breath, told the boy to slow down and pull into the right lane, where there was less traffic, and slowly undid his pants, unfurling the broad, copper buttons on his jeans where on the inside flaps were colorful printings of seahorses. The teenager gulped, and then laughed a little, and then turned down the radio as she rubbed his penis over his silk boxer shorts and then, with an unmistakable sound of pleasure, engulfed the purple tip of it with her mouth. The boy heaved and grabbed her hair. The sun blazed down through the window over her bobbing back, the two of them like animals in a broken-down piece of furniture, and they sailed under the University Bridge—there was an unexpected pile up, an accident on the Colorado Boulevard exit, and the boy looked up at the roof in dumb pleasure before they eviscerated the backside of an old woman's Honda. With his pants down he lurched through the window. Lily's face smashed the gearshift upon impact. She took a gash in the abdomen and woke up in the hospital with her jaw wired shut.

Without hesitating she tore the stitches in her side. She made herself hobble through the levels and squeeze through a fire exit just before the police arrived. She checked to see that the identification she'd been carrying identified her as nobody else but a dead woman from Wyoming named Clarissa Bentley (along with the car) and seeing it was, let out a sigh of relief and found a bathroom in a gas station across the street from Rose Hospital, hoping no one would catch on. There she vaguely dressed her wounds with paper towels and looked at her teeth in the mirror, a sadist's hard-on, and noticed when she spoke she choked on her tongue, and bought a sweatshirt with the cash from her pocket.

Upon waking up from his concussion, the boy, with his broken arm, nose, and severe head trauma, not only refused to tell the police what happened, but said that all he wanted to know was that she, whoever she was, was alive, and that he'd like her to return to him and finish what they started. Unfortunately, however, Lily knew that the law didn't cater to upheavals of even the most ancient sorts of romance, and went on vacation to Mikonos for two weeks alone in the summer of 2005.

CHAPTER NINETEEN

THE MUTATING SUBMARINE

Jeffrey and Nemo met at the Chinese Theater at the Arapahoe Crossings strip mall extravaganza. Though most people, especially Coloradans, wouldn't have cared to know that the original project, the notorious one Grauman built back in the 20s in Los Angeles, had required the dedication and gratuity of the entire Chinese continent, Nemo was already able to sense that these imported temple bells, stone Heaven Dogs and pagodas, were probably edified from the same cheap materials Americans used to make all their unsound structures look sound. Apart from changing over ownership three times, the theatre had been dragged into waste after its expensive flair faded out, and what remained now was usually empty, like an abandoned theme park, where people came to admire fakery or recollect a semblance of the real. But more fake than the theater was the actual presence of Jeffrey West-cott, hands reaching in his pockets for ticket money. The jostle of his fingers was so deliberate, so unreal, it could have charged admission itself.

"I'll pay for it," Nemo shouted. He shoved himself past Jeffrey and dispersed a mess of bills on the ticket counter. "Two for *Atomic Child and the Mutating Submarine.*"

The adolescent girl at the ticket booth clacked her braces and handed them tickets, staring past them through the window at the interstate rushing below the parking lot. Her wires caught the glint of sunlight disappearing behind the mountains before five o'clock. Though Nemo looked young enough not to pass for PG-13, Jeffrey, though only twelve, was stocky and long, with booming cherry chunks of hair. It was enough to wangle them passes to something other than the latest bit of saccharine animation.

Jeffrey said, "I'll get the popcorn," with the slowest wink, and before they knew it they were gathered in a huddle over the butter pump. Jeffrey said it reminded him of motor oil—his mother fixed cars. His father, a water treatment specialist and amateur artist, carved marble in his basement, and they both fixed up and rode motorcycles from the fifties.

"I don't like what they do to you at school," said Jeffrey, handing Nemo a straw for his looming trough of Dr. Pepper. "I know you didn't do what they said."

"I was sick that day," said Nemo.

"They're sick every day," said Jeffrey. "And besides, it shouldn't even matter masturbating. I think we're getting to that age, anyway."

"What age?" Nemo asked, knowing very well what age he meant.

"The age of, you know. . ." he looked away at a replica of Humphrey Bogart's handprints, carved from plaster. "Funny feelings. . .is what my Dad called it—who the fuck's hands are these?"

Nemo shrugged.

"Well, whatever. Funny feelings, you know? Things adults feel."

Funny feelings. Like the sparks from his hands? Nemo had funny feelings all over his body that his mind tried to map and control. But besides experimenting with his mother's back message tool, a hump of a machine with what looked like a duck's bill at the top he used to tickle his lower back, and once or twice a little bit lower, on the front, he was nervous at the thought of human contact.

"I don't know about those feelings," he said, sipping his straw.

"Yea," said Jeffrey, hopping a little in place. "I guess I don't either."

The theater was almost empty save for the two boys and a couple, maybe a man and a woman, who were already busy assaying each other's flesh. Enmeshed in zippers, moans and movement, the occasional pink part emerged, an areola or belly button, they couldn't be sure, untreated by the sun. Especially since one of them used a long white coat to cover their faces.

Though Nemo and Jeffrey were more mature than many boys at Laredo, they couldn't help getting a little giggly in the couple's presence—they were twelve, after all—and that twelveness caused Jeffrey to make a joke about face-sucking aliens. Nemo followed it up with a tale of how he caught his parents humping in the bedroom, a fantastical, lobotomizing sight, and Jeffrey asked him if he saw what they were actually, physically doing, and, when hearing no, then gave his personal postulation that sex involved the woman slapping a man in the face with her breasts and, if then, when things got hotter, using her vagina as a sucking apparatus. Sexual Education as a course wouldn't be taught until the end of this school year, and, before then, it was common for most sixth and seventh graders to speculate with wild ingenuity on the unfathomable process of coitus.

"Did you know," said Nemo, "that when a woman reaches a certain age, she starts to bleed from her, you know," he pointed.

"Her kootch?"

He nodded.

Jeffrey was shaking in his seat. "I heard that's the reason they have to steal blood."

"What do you mean steal blood?"

"Like, you know, they need new blood to replace the old blood, or else they'll dry up like prunes."

"Women don't steal blood," Nemo laughed. "Come on. Where would they get it from?"

"I don't know," said Jeffrey. "But I heard they have a gland found in the brain, referred to as the PoonEx, that destroys a woman's ability to think logically once a month. It also helps them live longer. Because if a woman does steal blood, she becomes stronger."

"Like a vampire?" Nemo asked.

"I guess."

"Man, I hope that stuff never happens to us guys."

"Impossible," said Jeffrey. "The natural menstrual cycle for a man occurs on major holidays and around the age of fifty. And only if he's not doing the nasty."

"What's the nasty?" asked Nemo.

"I don't know, but my brother's friend said it costs a lot of money."

"Wow."

"But then again, my brother's friends aren't the smartest bunch." He crooned his neck onto Nemo's seat, dizzyingly close to his head. "You're smart? Aren't you Nemo?"

Nemo clucked his tongue. He looked down the red velvet rows of burlesque theater seating. The plaster architrave with Lu's, Fu's, and Shou's circling above the curtains. "Not really."

"Oh come on, you're super smart. You probably know everything about sex."

"Well," said Nemo. "I did hear that it has something to do with producing babies.

And that when a woman bleeds she's probably not doing it from her brain, but her uterus, where the eggs are."

"Eggs?" asked Jeffrey, shaking his head. "What eggs?"

"The ones men fertilize with something called sperm. They're like. . .little tadpoles."

"You're blowing my mind."

"My mom gave me a book."

"Does she menstruate?"

The couple in the back row made a snorting sound.

"I think so."

"From her, what did you call it, Boarface?"

"Uterus. I think so. But we don't talk about it much."

"That really sucks for her."

"Yea, I guess it does."

"I'm glad I don't have eggs."

"Me too."

"Come to think of it, I don't think I like the fact that anyone has eggs." The curtains were slowly drawing from the screen. When the lights dimmed Nemo became conscious of every part of his body. And Jeffrey's. His little shifts in the seat, were they towards him? And if they were, why?

What longed for that magnetism, to tip his knee out towards his?

"I know what you mean."

"I mean, take girls, for instance," Jeffrey whispered. "I want to be friends with girls, but I don't want to kiss them. I want to know them, but I don't want to hold their hands. Some of my friends, they call me a 'pussy.' They think I should learn to pimp a bitch."

"Yea," said Nemo, mesmerized by his voice, smiling because that was all he could do. "I mean no—I don't think you're doing anything wrong."

"I don't know," said Jeffrey. "Maybe I shouldn't be talking about this. . .you won't tell anyone, will you?"

Nemo took his fingers and locked his lips shut, tossing the invisible, airlight key into a place rows ahead of them.

"Not like they'd believe the masturbation king, anyway," he said.

Jeffrey smiled and punched Nemo softly on the shoulder.

"Well at least you're not the masturbation prince."

The lights went low, disappeared, and the boys were left in darkness. The couple behind them seemed to slake their carnal thirst, and though Nemo was nervous, Jeffrey seemed comforted. He was snuggled in his jacket—a warm tweed coat with fat buttons snapped up his neck like a gorget. He ate the popcorn fast and with so much energy, in a way Nemo supposed most children other than he did. With what could have been mistaken for violence he made it disappear before the previews were half-finished.

"Spaory," he said, mouth crunching on partially-popped kernels.

Atomic Child and the Mutating Submarine then began. The first shot featured a panoramic sweep of the Pacific Ocean accompanied by spraying sounds of spume. A future flash; many years after where the film would begin. In an epileptically high-resolution explosion of light, the hero, Atomic Child, from one of his many trysts beneath the earth's mantle rocketed to the surface in search of a nuclear bomb on its way to Paris (already an inaccuracy—Atomic Child's first and only nuclear bomb determent was being launched into the heart of East India). His lips were pursed in acceptance of his purpose. His eyes were dark with any adventurer's sense of weary and usalvageable sin. How amazing it was, to see one's heroes live. To see one's heroes take flight.

Adapted from a series of gritty, postmodern comic books by the cult-famous author Salazar Johns, the thrust of this film revolved around the virtues and failures of a post-WWII superhero by the name of Alan Lyte. According to Salazar's original storyboard, Alan's birthmother, a Ukrainian special ops soldier stationed in Japan, codenamed Golochka, had emerged from the wreckage of Nagasaki following its decimation miraculously un-harmed. Somehow, she'd survived the megatons of radiation and hellfire without so much as a scratch, and was found wandering nude, visibly preg-nant, and emitting a soft blue glow through the stultifying ash and bones-moke of southern Japan. An American pilot, and topographer, George Hale, photographed her from an altitude of four thousand feet, and showed a de-lighted and embarrassed room of Pentagon war-strategists negatives of what might as well have been a star-nymph. Soon enough, interest was encoded via a vast spy net; Galochka was airlifted into the heartland for study. It was deduced that, for cabbalistic reasons, the Ukrainian alias possessed an inbred tolerance towards radiation; after subsequent tests, the lab experts concluded that she could absorb it internally, and neutralize it through a detoxification process no more unpleasant than the daily human expulsion of fluids.

The child she became impregnated with was soon carried to term. On the day of his birth, in line with the official end of the Second World War, the tickertape parades on the streets of New York, Golachka died from a mas-sive hemorrhage. Nasty business. "Alan," she'd said to her delivering doc-tor, as light began to leave her eyes. "Name him Alan, after his. . ." before she expired. She left no history behind. The only thing she bequeathed was a breath-filled boy and a clear lack of directions for him to follow.

There was no one, as it stood, beholden to do diligence to Golochka's last request, especially for the dubious nature of her home country and the contra-Western politics it was just beginning to pioneer. Thankfully, the military scientist who took him into custody, Eustis Lyte, was a kind, and lonely, if desperate, man, who relished the responsibility of raising a child for the company it provided just as much as for the research potential. Alan, he called him, in good faith to the mother. Followed by the surname handed down from his own father. In a few short moments, a legend was born. Alan Lyte, Atomic Child, slightly different, slightly great, slightly disturbed. With the help of Eustis, electrifying genetic abilities came to fruition. Alan found himself able to heat anything he touched with his fingers; at first, the effects were unstable at best. Fires broke out, buildings were incinerated, a person or seven were reduced to utter char. Emotions were the key to Alan controlling his powers. Inner stability translated to miraculous heroism. Instability gave way to havoc, and horror.

Time passed as Alan trained. Forces reconnoitered within US government branches, and the American political landscape shifted from post-war capitalism to combating the Red Threat. Alan Lyte's custodian, Eustis, who'd raised the Atomic Child with two parts folksy Midwestern morality and one part scientific Darwinism, ended up roped into the whims of a Pentagon subsection named N. A branch with no apparent timeline, there was no telling how long it had been around. A cultish element comprising its ranks casted a Mason-like shadow over its identity. Rising quickly and furiously to power, its archetypal cronies, with a mistaken spin on the future, and a motley moral code to accompany their views, spearheaded enterprises bent on exploiting both domestic and foreign policy. They had no concern for collateral damage. They began to run the government from within. Alan Lyte, following strategic coercion, manipulation, and the horror at witnessing the torture of Eustis's younger sister, Liddy, ended up surrendering his services to N's dark dido, and became its official combatant, its indentured hero, fighting for a side of America whose ethical character was up for debate.

Through his naively endearing efforts, however, Alan always seemed to try and service some sort of good. Even when acting under suspicious orders, he remembered Eustis's advice: "Sometimes it's okay to lie. . .as long as that lie serves a greater truth." Alan lived in a state of constant conflict; a special being in a not-so-special world. Identity crisis pursued him at every bend, drowning him in soapbox existentialism.

One of Atomic Child's first battles took place in issue number 9: a dirty bomb was dropped on a naval fleet off the coast of American Samoa (by British Guy Fawkes radicals in the comics, Ukrainian terrorists in the film) in the late fifties, at the height of the Cold War. After years of training, Alan Lyte—by that time equipped with the bells and whistles superheroes take for granted, namely a thaumaturgical suit that allowed him to channel radio waves into flight, and a host of weapons with which to expend his strength (the Lyte-Staff the most famous amongst them, engineered by a rogue military specialist with a taste for dissent)—launched into action, rounding up criminals for a painful allotment of justice. These epic battles usually ended in dissections of the motives of 20th century terrorism, and the morality of preemptive defense. The choices Alan was forced to make tended to be ambiguous, neither wrong nor right, a product of evolved ethical thought, and the ability to cogitate with nuance.

Over time, Alan Lyte grew arrogant. In line with the endless encomium he received from the officials at N, his ego was in regular need of taming. Most Americans viewed him as a protector of the peace; smaller amounts looked upon him as a government lackey, who'd been fed jingoism as if through the teat. Salazar's authorial hand, a good distance through the series, came to introduce his greatest nemesis, to complicate the moral mire even more thoroughly. The villain took the form of another boy born from the flames of Nagasaki, who'd been raised under the auspices of the Soviet flag. During a later reveal, he turned out to have the very same biological father as Alan himself—a massive dénouement, as might be expected. This evildoer/half-brother, who deemed himself Siege, but whose true name was Hayashi Nakamura, built a cognitive machine that prompted him, based on shared genetics (one half of which were stolen from Alan Lyte's military phlebotomist), to impact the actions of the other. C.O.R.D., the device was called. Cerebral Ovular Redaction Device. Whichever half-brother operated it had the ability to partially impact the actions of the other.

As a Third World War loomed, threatened by separatist Chechnyans, Alan Lyte, predictably, sprang into action to keep a warhead from being docked at the port of Oakland. Since his actions were half-controlled by his half-brother, however, he ended up sabotaging his own side's plans; though the bomb itself was deactivated, an unconsciable amount of American civilians were murdered brutally, scorched by Atomic Child's Lyte-staff, as it exploded in a biblical sea of radiation. He was defamed by the American public shortly after. Subsection N abandoned him as an asset (concentrating on a new genome project instead; later to become another of Lyte's villains), and Alan himself, after learning of his half-brother, was forced to seek out the true meaning of justice. The last few volumes, before the author changeover, were devoted to this internal battle being fought within the troubled hero's mind; he wrestled with the concept of good versus evil, and explored the ambivalence of empire. He made a controversial move in book six, after his self-revelation as a homosexual, to bed his sidekick, Sputnik, a WWII Jewish war vet with superhuman intellect and a chip on his shoulder. Theirs developed into a deep, and insistent relationship. Salazar's readership spiked during that period behalf, whether he'd meant it to or not.

Since the film version, however, had been directed by Ashton Burns, a man known for expertly converting grade A concepts into grade D narratives, one had to wonder whether any of those subtle aspects would rise to the surface. Jeffery Westcott likely wouldn't know better either way; it was safe enough to say he didn't preoccupy himself with deconstructing the pathos of comic books and science fiction with the same amount of seriousness Nemo took to them. Instead, he reacted like any good moviegoer should have, with full body cringes, eye bulges, and expressions like, "Nemo, didya see that," squealed with whispery delight. Nemo was obviously a lot tougher of a customer. This was for many reasons, not the least of which being his lack of real friends, and the subsequent identification he forced himself to make with worlds beyond the mortal purview. As he observed the screen with a skeptical eye, he tried, for instance, not to betray the sheer mental dizziness he felt when he saw what Ashton Burns had done with his favorite character, Eustis Lyte, depicting him in silhouette, solely for comic relief, as a man diagnosed with somnambulism. What was worse, he thought, than having your heroes portrayed as flunkies, nimrods, or fools? He suffered for every poor choice. A film was not a comic, and vice a versa; this Nemo knew. But essence was essence. Indelibly. This he also knew.

Jeffrey said, "I think this is the best movie I've ever seen," and, as the first twenty minutes concluded with a spectacularly under-earned scene of Atomic Child redirecting a dirty bomb into Antarctic Defuser Zeta, where he deposited all rogue weapons, tilted towards Nemo, just a little bit.

"I know," said Nemo, biting his lie. He couldn't keep himself from watching Jeffrey's leg, wondering what would happen if it came a little closer, and consequently letting it sway his thoughts, like a vigorous narcotic.

"Great special effects," Jeffrey whispered. "Don't you think?"

Nemo murmured his agreement, but inside his stomach was stewing, firstly for the proximity of his new-found friend, and secondly for wondering why so many dark, yet captivating ideas had to be made so bright and innocuous for the American public. Nemo thought it must have had something to do with CGI. Computers were capable of producing such beauty, but at the same time corroding that beauty in a membrane of kitsch. This was evident in the emergence of the notorious Mutating Submarine—what was supposed to be a self-enlightened creature of mechanized proportions according to the original story, birthed from the leftover of Japanese nuclear waste when shoveled into the North Pacific Ocean. In the film adaptation, however, this inhuman byproduct of nuclear exegesis was given an actual, HUMAN pilot, defeating the entire metaphysical purpose and philosophy of its existence. A small, yet massively transformative difference. The director then appointed Siege for that position as if on a whim. Hayashi Nakumura, amongst other impurities to blot the original plot away, became more of nincompoop than actual villain, the blundering cliché, piloting a big hunk of metal he'd had assembled from pieces of post-war wreckage in his lust for unattainable power. It was such a shame for Nemo to see what was supposed to be a fable of nihilism versus suchness now made digestible and soft. What beautiful concepts corrupted by the bagatelle of artificial sound, a marketing scheme, and light.

As Nemo became agitated, Jeffrey Westcott's knee touched his own, lurching him back into cloudy carelessness. His left hand buzzed a little bit, and Nemo became afraid to lift his Dr. Pepper to his lips. He kept it hovering above the cup holder, and, compromising everything he'd ever learned, all his fear and what now seemed to be his last human line to the social salvation of middle school, leaned his knee back. He pressed it a little. But then he found something strange was happening, something he hadn't expected: Jeffrey wasn't retracting his leg at all. In fact, he was pushing back, and his hand, a lithe extension of powerful fingers, floated over his own knee and stayed there with a pinky touching the edge of Nemo's pants.

On screen, Atomic Child said, "That's why I live in this great country," referring to the US, after smashing the Mutating Submarine into oily detritus. He issued this statement to the press: "Because even if we don't agree with our leaders, we have the right to disagree. Unlike those who have been corrupted by the idealisms of a once peaceful people turned wrong. I, as sworn protector of liberty, promise to obliterate the crux of our enemies."

Nemo remembered that, in the actual books, Atomic Child—as Siege tapped into C.O.R.D.—began to attack the crowd of his supporters against his own will. He murdered more than fifty innocent Americans on Venice Beach. Afterwards, as the Mutating Submarine sank into the depths of the Pacific, Atomic Child escaped from an angry American mob, trapping himself in a compound, derived from the Fortress of Solitude, deep in the Arctic, to avoid taking more lives. Thus was his saga: protector and murderer, representative of opposite polarities simultaneously, all lost to simplification and fire.

Jeffrey reached out towards Nemo and touched his knuckles. Nemo touched back, arching his in a spasm, and before they knew it the two were calmly interlocked. Nemo, not for the first time in his life, felt repulsed at himself. Felt wrong. He remembered his father and his blustering lips, his mother and her secrets, opposite sexes, *The Manaton* and the empty box and the dinosaur in the woods. But he also couldn't help from feeling like he'd discovered a new hope, or maybe a new universe of touch and grandiosity, where two people, being together, felt right when together, and laws could be wrote and rewritten.

Lowering himself into the seat so his deerstalker cap fell below the line of sight, Nemo turned to Jeffrey and looked at the way his chest breathed—

so quick. Atomic Child, in his white leotard, entered into a conversation violated by the artfully artless sensibilities of the director, but Nemo was lost from the plot by then. How could he be feeling the way he was towards another boy? It was shameful. It was so unlike any male of his family was supposed to feel, and thus, a little dangerous. This was more than a physical experiment, as some boys played out, this was a true, genuine crush, one boy appraising the shoulders, lips, and idealized vision of another boy to a point where the outcome seemed palpate. Though neither he nor Jeffrey noticed, a little electricity crackled between the tips of their distal phalanges and, as if he didn't have the choice, Nemo sprung from his chair and kissed him on the left cheek.

"NEMO!" he heard a voice, and before he could turn around his father was upon him, bounding over the rows behind where he'd been disguised in a denim shirt and ruined blond toupee. Lily was in tandem in her lab coat. "What the hell do you think you're doing?"

"What's going on?" asked Jeffery.

"I'll tell you what's going on," said Lantana. "Perversion!"

"Try and calm down, Corn Cob," said Lily. "He's just a friend."

"A friend," growled Lantana. "A friend?"

"We didn't want you to exchange in naughty behavior, Nemo, regardless of sex or agenda."

"How dare you," said Lantana. "Tickle tongues with men."

"Please don't tell my mom," said Jeffrey, eyes bleary. "Please, please, please."

"You followed me to the movies?" asked Nemo.

"We wanted to supervise your social dealings. It's your first time out with a citizen, and we have secrets to keep," said Lily. As she spoke she seemed to be directing her words not only at Nemo, but her husband.

"By ambushing me?" asked Nemo.

"Perversion," said Lantana. "Abomination."

"I want to go home," said Jeffrey.

"It's okay," said Lantana, not soothing his son, but himself. "This can all be fixed. I know what to do."

"Corn Cob," said Lily, blinking. "Try and relax."

"Don't you know that a man and a woman are supposed to be together?" he asked. "Adam and Eve."

"Yes," said Jeffrey, answering the question himself. "Yes. I do. I didn't want him to kiss me. . .he's a faggot."

"Easy with the language, kid," Lily said.

Atomic Child whispered diabolically, "Because I'm American you son of a bitch." And Siege, in a rocket pack suit that had never been glimpsed before in the original story, soared towards him firing twin rockets.

"Abomination," wept Lantana. "Perversion."

"Calm down, honey," said Lily, escorting the two boys from the theatre. "There's nothing in this world that can't be understood. Maybe we were too hasty. . . ."

"I can't believe I felt sorry for you," Jeffrey Westcott said. "Wait till the kids at school hear what you tried to do. They'll murder you!"

Nemo, a lot like the film he was driven from, felt far too gelded to cry. Atomic Child, in his incoherent battle with Siege, screamed something like, "Stripes and Stars!" He was led by his mother past the Foo Dogs and pagodas into the parking lot with Lantana sobbing loudly behind them.

"Perversion," he whispered, unlocking the door to their Saturn. "Abomination. Mutation."

"It's okay, Honey," Lily whispered to Nemo as she shut him into the backseat and repeated her mantra. "Whether you know it or not, I'm always on your side." But as she said those words she seemed to possess anything but strength. Jeffrey kept his face and eyes beaded towards the window, shoulders and legs firmly crossed. Lantana blared Queen's Innuendo album and bore his teeth down at the road, reciting, "Maniscus, Manaticus, Manu," over and over again.

Nemo thought of the gun below his bed. Dormant, and forgetting about itself. For the first time in his entire life, he wished he'd been carrying it.

Later that night, to relieve stress rather than by necessity, Lantana went out on the beat in East Aurora. Most of the p.m. hours were spent relieving crack heads of their pipes, halting a few shoplifters, stopping one homeless man from beating the hell out of another homeless man for reasons neither of them could remember. When he got into the a.m. around two or three, he found a horde of prostitutes attempting to kill a John for his wallet, and, without bias, kept it from happening. By four thirty he was in East Denver, and, after a couple of drunks heckled him about his costume, trounced them something awful with it. With his club bloody and mind spliced from a lack of sleep and what he'd seen in the theater, he settled down on a curbside beside the capital building and stared into the lightless sky. He thought of his son. Felt a mixture of disgust and guilt. How could his beautiful boy care so little for his own future?

19th century light posts were stretched up into dross, and the white granite columns and architraves they shadowed were besprinkled in spurts of city snow. If there really was a gold rush, commemorated in 1908 by the leafing of the capital dome with gold, than that bit of history was cornered and forgotten by Pennsylvania and Lincoln in a hidebound little square. It reminded Lantana of how little his state, his country meant to the world, as a lush, revolving mineral cluster surrounded by vacuums, and how any country, and its perception of eternity, could be ruined by what humans did best. Nothing. As he pondered he stared up at the sky in the way any sad, anachronistic philosopher might. His knees and arms were pink from the cold and the club was stuck tight between his thighs.

Some ragged wanderer dressed like a wizard with a walking stick and a shopping cart, passed by him, stopped, and said, "Do not tarry, young Emperor. All things are made clear with the dawn."

Lantana paused, and then picked up a clump of ice to hock at him.

"An emperor?" he said, winding up for the toss. "Do you see a crown of fucking leaves?"

CHAPTER TWENTY

PINOCCHIO

On the eve of Nemo's sixth birthday his mother introduced him to the creature called butterfly at the very same time as a gun. Summer thunderstorms screamed over the pried-open plains of Arapahoe Falls. Towards the south tornado warnings wailed and thunderclouds krakoomed ever closer. But inside the fortress of the Zatkin house, under the incandescent stars on Nemo's ceiling, a birthday had been carried out, and concluded, with calm. The birthday cake was eaten. Nemo had watched Pinocchio twice on a Magnavox with a cracked top his father gifted him, but was careful to fast-forward through the nastier sections, the ones featuring a craven black whale with silver teeth.

When he looked up Lily stood in the doorway. Her body was powdered by light from the hall, and then what seemed to be an additional, more ephemeral light from somewhere that wasn't quite anywhere. In each of her hands she held a box. One was pocked full of holes, and the other looked heavy, like a block of pig iron, and was visibly harder to lift. Tilting her head, she walked into the dim shadow of the television until it could be revealed she was smiling.

"Happy birthday," she said.

Nemo leaned against her shoulder as the sky outside moaned. He wore a pair of Halloween pajamas modeled after a frog that he'd received

232

from a classmate's mothers. He pulled the big-eyed bonnet over his head, knees to his chest, and rocked.

"More presents?" he asked.

Lily nodded her head as another flash came from outside.

She placed the box with holes in it on the bedside. As she did so, a dry, anxious twitter tapped away inside. It was a sound that Nemo immediately hated, but found himself fascinated by, in the same way his nostrils longed for gasoline whenever his mother pumped. Lily slowly pried open the lid and with one hand cupped the exit. On the inside was a peablue butterfly with half-drawn, gossamer wings.

"For you," she said, taking what seemed to be a thin thread attached to its thorax and tying it tight around his fingertip. "Lepidoptera. Many births."

Nemo held the creature before his frog's face, crossed his eyes, opened his mouth as if to swallow it. Every time he breathed out the wings shuddered a little. Lily said, "They come frozen from the place I got it from, so it'll take some time to wake up."

Nemo took his finger and barely touched the edge of a wing tip, which jerked back.

"Can I name it?" he asked.

"Sure," said Lily.

He looked at the TV screen.

After a moment it was Pinocchio who sat on Nemo's thumb. Lily took the other box, the heavier box, and placed it beside the other on the bed.

"Now this present," she said, "is to be kept a secret. Which means that only you and I can know about it."

Nemo looked away from the butterfly.

"You and Dad?"

"No," said Lily. "Not Dad. This is a gift for you, and nobody else. I'll even forget that you have it eventually."

"Can I open it?"

"Of course you can. You roll these numbers to the middle—just like that."

"Really?" Nemo said, opening the box to stare down at a Sig Sauer. As he did so, the small Peablue began to lift from his finger, just barely, before settling back down.

"Yes."

"Is it real?"

"Loaded with eight bullets."

"But what do I do with it?"

"Protect yourself."

"Protect myself?"

"If you can."

She looked at the pistol as if wondering why it had appeared. Nemo ran his finger over the safety, and then, as if it had refused his touch, returned it to his lap. Pinocchio the Peablue began to rise higher, and higher, until the tug of the thread drew it down to Nemo's knuckle. That same knuckle and finger gripped the trigger, but refused to go so far as to pull.

"Keep it safe," Lily said. "Keep it for those who intend you harm. With this gift, there are no wishes. Just life how it is. And decisions."

Nemo nodded.

"Happy birthday," she said, and creaked up from the bed, leaving Nemo, much like the peablue, aposematic in the window-rain.

That night the butterfly flew frantically, attempting to tear itself from the thread. The next morning it worked so furious that Nemo cut its line and watched it flap to the ceiling. He asked his mother to buy him some flowers, so she came home with o she came home with some Gerber daisies, which Pinocchio stuck its proboscis into and fed. which Pinocchio stuck its proboscis into and fed. At night, it joined the stars and moons on the ceiling, thumping, and falling, and thumping again. Soon it seemed to realize that its heavens were illusions so it smacked against the window instead. A few days later, in the morning, before breakfast, Pinocchio seemed to tire, and although Nemo tried to offer it the nectar from daisies it eventually came earthward and turned over on its back. Its wings slowed. Its legs stiffened. The boy placed the carcass in an envelope and put it inside the safe.

The gun, he noticed, was still so shiny. It looked as if it could never age.

The peablue, Pinocchio, however, crinkled in its envelope as he shuffled it underneath the steely muzzle, and prepared, with relative indifference, to forget about it for years.

CHAPTER TWENTY ONE

SHE DOESN'T SLEEP

HOMOPHILIA

A *Manaton* Administered Exam

The following exam, conjured by the mental greatness
only accessible in Aesop Mac'Cool, is an experiment
deviating from the Socratic methodology of oral dictation.
It will be conducted by electing the best possible option
from four or more possibilities. Good luck and fuck you.

Manu.

QUESTION ONE:

What do homosexuals eat for breakfast?

 a) Tongue, broiled ham, fried eggs, fruit, and rolls.

 b) They don't, in place of a larger lunch.

 c) Infants.

 d) Both A and C.

QUESTIONS TWO:

If you see a homosexual walking through the main business district of your resident city, what is the best way to identify him?

      a) Orally.

      b) Psychically.

      c) Digestively.

      d) With the enchanted spectacles of Yur.

QUESTION THREE:

If you happen to notice any symptoms of Homophilia in yourself, what is the best method to expunge it?

      a) Cry.

      b) Remove your testicles.

      c) Kill your father.

      d) All of the above.

QUESTION FOUR:

In what geographical locations is homosexuality a frequent practice?

      a) China.

      b) The Yucatan.

      c) Scotland.

      d) Nowhere.

QUESTION FIVE:

What should you do if you are touched, or come within contact of a homosexual?

    a) Wash vigorously.

    b) Make moral amends with a priest or belief-appropriate religious leader.

    c) Throw yourself into a Polynesian volcano.

    d) First A, followed by C.

"Dad," said Nemo, letting *The Manaton* fall into his lap. He hated the ragged tome, the amount of devotion his father gave to it. The fact that Lantana treated this absurd, miscompiled bible of random circumstance with more authority than the entire 21st century, made him doubt the previous twenty. "I don't know how to answer these questions."

Lantana stood above him with his arms crossed over his chest behind a row of luggage they were planning to take with them, on what he said would be a "vacation."

"It is important that you answer every question," he said. "For it will help you understand the degrees and consequences of the. . .vulgarities you pursue."

QUESTION SIX.

How do you know you're homosexual?

    a) Someone told you so.

    b) You feed upon the blood of the innocent.

    c) You've stolen the enchanted spectacles of Yur.

    d) None of the above.

Nemo frowned and, without looking at his father, thought, quite morosely, D.

"Well," asked Lantana, putting his face and nose near the page. "Which is it?"

Nemo looked into his eye, saw it tremble and shook his head.

"I don't know. They all seem like such good answers."

The next days Nemo spent away from school. Apparently, there was a death in the family of a nonexistent uncle allowing them all to take a vacation to Carl's cabin on the northern coast of California, in a tiny, wealthy village called Mendocino. No one knew how he'd run into such accommodations. As far as the Zatkins could see, Carl lived in a scummy, pee-colored cube on Washington and Colfax in west Denver, and worked as. . .Nemo had no idea. Men like Carl, Lantana once put it, were employed by the world itself, and therefore were compensated in turn by the world. Which was a nice way of saying he was a criminal.

On the plane ride over, while his parents remained quiet, Carl talked for two and half hours without a single pause about Dr. Seuss, his story "The Butter Battle Book" and its pro-communist slant while he got drunk and ended up falling asleep in the bathroom before landing. In the airport they hailed a shuttle to the rent-a-car company and, for some reason, didn't have to pay for it. Carl then disappeared for three hours and came back with a tight wad of twenties.

Passing off the Pacific Coast Highway, Nemo was happy to leave his home behind. He remembered the feeling he'd had, the one telling him to draw the gun from its safe, to hold it before Jeffrey Westcott's cherubim face, and, not fire, but make him think that he could. That feeling scared him, and he decided that the gun should be kept forever interred. Maybe.

As they passed to the coast, he was taken by the chimerical qualities of northern California, Cyprus trees climbing to excessive heights and billowing like mizzens before the ocean. There was the smell of coal charring fish and, as if intrinsic, the unexcessive people that cooked it. In the Focus they'd rented they pulled into the cabin located on the outer fringes of Mendocino village near the Hill House Inn. To the west of the cabin was the ocean, and to the east, Redwoods, green ground, and lush Victorian gardens. They were close to an old water tower, and further away from a nettle of homes adorned with bohemian expressions like pink flamingoes, serenified Buddhas, lilies and gertians, and there was the smell of light, the sound of light, playing off the picket fences and storefronts.

The moment Carl entered into the Mendocino he pulled on a ski mask.

Lily asked, "What are you doing?"

Carl didn't answer.

"This is your cabin?"

Carl looked at Lily, the mask worn so badly that only one of his eyes popped out of two conjoined holes like a sock puppet's.

"It's as much mine as it is my ex-wife's," he said.

"You were married?"

Carl slapped his fingers on the dashboard. "Oh yes."

Lantana was snoring, spandex puffing with each deep breath.

His dream: attempting to assemble a model car, a 1957 Dodge Torqui-flite (it had a push-button transmission, and thus was a piece of shit) with no glue.

The ocean breeze came in through a crack in the window, and Nemo felt, in a place like this, his family would have to become normal, away from the boisterous morals of stiff-jawed Christians who believed in set moral postulates as if they'd been pulled from a pop-up book.

"What is this place?" Lantana snorted awake, feeling instant reprieve from his nightmare.

Climbing from the car his eye unstuck to the ocean. The sightline of stratocumulus sky. He stretched his arms and, plodding out towards it, waded straight in without minding his clothes.

"Wait for me, Licious," Carl called, and he followed him, skimask and all, into the spume.

Lily opened the cabin's front door.

"A place like this should be good for you, Nemo," she said.

It was the first thing she'd said to him in hours, and quite possibly the last for the day. Immediately after the words left her mouth she retreated to the first bottle of alcohol she could find, a Riesling chilling in a small refrigerator. Nemo, watching her, wondered how a person could promise to protect him, build a wall to keep evil forces at bay, and sequentially despoil it by chiseling out the mortar? Her normal ambiguities perplexed him.

Out the window he could see his father and Carl, two massive turds being lulled by the tide, and felt a little sick. But mostly he thought of the face of Jeffrey Westcott, those fingers that touched him, and then made fists, and then screamed out words like, "They'll murder you!" And even if Nemo was safe now in some glen of Eden where the air was warm and easy to breathe, he would have to return to the land of idol-worshippers eventually.

"Hey Licious," Carl yelled, floating on his back in the ocean. "When I was married, I used come out here to shit and nobody ever noticed."

Lantana grunted his approval. He ruminated for a moment over the safety of Steve Two, who'd they left in the trust of a questionable cowhand, and friend of Carl's, named Merl Takote, and his buffalo ranch in the hills near Golden.

"And guess what?" he chuckled. "I just did it again."

The sun was orange beyond the clouds.

When night fell, they ate a meal of free-raised chicken stuffed with arugula, locally farmed wild rice, polenta, and currents, cooked by Carl in the modern granite kitchen with unexpected precision. Lantana surveyed each bite with the tireless scrutiny he gave to all his enemies, and then held his palate to the same standards—organic food was elitist. Carl seemed calm enough, but often could be seen glancing out the window. While Lily ate she murmured and avoided eye contact with everyone. The night carried on like this in relative peace, and with sensuous, prolonged mastication.

As Nemo tried to sleep later on, however, in a cold, seaside cot, thoughts of Jeffrey trip-wired through his head. The face of the boy slid closer to his, the brass-blond eyes widened, flashed recognition, as if they'd just opened from a coma. Though after a moment, the proximity turned heavy, and the blond boy was sucked into a polysemous space. The onset of slumber, coming on quick. Nemo heard the words of his father, first softly, and without meaning. Then louder, as if in universal decree. Lantana sounded distinguished in dreams; he could have been broadcasted over television sets and radios the world over. "Nemo is not a normal boy. He never will be a normal boy." Diplomatically, like a politician, his toga starch-ironed. A pit opened in the twelve-year-old's stomach. Lantana's booming voice again, "Nemo is not a normal boy. And by not being a normal boy, he is, in fact, little less than normal. The ancients decree: Normal is not normal. Or was it not normal is normal? Where was I?" Nemo felt as if every person in his life, each and every dear one, was silently asking him to become both average and strange, both innocuous and terrifying, with so much insistency that, if the charade didn't stop soon, he would be capable of casting a deranged, murderous venom upon the world.

His eyes bleared open for one last time before the sandman took him. He saw the ceiling and noticed a shape formed by a little sealight leaking through the drapes.

After almost an hour of stirring, Nemo's thoughts were too fast to find rest. He creaked down the hallway in search of movement. On his way he heard someone humming (or was it groaning?) from the living room. Peeking around the corner was Lily in her panties and bra sitting in the sycamore.

"One day, my darling," she whispered to herself.

"One day, my darling, we'll be together."

She was sipping white liquid from what looked like a test tube. Her eyes were closed, but they moved beneath the lids, and the liquid was the same consistency, and color, as the one Nemo had been made to drink the day he was at home sick before the rumors started. She'd said it would help clear his sinuses.

Above her were photographs of men with moustaches. The walls were made from the local cyprus, and adorned with shelves, at least seven, that carried model watercrafts. Lily's mouth was a little open revealing her two lost teeth, gaps in the back of her jaw, black, where a metal plate was in place. A brass lamp gave off a bitter hump of light, and as she hummed Nemo saw her skin glow. A phosphorous hue burned beneath her skin and, in that burning, organs could be seen. Nemo's foot pressed down. The floorboards moaned. Lily looked up with wild eyes.

"Corn cob?" she said, hiding the vial. She took a towel to her body. "Not much crime in Eden, eh?"

Upon hearing no response, her eyes relaxed, and she went back to sipping and humming. Nemo retreated to bed. Apparently, he thought, as he stared at his hands, he wasn't the only one with a tendency to issue light.

CHAPTER TWENTY TWO

STEVE TWO'S SILENCE

Steve Two broke free of the Zatkin home when she was just more than two years old, and, out of line with Lantana's ethos, may have been allowed through the back door by the unlatching of a particular lock (on purpose?), exposing her to the boondocks of humanity.

Lantana always felt it a fact that lions, like cows in the land of India, were meant to be worshipped above all other forms but man, and that only man, and only with his bare fists, was allowed to face one in hand to hand combat. But unlike the joy he felt with the birth of Nemo in 1994, Steve Two's cloning left him weakened. To begin with, the lioness reminded him of the first Steve, and the pain he'd felt when, before Las Vegas, before Colorado and after Fearghas, the creature fell victim to its own fool's errand, chasing a rabbit off a cliff.

He remembered that they were mourning Fearghas in the Annieopsquotch Mountains (as requested by the Scotsman years ago) casting his ashes and a terse encomium into the frigid Canadian wind. Steve Two was as somber as a lion could be. He sniffed at the urn occasionally. The snowshoe hare was terrified when its tired ears egressed from the thicket to find a four hundred pound African animal in the middle of a North American snowstorm. Before a second passed, it was bounding towards the chasm with Steve lumbering clumsily after it. He seemed to know the drop was coming, and still ran and ran, and with such silence, such apathy. He skittered and fell with his belly to the sky. He didn't even make a sound.

Steve's death changed Lantana, just as much as his father's had, if not more, and made him feel inferior to the mythos of such mighty animals, and the fact that they were prone to ending their lives just as a human could. He thought of the African proverb Argyll once told him in a moment of drunkenness when he was fifteen:

A Grandson goes to ask his Grandfather a question.
Grandson:
Is the lion the king of the jungle?
Grandfather, albeit curiously:
Yes, but why do you ask?
Grandson:
Well, if the lion is the king of the jungle, then why, in all the stories that I read and hear, man will defeat the lion? How can this be true?
Grandfather, warmly:
It will always be this way until the lion tells the story.

When Steve Two was born from a test tube, Lantana remembered him growing into something small so fast. She had tiny blue capillaries in the open pigments of her eyes, a triangle body; the tendency to fumble about in playless curiosity until collapsing from exhaustion and mewing and purring at her master's purple toes. She was a hungry girl early, and loved to eat. Or maybe she liked to eat because Lily fed her so much, and got used to unlicensed gluttony. Like most holy creatures in un-Christian antiquity, Steve Two was born a combination of the sexes. Though Lantana thought this was correctable in humans, and would have been his own son, he would do nothing to change the fortune of this new life, this reincarnation. He would do nothing but give her love and protection in attempts to rewrite, what he saw to be, his own failure.

When Steve Two escaped that day, Lantana had what could have generously been called a breakdown. Apart from drilling everyone in the house

as to their involvement, including his nine-year old son, who was perus-
ing through the *Odyssey* with unchildly quickness, he blustered around
Arapahoe Falls, not caring whether or not he'd be considered strange for
asking the whereabouts of a lion. He went door to door. He harassed
children on the playground. He bullied teenagers and women with baby
carriages. It was when he entered the Jicarilla Heights, however, that he
finally found her. Dorado Avenue, the gem of The Heights, and the ruby
of The Falls, where the wealthiest lived. The houses looked like sleeping
furnaces, creatures from a world of walking machines. With assortments
of pale eyes glowing from their dormers, stanchions rooted deep beneath
the ground, they prepared to heft up their roots and stalk for blood across
the land. Lantana in comparison was an angry speck challenging their
rooftops to war. The one on the corner had its back to a shallow river, the
Smoky Hill Creek, where in 1859, the white man settled, following the
California 49ers and their news of gold while paving a trail to the Rockies.
It had an old medieval steeple on top of it.

In front of that old tower-house Steve Two was cornered. Rain
poured and poured, a biblical deluge. She'd killed a house cat, a tabby,
removed its flesh and fur in leonine pleasantry before it finally died, and
was now being corralled by that tabby's owner. A big game hunting rifle
capable of slugging elk was cocked to his shoulder. The cocker himself was
middle aged, well toned, and most definitely experienced in killing, with a
look any accomplished hunter would get in his eyes before extinguishing
something so majestic as a lion. Steve Two growled and licked her chops,
seeming so entirely unaware.

Lantana came up from behind the man and said, "I'll give you
two seconds to drop your gun and then you can decide whether to fight
or flee."

Making a *Wha* sound he whirred to Lantana, and the lioness dug
her claws into his shoulders, spun him and grizzled the Adam's apple from
his throat, leaping forth with the wordless reasoning animals give for their
actions. She picked it clean. The man fell dead. Lantana was strangely
fascinated by the gore.

Afterwards there was the problem of stowing the body. Thankfully the attack happened at nighttime, and no one had seen through the rain. Lantana called Lily and had her pick up Steve Two in the old Cutlass they still had at the time, went down to the creek, and dug a hole, and put the body in a trash bag. He waded into the river and used a mess of concrete bricks from a nearby construction site to bury it beneath the silt. It was the very same creek that, year after year, Lantana would return to with a yahrzeit for his father. Its current reminded him of how things could die, quick or slow, but usually quick. It reminded him of the reason why he sheltered Steve Two, who he hoped would never again lust for violence, and of what he'd become. How his hands, strong and tireless, had hidden, and buried, dead flesh.

CHAPTER TWENTY THREE

𝗗𝗔𝗣𝗛𝗡𝗘

"You must be one of Carl's friends."

The next morning Nemo awoke without barely having slept and walked around the corridor to the living room where last night he'd seen his mother effervescing. He passed into the kitchen thinking of how to broach the subject of the strange liquid, the one she'd fed him when he was once ill, but instead of his mother, or Lantana, or Carl, or a kitchen with hopper windows, buttercups and aloe plants, there was a nude woman with drowsy buttocks whisking a bowl of pancake batter. Nemo tried to retreat but she turned around and smiled at him. She had a full truckload of body, a cab of blond pubic hair, with something Nemo considered feral sitting shotgun inside. But for some reason, he wasn't afraid of her. He was embarrassed by her, but not fearful. Maybe it was in the way she forced her eyelids tight, like veined petunias on the verge of their bloom, or had such a full smile that happiness and calm could be drawn from her lips, like their nectar. Maybe it was the fact that she was implacably unclothed, and the sight of bare skin made Nemo giggle. Or maybe her skin was so red it looked pained, and he was confused by its ineffable strangeness.

"You must be one of Carl's friends," she said, dripping the batter into a skillet. As she moved across the room she used her toes as stilts before flattening them and their feet against the tile. The middle of her stomach had a little bit of fat arranged in a pear shape, and her underarms sagged, but her chin was strong. "Do you know where he might be?"

Nemo shook his head. "No ma'am. I thought he was here."

"Well aren't you polite," she said, mouthing Ma'am to herself. From the counter she picked up what seemed to be a long, half-smoked cigarette—but more elliptical—and set it to the burner on the stove.

She sucked on the tapered end of it, drew in her lungs, and phewed out smoke in a sigh so long and luxurious it made Nemo long for tranquility. Seconds later, as if in the onset of pathology to counterbalance that promise, however, her eyes became smaller, and the teeth revealed in her smile, if even possible, became larger, and shinier, than before. She settled her shoulders in repose. Nemo watched her do this with curiosity. It brought up a memory, not all that distant: observing Lantana sneak a cigarillo in the back yard celebrate his first major mention in the *Washington Post*, late at night. For some reason, the gesture appealed to Nemo. The fire, the paper, the wheezy inhale. So much so, in fact, that he set off to recreate the scenario. A silly enterprise, in retrospect; an impulse to mimic the movements of a stormy man. He remembered setting off on a journey through Arapahoe Falls, shortly before suppertime, skirting the shallow ends of the reservoir with a half-block of orange post-it notes in his pocket. He picked weeds, flowers, species of grass, and, with surgical precision, stuffed them into paper squares. Sometimes he mixed floral combinations. He found himself enjoying the ritual of it all. He tried it ever so often for a couple of years, sneaking into the bathroom after bedtime, opening the window, and watching the mirror for signs of Lantana in his demeanor while he took a small puff or two of the neighbor's zoysia grass. This, of course, was until his tenth birthday when he lit up on poison ivy and was sent to the hospital on a respirator. He tried not to let that memory affect his current mood, however. He was far too intrigued by the company.

"Oh?" said the woman, who caught Nemo sizing up her drug. She looked around and shrugged. "You wanna try?"

Nemo nodded. "Alright," and found himself hacking on a forest of sweat and molasses. Daphne laughed and said "Right on!"

"What's your name?" Nemo croaked.

"Daphne," she said. When she bent over to shake Nemo's hands her breasts folded over her stomach, two gigantic nipples the same adobe texture as the tile seeming to greet him.

"Wow," said Nemo, in response. He found his thumbs most fascinating, and brought one of them with his hand to shake hers.

"Well hey there, Wow," smiled Daphne, unquestioning. "Nice to meet you."

Minutes later they were eating pancakes together, but to Nemo no cake or waffle or meat or fowl or anything at all ever tasted better. The fork in hand. The ruche of warm batter. The violence of syrup. It was all like a hunt. Daphne's breasts sat with them on the table, but unsexually. Her nipples were hard from the window breeze, at sort of an upward incline as if broadcasting signals to airplanes. She told him a little bit about herself: "So I came from this little town in Nebraska, you probably wouldn't know it, it's called Box Butte, and it's a terrible, backwater shithole. Small. Insignificant. Some towns are built just to keep Jesus alive and kicking," she laughed a little, took another pull off her joint, held it in her lungs. "You know what I mean? It's, like, the great American fucking conspiracy," she said before exhaling.

"Totally," croaked Nemo.

"I don't think our forefathers, Jefferson, Lincoln, Waldo, whatever, I don't think they would want to grow up in a place like Box Butte. Fuck no."

"Fuck no," Nemo repeated, nodding vigorously with his gigantic cap all wayward down his left ear. All he could think about was food.

"Just wanted to get out of there."

Nemo squinted up at Daphne and, as he saw the joint simmering, attempted to pick it up for another hit, but before it touched his lips, asked, "Why are you naked?"

"Well," she said, with her hand at her chin and eyes dreaming to the ceiling. "I believe that the body is not to be looked at with shame."

"What do you mean?" asked Nemo, thinking of his own body, and the almost immediate sense of churlishness it seemed to respond with.

"It's kind of like my car, Wow. A car for a woman who wanders. I maintain it, I sleep in it, I let it carry me wherever I need to go. And I feel like the shape or size is as meant to be."

Nemo sucked in some smoke in thought, feeling unerringly cool.

"Don't worry," she said. "I never get sick of answering that question."

The front door to the cottage opened and, without allowing herself to be startled, unlike Nemo, Daphne crossed her left leg over the right and continued to eat. At the entrance to the kitchen stood Carl, eyes wider than Nemo had ever seen them before, in a seersucker suit with a lavender tie and holding a bag full of oranges.

"Hey there, lover," she said.

Carl chewed on his lip, eyeing the joint, and walked on his boat shoes into the kitchen. He sat down at the kitchen table with the two of them, set the oranges below the chair, and took a hit.

"Pass the syrup," he said, exhaling.

"You two know each other?" asked Nemo.

"We were married," Daphne said.

"Really?" asked Nemo, withholding the urge to comment on the fact that Carl, of all the men in the world, was more worthy of judging a crapping contest than becoming a husband.

Carl scoffed. "If that's what you want to call it."

"That's what it's called," said Daphne, elbows squeezing her breasts together as she set them on the table. "Marriage. Man and wife, for nine wonderful years."

"I didn't say it," said Carl, taking his fork up to scratch his chin. "You did."

Nemo refilled his orange juice.

"When did you get back?" Carl asked. "I thought you were in Barcelona."

"I got bored," said Daphne.

"In Barcelona."

"Too much dancing."

"You mean you ran out of money?"

"Not these days," she smiled, sifting through another bag of verdant shake to roll a second joint. "Business is good."

"I bet."

"What's the deal with you?" she asked. "You just show up here out of the blue. . .with a twelve-year-old."

"He's not mine."

"Thank the stars."

"I came here with his parents, Daphne," Carl growled. "To give the boy a breather." He tousled Nemo's hat. "We weren't expecting company."

"Is he sick?"

"Something like that."

"Nothing a little time cruising the Pacific breeze can't fix."

Nemo looked at his pancake and laughed hysterically, drawing the attention of his tablemates.

"Ah, fuck," said Carl, pointing his thumb. "Look at him, he's stoned as a goat."

"He's just having fun."

"If his parents see you, see this," he swooped his hand over the paraphernalia, rolling papers and ash. "They're going to kill me."

"Oh, come on," said Daphne. "It's just a little bit a herb."

"You don't understand. His father's a little bit of a. . . ."

"Fascist?"

"I was going to say visionary."

"How long do we have before they're back?"

"They're due anytime now. Went sight seeing."

"Well, that'll be quick," said Daphne. "Not much to see. I'll just put on some clothes and light a candle. They won't know the difference."

Carl's knee began to bounce, and then quake furiously against the ground. The pot had probably been just as bad for his paranoia as the naked woman with her ass sprawled across the chair.

"Won't work. You've got to hide."

Daphne lowered her neck to the table. "Won't work, darling, or are you afraid your friends won't like what they see?"

"I like you, Daphne," said Nemo.

"I know you do, sugar."

A car pulled up the road outside along the efflorescent coastal homes. In a city like Mendocino, where there wasn't much traffic and a lot of open sea, only the barest, most pillowed feet could pass undetected. Carl ran to the window and ducked.

"You've got to hide," he whispered.

"Nu-uh," said Daphne. "This is my house too."

"Come on," said Carl. "Come on, come on. Do me a solid."

"No."

Nemo, looking direly at the table. Hissed, with bravado, "Sugarbowl."

At this sight, Carl took Daphne by her hips and forced her into a broom closet with an espagnolette, locking it behind her. She banged her fists, but after he whispered a few words that just from their tone sounded like promises, she went quiet. Carl went into a frantic hop around the room with a can of vanilla aerosol, stuffing plates into the sink along the way. With a sponge he sopped off the ash and jettisoned the joints into a small plastic baggie, along with the weed, before hiding it beneath a kidney-curved loveseat in the living room and heaving open all the windows.

"Shit, shit, shit," he said as he finished covering up their tracks and fell into a seat at the table. Through the cottage door came Lantana, and then Lily.

"Are we having pancakes?" Lantana asked, noticing his son at the table, who, apart from having his plate stacked with enough batter to block a small flood, grinned at him stupidly.

"I thought I would surprise you," said Carl.

"Well, thank you Carl. I am hungry," said Lily, pulling a plate from the cupboard. Her hair was back in a wide coda. She was wearing an Aran sweater over another sweater, a pair of military issue khakis and a scuffed pair of auburn pumps. "What is that smell?"

"Like skunk," spat Lantana.

"And how are you feeling this morning, sweetie?" she asked Nemo.

"Fuckin spectacular."

"Language!"

"Dare you talk to your parents that way?" asked Carl.

Nemo was crouched behind his fortress of pancakes, all of which he'd horded, holding his knife and fork in his fists. The tip of his cap and eyes peeked out from the top of the stack. "Well," he mumbled. "I realized that I'm kind of like. . .a car. A car with a wandering driver. And my body, my mind, everything that is me, is exactly like a fucking car."

Lantana, if not a sore thumb, than a broken one on the Mendocino landscape in his clinical garb of Spandex and what quickly became nothing else but a muscled chest and long legs, glared at Carl.

"What the hell is going on?"

Nemo, making his hand travel over imaginary, rather handicapped waves, said, "I'm cruising the Pacific breeze."

"What happened to your eyes?"

"He must be allergic to something," said Carl.

"He's got no sensitivities."

"Then he must have slept bad," said Carl.

"Yea," said Nemo. "I did sleep bad." He looked at his mother, who reached out to fork away one of his pancakes, but as she did so he threatened her fingers with his butter knife. "No."

"But you have them all."

"They're mine."

"Nothing belongs to anyone," said Lantana.

"True," said Carl. "But I can make more."

"You can't have these," said Nemo.

"I can have whatever I want."

All of them turned their heads to a crash they heard in the broom closet.

"What was that?" asked Lily.

"My friend," said Nemo, digging his hand into the top of his stack until it left a deep pit. He then took the batter and rubbed it between his hands. "She's from Box Butte, Nebraska. Like Jesus."

"Your kid's stupider than malt balls," squeaked Carl, coming between them. "It's just a possum in the closet."

"A possum?"

"Need I repeat myself?"

"Yea," said Lantana, climbing from his chair. "You do."

"Be careful, Corn Cob," said Lily.

"Oh come on, man," said Carl. "Just take it easy."

Lantana, seeming much less brave than usual, poised his body to open the door, nose forward. His free fist was prepared to strike.

"Ahhhhhh!" he screamed. "Nudists!"

"Nudists?" screamed Carl. "Multiple?"

"How big is that closet?" asked Lily.

"So nude," Lantana said, hopping across the room. "So clotheless."

"What do we do?" whispered Lily, trying timidly, from her seat at the table, to look into the dark closet. "Are they here for clothes?"

"Just calm down, everybody," said Carl.

"What sort of place is this?" said Lily.

"An evil one," said Lantana. "No rule of law. Nudists, Tush, they don't function like the rest of us. They roam the night in search of acceptance, spewing genital acceptance over everything in their path. I should have known, on this woebegone coast. The invasion, it begins here."

"There's no invasion, Licious" said Carl. He thrust himself between Lantana and the closet, holding up his stubby palms.

"The nudist (singular) in the closet. . .is my ex-wife. . . ."

Silence.

"She wasn't supposed to be home."

"Home?" said Lantana.

"We own it together. . .joint lease."

"He's telling the truth," said Daphne, emerging from the closet and unfurling her flesh to towering heights. "Carl and I go way back."

"I thought you said your ex-wife died," said Lantana, now allowing her bounding nakedness to form one shape, as opposed to the many his mind's eye had conjured.

Carl scratched his head. "I was speaking figuratively."

"You're a ghost?" Nemo gasped, peeking out from his turret. "No shitting way!"

"What wrong with you?" Lantana asked him.

Nemo, using the molasses and his fork, began to make explosion sounds.

"We got divorced four years ago," said Daphne, waiting for them to let her pass. Upon doing so she leaned on the kitchen counter. "Carl couldn't handle certain aspects of my past life. So we drew the line."

"Why don't you ask her what those aspects were?" asked Carl.

Daphne sighed.

"Come on. They have the right to know."

"Dirty communists," said Nemo.

"Alright," she started, sitting down next to the child and patting his bleary head. "A long time ago, and I'm talking a long time ago, when I was getting out of high school, I took all the money I'd saved, including the rainy day fund from my mom's dresser drawer, and," pointing to her soft, furred genitalia, "made myself whole."

"Isn't that illegal?" asked Lantana, suddenly afraid of the what he'd felt staring at Daphne, watching her widely immortal female hips that, despite their berth, could still make him ponder naughty acts.

"Of course it's not illegal," said Carl. "It's just wrong."

"It's not wrong," growled Daphne.

"You are weak," Nemo yelled at his fork. "Indulgent"

"Sure it is," said Lantana. "Boys are boys and girls are girls. Just like up and down."

"Well," said Lily. "There are exceptions."

"Amongst antelope," Lantana snorted.

"Then give me a set of hooves," said Daphne.

"See why I couldn't tell you about her?" asked Carl.

"I loved you, Carl," said Daphne.

"And I loved a woman," said Carl, a hint of forgotten whimsy warming his cheeks. "Not a. . .whatever you are."

"Don't call Daphne a whatever you are," said Nemo, suddenly so poignant that they all, especially his father, who'd particularly felt the result of that poignancy, became afraid. He then returned to his project. "Dead or alive, she's still a something."

"But buddy," said Lantana. "Daphne told a big lie, and that was wrong."

"I didn't tell a lie," said Daphne. "I was a woman. I always was."

"You weren't a woman," said Lantana. "Which is why you had to have a surgical procedure to become one."

"Who are you to say who the fuck I am? Sure, I had all the equipment a boy should have, but insides aren't outsides. A higher being doesn't write the truth on your forehead. It was in my genes to be a woman, but I couldn't express my biology with words, so I had a doctor do it for me." She tapped her toes against the ground. "That's how identity happens, asshole."

"See, kiddo," said Lantana to his son. "This is a classic case of the transgender rage."

"Amen," said Carl.

"Corn Cob. . ." seethed Lily, before retreating angrily from the conversation.

"No, what we call this is dysphoria," said Daphne. "People who are so sad about their own lives that they need to make others feel bad about theirs. Grade school shit."

"Grade school is shit," said Carl. "And lies are lies."

"Don't listen to them, Wow."

"Wow?" asked Lantana.

"Daphne made me pancakes," said Nemo, suddenly turning around in his seat with his elbows on the chair frame.

"Anyone can make pancakes," said Lantana.

"But hers are really good."

"So what?"

"So. Can someone who makes pancakes this good be all that bad?"

"Yes," said Lantana. "Yes, he can."

"Unfortunately, the true answer to my question requires far more litigation than can be summoned at this precise moment."

"What the fuck are you talking about? Litigation?"

Daphne, with her second arm folding across her breasts in a secure and biological trap, looked proud. Lantana and Carl, fey, yet hungry enough to forgo the morning's ilk, took enough restraint to shut their mouths and agree that food would be best for everyone, just to calm their nerves. They ended up allowing Daphne to prepare their pancakes in a worn paisley bed sheet, which she wrapped around her undeniably mannish shoulders in, what was for them, a fitting, biblical fashion.

Old Testament.

The pancakes, Lantana admitted internally, were fantastic.

The high Nemo had passed unnoticed as, post-breakfast, he napped in his cot. Of all things to contradict the bright madness of his morning, was a dream of him being devoured by a sea monster. In that dream, he was captain of a ship, a brawny wooden man o' war pumping towards the Indies as the sun reached its peak in the sky. A long black serpent rose from the water like a seething hook and unhinged its slivering fangs. Darkness fell and the clouds gathered in a net, and when its mouth closed Nemo experienced first-hand what it meant to peel away a seductively red apple of youth and find black beyond black beyond black below the rind. His body, his mind, his fear. All alone. A boy decomposing in the beast.

But when he awoke the air returned to him. He was alive, and enthralled with the simplicity of his wants, what it meant to open the window and find that the light from the evening sun, even if dislocated, fading, or tired, was in the company of other light, that of the moon, supplanting itself in good will.

In the living room were Daphne, Carl, Lantana, and Lily, playing an intensifying game of Scrabble. It was nearing night, they were drinking beer, Anchor Steam, and Nemo wondered when the lull in his internal storm would be dragooned, when he'd be thrown into another battle against what must have been his father, for he lost skill when battling with himself. At an early age he'd learned to feel content with the suppliant mystery of his mind; it was people with the bane of insecurity, a rife of talent and a hog's head of anger to exacerbate inadequacy that excelled in stifling his happiness.

"Come on over, Wow," said Daphne, to the horror of the other men. "You can help me play."

"You shouldn't even be here," growled Carl from his seat.

"Just as much my house as it is yours," said Daphne.

Carl swilled his beer. "Fucking California."

Although they seemed to take issue with the fact that Nemo wound his way to her with red-cheeked warmth, they returned to attacking the board, and forewent the decision to correct her on his actual name.

For hours they played, baking frozen pizzas in the oven, and when Daphne excused herself with Carl to speciously puff a little fatty outside, Lantana and Lily played ignorant. Nemo wasn't allowed to participate, of course, they still thought that twelve years old was too young for him to know what drugs were. To them, the world and its chemicals, though they'd informed him of the effects (especially Lantana in his cautionary tales of LSD) were pugnacious to anyone not deranged or depressed enough to imbibe them. Either that, or they were just too tired to explain.

Daphne and Carl returned stew-eyed and they resumed playing. Lantana got a call from Merl Takote, saying that Steve Two got her tail stomped by a buffalo. "Some fucking lion," he said jokingly, and Lantana, in response, vowed to bash his face. Nemo came up with a five-letter word, ALPHA, which won them a double word score. Lily spelled QUIT. Carl, HAPPY. Lantana spelled HE, and became somber at the point total. Nemo thought then of Jeffrey Westcott. The next word he spelled was ALIVE.

When he made sure Lily was asleep, Lantana stalked across the cottage and, before passing through the Creole-French doors leading to the deck, pried open the entrance to Nemo's room. The boy was sleeping soundly, nose in the pillow, below two or three boughs of ivy twitching to an unseen wind. He'd cleaned out a little sterile place for his yarmulke on the nightstand. Lantana couldn't help but force down a smile, thinking of all the remarkable thoughts a boy could have. He remembered how, about three years ago, he tried to teach him the apparitional miracle of building model cars.

They'd sat in meticulous, practically painful concentration, until the Cadillac Fleetwood began to resemble its shape atop a carpenter's desk in the garage. They were both so tired afterwards. And hungry. The season, he recalled, was something in between spring and summer, and the temperature, elastic, unsure of hot or cold; Nemo admitted his interest in butterflies, Lepidoptera, the creature of multiple births. Lantana nodded as his son explained the baryon elements of pupal cycles, and took genuine interest in the subject.

Now, Lantana left his son's room, slipped on his golden sandals and toga, picked up his club and stepped outside towards the beach. It was true that these days he only felt himself when he was The Savage. His other personality, a plinth of fears and wants, remained in his alleatory past.

On the shore, the rugged, inestimable nighttime water rushed up the creases in his toes. He looked out into the soreness of the moors. A piece of driftwood was saddled to land by the waves, and glugged up and down against his ankles as if nudging them awake. Lantana looked down—in the flotsam was a corked glass bottle with sloping shoulders and a dimple on the bottom. On the inside was a yellow piece of paper. Thinking of all the appropriate clichés of star-crossed romance, Lantana clawed through what was left of the driftwood to wrench it forth. He then pieced apart the algae and held it to the moon.

Dear Lantana,

You are hereby chosen by the hierarchal mandate of the great fuck you to climb on top of a mountain and die.

Angrily yours,

God

"What the fuck?" Lantana asked the bottle. He removed the note and read it again.

The words were real. Dry and sincere.

Suddenly he felt afraid. There was no one, no one but Lily and his dead father Fearghas that knew about the 'Great Fuck You.'

He looked into the darkness from whence it came. There he found something to look at—a light, a small boat, chugging along off the shore. God knows how far away it was. Lantana glanced at the bottle. He broke it and leaped into the sea. His body was strong against the current, deltoids against the current's tug, little and swift, sucked into his lungs. He got drunk on salt. His eyes blurred. He thought about Nemo, and the fact that he was so smart, so sure of who he was from such a young age. Lantana never knew a thing about himself save for the fact that he needed to fight to live, that he was too weak to withstand the quotidian current, that he was a scrappy son of a bitch, a meteor, a comet, who'd leave the world just like he'd come into it. But still he swam. A flame in the water. He ignored whatever flipped beneath. His body began to drag with the tide and he couldn't see the boat or its light on the horizon. When he saw the moon and the stars occasionally above him as he came up for air, the water filmed through and netted the splendor of six shining wings on the sky.

CHAPTER TWENTY FOUR

MIMESIS

The death of Fearghas monumentalized Lantana's decision to marry Lily the summer of 1974. He latched her with a ring because she was the last vestige of his father's sandless exodus from life, and the private white-ribbon affair they had was officiated at a Boston courthouse before a lipless woman who pronounced them bound before the end of six minutes. Lily seemed unsure when she said, "I do." She was listless as they drove off in the Cutlass. That evening, after a short trip, they silently sanctified their desanctified union in a hotel north of Central Park in Manhattan, and ate oysters at midnight in Midtown. Lily got real drunk and flirted with their waiter, who Lantana promptly beat with a serving tureen. The next morning he went to collect his inheritance at the Withal Trust in a tattered Lacoste shirt, his last pair of jeans, and a billfold bruised to the stitches. The banker passed him the check as if he were bequeathing the sun, and let it seethe from his fingers with amused, almost Godly gravitas. When Lantana's eyes adjusted to the numbers he understood why; it would have been sufficient to buy them not only out of the murdered ligature they called a home, but into a small castle in the hills of Tuscany or some far off picture-book fantasia.

It was really that much.

And that muchness might have been the reason that Lantana made a break for the city of sin and starving darkness. Lily was already settling in for classes in Colorado while he, signing the last of the death documents away, prepared to load the piddle of his belongings, his thoughts of fortune, into the Cutlass and shuttle down 90 West. Somehow he just ended up veering little by little from 76 to 15 South, and before he knew it his windows were open and his hair was soaring with an arid, dooming wind, and in every pocket of his person were his father's words now evanishing down the southland rise.

He found out quickly that it was easy not to call Lily, to aerate into the desert, where many people came to disappear in the same fizzling manner as its molecules. They were married, anyway, and marriage was what adults called 'forever.' When they could. For weeks he didn't phone, and it didn't seem like she tried to reach him. He began shooting craps at The Empire, a fortress of gimmicky artifice modeled after Ieyasu's Japanese Shogunate, and before the end of his first month had established himself as a young shrewd shooter who gambled in the silent, serious way. He would return to his penthouse suite two floors from the veranda without a woman each night, of which there were many to return with.

Whenever a voice in the back of his mind asked him why he was doing this, why his father had raised them under a grand lie of penury, why he'd avoided Lily, why these questions kept on surfacing to the scrim of his loosely jumbled mind, he would fill a riot shotgun and his pockets with 9mm Parabellum buckshot and go into the desert in search of vultures. He'd let the barrel drag against the ground as if grazing for food, move slow and steady, finger to the trigger. He'd search the sky for shadows. He'd lie on the ground and pretend to be carrion. He'd unroll a slab of rotten meat. He'd wait for them to come, for the vultures to feed, and then show them, for their last moment on earth, the consequences of their scavengry.

In his second month of his stay he met Carl—a quiet and troubled boy back then just like he was now. He'd been running from a hit the Yakuza put on him in San Francisco for doing something he called, with a smirk, endlessly incriminating. He dressed in a seal-leather jacket every day (it was markedly the only nice, or expensive, thing he had), beaten down Florsheim loafers, and despite claiming he'd lost most of his money on roulette, Lantana knew that his wallet had gone towards less sure bets like booze and long legs. The way he looked at women was almost prosecutable in itself, and alcohol, a mean exasperant. He twitched a lot and scratched the right side of his face, right between his chin and cheek.

But as far as friendships distended, Lantana remembered theirs as serendipitous. Carl, who never shared much about his roots save for the fact that he was an army brat raised in practically all of Europe who got involved with some 'bad' sorts out of high school, after something 'bad' happened, was looking for a person to impress or emulate, someone a little wiser than he. He was also looking for something to calm his bunny-hopping libido, the one he feared would end up getting him syphilitic or, quite simply, shot. Lantana was looking for a vessel to impart his missing father's words upon, and whatever he and Carl started began out of necessity as opposed to desire, in tandem with the miserly miracle of Las Vegas.

Carl and Lantana worked together on everything, and Lantana was happy to share the money with someone other than himself. Apart from his inheritance, he was taking home a good grand or more a night, and Carl had been sleeping out of his Pinto. They rented a spacious two-bedroom apartment near the Strip in a complex called Desert Shadow, and Lantana slowly unreeled the secrets *The Manaton*. He did it ostentatiously to make his disciple feel like he was incurring the sharper end of a secret. Carl didn't even nibble before he bit. He stopped sleeping around after finding sores on his feet and hands from what turned out to be the early onset of his first of two mortal fears, and began studying every day, memorizing Mac'Cool line by line, and at night would meditate below the starless sky on the roof often without food, sleep or drink.

Sometimes, and without a set schedule, they'd still find time to go into the desert and kill vultures. Lantana, at first just a little dumb on booze, would murder anything that flew. Carl often shot at cactuses, or blew the needles off yucca plants, mostly because he was squeamish about killing anything that wasn't human. Lantana began to feel that anything living in the desert was a scavenger, and thus deserved nothing but a scavenger's fate, which was dangerous, but poetic, and incurred Carl's respect.

The idea to begin boxing had been Lantana's idea—not Carl's , as he'd later tell his wife, so as to make his bloodlust seem less inbred. Skittering up a spire of what began looking like endless success, Lantana was simply searching for a way keep himself grounded, balancing the scales of favorability. He wasn't used to such winning streaks, which he'd been having lately in every casino the Strip offered. If he could win every turn at roulette, every hand of blackjack (which appeared to be happening more and more) then he'd take his charmed luck into the ring. See if the same rules, or lack of rules, applied.

Coral, a modern day Coliseum, resided below a nightclub, also myopically called Coral. Twin brothers, from East Coast old money, managed the latter, a hand-me-down from their silk robe wearing New Jersey father. The ring itself, however, two elevator levels below, was run by a man named Donald Snikes, who, apart from being immensely strong, wore more than nine rings, mostly skulls and snakes, on his bark-dark fingers to further haunt his image. At first glance, he looked less capable of running a ring as he did at being inside it. When he and Lantana met, accidental observers may have been reminded of a nature documentary; the type where two antelope sized up each other, and sharpened their antlers over a coveted doe. The saving grace her was that they had less to earn from warring against each other than they had from warring for each other. A relationship of remarkable convenience shored up by a lack of competition.

"You like to throw fists?" This was the first question Donald Snikes asked, his rings grating as he massaged his left hand with his right hand.

"I've thrown them," said Lantana. "And they've landed where they've needed to."

"You're not that big," said Snikes. "Most dudes who come in here are big."

"I'm winning big," said Lantana. "Does my body need to be? It can hurt people, that much I know."

"I don't know you," said Snikes. His hands went to his sides, loose, and ready.

"Do you need to?" said Lantana.

"Not in this instance."

"But you need to see what I can do?"

"Now that's critical."

He nodded Lantana towards a hundred pound hanging Everlast bag. The young man walked up to it, kept a straight face—not a hint of smugness—and put one fist through the filling. Upon retraction, a sizzle of sand piled onto the floor.

"I'll pay you for it," said Lantana, wiping his knuckles.

"I'll pay you for it," said Snikes, grinning like a demon.

Lantana, under the ring name Buck Zatkin (chosen for the obvious implications of his rodeo-bull's frame), began fighting for small pickings, without complaint, but after he flattened most of the middleweights, was tailspun into high-staked matches with anyone brave enough to risk murder. He even fought an accomplished heavyweight, Manny Knox, and, in what would be swept under the blanket for the pugilist's aspiring career in years to come, pummeled him down before the third round. He became a fascination for young drunks and adulterers, men who dragged prostitutes on what they tried to call dates, and spent so much time in Coral that the ring became the catacombs and he, the slack-jawed beast who roamed them. Fights became easy, so did money, and one night, after he won a big match, so did forgetting his wife, whose genitive activities lasted until six a.m. with two women in the toilet of his dressing room whose genitive activities.

Oddly, during Lantana's wild days, Carl became a locus for moral righteousness, and spent time and words trying to pull Lantana from his thrills, which in their darkest moments turned into an LSD bender two weeks long that found its apex in a leap he took off the tilting, swirling S of the Sands Hotel. He dove backwards, legs in a pike. He twirled like the greatest human acrobat. He had a grin on his face, was wearing a jester's hat, fastened with a strap, and warbled something like, "I can see!" before impaling his eye on the hood-icon of a recently parked Mercedes.

During this time, especially after the accident, the vulture hunting also picked up, which Carl refused to engage in anymore after Lantana, while tripping balls one hot day, mistook him for a six-foot tall lizard and tried to shoot his tail off. Afterwards the weekends involved Lantana alone in the desert, firing at what he thought were vultures, but could have been angels, or devils, in the sky.

After time, winning became more of an expectation for Lantana rather than an endeavor. He didn't even have to be shrewd, as he did at the card table. In the ring, he was power. The sort that verged ultimate. He began to convince himself that there was some cosmic kismet imbued in his decisions. That the thoughts he had came in line with a purpose greater than anyone else's he'd known. Death was laughable. Yes, some holy guardian maintained plenary control over the winged tornado of his existence. If his life ever seemed chaotic, it was because purpose itself was chaotic, and you had to work within one's personal cosmic system to get anything accomplished. Lantana would never lose anything he didn't want to. A fact of which gambling was practicum. He was the amoral table tentacle that had no quarrel slurping the pockets of both his friends and his enemies, as well as the first one to leave if he felt the winds of circumstance trying to convince him of their existence. At that point he'd rise nonchalantly from his bucket chair and, like the humble brawler he truly was, volksmarch away without forfeiting a dime.

Time went by like this. Carl became more and more serious about *The Manaton*. There was the incident when he became so serious he attempted to remove all the vaginal-looking artifacts from the house, and Lantana stormed out before attempting to trounce him with a toilet seat he'd tossed in the trash. But for the most part they lived in a breathless little limbo. Money flowed and emotions were soft. There were very few things to really talk about. Until one night when Lantana lost.

August 12th:

Lantana was gambling at The Empress, where players, dealers, and security alike had found him out as, not a cheater, but one of those slick, and now one-eyed youths (not as unusual as it might sound in Las Vegas) with enough brains to make their pockets a little lighter. A virus in the system. An ineradicable germ. On this summer night, however, Lantana would meet his match. The beginning of the end. It would happen at the blackjack table, with a dealer who seemed to be suffering from pinkeye and a taste for bad bouffant haircuts. A man with a nametag pin, copper, and aslope, that dubbed his glitzy spirit: Warbuck.

Lantana was in the Dynasty Room, a commanding, matted area rimmed with glass cases, filled with full suits of Samurai armor. Each one donned a sloping helmet featuring deer horns, fish, or some god of longevity. Lanterns swung from red velvet cables, and light-skinned women dressed as Geishas swaggered through the ranks with martinis.

At first, Lantan seemed to be running the table. He snapped up a series of difficult wins in clinchers so miraculous they seemed suspicious even to him. Each hit came out narrowly in his favor. He exhaled deeply when he hit on seventeen, for instance, and pulled a four. A four. How preposterous. Not typically this reckless, Lantana found himself admitting that he'd developed a mischievous burn in his belly. Something within him, something violent, and careless, wished to challenge his luck, see how far he could take it. He played this way for a few more hands. He hit on 18, and received a 2. On 16, a 3. The obviousness of his fortune began to frighten him, and he soon decided to pull back. By the time the dealer had changed to Warbuck, he had abandoned his daring, and returned to his normal, careful self. He never wanted his impulses to overtake him, he knew. He didn't want to become cocky and discount his gifts.

Warbuck dealt Lantana two kings, fresh off the draw. The infallible winner thought for a moment that he might have hit again, maybe received an Ace. But he immediately discounted the very idea, thinking he'd already gone to far. He went inward, sucked on his teeth, and did what any judicious human would have.

He didn't put down a lot of money on the table. A couple thousand dollars. Nothing compared to previous bets. He just wanted to pay homage to his endless winning streak.

"I'll stay." He swiped his hand in secure surrender of the deck. He'd won. He knew he'd won, as he had so many times before during his stint in Las Vegas.

Warbuck looked at him, and Lantana swore he saw the faintest trace of a smile as the old, itch-eyed dealer flipped his Jack and Ace to the velvet. One club and one diamond, each one gory, and scintillating.

The Dynasty Room went silent. Warbuck dragged off the chips as if they'd been more important than all the others he'd taken that night, or any other night, since his streak had begun. Lantana had no idea what had happened. For the past few months he'd felt like he'd been living inside a wind tunnel, one carved out for him by the architects of his future. But now here he was. Foiled. Mistaken. Spurned from his highway of spoils. For Lantana, from his largess and his winnings, two thousand dollars could be chalked up to pocket change. But that wasn't what he was afraid of losing. He'd been convinced, ever since arriving five months ago, that, under no circumstance, could he, or any extension of he, be taken for a fool. That he'd been anointed by the death of his father to live on in sanctity and pleasure.

He accused Warbuck of cheating. Pinkeyed and pulling his tuxedo vest from Lantana's rough-housing, he denied the charge with almost suspicious avidity. Lantana stared at the man as if he'd been responsible for the descent of modern society, then cashed out the rest of his chips, and stomped across the El Cortez carpets of the main slot floor with their allotrope locks of kitsch in a manner never before witnessed in this cool and clever young man. Sure, people thought he had a control issue. But what active 'resident' of Las Vegas didn't have a control issue? Most men who frequented the tables looked closer to dead than alive. Some even injected their cheeks with Novocain to make their poker faces clinical. Lantana, however, and with the worst poker face he'd ever mustered, a poker face that worked against his poker face, lost 92,000 dollars that night. And then, over the next week, another 130,000.

And this was when the fighting went bad.

Lantana flew into rages when anyone, anywhere, brushed his bristling nerves. Without warning he'd lay bodies to the tarmac along The Strip—just for a stray eye or grazed knuckle—and then clop away muttering of the law. Coral, where Lantana (AKA, Buck Zatkin) was immortalized in combat, began to emulate his luck at the casino. After his week of losses at slots and black jack, he began his month of losing in battle. This wasn't because he lacked the strength to deal out anything less than a cosmic jackhammer of an uppercut, of course, but because, in his opinion, that he'd been sabotaged. Possibly by himself, but most likely by someone else.

He began to fight his opponents like he was drunk. His punches landed in what might as well have been the stratosphere. He suspected the managers of feeding him drugs, of sneaking barbiturates in the water, to make the fights more interesting. When he finally accused Donald Snikes of slipping him roofies, he received a grievous scowl, and was banned from Coral for what was said to be a few months. But Lantana, still unready to accept that he was susceptible to the whims of ordinary circumstance, went loony with paranoia, to the point where he felt everyone, even Carl, was trying to steal his inheritance, trying to conspire against him to destroy his great destiny. At Coral's front doors he'd scream on the weekends: "Give me back my right eye, you scheming bastards."

Carl began to attend to him in the sinking hole his bedroom had become. Lantana lay in the corner of his beaten-down Desert Shadow condo, on a beanbag beside the cot, gaining weight and stench and scribbling terrible poetry.

> *Twas the night of 1967,*
> *That my father trust my soul to heaven,*
> *And now, in the year 1974,*
> *My eye got fucking gouged out!*

The money was still around, there was too much to deplete, and the rent was paid on time. But Lantana spent most of his time sobbing and raging until one night he lost everything anyone could have called his wits and, taking his shotgun, lumbered off into the desert beyond Las Vegas in the only article of clothing he liked to wear during those days: a pair of blazing blue Spandex. He'd accrued them being a 'big winner' at The Empress back when big winners were forever, and unlike his money, they couldn't take it back. He also took his bankbook with him, his wallet and his father's empty box and *The Manaton*, and trudged barefoot across the rock and sand to somewhere in the East. He walked to the skirt of Nevada, neared Lake Mead and went north, and then east, and he thought if he walked long enough, far enough, the Rocky Mountains might unroll like a tapeworm. He fired at vultures, prairie dogs, anything, until the buckshot was gone and he thrashed the shotgun against a tree. Las Vegas had cheated him, taken his eye and his pride along with it, but because he, as more than a man, as a Lantana, was capable of controlling his own destiny, he continued to walk until he chose to walk no more, which was actually quite far, somewhere in Utah, in a valley of hummus-pink stone. The sun furrowed down him, and even he, with his altered plutonium blood, began to thirst. He could do little more but sit and stare blankly at the boulders scrawling ruins on the sky. He got naked, and, in attempt to relieve the heat from his skin, even allowed his Spandex to leave his body. His penis spooled down the rock in a frowning sausage, and the sun burned and burned, and he waited.

"I am my own destiny," he said. "I am my own Lantana."

A dark circle of sand razored out from under his feet. A jolt of pain spasmed his stomach. He remembered falling to the ground and hugging himself, the atmosphere shaking and buzzing with a membrane of tumult as a dot of fire, small at first, but then bigger, warmed the sky. As it got closer he tried to study it. A brown, starrish entity. It came down and down and, upon contact, blew his body backwards.

Struggling to his feet, the world was acid trip bright, with an added shade of festering onion yellow. He crept towards it, blood on his legs. From the smoke a looming pile of what looked like junk mopped out into the sand. It moved as if, below its bulk, were tiny multitudes of feet and toes, creaking, staying its course, until feet before Lantana, halting. Bare nude and even barer of mind he watched it. Then it quivered, taking up a suckling of sand so visible that it resembled a drag of smoke. He covered his eyes as the pile inflated, as it heaved all the air around it into its body, and pushed only a small bit towards the tip. It looked like a steel Zeppelin wrapped in fisherman's trawl. Lantana lifted one hand to wave at it.

As if in response, the Zeppelin burst and viscous liquid shot into the air. Lantana was bathed in its mercurial foam as its midsection split in half, and, from the drizzling effluvium, outcurled six wings. The sparkling feathers contained shreds of aluminum, bike handles, toilets, hubcaps, baseball gloves, nickel alloy, tubing, old shoes, pocket mirrors, cutlery, all of which reached out towards the sky, and soon Leonard realized exactly what existed before him—the human face, the human body. The male body. Clothed all too vividly and somewhat scandalously in a glimmering blue sequin lounge dress. The brown eyes smiled, akimbo between seashell earrings and fittingly parallactic Nashville-thick sideburns that bristled like the beard on an eagle. The lips parted, a schmaltzy gold. The hard, tubular chin looked down and measured its hands, flexing them strong as the great wings shivered in their sockets. It was then that Lantana found himself looking real hard, on the verge of panic, into the creature's eyes, and then its face, all too familiar. It gazed back at him calmly. Peaceful and at ease. And with no visage, he realized, other than his own.

"Who are you?" he remembered asking, embarrassed of his nudity.

"Iuetitia, Pietas, Dignitas, Gravitas," it said, in a voice that boomed. "The other you."

"But why?" he remembered asking again, being so tired and thirsty.

And he remembered the creature answering his question, but didn't remember what it said.

As Carl recounted it, he found Lantana in the Mojave Desert after tracking him for over six days. It had been remarkable that the man was still alive since he'd walked the length of two states. Carl brought him to colorful Colorado, per request, and en route was silently furious when Lantana, in what seemed like a fit of denial, convinced himself that his own will, and not Carl, or his devotion, had led to him surviving the desert.

"I chose to live," he said, calmly tipping his head to window in the passenger seat. "Death won't come for me unless I let it. This I know for sure." He looked to the cloudless horizon. "Fucking scavengers."

Though Carl was no less than offended by these words, he nodded over the steering wheel, and said, "So it goes, Licious. So it goes."

Lantana appeared as if abandoned at the doorstep of Lily's dormitory at Anderson East, on the Boulder Campus beneath a bridge of walnut trees. He was wearing his Spandex and a white cotton tank top. He looked clean, fresh, had a smile on his face, and the *Denver Post* aspraddle in his lap. When she saw him she recoiled, and then, as if being tugged by an invisible line, they snapped back into the ruptured conundrum of love they'd shared before, at least for a moment, before Lily hinted there was a deeper discussion that needed having. She nudged herself away with her hands. Her wedding ring was not around her finger and she had a peregrine hue of distance in her eyes. Lantana, however, put his palm to her mouth as she tried to continue, and told her that were some things not worth saying.

"But," she muffled. "So much has changed."

"Tush," he said. "Marriage is forever," and introduced a new ring, a larger ring, a ring with more than sixteen diamonds arranged in an undecagon of splendor. "Now," he said, placing his hand on the small of her back. He pushed her towards the dormitory. "Let me tell you of my inheritance."

Lily seemed to resist, but then allowed his fingers to guide her wherever they wanted. She remembered how, almost thirty-five years ago, she'd stood at the open door to his '67 Cutlass and said, "If you want to walk the tight rope alone, or even if you join the Flying Wellendas, then you're going to plummet without me. I swear to you." But now, Lantana had become more than a Flying Wellenda. He'd become the tightrope itself. And now she was the one who wanted to plummet. To fall, silently, into doom.

CHAPTER TWENTY FIVE

AT SEA

Nemo was asleep for a few hours when he awakened to the sound of a gong.

"Son of Lantana," said Carl, banging the gong again. "Rise. It is the time of your pilgrimage."

He was shaken from his sheets by BONGGGGG BONGGGGGG resounding off the western coast of California. His bed had been moved while he slept. Now he was on the edge of a cliff in the middle of the night with the sound of water drizzling up the rocks. The gong itself was massive—God knows where it came from—tooled with anfractuous dragons, and Carl was dressed in a red *fundoshi* wavering a mallet of bamboo and smelling, palpably, of booze.

"You might ask me why I am here, and not your father, or where you are, or what you're about to do, or why the fuck," he hiccuped, "I married a man, and the answer to all of those questions would be: yes.

"Now," he slurred, the fundoshi riding the tense little interstice between his ass cheeks, "let me tell you a little bit about myself. I was born dead, literally stillborn for three days, but now I am alive. I've been married to six women in five different countries, you won't find me in the phonebooks, and I am sworn to your father by the order of *The Manaton* to serve him till the end of his days."

"I'm cold, Carl," said Nemo, grabbing his elbows.

"That's because you're Homophiliac. But we can fix that. Manu!"

Carl looked himself over, practically naked, and watched his own calves wobble.

"Take a little bit of this," he said, handing Nemo some of Daphne's pot, which Nemo grappled for gratefully. Carl relit it, and, upon puffing, began to cough, before handing it to him. "That'll warm you up."

The boy continued to suck on the cigarette almost without thinking, the harsh, skunky fumes, but it was true—after a moment he did feel a little warmer. Sliding from his sheets he came to stand before Carl, poised on a briny stump, his hands on his hips. Then he smoked a little more of the joint. Then a little more, and Nemo had a little more too, and, as opposed to doing anything they were supposed to be doing they formed smiles and began singing "Conjunction Junction" before Carl shushed them and resumed.

"See that boat down there?" he slurred.

"No," giggled Nemo.

"Look, man," said Carl, sucking the legs off the joint. He pointed to a tiny white blot in the sea, a rowboat, swishing at the bottom of the moor. "It's a boat."

"Yea," said Nemo, rubbing his eyes. "I'm hungry."

"Well," Carl said. "Down in that boat, there's a bunch of tasty munchies."

"Munchies?"

"Food. To eat."

"Really?"

"Sure thing."

"But why down there. In the boat?"

"It's my secret, fucking nautical stash."

"Nautical?"

"So no one will find out."

"But it's so far away."

"Don't worry," said Carl. "There's a path. I'll take you there."

And Carl did take Nemo down the path to the bottom of the moor.

As they moved closer the small boy sensed a spell in the weed, chasing away time. He saw the boat, a small, crepitating dinghy snagged to an excuse for a pier. The sky was full of stars, but the ocean was turbulent.

"Go on," said Carl. "Go see for yourself."

"But there's nothing here," said Nemo, tumbling in. He smelled fish. Under the bough of the boat there was a canvas sack. Half-soaked.

"Look closer," said Carl. He picked up something from below the pier.

"Where?" asked Nemo.

"Down, below the stern."

As Nemo bent down, Carl, yowling, fanned a machete in his right hand, above his head, and slashed the rope loose, sending the boat out to sea.

"Carl, wait!" yelled Nemo.

"See that islet over there," Carl said, pointing the blade to a mound of earth jutting from the ocean, not too far away, but far enough away to require nautical savvy. "Just grab the oars and hinge them in the joists. In your sack you'll find instructions. I'll see you in two days."

He turned away.

"But what am I supposed to do?"

But the rangy figure was already giggling his way back up the cliff-side. Nemo turned to the water and, feeling the tide hale him further off the coast, touched it with the thought of swimming. It was far too cold. Inside the sack were two nautical flares and a piece of notebook paper with chicken scratch, numbers, what could have been a map but looked more like a four-year-olds' rendering of a moose. As he tried to decipher it with weedy eyes, a heavy wind picked up and snagged it from his hands. Water spilled into the boat and he fell backwards.

"Hee hee," Carl could be heard sniggering above the waves. "Hee hee." But his voice soon disappeared.

Coughing from the salt spray Nemo gripped one of the nautical flares and, after toggling its lid, calcium phosphide cauterized the air. He waved it in a circle, screaming, "Carl, the map! Help me," thinking about nothing but the fact that, hours ago, he'd been sleeping in one of the most beautiful parts of America, an Eden, and had been pleasantly stoned, but was now lost in a lenticular nothing, a lightless part of the globe where the stars weren't bright enough to guide him. No one seemed to notice as he rocked away and away and finally his throat felt hoarse from screaming and he settled back with the flare spitting from where he stuck it on the bow of the ship between two pried apart planks. Nemo sat against the stern, sulking as he looked for land. A few moments later the flare squeezed from its perch and, frightened at the distance he could see it sink, fumblishly prised up the other one. He took handle on the oars, flare in his teeth, and tried to row, but his arms became sore quickly and he gave to the tide. For almost an hour he forgot his predicament. He got lost in thoughts of old comforts and whether they'd actually been comforts, fearful memories, dreams of beasts, but then stood up screaming and wobbling the flare, finding that he'd drifted further away from the mainland and towards nothing. He saw no island, only water and water. The sad, foreign society of water. He didn't want to know what circled beneath, and instead curled up in the bottom of the boat and pretended he was alone inside a larger womb of wood, holding the flare as it faded, with one tired arm, into the seaborne empyrean.

Later he awoke to a sound that startled him. He jolted his head and saw nothing but moonlight, liquid, maybe a shape like the back of a shovel falling beneath the waves.

Later than that he awoke to what might have been a storm. The fringe of a storm. But small.

Even later a seabird came to roost on the portside. One of its eyes had gone blind, and it searched the space between the planks for food with dizzy compulsion. When it opened its beak the most delicious sound spilled forth. It had a white underbelly, twig parts for legs. It seemed to find something in the space between the planks, for it chortled and reared its head up as if to swallow, but then whirled its beak in delirious diffidence, and with the tedious thrill of the insane.

Near morning—the sky through his closed lids was yellow—he awoke to the sound of human voices.

"Is that him, Aggy?" asked a man with a weasel-pitched gobble.

Nemo stayed quiet.

"Yea, that's him," said the second voice—a lower, more cranking purl.

"Is he alive?"

"Don't know."

"I don't care if he is."

"I know you don't."

"Don't like alive."

"So throw yourself in the Goddamn ocean."

"I will one day, Aggy. And won't stop talking. Even when I do."

There was the rush of waves, but Nemo's boat was anchored. The bough tipped up and down.

"But I guess He needs him," the higher voice said. "So says the book."

"So says Him," said the other man.

"And the book."

"You are a fucking factual inaccuracy."

"Agreed," he sulked, and they stopped for a moment. "But don't say such things about the book."

"You didn't even know the book until we showed it to you."

"Did too."

"Bull shit."

Nemo pretended he was asleep, or unconscious, anything but afraid as two fat boots smacked to the floor of his ship. The rubber soles creaked loud as old driftwood, and though the smell of the large man's clothes was clean, his breath was saltier than the sea as his shoulders hoisted Nemo off his boat and placed him on the surface of something much larger. Then he heard the voice of the smaller one, like a bitch in heat, skittering on the deck. A motor panted somewhere, and upon opening one eye saw the sky was a moving thing, taking Nemo along with it, somewhere in purposeful direction against the waves.

The small one laughed a little, and Nemo heard the sound of eating.

"Big fish," he said through his chewing. "Fearful of the pond."

Lantana found Carl sleeping in his fundoshi on the cliffside in Nemo's relocated bed. He had a bottle of Mad Dog 20/20 shoved between his legs, it was almost empty and partly covered up the fact that one of his testicles leaked through the cotton like a waxing zombie moon. Lantana was dressed in his hero fatigue, his flaring red toga and titanium club. He was a living obsessive-compulsion, dressed up even on vacation. He'd been awake and one could see the insomniac in his eyes. He was man who didn't like to sleep because it made him vulnerable, and unable to carry out the particularities of his trade. His vocation was subject to more than a little change. Acts of heroism were accompanied with loneliness—no triumph was meaty enough to sate his appetite for praise. He searched for vindication like a drunk for misery, sacrificing whatever he could for that next bump of approval. Scars simmered up his ankles and arms. There was a fat, fresh one down his cheek. He was wet, and tired. His skin burned by morning. With his golden sandal he nudged Carl's cheek and the salty clams flickered right open.

"What happened to you?" said Carl. "You look terrible."

"Where is my son?" asked Lantana, leaning on his club. He limped off what seemed to be a bad ankle. "Tell me, now."

Surrounded by last night's evidence of debauchery, his cohort grinned.

"I sent him on a quest."

"A quest?"

"Licious," Carl said, rubbing his eyes. He stood up on the cot and stretched his arms to the sky. "I was saving you the grief of having to re-program that kid, as well as convincing you I had no idea that woman I married was a man. No idea!" He licked his lips. "You've got to trust me. This'll work."

"What did you do to him, Carl?" Lantana asked.

"Nothing too crazy."

"Nothing like what?"

"Oh, you know? Typical stuff."

"Such as?" he gripped Carl's wrist.

"Nothing, man," he whined. "Jeez. I just sent him out to sea in a rowboat to find an Osprey egg on an island off the coast, or something."

"A rowboat?" Lantana's other fist tightened around his club. "Or something?"

"Relax, Licious. He's got nautical flares and a map I drew on some napkin. And a bag of chips, depending on how many bags I bought. If I bought two bags of chips, than he has one, but then again, I've been known to eat more than my stomach can take, especially when I got the herb on hand," he held up his diminished bag of pot. "But yea, your kid's on a boat; reminds me of this time I was a kid and my Dad took me fishing and before we set out he dared me to touch some woman's tits—because she had these iron set of double D's, fucking monstrous, at this chicken and waffles bar, Hadleys, around six a.m., this was in Louisiana when we were stationed at Barksdale—and when I touched them she slapped me in the face so hard I got a concussion and was sent to juvie for six months. Tits, Lantana. All 'cause of tits. You think the same God that created us created tits? No. I think there are two Gods. One for all of us who wanna touch tits without repercussion, and one for everything else.

"Jeez," he threw his fists in the air. "How could she have been a man, Licious? I loved her. I fucking loved her!"

Lantana took Carl by his *fundoshi*, pulled it off, and threw it off the cliff.

"Oh come on," said Carl. "People know me around here."

Lantana pushed Carl and his wattle of a penis aside. He set his hand above his eyes and scanned the western seaboard. Nothing. Above him was a morning trying to escape the tide of gulls and ospreys, a sun fleeing the coast from flapping wings. Then, without noticing, he found he was gripping the empty box in his right hand. His fingernails were warping the roof of the vinyl. He wasn't sure how long he'd been gripping it, last night, a lot of nights, were blurring together in some collapsing monstrance of violence and glory. The great 'fuck you.' In his mind, thoughts of his father made him feel just as vacant as what was inside that box, just as lacking for answers and history as the old Scotsman had ever been.

"Look," said Carl. "Don't worry about Nemo. He'll be fine."

Lantana, teary-eyed, punched Carl in the face. In his other hand he twirled the empty box with his fingers lingering over the ocean, before feeling sinful and placing it back inside his toga. That was the only place to keep anything safe, including the anythings he hated.

The thought came to him of dying, and not necessarily of him dying, but people dying in general, a boy lost at sea drying up with the sun, desiccating with time against the bilge of a boat until skin turned to tarpaulin and thought: was that what you put inside a box for hopes and dreams? A boy's skin like a dried frog's? Nightmares could fill a father's mind when imagining the death of his (even if bi-curious) son.

"I need to get laid, Zatkin," Carl said, lying naked on the coast of Mendocino. "Yea." He stretched his arms and legs, taking another joint to his bruised lips and lighting it. "That'll do me good."

CHAPTER TWENTY SIX

LANTANA AND THE BATTLE FOR KANSAS

In 2003, Lantana, The Savage, Zatkin, watched the sky over Kansas for signs of impending doom.

In that forlorn sea of cattle, wheat, corn, and sorghum grain, he'd come to Finney, following the anonymous, electronic chortle of a villain calling himself The Brother who apparently had a nuclear bomb aimed and ready in the direction of the Sunflower State.

Lantana watched the sky, his toga still in the humid Midwestern slough as the sun made hell of his retinas. He wasn't sure he even believed the fact that The Brother existed, that this anonymous, self-proclaimed villain, in all probability, was some sex-deprived soul out of Ohio with a mouse pad and a pink, pimpled penis. But still, when The Savage was taunted on his rarely attended website, **www.whalebone.com**, into foiling this unfoilable crime, there was no other choice but action, fueled by boredom and egoistic woes.

In the middle of Finney's town square, which was really less of a town and more of statement on the sadness of Middle America, he found a small, silver present box, wrapped in white ribbon. It sat on a raised stone divider.

He fumbled it open, tired, and hungry. On the inside was a Ken doll, wearing a toga, with a painted-silver cue tip meant to be Lantana's titanium club, and golden sandals painted on the feet. Beside the doll was a tape recorder and he held it to his ear and pressed play.

To forget your brother is not a little sin, said a voice that seemed incapable of not laughing. It is the destruction of Kansas.

The voice clicked into static, and Lantana, after securing the video camera he'd placed on a tripod and aimed 95 unmeasured degrees, looked to the sky.

On a rooftop no more than fifty yards away, Lily watched her husband stumble. She watched him through binoculars, spread out on her stomach. He didn't know of her presence, and she hoped he wouldn't know. Ever since the birth of their son Nemo, and the lethargic growth of the lioness Steve Two, and her husband's lapse into a careerism so fanatical that he'd forgotten her right to exist, she'd felt this desire to make herself exist, like a shadow nailed bloodily to his heels. She thought about what she'd begun building in the fourth garage of their house, a place they referred to as The Gravitas. She removed a vial of milky liquid from the pocket of her labcoat and let it slip between her lips.

In the sky over Kansas, The Brother's threat became a reality. Lantana almost laughed upon seeing it, shiny and white, and then began to hop in place. "Holy shit holy shit," he tittered, clapped his hands. "Holy shit." He turned to the camcorder. "You'd better be recording."

Lily, looking above through her binoculars, saw the unspeakable pitching through.

After Lantana finished his dance, and the sweat beaded into his eyes, he then realized he had no idea what to do. How exactly did one stop a nuclear bomb hurtling towards the great state of Kansas? He thought of various scenarios, particularly the one he was standing in right now. Then, he remembered the night he fought the Kraken. How he'd flown into the beast's raging oculus under the countenance of heaven and ayahuasca, and how he'd seen the stars, spoke to them, and asked them for opinions, and then suffered their imminent wrath. It was one thing to battle an illusion, but another altogether to battle what one once thought was an illusion after it too quickly became a reality.

"Oh fuck," he said, and then resorted to the only thing he could think of. From his duffle bag, he removed what Lily had once defined roughly as a laser rifle, even if, in a more generous opinion, it looked more like a potato launcher. He'd taken it from The Gravitas without telling her and wasn't even sure what it would do.

"Alright," he said, aiming it skyward. "Okay."

He pulled the trigger.

"Alright."

He pulled the trigger again.

"Alright," he said. "Alright."

Apparently what it did was not work.

As Lantana let the rifle slip to the ground Lily covered her mouth and chuckled. Even as what could have been death approached them all, Lantana could still make her laugh. He was like watching a one man improv. She observed her husband as he raged at the ground. He tore off his toga and tossed it to the sky. From the inopportune town of Finney, Kansas, a few men and women and even children crept out from the barbershop, a bank, and a bar. They watched this savage in his primeval tantrum and then shaded their eyes to the sky.

Lily stood up upon what she thought was the local radio station, leaning a little on the crossbars of a midsize antenna. She crackled her knuckles and whispered, "Ready, Father?" Lantana, mostly naked save for his Spandex and sandals growled and scratched at his chest, stared at the falling bomb. Lily lifted her arms. He stared at the falling bomb as he'd stared at The Kraken, and then, with all his lungs, screamed. From Lily's fingers emitted a light, a serpentine twist of electricity, in tandem with Lantana's howl. The bomb stuttered and hung in mid-air. As if timid, it diverted meekly to the west, disappearing slowly over the flat horizon until there was nothing but sun and serenity.

Lantana watched it flee from his vocals and, after a moment of drooling, smiling, began leaping, yelling, "Did you see that?" And spun through the square, frightening townspeople back into their stores. "Did you, huh? Did you? I, the mighty Savage, have saved Kansas with nothing more than my might roar. I am America's greatest hero. I am what you all want to be."

Lily then, closing her eyes, was able to guide the acceleration of the bomb, as if she were its ancient Soviet guidance system, and then deposit it in a place she knew would be safe, over the plains, under the radar of Lowry Air Force Base, into the suburbs of Broomfield, Colorado, using only her mind. There was a bunker she'd prepared for situations like this—a woman, like many of her generation, who had doom built into her instincts as familiarly as hunger and thirst. Twenty feet beneath the ground in a hanger in the side of a dried down reservoir, she released it, and then fell gasping to the ground. She smiled and hugged herself, body shuddering with youth. She felt pleasant pain, her insides sore.

"Number One," Lantana boasted, hands on his hips, as his wife, unknown to him, fainted. "That's right—hold your autographs, baby, this world needs a number one."

CHAPTER TWENTY SEVEN

HELL OR ANTARCTICA

Nemo travelled on the boat for days. He remembered it was the smaller man, the one called Peccadillo, who with a bored and unsatisfied air of ennui, flicked his cheek with a sharpened fingernail, and slapped it just to make sure he was awake, before injecting him with the sleeping drug. After that, he awoke in lightless room, walls of wood, where there was a little light slipping through a dank port window, and a starved smudge of clouds, and sea birds. When night came he felt disembodied. In the darkness, the lost light adjudged from the window noshed his sense of space and time away, little by little, especially when there were too many obstacles for the stars. Sometimes the boat seemed to change direction, or maybe it was the work of the waves, the chugging that awoke him, the drummel of rain, reminding him of his confinement.

Whenever he fell asleep is when they came. He knew they came because in the morning there was food on a peeled plastic platter. There was milk and meat, a little corn porridge. He ate abstemiously, and rationed. Whoever it was who'd imprisoned him was intent on keeping him healthy, even remarkably so, with a certain quality of freshness to everything he ate, and soon he found that he was not simply within the jurisdiction of torturers or murderers, but someone intent on his blindness, like stonemasons or other, less savory guilders intent on hiding their domain.

He remembered his father and mother. And Jeffrey Westcott. He dreamed in bursts of inaction and longing, of not being able to walk, or having his knees crumple beneath him. Prickles of blood awaited him in the morning along and down his forearm. He felt like he'd awoke on the fringe of a coma, but unlike before couldn't dig up the strength to become afraid for himself or call out.

One morning beyond other mornings he awoke in a different room where there was light, small portal windows and a humming sound above and below him and bumps in the ground. Little hiccups. His ears were plugged with nothing but air, and he was in a stiff seat, blue canvas, across from a very handsome old man wearing a furry, and noticeably too hot, Ushanka.

"I'm not interested in most of what you're going to say," he said. He wore straight-legged jeans, and a button-down white cotton shirt with an Aztec border, where six spear-armed Indians in leather breechcloths and warbonnets made their stampede.

"You can ask questions, but it doesn't mean I'll answer them."

"Where am I?" Nemo asked.

"You're on a plane."

Nemo looked around him, adjusting to what he always felt was a Mesopotamian sort of light found on aircrafts. It was a small plane, and stenciled squares of land monotonized the horizon out the window.

"Where are we going?" he asked.

"To get The Book."

"Why?"

"Next question."

"What's your name?"

The older, handsome man smiled. "Call me. . .B."

From his side he drew a large carving knife, a Kukri, holstered in lambskin. He removed the scabbard and set it on the tray between he and Nemo, where he could see it better.

"What is a knife?" asked the man after a moment.

Nemo looked at him askew. There was a comical aspect to him, dressed as someone who took himself too seriously.

"I asked, what is a knife?"

Nemo then realized this was his question to answer.

"I don't know," he said.

"It would be better if you try."

"Well," said Nemo, hating why, as opposed to fear, he felt a ticking slowness in his fingers and brain. "A knife is used to cut."

"And?"

"I don't know."

"You do know."

"But. . . ."

"Pick it up."

Nemo obeyed, picking up the knife, too heavy for his hand. He took it with the other hand and held it before his chest.

"Now answer the question."

He arced the Kukri to the left.

"To hurt?" he asked, more guessing at the man's desires than the knife itself.

"Yes," said B. "And no. A knife can do too many things to be referred to by just one word. A knife can be used to kill. A knife can be used to share. I had a brother once, who shared everything with me. He was, in essence, a big, beneficent blade."

His mouth opened wide, not in a smile, but in readiness to swallow something arbitrary.

"What do you think about infinity?" he then asked.

Nemo began to put down the knife.

"Pick it back up," he ordered, taking his hands to his knees and leaning forward. His teeth horsed out between his lips.

"What do you think about infinity?" he asked again.

"It makes me scared," Nemo said, watching the sliver of blade tremble between his crossed eyes. Due to the drugs they'd been giving him, 'scared' was something he knew but could not feel. "Like bats and the ocean."

"Well, that's pretty damn specific of you," B said. When he spoke his pupils remained still, so much so that all those comical aspects Nemo had seen in him before began to evaporate. "There's an order of things, isn't there?" he asked. "Like a food chain."

"I don't know," Nemo said.

"I remember, when I was young, staring at clouds in the sky like they were little presents from heaven. . .sheep and bunnies and tiger cubs. Fur. So I started to look at them everyday. I just loved all those faces from God, up there and unknown, sleepy angels with perky wings and even. . .perkier ambitions." He bent down, began to remove his boots. "But then I realized that white, fluffy clouds could become steaming cirrocumulus—as if they had teeth—and beyond them, if you went high enough, a vast ionosphere, and beyond that ionosphere, ozone, and beyond the ozone, a thing called space, and beyond space, more space, and more space, and more space, and more space, and more space, and, well, it just didn't stop going, you know."

Nemo nodded, head dipping towards the knife.

"But," he said, watching the boy suddenly with shocking interest. "You seem to be a person who knows much about nothing. I can see it in you, right now. You're a clever boy, and you're going to turn into a brilliant man. We'll have too much in common for either of us to be friends."

"Can I put down the knife?" Nemo asked, feeling weak in the arms. They were already shaking a little from the weight.

"After you do something for me," said the man in the black Ushanka. He set his boots against the ground, came out of his chair and crossed the airplane floor, warping his steps, to Nemo's level. His breath was scentless, but the smell of his aftershave was so cheap and heavy it could have made the air-conditioning cough.

"You're going to cut off the very tip of your least necessary finger," he said.

Nemo blinked.

"You're going to cut off the very tip of your least necessary finger. As a choice."

Nemo shook his head at the knife.

"No."

"Oh, yes," he spoke to him like one should speak to a child, but too sweet.

"I can't. They're—they're all necessary."

"You can," he said with enthusiasm, even friendliness. "And when you do, you'll realize that you're wrong. See, the point of most exercises in dispelling denial," he took the boy's hand, made it grip the knife, "is discovering something new about yourself." He forced it towards his left hand. "I'll help you choose."

"Sir."

"Call me B."

"B?"

The cowboy pulled the boy by the hair and stuffed his face to the table.

"Get ready."

He took Nemo's hand and made it hold the knife to the other hand, which he pinned down with his elbow.

"Now watch it as this unnecessary little nothing leaves you," he said.

"Please don't."

"No apologies. Concentrate. Watch what happens. Slow as it goes. Permanent as a piece of marble from the dick of the David." The knife broke the skin. "Through, through."

Nemo screamed.

"The bone."

"EEEEEE!"

"There," said the man, hand and stampeding Indians splattered with what seemed to be the terminal endings of their hunt. "All done. Now isn't that better? So much easier to see how beautiful things are after they're gone."

Nemo bucked over his hand, holding it, rocking and too numb to shed tears.

"Oh, come on," said the handsome man in the black Ushanka, making a fist around the dissevered finger. "Don't be so dramatic." He began to laugh and nudged him with his fist, almost kindly, before shaking his head and taking a bottle of Wild Turkey from beneath the chair. He unscrewed the bottle and took a little swig. Firewater down his chin.

He then took it and dumped over Nemo's hand, soaking his clothes and seat with blood and liquor.

"The pinky is the least necessary digit, Manatonian," he scolded. "It's not like I asked for your hand."

CHAPTER TWENTY EIGHT

THE MAN IN THE BLACK USHANKA

1939.

1939, October the 16th.

1939, October the 16th, and two Barrage Balloons trundle in flames over the Forth Bridge. They are sweeping, silent, dying Gods. They turn the sunset diuretic over Edinburgh, bowels loosing through nylon skin, and cascade beyond the bridge to the River Forth, their last, laborious sizzle of altruism fraying and moaning beneath them. Concrete Dragon's Teeth jaw down the beach between Cramond and Cramond Island and, off shore, the surf seems to quiet, humbled by the staler lulls in war. Blackout curtains seethe across window-panes, candles sputter up, radios sizzle; tired, frightened voices beat down the advance, tell everyone to stay calm. Some fortunate families flee to the Anderson shelters if they have them, and huddle to the walls, fearing the sirens. The anti-aircraft boom—can German dive-bombers fly higher now?—and occasional whimpers are heard outside as something, somewhere, in many somewheres, is razed to auriferous rubble.

In one Anderson shelter at the Corner of Balgreen road below a pill box, a boy, a thief, but not yet a murderer, who calls himself Jimmy because he likes the way it sounds—and no one else bothers to call him anything else—is offered solace by a man named Fingal, a successful barrister, and retired soldier. He is also the great grandson of Beamish, great grandson of Beamish, but of which Jimmy knows nothing. Fingal has a son about Jimmy's age, which, the thief approximates, is somewhere between twelve and thirteen, though he can't be sure, and that boy, Duncan the Second, was born what people call 'touched.' Jimmy, upon meeting Duncan, finds conversation to be impossible (not that he's mastered the art of lasting dialogue). All the boy does upon being asked a question is grow a wry, meaningless smirk at the sides of his lips, knead his fingers with bitten down thumbs, and say something of grunts, or foul bits of language, with spittle falling from his mouth.

Fingal makes conversation with Jimmy in the way a father might. Asks him where he's from, if he'd been separated from his family during the raid? Jimmy lies a little, says he's lost his parents, which is marginally true being that the woman he'd been born to, a Maldivian prostitute, abandoned him before the age of four.

The ground shakes in the Anderson. The air is stenched. Fingal grows a look of concern. "These damned Krauts," he says, looking to his son, his slug of an offspring, alert but drooling. "If they wanted to win a war, they'd be doing what we're doing, isn't that right, Duncan?"

For hours they keep in a tired little huddle. Duncan, in the corner, finds lint, dust bunnies, spiders, and other insects to toy with. When no one but Jimmy is looking, he pulls the legs off the bugs one by one and drops them in a small pile. Whenever Fingal turns away, he taps Jimmy on the shoulder. "Look," he says, and then nudges harder with his elbow. "Look!" And Jimmy is forced to take a glimpse. "I did." He hits his fists against his knees. "I did, I did, I did."

There is something artful in his arrangement of death, something that shows he's familiar with weaving hemiptheral tapestry. Jimmy pauses to watch, transfixed, as Duncan pulls apart a grasshopper before his eyes and splits apart its guts on the ground.

Fingal turns on the radio, and smiles occasionally whenever he sees his son fraternizing with something that isn't the wall. It's easy to see the boy has no friends. A dangerous child. Bred to be so, perhaps.

Finally they all try to sleep to the kettle-boom of bombs, the sirens, the muted calls for order, and when they begin to snore, Jimmy forces himself awake. Years as a thief have taken away his slumber; rather, he works best when the world sleeps. It's when people sleep that he loots the dead, the living, when he slips amongst the drunks and their inarticulate pockets, makes his own undernourished ones swell. Being unable to sleep at night is also the reason he always keeps his shoes on tight. Feet are the part of him he needs most. They separate him from the slow. He is convinced they are a gift from a divine benevolence. Endowed from a non-familial source.

As a thief Jimmy has looted anything and everything. He's stolen virginity, or what some endowed man's daughter named Alice Coddleflaugh claimed to be her virginity, entrusted on a deed as one would signify land, and spent considerable time figuring out what do with it. But tonight, while Fingal and Duncan sleep, Jimmy is strangely uninterested in theft. And not because he can't get away with it. Should he wish, he could easily nose through their belongings and lurch a penny richer into the warzone outside. Instead, he looks upon the shovel-chinned man sleeping with arms around his stomach, the rise of his shoulders, the knicks of their blades, and feels, for a moment, the need to stay somewhere and be someone that people can talk to.

In the morning he awakes to Duncan holding his arms to his groin. The boy is fat in his threadbare pajamas, and the normal amount of spittle he seems to produce, yellow, dog-like stuff, drips down Jimmy's left cheek.

"We going," he says. "Now."

"Good job, Son," laughs Fingal, strapping their belongings into a sack as Duncan rolls to his stomach. He then asks Jimmy if he'd like to spend a few days at their home until he finds a better place to go.

A cordial offering.

Jimmy nods.

Fingal pats his head.

Duncan slowly gropes his own testicles.

They emerge into light, expecting the death of all Scotland, but instead, the air smells clean, feet stir cobblestone, little pikes of smoke rise not only from blast sites, but chimneys and sewers. A boringly common day.

Fingal's house, like their Anderson structure, resides on the corner of Balgreen Road. It's a cozy cottage with a slated roof, and, upon entering, shows anyone worth a damn that money has been spent. Firstly, even the vastest of space appears off limits. Each room exudes an ancient sense of ownership. The dust itself has even grown ornery. Jimmy is housed respectfully in the upper loft, in the exact same room as Duncan, on a smaller bed. The lilac sheets look undisturbed, and as he crawls into them, feel like they might bleed. He's never touched something so clean, and that cleanliness, that mild intimation of sterility, makes his fingers feel like trench knives. He refuses to look at himself in the mirror, and remembers to sleep in his shoes, just in case the world, as usual, wakes up to recognize his betrayals.

"Digney," says Duncan, nodding off towards the bed with his loquat of a head. When Jimmy doesn't answer he repeats, "Digney, Digney," slamming his fist against the wall.

At the commotion, Fingal comes inside.

"What he means to say is, this bed was meant for Duncan's brother, Digney."

"But Digney dead," says Duncan.

"Yes," says Fingal, nodding his head sadly. "Digney is dead."

Jimmy decides not to inquire any further into the subject. He promises he'll be careful with the deceased brother's belongings, but still stays cautious, afraid of what Duncan might do should the fragile constructs of his universe be disturbed. The room is glaciated in what isn't the past, but a clear lack of effort, and that laziness is monitored incessantly. If Jimmy tries to organize his meager belongings, Duncan flails them around the room. If Jimmy tries to wash his face, Duncan throws tile grime or chimney soot on his forehead. Daily, since neither of them go to school, it's customary for Fingal to instruct them on what he calls the Ways of the World. And it's in that instruction that Jimmy first learns of the first thirteen chapters of *The Manaton*.

Their daily lessons begin at seven a.m., in which Jimmy and Duncan, following tea and toast, make their way down to the basement. This is a small, limestone structure with a water-warped mahogany table, two chairs, and an abused blackboard that can hardly be spelled upon. The walls look fat, pregnant in places, or riddled with tumors of dirt. Light or rain ekes its way through a crack, ushering in the aroma of sewage.

At first, Jimmy finds solace in this new education. He teaches himself how to read, but only barely. If anything, *The Manaton* provides him with grounds in which to advance his command of the English language. The only problem with that, however, is that all other books have been banned in Fingal's house, and, if anything unorthodox were to make its way through, punishments, severe ones, would take place, or so was decreed early on.

When teaching, Fingal treats Aesop Mac'Cool's words like a puzzle of infinite propriety, and often stretches the lines and sayings far beyond probable meaning. Over time Jimmy notices these exaggerations are purposeful, and expertly placed. As Fingal explains over and over, Beamish, in an act of cultural, intellectual, and philosophical betrayal, was cruelly torn from the final chapters of his own book, which he founded and wrote decades ago. This thievery was enacted by a piratical-turd of a man who called himself Aesop Mac'Cool, who is, quite openly and to this day responsible for all of their ills. The spiritual equivalent to Beelzebub, and the boogey man, cultish and bloodthirsty, lurking behind all misdeeds.

Over time, Jimmy begins to sympathize with these poor, disenfranchised people, these creatures from a society galumphing about in search of home, a home of whose origin resides in the unknown, final chapters of Beamish's text. Who wouldn't sympathize with such sadness? Incurred by an enemy within their reach? Apparently, at the end of the book resides a detailed map to solace, a land of peace, and eternity, and kindness. One day they hope to reclaim what is rightfully theirs.

By any means possible.

The boy, Duncan, who he'd first perceived as a threat, becomes marginally sweet. Jimmy sees that as long as he doesn't disturb his oblong sense of disorder, Duncan always offers him his chocolate rations, saying things like, "You eat," and then smiling while Jimmy chews. Fingal is a generous man as well, almost suspiciously so, at times, and, though visiting with the neighborhood boys is forbidden, buys Jimmy new clothes so he'll look presentable before the dirty, time-warped family mirror. He also, upon much request, brings him home a copy of *Frankenstein*, which he reads in less than two days, and then proceeds to reread for weeks to come. It's so uncommon for such a thing to make its way into their home that Jimmy feels elated, like an honored emissary from a respected land abroad. *The Manaton* is studied, and soon Jimmy is just as ready to interpret the text as his peer, and excels in doing so (which isn't much contest versus Duncan) until he genuinely hungers for more. Duncan is given additional assignments, all nocturnal. Assignments specifically not meant for Jimmy. Whatever brutal tasks the boy's forced to undergo are kept veiled in secrecy, but it's known that in order to train his muscles he jumps rope with the iron linked chain he keeps on a shelf in the closet. His triceps grow monstrous, his shoulders wider than a hangman's beam. He snarls strength at every lift of the links; his eyes pop from his head.

"Take off your shoes, Jimmy," Fingal tells him often, noticing the boy wears them as they'd fed into his flesh.

"Even when you're at war, you take off your shoes. Open feet help for concentration."

London is bombed in 1940, blitzed, and there are dark rumors in the land of the Reichdom. In Fingal's house, however, life is still happy, and he resolves to calling Jimmy 'son,' which leads to Duncan calling him 'brother,' and leads all of them to laughing and studying, celebrating birthdays, divining presents. Soon, towards the time when Jimmy turns fifteen and the war has swept through Europe, talk emerges about a man by the last name of Sikophsky who's established himself in Edinburgh, after fleeing Poland. Though Fingal never shares too much with Jimmy, he informs him that this man, this bastard of a man, is a descendent of the Mac'Cools, and possesses what they've always longed for: *The Manaton* in its entirety. The urgency with which he speaks of this contains no humor. He may as well be talking about a loved one's burial.

Another birthday passes, Duncan's this time, and the Russians claim the battle of Stalingrad. Duncan has grown into a fat, quixotic, but strangely sympathetic teenager. Aside from the fact that he occasionally has to be kept from torturing an alley cat, or bashing in the head of whoever regards him askew, he bestows Jimmy with half of everything he has, whether food, toys, even a bicycle, which he lends to the former-thief whenever he's beckoned to pedal his ashen ass to and from the market. He somehow stumbles upon some printings of Victorian pornography, and the sound of him masturbating is unforgettable. But at least he's found a way to curb what could have landed him in prison. Duncan is not a candidate for romance.

Fingal takes to his study a lot, drawing maps and writing letters, often skipping meals in long succession. The sirens wail. Soldiers ship out. Europe is sanded down to its skeleton.

One night Jimmy awakens to Duncan crawling into his wider, lumpier bed, from somewhere beyond the front doors to their home. It is past midnight, raining outside. Jimmy watches with one avid eye, before noticing that his roommate's knuckles, though washed, are still traced with blood, and that his fat, baleful face, is blushed with bruises.

"Where were you?" Jimmy asks, as Duncan stares at the ceiling.

The gummy teeth smile.

"My duty."

He then, as if drugged, falls asleep, knuckles crossed, without so much as toggling the bedsheets.

Nothing is said about the previous night while they imbibe tea and toast in the morning. As he teaches in the basement, snapping the board with his fingernails, Fingal looks mildly amused, though somewhat desperate in that amusement, as if he's gotten a simile of something he's wanted, but not quite achieved the goal. Jimmy and Duncan are approaching the age of eighteen, though Duncan looks more like he's thirty. With his shirt off at night, and his face mangled, he could be the battle-axed guardian to any netherworld or proverbial manifestation of judgment day.

When the lesson's over, Fingal approaches the two of them and, from an abused box, a barnacled, underwater coffin of a thing, pulls out the black Ushanka. He handles it as one would handle an artifact of divinity, letting the fur only tickle the bottom of his fingers before allowing it rest upon the table, and then taking two steps back, for proper reverence.

"Do you know what this is?" he asks them.

Jimmy knows what it is, but allows Duncan to answer.

"Beamish," he grunts. "Beamish hat."

"That's right," says Fingal, smiling at his son, before plopping it atop his prematurely bald skull. It tilts towards his left ear.

"After last night, you've earned it," he continues, nodding towards the dried blood on his knuckles. "And you'll continue to earn it. Manolitude. Manancer. Mana."

Duncan the Second laughs riotously and pounds the table with his fists.

"Earned it! Earned it!" He sings. "Earned it!"

"And as for you, Jimmy," Fingal coos. He puts his hand on the teenager's right shoulder.

"You're one of us, now. A Beamite. Always a Beamite. And know, that no matter what happens to any of us, that you'll always have a home. Here. In this house. Or anywhere we reside." He looks down at his pink feet, ten, perfect toes. "Which I see you've come to realize. One day, who knows, you might be able to fight for the cause. But we'll get there when we get there."

Jimmy looks up at him. "Manease. Manipulate. Mana!"

Later that night, before they go to bed, Duncan, in what has become his nighttime attire, a posy-pink nightgown trimmed with French lace, sits down next to Jimmy on the bedside.

"Brother," he says, his rumpled, fat buttocks tilting the mattress.

He pulls the Ushanka from its box beneath the bed, takes it out, and places it on Jimmy's head.

Jimmy shakes his chin and takes it off. "No, Duncan. It belongs to you."

"Brother," said Duncan, a little angry now as he tugs it back over Jimmy's head.

"I can't."

"Brother."

"I haven't done anything to deserve it."

"Brother," Duncan snarls. "Deserve what I say he deserve."

Jimmy gives up as the homunculus beside him smiles through whatever pall obscure his thoughts and morals from the world. He places his hand on his shoulder, pulls him to his chest.

"Brother," they both say, Jimmy sounding unconvinced. "Brother."

They repeat it until they fall asleep.

Later they awake to black upon black through the windows, the pumping of gunfire and screaming below. Jimmy jumps from the bed, drags Duncan towards the door to their bedroom, but before he can open it, his friend, his brother, slings him into the closet. He takes the chain he used to jump rope and ties it around Jimmy's waist, and then ties that waist to a section of plumbing.

"Duncan," Jimmy squeals.

"No sound," he whispers, face mad with veins. "No sound, brother."

He gives Jimmy the black Ushanka, places it on his head, pats it confidently before making his way to door. Jimmy struggles against the chains, saying nothing, no way out; he feels awed and protected by Duncan's freakish, Minotaur mount as he shuffles.

The door splinters open by a rainboot riving through the panels.

In the pitch, with debris at his feet, stands Apollonius Sikophsky.

His eyes are alight with a storm inside him, face and beard burning with moon. Wind blows through a fatuous, moth-eaten hole in the drapes. His lower lip's fastened to the cupids bow, and he dons a tent of old peacoat. A Welrod shimmers in his gloved right hand and his rainboots are stained bright with blood. He frowns with determinacy, looks upon Duncan, bleeding from his stomach by a shard of the door's wood and sidesteps the wideness of his head.

"This is the end," he says.

He lifts the gun.

Jimmy looks through the closet door, silent.

He remembers, "No sound. No sound, brother."

He remembers the word 'brother,' an Anglic breath, and then splinters, moonlight, 'the end.'

He remembers the fact that, until this very moment, until this moment that isn't quite over yet, he's learned to be something other than a nameless blight. It's almost as if there is no 'the end,' no 'this' moment in time, no 'this' lasting second, but instead, 'each' previous second, 'a' gun to Duncan's head, 'eternity' in what is called death.

"Brother," says Duncan, tears ebbing from his eyes.

His attacker becomes surprised and confused. Jimmy goes over all the tenants of *The Manaton*, searching them to make magic to appear before his eyes, through the blinds of the closet, through the sound of Duncan's weeping, through the reality of what it means to lose.

"I'm no brother of yours," says Apollonius, and with his hand a snake constricted, hisses fire.

Jimmy finds his way from Fingal's closet eventually. He pulls himself from the piping in the wall and crawls towards Duncan's deadness, kisses his forehead and caresses the unified fur of his brow. He finds Fingal slumped over the banister, the third step, a hole through the back of the head. The front door is open, it's sunny outside, and there's still good milk in the icebox. Jimmy eats, and then drags the bodies and burns them both in the chimney. Makes a fire. Watches it crackle. The soot and bone fragments he places in the Ushanka's box, and the Ushanka he places on his head. The box he empties over the Firth of Forth. He takes over the deeds to Fingal's estate, creates a forgery saying Fingal had gone missing while on mission duty in Java. Jimmy purports his name to be Duncan, and provides the documents to match. Soon after, he sells everything; he lets his toenails grow long, and sets to wandering the planet in search of the one called Apollonius, who, one night, years later, he finds in a whorehouse in Prague, and strangles, ever so slowly, with the chain his brother once used to jump rope. He makes it last long. He explains to him that, in death, all can be made beautiful. "Infinity," he says. "Your death is infinity. I am your beginning. No end in sight."

He ships Apollonius's broken body to his wife's address, where hopefully, if there resides a son, or daughter, he or she could be there to open the casket, and shriek upon the mangled corpse inside. In the following years he starts his search for remaining Beamites, as Fingal had pointed out over various lectures. Cousins, mostly, and a couple of tired friendships. In his late twenties he discovers a boy born to a woman who claims to have once been the recipient of Fingal's seed, during his time as a soldier. She's a hooker from France named Jacqueline Blue Bovie, and the boy, who's then just turned twelve, she introduces as Agamemnon. She's convinced he is a reincarnation of the king of Mycenae, she tells him. Information derived from a diviner in Toulouse who sips absinthe and, while euphoric, convenes with Delphic oracles. After little to no discourse, Jacqueline is happy to give him away for the cost of a new bed frame, which she desperately needs. All this as she reaffirms, "Oh yes, he is the son of Fingal. How could be any other? Look at the way his blood boils, just by touching him." She slaps the side of his bronze-blond head. "See how he seethes? A little dignitary if I ever saw one. Ready to ascend his rightful throne." Jimmy dubiously pays the sum and takes the boy home. Agamemnon doesn't speak a word until his nineteenth birthday, and his first syllables, with murderous undertones: "How dare me betrayeth, Clytemnestra?"

Peccadillo, in stark contrast, seems to appear out of the nothing. Begins stalking Jimmy, who was now renamed Bartholomew, and Agamemnon along the streets of Manhattan after they've taken up temporary residence on the Lower East Side, behind a corner grocery, in a ratty basement dwelling, to build prestige and regroup. His original name is something like Peter, or Phil, and, due to circumstances he refuses to detail, lived on the streets of Brooklyn most of his life until taken in by a Italian parish family in Flatbush, Queens. He then attended a Catholic school called Saint Augustine's, and did quite well, strikingly well, before being expelled for spreading thoughts of onanism. His foster father disowned him soon after when he got involved in something like the mafia, Cosa Nostra, and began drawing in dirty funds. He has relatives, as he describes it, from a side of *The Manaton's* conflict he prefers to forget, or fight, and apparently, they prefer to forget him, too. "I wish to destroy my maker," he likes to say. "To return power to whom it's due."

Bartholomew is not easy to trust, however, and thinks the small, squeaky peccadillo of a man for a spy, a supplanted element of the enemy in his midst. It isn't uncommon for Jimmy to see Sikophskys everywhere, traversing air, sea, and earth. When Peccadillo admits having access to a weapon of mass destruction, something left over from his organized days, a contact originating out of Christchurch, New Zealand, with hands in many puddings when it came to international terrorism.

"How easy it is to make a little sin," he often says, without information attached.

He is a talkative and scary boy who grows (though only slightly in height) into a more talkative, and even scarier man. In the year 2003, following years of meticulous planning, and time spent off the radar, he purchases, stows, rigs, and finally launches a nuclear bomb at Finney, Kansas, in hopes of confirming a suspicion of his, unapproved by Bartholomew: that The Savage, an amateur crime fighter roaming the Rockies, is the son of Fearghas Murdoch Sikophsky.

"You think everyone is a Sikophsky," says Jimmy/Bartholomew, in response. "You have to learn that these. . .Manatonians. . .are craftier than snakes. They would never let themselves be exposed in the open with brazen disconcert."

"But great leader," responds Peccadillo. "Does not a thief who excels in stealing, not take his prize right before the owner's grasp? Do not discount these obvious flourishes. Do not think you've already been beat. These vermin, they survive because they adapt. Just like so many an insect."

Peccadillo's gamble, however, ends up generating some genuine suspicion. Details come to light in the wake of the bomb's deflection—a through line is established. Setting up a tail on a woman named Lily, Peccadillo discovers that the Savage's alias might well be Zatkin, one of the sixteen possible identities assumed by the Sikophsky brood worldwide. This following the disappearance of the one called Fearghas, a mysterious keystone in the movement, with hundreds of possible altar egos.

"T.H.E.Y. creeps through the web of all things," Jimmy/Bartholomew likes to say of his men. "T.H.E.Y. is an indestructible firmament in the weave of the world. We are as essential to its function as sun, earth, and air."

And what for this acronym: T.H.E.Y.?

The syllables themselves could be thought to have come about soon after Fingal's death, branded in Jimmy's brain the precise moment the bullet came for Duncan's. It happened in a way that seemed spiritually flawless, as if passed down in the frosty breath of ancients. Though as with most identities, T.H.E.Y. begun as a counter-revolution. As immortal in spirit as the muzzle of a gun. Testosterone Heightened Enforcers of Y might have taken the contemporary stage in explanation and etiology. Yet even those words contained dubious roots. As Jimmy/Bartholomew should have known from his studies (whether he does or not remains to be answered), battles evolve from older battles, vengeance from revenge. While T.H.E.Y. has now been equipped with the means to navigate the hyper-real society of the now, it's impossible not to doubt its verity. As they swear to reunite their kind, kind itself becomes a peculiar word to use, for none of them can actually claim, in any avenue or vein, to have a genuine connection to the faceless creature in the furry Ushanka known in tradition as Beamish. But in all honesty, what people can provide such history? And if they can, is it not affixed to hate?

CHAPTER TWENTY NINE

IN THE BRAIN OF THE BEAST

The rest of the day Nemo spent curled over his missing digit, and, as night came, he was introduced to his cell, a dingy, watery circuit of a larger building, cold with marine wetness. He attempted with every part of his person to stave off the sleep drugs by digging his full hand's nails into his arm. As he neared the fringes of dreaming, he realized, with whatever they'd been injecting him, that forcing himself to stay awake could turn the moist air into a hot sky of angry stars, the cracked concrete ground into kibbled earth, and the walls into something like glass. His thoughts were concealed, but still they came to him, came to him in the way a new world could, and he saw himself reflected in the wall; he saw his skin ruck from his shoulders and, from his back, two growths, wiggled and spread into silver and skeletal wings, with dashes of pink, and two more from his lower back, and another couple from the flesh above his ass. His bare chest hillocked with a set of ample breasts, and his crotch, a tapestry for apparition of his penis, was neither present nor concealed. He found himself crouching, standing, then moving around his cell, and thought about Jeffrey Westcott, and when he did he thought he could see the boy, though mangled, in a brooding bundle of smiles and villainous sneers on the walls. "They'll kill you," he heard. "I think they're sick." And when he heard those words he realized he was truly nearing the place between dreams and sleep, as well as the edge of the cell, when there appeared lettering, scores and scores of lettering all around him, scrawled and jumbled. As he looked closer and forced open his lids, he saw words, sentences, instructions, paroxysms. One on each wall from top to bottom save for the bars of his cage.

WALL ONE

The events in the life of a human being are traumatic.
They are smuggled through a labyrinth.
If there is a monster somewhere inside.
If it wears a black mask, with two hollow eyes.
And they glow.
Then life will end with a child's breath.
And every drop of its blood will be a diamond.

WALL TWO

If there so emerges a monster from the labyrinth, than that monster needs to be fought.
Every human, pink and livid.
Is a hero.
Dying in the mazy jaws of a monster is better than never having battled one at all.
The beast combated tests its strength, just as much as the hero that tests it.
The monster, taking on all shapes and sizes, black horns, eagle wings, Tarasque talons, tooth-venom,
Is afraid of the hero, just as the hero is of it.
If there is great validity in both altruism and murder, then there comes the question:
Are they interdependent?

WALL THREE

A human must never reveal who he truly is, for each man,

In all of his faculties,

Is amorphous, and especially dangerous.

Even evil creatures.

Willing to do harm, should conceal their identities

from the public,

The truth might is too beautiful and terrible to stand.

As it goes for both heroes and monsters, each one has something in common with the other.

A disguise is needed to preserve individuality,

So that all us.

Can know.

Good from bad.

Footsteps were heard down the hall, and, in the murk, the hallucinatory stars, Nemo played prostrate on the floor with his eyes shut as tight as they could without sleeping. He heard the grunting of the larger one—it seemed as if he'd been assigned to his surveillance. He clinked open the door to his cage, snarling metal, halted, and the broad shoulders stooped down. He made low, droning noises. Nemo—busy earlier stretching his t-shirt to his elbows—tried not to flinch as the needle touched his arm, and shifted a little, just the smallest bit, to divert it to the fabric in his shirt, to a place he'd knotted into tougher layers.

His only chance.

The large one barked when the boy flinched, and then, gripping his arm with a big, purple hand, fell for the slight, pumped the syringe into the shirt and lurched away. He clanged the cell closed and disappeared into the relative brightness down the hallway. Nemo breathed out and collapsed into sleep, or something like sleep. He saw himself again as a creature with six wings. He had a great spear coming from his arms, as if molded, and before him was a beast, not a Kraken, but a homunculus with the sweetest eyes, the roughest hands, the flattest breasts, and enough strength to wrestle a hundred nightmares and their assaulting navies into the mantle. Lifting that gigantic spear, he drove it between its brain pan.

Beneath, in the barreled skull, was this shape pulsing pink:

And thinking that his mother, unlike his father, was the only person who ever helped him feel safe, he fell into dreamless REM.

After Lantana broke the news to Lily there was a moment of ambivalent calm. She walked across the breezy Mendocino cabin's living room, leaned on the loveseat, and walked back across the living room, and then outside to the heel of the porch, and came back inside and outside again with nothing less than wonder on her face. Lantana folded his arms across his chest, and then let them open, almost confused, as she snuggled her way inside. Husbands and wives like them felt that they endangered each other with acts of true intimacy. To Carl and Daphne, watching the two of them embrace, they sensed something awkward in the display. It seemed scripted, or even false. Sure, they could kiss, or occasionally make love in physically altered states, but even when their child became a common thread they still had difficulty convincing those around them of their genuine happiness. Since Nemo was one half of each of them, one half of each of them, they could act like they needed, in his mother's direction, they could act like they needed each other in this very moment. In some ways, they genuinely did—brains and brawns did undeniably work together, even as an effective cliché. But after the call came, the man's voice (one could tell he was small just by listening) nattering about ransom, a book, years of unresolved history, Lily and Lantana's relationship was reduced to the normal, quiet loathing, passive, aggressive, like the battle for Kansas, with Lily's larvate hate avoiding her husband, silently humiliating him from every invisible angle and postulate.

"It's just not right," said Lily, pacing back and forth.

"We'll get him back," growled Lantana, fingers fisting and unfisting at his sides.

"What could have happened?"

"We'll get him back."

"He's a little boy, out there, all alone, and it's your fault."

"It's actually his fault," said Daphne, pointing at Carl.

"We'll get him back," said Lantana

"What could have happened?"

"We'll get him back."

"Oh, my poor Nemo."

"Rain or shine, Hell or Antarctica, I promise to everything that I have ever lived or loved that my son, our son, will return to us alive, and, if I can possibly have any hand in it," his tongue spun round his lips, "the most fitting revenge ever conceived by any human in any time on any part of the planet called earth or any other planet, will fall upon my enemies with unprecedented animus!"

Lantana beat his chest.

"Manifilus. Morgasm. Manu," yelled Carl.

"Seriously," said Daphne. "What's the deal with you two?"

"Elevated subject matter," said Carl.

"Poor Wow," she continued, sparking up a joint. "Such a bummer."

"Bummer?" yelled Lily. "My boy's being held ransom by a group of international psychopaths."

"I wouldn't say international," said Carl. "They're fairly local."

"We're going to get him back," said Lantana.

"Then go get him back," said Lily.

"Can I come?" asked Daphne.

"No," said Carl.

"Yes," said Lantana.

"Liscous!"

"Any help is good help."

"Then let's go," said Lily, spinning the keys to the rentacar above her head. "Daphne, if you're coming, than you should probably know—my husband, the idiot standing right before you, is what America now calls The Savage."

Daphne cocked her head at the gigantic, fuming creature, head hung in shame, and seemed to understand.

"Far out," she said, and then chipmunked her cheeks with fresh smoke.

By that evening they were back in Arapahoe Falls. They picked up Lantana's Saturn at the airport and scrawled down La Pena Boulevard back to the house with the collected and arcane silence of pallbearers being hefted to their own funeral. Once they were in the garage, springs rattled the doors down, lights came on, and Lily, eyes and face ablaze, led them through a small door in the westernmost wall—one they wouldn't find without her guidance. One no one truly entered but her. Swearing Daphne into secrecy breakable only by death, she flipped on a massive light fuse to what might have long ago been a fifth and sixth garage, extruding by floor plan into a small section of the backyard. High vaulted ceilings of bolted sheet metal shuddered like the windy insides of an airplane hangar. Heaps of tinker's equipment, however—circuit boards, sheets of copper, microammeters, disemboweled radiators, hedges of stacked batteries, a Bell helicopter engine, clamps, shears, a dizzying aggregation of wrenches and screwdrivers scattered proximately like debris from a highway collision—stole most of the space away. Many of these wares had been used to fashion what could have been considered gadgets, which lay everywhere. To Lily and Lantana each one had its own particular meaning, and to Lily that meaning had developed into existence by days, even years of solicitous tooling, that wouldn't have been worth explaining without due cause.

"Welcome to what I call The Gravitas," she said, and, from a miserly coat rack beside a tumble of unpacked boxes, pulled off one of her lab coats and pulled it over the sweater she'd been wearing.

Before them, in the rough center of the bunker, was something large they couldn't only not describe, but ascertain use. A bundle of nine-inch thick rubber cables funneling electricity from an undisclosed location behind the series of steel cabinets piqued Daphne's attention.

"They'll be no introductions, only action," Lily said, coming between It and all of them. Lantana was the only of the four who seemed to find familiarity, but even he remained a little awestruck. "The pick-up is in two hours at Jones's Rubber Factory. You all know what that means," she looked at all of them with pity, or low confidence, as Steve Two, with her large, sad belly might stare upon a piece of rancid meat. "Now. Get my fucking son back."

CHAPTER THIRTY

BIRTH, LIFE, AND DEATH OF FEARGHAS MURDOCH SIKOPHSKY

Six hundred billion years ago, before time was time, before before was before, when when was a way to describe what, and the gate Exegesis 6B
was the only way two galaxies separated by an ocean of stars could supply
interplanetary connect, Fearghas, or, as he was once known, the—

Dear Reader,

The following chapter in The League of Somebodies pertaining to

Fearghas Murdoch Sikophsky has been removed by Subsection D,

subsidiary of the United States Military as of December, 2008.

Any inconveniences will not be disputed.

General Donald Grieves

Donald Grieves

Pentagon

(Subsection D)

CHAPTER THIRTY ONE

PROMETHEUS

"I think we were supposed to turn back on Downing," said Daphne, looking over the directions. They were written on a pad of notebook paper soy-stained by the bottom of a Chinese take-out box. Unlike before she was dressed, excessively so, with two sweaters beneath a rubicund monster of Gore-Tex. Lantana's Saturn, which was already on its last legs as far as freshness was concerned, smelled of sweat, dampened wool and sour to-bacco as Carl smoked a cigarette, setting his tongue along the filter ever so often before taking a drag.

"Yep," she confirmed. "Two blocks back."

"Then why didn't you tell me two blocks back?" asked Carl, spinning into a swift U turn.

"Relax, sugar," said Daphne. "You know I'm bad with directions."

"Goddamnit—Lily." Carl clicked his fingernail against his ear as they halted at red light. "Lily, come in."

"On this frequency, you will call me Gilgamesh," said the voice through the receiver that broadcasted to all of their ears.

"Fine, Gilgamesh," said Carl. "Why the FUCK did you stick me with such an amateur?" He pointed to Daphne with his elbow, indicating, possibly, that her simian parts resided there. "It'll just slow us down."

"You're the amateur," said Daphne, offended.

"Calm down," said Lily. "Do your job or I'll spoon your balls off."
Daphne chuckled.

"Now," said Lily, as the Saturn slowed to a crawl nearing Jones's
Rubber. Snowfall drifted without much wind, or hurry. Lily, miles away,
sat with her fingers in knots as she maneuvered the security console she'd
fashioned for Lantana's missions. It consisted of four computer monitors
stacked corner to corner, a wall of complex hardware behind them, and
one small, aluminum-framed keyboard positioned pristinely in front. Lily
repositioned the mouthpiece on her headset so that it almost entered her
lips, and then drew the clamp into her head.

"We've all talked about what's going to go down here," she said, trying to keep herself from sniffling. She felt as if she were speaking to Nemo
right now, trying to repair another cataclysm she'd allowed to take place.
"My son is the top priority," she resumed with composure. "I carried him
in my gut for eight and a half months. We shared the same heartbeat—he is
mine, and I am his. Blood is blood. No one can fuck with that." She paused.
"Understand that we are going to give T.H.E.Y. *The Manaton*, and hope for
a simple exchange."

"Oh, come on," whined Carl, stamping his feet.

"Do not challenge me," lowed Lily. "I have installed a microscopic
tracking device in Chapter 13, the one on," she shuddered, "The Musts of
Defecation. But pursuit of family takes precedence to pursuit of paper. So if
you want it you can get it back later. After my son is returned."

"Acknowledged," Carl sighed.

"I'm in position—*fzz—shtpp*," came Lantana's voice, fizzling in from
somewhere in space.

"Good," said Lily. "Carl, Daphne, proceed to the handoff."

"I don't—*fzz*—like involving Steve Two in this," Lantana said. "She's
not cut out for this sort of heat."

Lily paused. "She's a goddamn lion, Lantana. She'll be fine. Now,
Carl, Daphne, get in position."

"Who do these jokers think they are?" asked Carl, gnashing his al-
ready-gnashed teeth. "Think can get away with kidnapping? Back in the old

days, someone pulled this shit on us they'd be forced to eat themselves. Alive."

"They already have gotten away with kidnapping," said Daphne. "And eating oneself seems pretty extreme."

Carl chuckled, patting something, a large, seemingly comforting lump, between him and the door. "We'll see about that."

Both thankfully and unthankfully, East Colfax wasn't a part of town people really paid attention to. It was more like the part of town people pretended to pay attention to while, in truth, the entire state had shelved it years ago after finding its inhabitants couldn't yodel magic dollar signs with the rest of the noble mile high. The neighborhood gave off a meaty waft, now. A distinct cologne of castigation and sin. Carl and Daphne looked above them at a fifteen-foot tall flashing red cross above the entrance to a homeless shelter called Beginnings on their left hand side as they drove. It was something that, much like the people who passed under it, flickered and fizzled in the cold.

"Alright," said Lantana, amongst various clicks. "Look alive."

"Where are you?" asked Carl, turning his neck wildly.

"I'm in—*fzzzshp*—position," Lantana growled. "Now look alive."

They pulled up towards the parking lot at Jones's Rubber Factory. It had a lot of spaces, a lack of employees, and lay, as if dying, in the acherontic shadow of its niche industry. The foot of the building was fairly far away from the lot entrance, and they had to wind through an autistic distribution of lampposts.

Carl blazed up a joint.

"What are you doing?" asked Daphne.

"Shh," Carl said, taking a drag and tapping on his earpiece. "Just to mellow out."

"Smoking substances is not acceptable activity while ransoming my son," said Lily. Though no one else could see it, she was practically grabbing the sides of the monitors with her fingernails.

"Aw shit," said Carl. "See what you started?"

"Substances—*zzz*—*ftt*?" said Lantana. "Jesus fuck, Carl. Exercise—*fzz*—*shpp*— some dignity."

"I don't think this is the time," said Daphne.

"Come on," said Carl, sucking and puffing as hard as he could. "We've gotta prepare for the worst."

"Put the fucking drugs out, Carl," said Lily.

"Why should I?"

"Wow's life is at stake," said Daphne.

"Look," said Lantana. "Just—*fz—shpp*—stop arguing. You're arriving at the drop point. Keep—*zhp*—alert."

"Can you see us, Licious?" asked Carl, looking up through the window and waving like a lunatic.

"Yes."

"Carl, you moron," said Daphne, shaking her head.

The car began to swagger a little towards Jones's Rubber, red bricks stacked into one reeling pillar. Its sign droned on the third story, a hot florescent loop of letters. They were luridly cursive and blurred by an upkick in the snow. There was something seedily attractive about the building altogether, as if, in another life, as if, in another life, it could have been a burlesque San Francisco hotel, either that, or the site of some villainy in Gotham City, where someone would be immutably transformed by an acid bath.

"Get ready, the two of you," said Lily. She was biting her nails.

"I can see them, Gilgamesh," said Lantana.

"Wait?" asked Lily, clicking on her computer back in The Gravitas. She zoomed into her grid of Denver, and picked up a neon green silhouette of a vehicle growling around a bend, about a block away from the factory. "I see one bogie coming in slow from Downing. Look alive, kiddos."

"Carl and Daphne, I see you in the Saturn," said Lantana, scanning for movement. "And here it comes. The second—*chzp*—car. A Buick."

"Anyone in it?"

"Can't see. Tinted windows."

"Of course they're tinted," said Lily.

"They're pulling up right where they said they would," said Daphne. Fear was evident in her voice. "Right in front," she gulped, dipping down below the window. "We're twenty feet away."

"They're getting out," Lantana whispered. "*Fz—shtp—fzz*—stay tuned."

From the Buick stepped two men, both from the front doors. One was small and one was large, but they both wore masks of metal. Each casted brow was raised into a curious triangle, and they had reedy red ties. White shoes. The large one, who was enormous as he revealed himself, had a golden cape around his shoulders, and was wearing leather pants.

"I'm moving to full topiary view," said Lily, clicking in a command on her keyboard so that she could observe pedestrian and police activity around Jones's Rubber for miles. "You're all clear. Don't worry about having to let loose."

"T.H.E.Y." said Lantana. His voice dropped silent for a moment. "My Dad—*fjzpp—csssh*—was right. I should have paid more attention. I could have taken care of—*blzzzphshh*—is years ago."

"You're Dad was never right," said Lily. "About anything. Don't make this about you. We're here for Nemo."

"I always feared—*fzz—shtpp*—moment," said Lantana. "How do you go so long without meeting—*fzz*—your enemy? All these years—*fzz—hzzhp*—not a sign. And now, here they are. Wagering my own blood against me—*fzz*."

"Don't lose confidence," said Lily. "Straighten out your mouthpiece."

"What is confidence—*fzzzzzSHTPPP*—an excuse to care about yourself? All this time, I've worried about my rise. And why? *Fzz—zzhhpp*—to protect what?"

"Carl," yelled Daphne, surprising the airwaves. "Take control of the car."

Lily, alarmed, yelled, "If you fuck this up I will kill the two of you!"

Carl had misjudged the ice on approach and slammed, as opposed to pumping, the pedal, sliding sideways past the Buick and teed a light post crooked. He still held the joint miraculously in his hand. When they stopped, the rear left window was smashed out. "Duuuuuddddde," Daphne slurred, something in between duet and newt. "Pot is totally a drug."

Carl took what he'd been hiding in the side of the seat, a book, a different book, not *The Manaton*, and threw it out the window at the large one's head, which it pinged like a nickel against a copper converter.

"Grenade!" he screamed, and then seemed disappointed when he saw it wasn't.

Agamemnon canted his iron chin to the ground.

"I'm going in," said Lantana.

"Hold it," said Lily. "Wait for a visible on Nemo."

"That wasn't the book," whispered Daphne, holding the real one.

"Shut up," said Carl.

"That wasn't the fucking book, Carl," she said again.

"What?" said Lantana, suddenly alert. "Carl, give them the fuck-ing—*fzzz—shtpp—Manaton*."

"Everybody calm down," said Carl, holding up his hands to the air. "These assholes won't know the better."

The smaller one, Peccadillo, walked up to the book, a leather-bound copy of *20,000 Leagues Under the Sea*, and picked it up before scanning the skyline. He opened it up, read a line or two. He showed it to Agamemnon and they exchanged whispers.

"What were you thinking, Carl?" said Lantana. "What were you—*mzzp*—thinking?"

"I have this completely under control," he said.

"It's a book, Carl," said Lantana. "A fucking stupid book—*fzzp*."

"Licious, how dare you?"

"Thanks for involving us in your plan," said Daphne, ducking away from the window. Her hair was plastered to her chin. Her eyes bulged with fear.

"You don't even know my plan," said Carl.

"Fine," whispered Daphne. "Then fucking tell me."

"We're gonna ram their car with our car."

"Nemo could be in there, you idiot," said Lily.

"Donkeys. You're right."

"And the car's wrecked," said Daphne.

"Nuts," sulked Carl.

Agamemnon nodded towards Peccadillo, and, throwing down the book in instant rejection, they drew pistols from their overcoats and opened fire on the Saturn. A bullet ripped through Carl's cheek. Blood across the seat and window.

"Help!" Daphne screamed. "Help, help!

"I'm going in," said Lantana. "Aren't I?"

"Yes," yelled Lily, her teeth grit, her hands flailing before the monitors. "Yes you are, you son of a bitch! IN YOU FUCKING GO!"

"Okay," he said. "Okay."

"Be careful, you worthless idiot," she cried. "Nemo could be in there."

With a BOOM that made everyone go quiet, the machine called Prometheus rose from behind Jones's Rubber Company. Its heat crackled snow. Its engines seethed from the rooftop into the parking lot, roaring down like maddening doom with orange fire hawking from its thrusters. Its wings spread, folded from within a titanium hide; the engines moaned and boomed. They were of various soldered metals, cobbled together, ashen circuitry and steaming bifurcates of tubes misarranged as if built on a living testimony to Dada. As it moved it seemed to change in form, from an amalgamation of plating into a winged creature, with arms and legs outstretched, needled claws, and its chestal hub—Lantana inside masked in leather goggles, shirtless, with Spandex pants and his toga—gutted from the '64 Bonneville. Using his arms as extensions of the machines arms, and legs as the machine's legs, he dead-dropped into the parking lot ground and ruptured the concrete below.

"Where is my son?" he bellowed through a microphone dangling before his chin.

Agamemnon and Peccadillo opened fire but their bullets blipped away. On the back of Prometheus, from a hatch, Lily activated the remote release and Steve Two erupted in her fat majesty, rolling to the ground. Lantana crashed across the lot and, using one of his claw-arms, picked up Peccadillo and swung the gun from his hand. He held him to the Plexiglass encasement, pressed him against the glass in front of his one, fuming eye, and cringed as he erupted in laughter. Steve Two roared and, in a monster mash, lumbered towards Agamemnon, who dropped his gun, as was customary to those who took stake in *The Manaton* when combating such a beast. He ripped off his clothes, completely, and put up his massive fists. Lantana clunked towards the Buick and peeled off the hood. He looked on the inside.

Nothing.

"I can't wait for the moment when He takes back what's his," laughed Peccadillo from Prometheus's hand.

Lantana, with his mechanical arm, brought the man to eye level and began to squeeze. He gripped his fingers, increased pressure. The mask popped off and he saw how boyish, how familiar the small creature looked. Like he could have been a clone of a younger brother. Like he couldn't have known any better. Either that, or knew far, far too much. Lantana let him slither from his grasp and pull away towards his gun, which he stepped over and crushed mechanically and slowly, and with a look of tsk tsk in his eyes.

"You truly are a undeserving man," said Peccadillo, still smiling. He flinched from side to side as Lantana attempted to corner him against one of the factory's front walls. He noticed that the superhero seemed unwilling, or unable, to dispute his assertion. There was something grim, and undecided in his sad brown eye. "I'll be delighted to take from you what's never been earned."

Lantana gasped as he saw Agamemnon and Steve Two in epic struggle, her unmuscled body wrapped in his arms. He hesitated on his next movement. He saw Peccadillo trying to escape from his vision. He saw Agamemnon's arms move up through Steve Two's mane. He was strong, no less than seven feet tall, veins sprawling in his sizeable, slightly erect penis. He took his mask off, revealing a flash of dirty, bleached blond hair, blue eyes, a chin that had a scar down the heft to the base of the neck. Lantana decided to help out Steve Two, but a little too late to make a difference. Agamemnon caught the lioness's jaw, much like Lantana had long ago to the original Steve, but snapped it in two and caste her body aside. He lifted his gunwale of a foot above her face. Lantana screamed. Steve Two mewed. An explosion blazed through the parking lot knocking Agamemnon against a wall.

"Son of Fearghas," bellowed a voice. Another explosion. The handsome older man, nearing the end of his virile years, but still alive as ever, and sporting his Ushanka, was holding an M25 bazooka over his shoulder and standing on a concrete wall, dividing Jones's Rubber from the highway. His shoes were off. His socks tickled the ground. The first stovepipe rocket brought Prometheus to its knees; the second made a gash through the place where its autotronic liver would be, beside the hub, exposing entrails of oil and circuitry ooze. Lantana tried to reticulate the controls, but ended up spilling from the cockpit with his club and toga in an emergency rejection designed to save his life.

"Or should I call you The Savage?" he completed, betraying a blush. "This is very exciting. And a long time coming."

"I told him that," said Peccadillo. "I was the one who found it out."

"Yes," said the handsome older man, too tired to be patronizing. "You're very smart."

"I only wish we could have gotten him back then," said Peccadillo. "He's very slippery."

"Like a fish," said the handsome older man.

"A tired, spoiled fish," said Peccadillo.

"But that's to say that we're not ample huntsmen. . .that our nets don't caste wide. . .that we don't trawl. . .the seas, no matter how long, to rake up our bottom feeders for butter and oil."

Whenever the man in the Ushanka talked, he enunciated odd words with tedious flare, as if struggling with an evil form of Parkinson's. Behind him, shackled in chains, was Nemo, battered-looking with a band of seedy gauze around his left hand. His deerstalker cap was removed, revealing a half-eaten yarmulke and the gauntness of his face. He looked so unlike Lantana right now, so healthy for all the abuse. The sensitivity he'd betrayed naturally and tried to hide in the past was gone. As Lantana observed this, he thought about the message in the bottle and wondered: was this, yet again, another great joke? Another test lain out by a madman? But, the more he thought about that prospect, the more he realized that no one was trying to test him anymore, that all the testgivers, the monuments of manhood, were dead, and he was the only one left. What was happening now, this was real. Too real, and too damn extraordinary.

"Give me back my son," he said, only partially believing in his ability to follow through with his own words. He hefted his club. It felt heavy in his arm. He wondered how it could have been designed for him: this tool of justice, weighty beyond purpose. "Or I'll. I'll kill you. Manascus. Maniscus—"

The handsome man turned the left corner of his lip upwards. "Manevolent, Manevil, Manitus, Manasturbate, Manatic, Manurder, Mana," he said. "Mana." He held up his hand as Peccadillo and Agamemnon approached Lantana on his flanks.

"Mranu," Carl called out from the car in correction. "Mranu!"

"Shut up, Carl," said Lantana. "It is Manu, asshole."

"We have different views," said the handsome older man. He let down his bazooka to the tip of his foot. "See, you're what your people like to call a hero, but I can see you already know you've failed. Years ago."

Lily mumbled in fear, "He talks like a super villain, right out of a comic book. Even the tone."

"Super villains don't exist," sighed Lantana. "Not really."

"Buck up, Lantana," said Lily. "Now's not the time to lose vision."

"What are you mumbling about?" asked the handsome older man.

"Nothing," said Lantana, rolling his shoulders. "Fucko. Just me and you."

"Then imagine, the entire saga of your life," the handsome older man continued, tightening his grip on the bazooka, "is incomplete. Imagine it halved, drawn down the middle, shuffled, and then broken, like a pack of cards. Imagine that, after all the time you spent trying to make yourself heard, that you were only whispering. Imagine that, just maybe, when something is taken from you, taken from your blood, your people's blood, years and years ago, that it always remains taken, and that you're never whole, and that, throughout history, you can never be made whole until that something is returned." He stuck a toothpick in his mouth, crunched the tip off. He spit it out, swept it across the ground with the right toe of his cotton sock. "I mean, look at what you're wearing." He didn't laugh, but pointed the bazooka in his direction. "This mighty figment, this empty Somebody that you are, and your league of supporters," he cast his hand to the crashed Saturn and his son. "You're so overconfident. Maybe if my ancestors held onto the book, possessed it for years as you have, we'd be wearing the bright colors of freedom, and not the darker, more intimidating tints of war and fear. But what's a deprived man to do? We're all in the business of creating dreams, and you've given the world one to believe in. I could only wish for that sort of capability. To foster one real, shining thing."

"Who the hell are you?" asked Lantana, gripping and regripping his club.

"I am," he said, leaning forward on his toes, "the Tyger," he smiled. "The pen created me. The same pen who createth the lamb. We'll never understand why we're doing what were doing to each other, but we'll keep on doing it. I swear."

"Okay," growled Lily over the earpiece. "This is getting way too dramatic. Beat it out of him. Now!"

"Hold on Lily," Lantana whispered.

"Now!" screamed Lily. "Now, now, NOW!"

Lantana lifted his club reticently to follow her orders, but, as expected, the man in the black Ushanka turned toward Nemo with the head of the bazooka, using the tip to bother the edge of his yarmulke. "First I'll get the book," he said. "Then we'll talk a little more about our predicament."

"Give it to him," said Lily. "Right now."

"Okay," Lantana said, holding up his hands. "I'll get it. Just take it easy." He walked over to the Saturn, where Carl's bloody face was being tied down by his shirt, in a uncomfortable cinch, and pressured by Daphne.

"Nwo," said Carl. "Dwornt drew it."

"Stop talking," said Daphne.

Lantana yanked *The Manaton* from Carl's lap. He marched back across the parking lot with it trembling in his fingers.

"Okay," he said, holding it high. "Nice and easy."

The handsome man motioned to Agamemnon, who started to stalk towards him slowly.

"Remember," Lantana said. "Nice and easy."

"Nror!" yelled Carl. "Nror!"

YOU'LL RECEIVE NOTHING BUT THE RAW SKEIN OF MY TESTICLES
FOR MARGINAL COMFORT AS I SHED IT FOR SUMMER!!!!!!

"No," said the handsome man, squinting his eyes.

"What?" said Lily. "What happened?"

"Who is that?" asked Nemo, peering through his bloody eyes. He saw
grey hair and darkness in human form atop the pink neon sign of Jones's
Rubber, bits of it streaming into the snow like a smoke bomb.

Lantana's jaw had dropped the second he heard the words. His insides swirled with nausea. His club thumped his foot in what should have
been a painful manner, but he didn't feel a thing.

"Dad?" he said.

"Ay, you fantastic excuse for a bastard," yelled the man who was
once known as Fearghas.

He stood upon the neon sign, on the ledge of the E, with the same
Old-World brogues he'd been sporting back when he was. . .alive. His beard
was untrimmed, his coat was filthy, and strands of it were torn and fraying
around him. Some devilish mummy, free from its grave. Either that or the
fabled unconscious itself, a manifest tribute to the sublime eternity of fathers. Lantana hated his eyes for what they now told him. They immediately
made his stomach feel tangled in a manner it hadn't been since childhood.
"And there'll be no way this creature will be taking our ancestry away. I assume you got my message?"

"Your message?" said Lantana, dropping his club to the ground and
thinking of the bottle. "You're dead. . .dead people. . .they decompose. Your
ashes. Your ashes? I felt them in my fingers."

Fearghas hung off the Jones sign's E and, quite artfully, landed on a
lower story.

"Did you exhume my grave?" he asked.

"Grave?" said Lantana. "I. . .caste your remains. . .your remains. Off
the Annieopsquotch Mountains. I was there. I saw it happen."

"Well, did you have my ashes tested for DNA?"

"It was 1973. Argyll gave me the urn. It was—what. . .DNA?"

"How can you be sure I'm D-E-D if you don't test my ashes for D-N-A?"

Lantana gulped. His knees grew weak and almost gave out. Lily had been warbling into the mouthpiece for the last few minutes, but he hadn't heard a thing. "What the fuck is. . .where the hell did. . .Nemo. . . Nemo. . .wake up, Lantana!" Blips of her voice. Sweet. Inflamed.

"I saw you," said Lantana, trying to raise his finger to point at Fearghas, but not being quite able to. ". . .When the bus—"

"You saw nothing."

"I was there. I saw it with my own eyes."

"Which belong to me."

"This is crazy." Lantana grabbed his own face and laughed insanely. "I saw you die, splattered on the street."

"Ay," said Fearghas. "Maybe you did. But I didn't see myself die, and that's what's really important."

"But then, where were you?" asked Lantana.

"Where was I indeed," he said, scratching his beard. "Why? When? How? Where do fathers ever go, my boy?" he laughed. "How many deaths could really kill me good? Certainly a question for the philosophers of our time—fuck all. Certainly a form of enlightenment."

The handsome older man looked at Fearghas with something that was not fear, but utter disdain, and maybe fortune, as Carl fumbled from the Saturn using Daphne as support. The bullet had gone clean through the tissue in his cheeks. He was using his shirt to cinch it up.

"Fleargris?" he asked, left molars visible as he spoke. "Riz zat you?"

"Who the fuck?" asked Fearghas. "Riff raff bastard. . . ."

"Cwarl," said Carl, reaching out to shake his hand. Agamemnon growled. "Cwarl Nrarmura. I'b herv swo mutch bout vou."

"Hello," said Daphne frightfully, as she stumbled beside him.

"I have no time for freaks and fools," Fearghas said, turning away from the two of them. "Argyll Two?" he screamed up towards the roof.

"Ay, Fergie," they all heard.

"You got that sniper rifle at the ready?"

"Sure do Fergie," the voice again. "Right at the mad bastard's brainpan."

"But you're dead," said the handsome older man, bazooka lilting in his arm as he squinted his eyes at the figment, dressed in layers of winter jackets atop the roof and highly drawn kilt socks, mad glass oculus glaring. He talked not fearfully, but with inquisitive interest. "I killed you myself."

"No," said the man called Argyll Two, "I'm in infinity, where you left me. And that's forever. Remember."

"Impossible."

"Give yourself up, Duncan," said Fearghas. "We have lookalikes all over the globe. We have ears where humans can't hear. We have fingers where they can't scratch. With your kind gone, we'll be free to practice our ways in peace. Come quietly or in a casket. Same to me."

"Dad?" asked Lantana, suddenly feeling very young, and very meek for the first time in years. "What the. . .what the hell is going on?"

"There's no time boy," said Fearghas, now swinging down to the parking lot and putting his hands on his hips. Lantana wondered, upon looking at him, exactly how old his father would have been by now. His beard both gave and detracted more than fifty years. Argyll Two looked like he'd been exhumed from the Pliocene. "Just know that the BASTARD standing before you is no one else but a descendent of one of the worst, most cowardly creatures the earth ever shat." He came to stand beside his son, proving himself more than an apparition. "He is the great grandson of none other than Beamish." He paused. "Duncan."

"Duncan?" said Agamemnon.

The man in the black Ushanka smiled.

"Yes," he nodded ruefully. "That's my name. And though you certainly have earned yourself an element of surprise, my dear, usurious Fearghas, ancient Manatonian, manifestation of pestilence, bigotry, and hate, you talk as if we are but antibodies to a virus you created. But the truth is that we, too, have our doubles. Our lookalikes and protégés—they become more numerous by the day. Don't think you have the monopoly on surprise, evil sun. Don't think, that even upon this day, if you defeat me, I will cease to exist. Eternity resides at the gate of my demise. I see that now. I've seen that for a while."

Meanwhile, Nemo was keeping quiet with his eyes towards the ground.

It was better that way, better noticing the finger of his captor, making a small circle over the trigger. At first he thought he was on the verge of blowing both of them into the Styx, but then he saw that Peccadillo was missing, and that a tiny body was busting up the rungs of a ladder towards the man who called himself Argyll Two, squinting through the lens on the roof.

"Look out!" Nemo yelled, the words spurting past his bloody lips. Everyone, from demoralized Lantana to frenetic Fearghas, turned their heads.

"For history," Peccadillo squealed.

He and Argyll Two struggled, pulling at both ends of the gun. A shot went off.

"Ach!" squawked Fearghas as the bullet hit his shoulder. "I've been kilt!"

"Oh, please save him," cried Lily through the microphone. "Oh, please, Lantana, if you care at all, if you're at all a father, then lash out and make it known. You foolish, foolish hero. Do what it is you're meant to do!"

But Lantana was already on his way towards Nemo. His legs, they impelled themselves. He was through with lies, with rebirth and false mortality. Unlike his father, he was ready to end his many stages of reinvented youth and simply travel on into death. There were some things a father evolved to understand. One of those things was a son's smile, or his laughter, his frown, even the sound of his tears. He had a right to watch him live and suffer, thrive and crawl across the wasteland of adolescence into what would one day hopefully retire into a tired fata morgana of adulthood. Why had he been so insistent on making him into a carbon copy of himself, he wondered? Why had he had to pass on tradition with fury, illimitable foresight, and coercion? A slight, passing fracture of happiness in the mirror of his brief, and terrifying life appeared. It was his right and his instinct. His indisputable end. To protect the future of his loins.

"Corn Cob," said Lily. "I love you, baby." She began to cry into the receiver, unsure of whether or not she was actually sad or just afraid that a portion of her life was coming to an end without her ending with it. "I know what I say to you. To us. There have been so many lies."

The highway quivered with its quake of traffic. Lantana's golden sandals crinkled in his steps. The snow fell before his eye and convinced him, as he'd been convinced long ago, in his bedroom when he was fifteen, that he was seeing the silhouettes of wings, silver, terrible, orgiastic things, separating him from all the years he'd wasted on the ambitions of others. Maybe everybody wasn't like somebody in the end. Maybe there were a million different variations of the self. He wondered if he'd ever really know anything. And whether or not he'd actually care to. Some people lived this way. Wondering if inside a dream.

He reared his club above his head.

He leapt from the ground.

His toga sloughed in the winter wind, a bright and audacious diamond, and the S on his eyepatch, a window to the past.

"Dad!" screamed Nemo.

A shot was fired by Agamemnon and the boy's father plopped to the ground. Nemo's scream ripped a tunnel through the snow. The handsome man turned towards him, betraying what, for the first time in his own life, was the supposition he'd forgotten something. His second toothpick fell from his lips. From Nemo's fingers came a crying light, turning the world into one congealed artifact. The handsome man, once named Jimmy, once named nothing, and now thought to be Duncan, a lie to some, a prophet to others, a descendent of Beamish, either way, was caught inside its flow. Prometheus, pilotless, with its damaged innards, rose from its knees like an undead beast and hammered across the concrete to Agamemnon. With its metal claws it ripped him in half at the groin. It smeared the bloody waist across its pink Bonneville chest. It then crouched, and let out a low, bemused moan, before leaping, sailing to the top of Jones's Rubber and flattening Peccadillo's guts through its foot. Jimmy aimed his bazooka. He held it up through the target. Prometheus turned and seemed to look at him with one deranged mirror of an eye. Then, the bazooka drifted to his feet. The tired, bookless, thief in a man-suit walked off the concrete rampart, made a little half circle. Then he aimed the bazooka in his mouth, warhead at the nostril, clicked the trigger, and, thinking of nothing but infinity, fired.

Fearghas looked up and laughed, spitting out blood.

"Now that's what I call creation," he sputtered.

Prometheus jittered its arms and legs, made a ruptured sound somewhere within its belly, and with the closure of a masterless marionette, toppled from the factory. Fearghas watched it with the amusement of a boy enthralled by the cinema, a smile widening on his ancient lips. He watched it as it landed right on top his head, and groaned with the sound of failure, before, in a brief, maniac's rage, it proceeded to rip him to utter pieces, crawling all over his body with its sharp, rusty limbs, and dissembling what lay below.

CHAPTER THIRTY TWO

ON BURYING AN ATOMIC BOMB

The aftermath of what Lantana would call the 'Real Fuck You,' was sterile, needfully timeless. The survivors all picked up their injuries and made their way to Rose Hospital. Steve Two died on the way. A sound of relent issued from his throat, and his lungs crumpled like a dead spider's legs. Carl was patched up with sufficient scarring. The ER surgeon told him he'd see a big difference in his face when the bandages came off, but that his brain was healthy and pink. Lantana lost one of his testicles, but fortunately, upon removal, the doctors found that it had been cancerous—he'd have to come in to be re-examined in two weeks—and Nemo was treated with antibiotics for the advanced stages of a staph infection. Fearghas, who's identity was revealed as a man named Dennis Sinclair in the criminal database, with a wild beard and clothes dating back to the forties, was pronounced garishly dead on arrival. When authorities—a couple of cold, stiff-lipped sheriffs— asked about how this had happened, they all corroborated the same story:

"We were attacked by hoodlums."

"What did they look like?"

"Large. Small. Lots of colors. Maybe communists."

"Communists?"

"Who knows."

"You said colors. What sort? White? Black? Hispanic?"

"They all wore ski masks."

"So you couldn't see their faces?"

"No."

"Then how did you know their skin colors?"

"We don't profile. We're easily offended."

"But then."

"Eastern European, I think."

"And the lion? How the hell did it get here?"

"We don't exactly know, Sir."

"Well isn't that convenient."

"There's nothing convenient about it."

"Don't be a smartass."

"Sure thing."

"I don't know. . .something seems fishy about this whole situation."

"Fishy indeed! We just want to go home and see if it stops stinking. It's been a terrible night. Please contact us with any further questions. We'll surely answer them. God bless."

Lily arrived at Jones's Rubber as they fled and disposed of the bodies of T.H.E.Y. Later she'd bury them at the same creek Lantana had laid down the hunter. Making a few small repairs, she looked around for suspicious company, and, from her hands, the same sort of electricity ushered out as had from her son. She didn't pause to marvel upon the ease with which she could summon it now. It twisted from her fingers, whirling in viscid curlicues. Prometheus shook to some form of alive, wavering on its legs, and, as she twisted her wrist, heated its engines, clanging. The wires snaked with fire. Its body lifted and fluttered through the snow-flurry, increasing in speed, dragging its shredded bulk southward like a corpse on an invisible lure. When Lily closed her eyes she could now see through the vantage of her creation, the front visor where Lantana had sat earlier. She saw herself through those clouded dead eyes, as the mechanical beast, soaring through snow, meandered its way back to The Gravitas. When she finally opened her eyes, it had landed in safety. Its resumed a stoic, warlike stance, and de-activated. Oil spattered the ground its body like incontinent urine. No one had seen its passage, she knew. Snow in Colorado could stay strong, and she knew how to disguise things in a storm.

Two days later, her family returned from the hospital. Everyone seemed to walk as if attached to the strings of a lethargic puppeteer. The man who called himself Argyll Two showed up at their door around the same time, claiming he had a right, an indelible right, to see, and mourn, for Fearghas's body, which he knew was not customary to the Jewish tradition. But after begging, and breaking down a bit, they let him. He claimed that he was actually not Argyll as they'd assumed, but Aargyll, with two A's, and was the fraternal twin brother of the deceased former. As to how he also happened to have a glass eye, however, or how he knew of the direct manner in which his doppelganger had died, he wouldn't share, and, after the coffin was unstapled, stared peacefully at Fearghas's reassembled parts, wrapped in a tachrichim, like cheesecloth.

Though they wanted a private memorial at the cemetery, a hired Rabbi with a last name like Berkowitz had come through hours earlier, mostly to instruct Lantana in the traditions he might not have been able to carry out on his own. This was the chance for Lantana to conduct his father's funeral on his terms, anyway, and he wanted to do it properly. To have a member of a religious order make sure the old son of a bitch's fate would be sealed forevermore.

After the Rabbi was dismissed, Aargyll, as he'd overheard, tore the edge of his lapel. It was his extent of Jewish custom. He crept up to the coffin and said, to the shrouded body, "you saved my brother. I only wish I could have saved you."

He looked mournfully at Lantana.

"You, too."

Lily sat on the front porch, watching as, following his final words to Fearghas, Aargyll with two A's slumped away into a modest Toyota Camry, and puttered around the corner of their cul-de-sac, never to be seen again. For the first time in years, Lily was smoking a cigarette, a hurt little Salem, and her fingers were trembling. Lantana hadn't talked to anyone since the incident, concentrating instead on whispering to his model cars, and listening for answers. Nemo opened the front door and sat next to Lily, inhaling the smoke from her fingers.

She handed it over to him and he took a drag, thankful to indulge a fascination.

"Why didn't you tell me?" he asked, exhaling.

"Tell you what?"

"What you fed me. . ." said Nemo. "The sticky liquid. I saw what it does to you. In Mendocino."

Lily shook her head.

"You're too young to understand."

"Too young to understand what?"

"Anything," she said. Her pupils were small and bare. Strangely, in the cold and wind, she wasn't wearing her lab coat. She wasn't dressed in layers at all. Instead, she was wearing a tee shirt, straight-legged jeans. Her forearms were frigid with pink and blue veins.

"Sometimes people aren't allowed to pursue their dreams in public, so they have to pursue them privately."

"Mom," said Nemo, putting his tiny, twitchless hand on her forearm. "It's never too late to do what you want to do."

Lily looked at Nemo, not tears, but redness forming at the edges of her eyes. She thought about death. About nature. She could have been a leaf from an Empress Tree, spinning violently and free into some Eastern wind. She imagined herself smiling to another man's eyes. She imagined herself feeling truth in her voice as she spoke to him. Then she receded to reality, remembered who and what she was. The choices she'd made flooding into and over the frozen Colorado horizon.

"It's never too late," Nemo said.

"Oh, kiddo," she said, touching her child's forehead. Beyond him, across the street, she saw the man he couldn't see, the man with a beard, the ungodly eyes, waiting so quietly for her soul. He waved at her. She didn't wave back.

"Oh kiddo," she said, full of familiar terror. "For some people. . .it is."

Later in the afternoon, Nemo napped. Lantana was still silently working in the garage on finishing his third model Mustang. He hadn't eaten anything at all. In the hallway next to her son's room, Lily unrolled a ladder from the hatch door to the attic. Taking a deep breath, she climbed inside.

She creaked across the old floorboards with a tact she'd learned to perfect. At the end of the attic were dust-eaten tapestries, sheets and cardboard boxes without labels. She swept the tapestries aside without care. Behind them was a heavy steel door. Jiggling a set of keys, she found the correct one and cockled the lock open. No one ever used this room but her. No one knew how to use this room but her. She pulled on the latch, scraping a familiar divot along the wood. Behind the door was, what her thoughts were telling her, should have been called a monstrosity. But since she felt like her thoughts were only partially her own, she took the statement as ironic. She called it a miracle instead.

The jowls of the man in the cavern behind were brittle where he was suspended from hooks and straps of leather. He had a cracker of chin, a molded cheese of chest and black-lidded skin over empty eyes. Tubes sucked and sprawled from punctures, attached to batteries and generators and casks and cylinders. A papery ventilator stemmed to a tracheotomy and made the lungs dryly expand. At the end of a bag originally intended for blood or saline, a liquid the tint, but not thickness of Maalox, slowly dripped into the plastic. He was being milked like a desiccated udder.

Lily, stoppering the flow, transferred that liquid to an empty vial she kept, amongst others, in a band inside her labcoat. After sipping it, she made an appreciative sound. She said, "Oh, Dad," and smiled wide. "I don't know what I'd do without you." And as she drank her body started to glow. She was seized by the sensation for a moment, of being filled with youth, and then shuddered with release. The man before her was alive. In between death and hell. She remembered all the things he had done to her. The times he'd hurt her by her mother's command; the times he hadn't believed in her, and hadn't known what it meant to be a father. She walked up to his face, caressed his cheek, and then turned to walk away. He'd forced her to do this to him.

As she closed the door, in a mirror on the opposite wall, she thought she saw someone looking at her. A basalt slab of chin. Two iceberg eyes. The man with the violet Himation she'd seen at the gas station the day of the accident, while making love to her husband months ago, minutes earlier across the street. An adolescent figment. Her dybbuk. With her since that first time she tried to take her own life. His green teeth smiled through his beard. Beside him, in a pool of flesh on the floor, was the woman he liked to batter. She was sleeping.

In a gentle voice, hands brittle and suspended like a puppet's, he said, "There is one thing alone that stands the brunt of life throughout its course: a quiet conscience."

"Why did you choose me?" she asked, creeping towards the mirror. "I have nothing to give myself, nonetheless you."

But upon receiving no answer, she nodded her head, accepted the silence and sobbed. The apparition in the mirror disappeared. She remembered where she'd heard that line before, in her youth when she tried to survive reading Euripides.

As she climbed back down the attic ladder, and then down the stairs, she saw a sleekly dressed man standing in the beveled glass window, rapping his fingers on her door. She wondered if he were a hallucination—she knew she was prone to hallucinations now. Something had happened to her brain; in her calmest moments, when no one was looking, manifestations came from her, begging to be noticed. But this man, he seemed to stick to the ground in a way that was heavy, and purposeful. When she undid the lock and twisted the knob he looked upon her with suspicious calm. He had less than a trace of nose, and his chin was unmanly, fatty and fawnish. His eyes headed their way up towards the attic, while straightening his double-simple tie.

"Are you real?" Lily asked him, his Italian dress shoes just outside the doorway.

The man, now holding his hands before his groin, smiled piteously, and took a couple steps forward.

"I'm afraid I am, Ms. Zatkin."

"Oh," said Lily, as if relieved. "Oh."

He removed a badge from beneath his coat, a shyness to him as he did so.

"Daryl Carmichael. F.B.I."

Lily spent a moment attempting to deconstruct the acronym into other, less serious implications, but it did little good. She was on firm ground now. She knew what awaited her.

"You need to come with me."

"I've done nothing wrong," she said. She looked up at the attic as if to incriminate herself. "Why—why are you here? What sort of behavior. . .you shouldn't have ever come to my house! You have no right to be here. . . ."

"Well," said the agent, holding up two identifications, one in each hand. Clarissa Bentley and Lily Zatkin. His feet were quiet against the hardwood. He had sympathetic eyes. Since he'd joined the FBI years ago, homes had become less private than sidewalks or public parks, but, in all truth, it didn't matter. To Lily, he was a suit like all suits. A suit to take her away.

"Apart from the warrant I have for your arrest on statutory rape," he said. "The family of Ms. Bentley thinks otherwise."

"You've got to be a Goddamn joke," Lily laughed.

"I'm afraid I don't have a good sense of humor. But I might be funny to look at. That might be true."

"But after everything I've been through—all that I've suffered. It's not like I hurt anybody. You try living the life that I have and come out on top. It's not easy."

"I know it isn't," the agent said as he put on the handcuffs. He escorted her out her own front doors while her child slept and her husband played, past the mammoth pillars on the porch and the unkempt wilds of frozen lawn. She laughed to herself quietly. She decided not to struggle. "What woman with a brain to gamble doesn't know that you've got to fight for your every last breath? Have you ever smiled? Did you ever mean it? Come on, Mr. Joke. Do you really think you're that funny?" He locked her in a set of handcuffs. "All you men, beasts, toddlers thieves, pugilists with the world in your corner, you never have any idea how hard it can really be for anybody else. Ignorance, Mr. Joke. Ignorance in a suit. It's driving our society off a cliff."

Lantana raged at his wife's disappearance, calling numbers and agencies that wound his hours into one self-anodizing paradox. But after a while, his anger softened. He took to wandering the house for clues of her criminality, still in disbelief at what he'd fine. The attic door had been left open when the agent took Lily away, and so he crept up the creaky stairs, more fearful with each step. He knew that couples kept secrets from each other. But what Lily had been hiding from him in the attic? This corpse, this piteous half-life? The stuff of a serial killer. A collecter of human skin. A dull sense of unknowing ensued his discovery. He sat on his back porch and smoked a stale cigarillo he'd saved for too long. He felt afraid of the fact that he'd loved her.

Nemo, in the meantime, paced back and forth across his room. With his fingers he tore down the stars on the ceiling. Who were his parents? What did he know of family? Had his mother been a witch? A demon? A sadist? A genius? More than abandoned, he felt finished. He felt tired of trying to be awake, and ahead of the next idiot's step. He went beneath the bed and opened the safe. He was not the type to hold a pistol to his own head, but he wondered if he was the type to hold it to another's. He wasn't thinking about the man called Duncan, who'd tortured him, but didn't have a head to speak of anymore; he was thinking about Jeffrey Westcott. The true source of all his pain. His first foray into trust, completely spurned, thrashed aside and left to die.

He decided to follow Jeffrey on his rounds at the basketball courts. He tracked him to Broods, where he bought cheese puffs, and back to his house, with the avidity of an ambitious caterpillar. He faced him in his driveway—it was evening, there was no one on the street—as Jeffrey prepared to skitter on inside, back to his remarkably warm family. His house was a lot more unspectacular than Nemo thought it would be, with a simple concrete porch, brick stairs, and a gambrel roof. He took the gun from his waist and, skittering up alongside unseen, held it out to Jeffrey. Cheese puffs spit from his mouth; he coughed, and tried to speak. Nemo flicked the gun forward, indicating adequacy, and, looking around for witnesses, directed Jeffrey through a path to the local neighborhood park, which was always empty. There he stood him up against a plywood fence in a shadowy alcove behind some wild fescue. The sprinklers hissed on and soaked through their shoes.

"Why?" asked Nemo, not even sure if he cared about the answer as he pushed the pistol into Jeffrey's breastbone. The boy quivered. Nemo could tell he was afraid to speak.

"Tell me," he yelled, thinking that maybe he was like his mother. That he, too, would do something terrible, and, as was meant for him, go to prison, and grow into his cell like an elephant in a dog crate.

"Tell me!"

"I was scared," huffed Jeffrey. "Okay? I was terrified."

"Not good enough."

The pistol he then took to his head.

"You're crazy," the boy said. "You're a fucking psycho."

"I'm tired," said Nemo. "I'm," he stuttered, severed pinky bleeding a little bit through the gauze. "I'm confused."

"Nemo," said Jeffrey, eyes darting to the gun again and again.

"What?"

"I really mean it, man. I was scared. . .Don't you ever get scared?"

"Do I ever get scared? Nemo laughed. "You have NO idea."

"Then you understand."

"I understand that you're a coward," said Nemo, the pistol harder and harder against the skull as his face moved closer. "A fucking coward."

Jeffrey, with a smile, a demented, ambiguous thing that, in the last minute, had gone beyond afraid, crawled across his face. He put one foot forward. One arm forward. He leaned in closer. Nemo watched him do so with horror, and allure. He backed up from the fence. His neck cocked back and then forward as Jeffrey kissed him.

His tongue went deep, before pulling back. He began to rub Nemo's crotch over his jeans.

"You're right," he said, sweat on his lip.

That evening, after the adolescents had spent some time exploring each other in the park, they found a trashcan and, following a couple of vows and apologies, disposed of the gun, shook hands, and agreed to never speak again. It was a necessary conversation. Nemo was changing districts, anyway, and would never enter Smoky Hill High. He knew that the world was much like him, raw and unformed. There would be no room for commitments, and all former identities would have to be left behind.

After some detailed snooping, Lantana searched Lily's purse, and discovered maps providing the apparent location of what seemed to be a nuclear bomb. A nuclear bomb the great-great-grandson of Beamish had stowed in storage shed near their house, in Broomfield, Colorado, for some unexplainable reason. Lantana knew this was the last thing his family needed. Not if he cared at all about his son's future. What would happen if the feds returned and found that information? He wouldn't be spared the cuffs.

The next day, Nemo and Lantana thus made their way towards that shed, tacit, slow-moving, to uncover what T.H.E.Y. had been hiding, and for a reason they never would quite know. Nemo found the trip long, but soothing. Spring was coming. Snow was melting. The sun was bleeding down, Jeffrey Westcott's lips had forever changed the construct of his memory, how he would come to view past and present. Both sensations were warm.

As Lantana fretted, the map was as correct as it could have been. With a forklift, a tarp for privacy, Carl, Daphne, and a whole lot of patience, they gradually excavated a 50 megaton capsule, which they suspected was old and nuetralized. They transported it carefully home in Merl Takote's pickup truck under the tarps, secured by bungee cords and tough vinyl ropes. It seemed a poor idea at the time, but it was better than no idea at all. When they arrived home, they loaded the bomb into the third garage, and went to snag Fearghas's coffin. Carl and Daphne, in a stroke of not altogether unusual happenstance, had gotten together after the injury, being that Carl, for all his uncomfortabilities with gender, all his insecurities, was disfigured, and because of it a marginally changed man. He and Daphne held hands almost violently as they readied themselves for the funeral. Whenever she walked away, even to the bathroom or for a beverage, Carl became anxious and looked to his toes.

In the back yard, they prepared to bury the bomb. All, save for Nemo, wore half-torn ribbons on their right breasts. After they began to dig, it took them hours. Lantana, along with Carl, had done their homework to find out whether the bomb was dormant enough; after determining it was, they began the ceremony. Beside Lily's greenhouse they'd created a massive crater. They forklifted the bomb down into it, this ovoid, dirtied-white, broken down capsule. If someone made a mistake, if it was still active, the only way to know would be if one day it exploded and sent Arapahoe Falls to the moon. When Lantana saw it nestled in the soil he felt like he was burying his own Terra Cotta Warrior. The letters across its hub read Tsar Bomba, like the one Lantana had screamed away at the battle for Kansas, and he scratched his head. Did they all have that inscription? Nemo looked down at this dark, human secret. This ability to harness light into death. They began to heave dirt in the air.

"Well," said Lantana, sticking his shovel in the grass. "This isn't right."

"What isn't right?" asked Nemo, back in his deerstalker cap. His eyes were wide and somber.

Daphne, tying the bottom of her shirt above her navel, said, "I'm getting all sweaty."

"Carl?" said Lantana.

"Licious?"

"Give me a hand."

A couple minutes later they came outside lugging the casket. They were going to take it to a Jewish funeral plot in Denver, but plans changed last minute. Holding it over the Atom Bomb's grave, they opened the lid and let Fearghas's reassembled remains tumble out like packings for a picnic.

"Are you sure about this?" asked Carl, putting his hand on Lantana's back. Today, he wasn't wearing his Spandex, but a pair of sweat pants to the middle of his waist with a Van Halen logo across the asscheeks.

"We already paid for the plot," said Nemo.

"It's my father," claimed Lantana, removing something from his pocket. The empty box. He dropped it to the ground, kicked it in. Then, upon further reflection, he ran into the house and returned with his toga and shiny titanium club and threw them in with it. "It's my father. And I want him here, in my backyard, just so I can make sure he stays there, with the nuclear waste."

They all nodded and continued to shovel dirt. Nemo covered his nose from the smell. As they continued, Lantana handed him a plastic grocery bag, torn through at a couple ends. Inside was *The Manaton*.

"I'll leave this one to you, buddy," he said, clopping him on the head with affection.

Nemo held the book over the open grave. He watched his father shoveling dirt. He felt so sorry for him, as if Lantana, as an aging man, was only now beginning to understand how capacious the universe was. Unfortunately, however, it was also getting late. His sun was setting. His horizon, rising up, so quick, to meet it. How much more time could he spend in the daylight? He'd made home, a child, and in the process his beginnings had passed into twilight. In some ways he was as old as Nemo was. In some ways, his spirit was just beginning to take flight. In his sweatpants he turned to glimpse his son, so it seemed, just to see how far the boy had come, and then returned to shoveling, with patience and grace, as if slowly digging out his ethical code.

"Are you gonna throw it in, Wow?" asked Daphne, wiping her forehead. Carl, with his scar festering from eye to chin, looked over his back and paused.

Nemo's tiny, four-and-a-half-fingered hand trembled for his father, his mother, and all of their posthumous dreams. It trembled for the hateful words and tender touch of Jeffrey Westcott, the sensations of hope and disaster he'd felt as they'd been his very last. Should he do away with this bane on his family, he wondered? What had destroyed his and his mother and father's life for years without mercy or care? He looked above him for a sign, an answer, a shape in the clouds, a shape like the one he'd seen on the ceiling in Mendocino, his childhood room and in the brain of the beast. There was only an empty, vast blue sky spinning off into the ineffable.

ANOTHER EXCERPT FROM THE INCREASINGLY MATERIAL JOURNAL OF MALACH DENNY

The more that life knows itself, the more it begins to take form. Yes, I am older now, which means that I have come to understand time, days, years, even weeks, I'm proud to say, as postulates to track my physical progress. I have approximated that I am approaching my early fifties in earth years, and that, along with that approximation, a sense of nostalgia, accompanied by restlessness, has settled into something like my heart. As a supposedly immaterial Malach, I am now afraid to die, for as I look upon my maker and the weaknesses that take hold of him day and night, I see that, just to touch, just to feel and think, is more precious than anyone gives credit for, and that to lose those possibilities: the closest plenary equivalent to hell. Anything that exists doesn't have the capacity to really understand a single second for what it is. How, in every imploding instant, the eyes and eyes of others are furious at work. My wings don't function the way they used to, and the rest of me has followed suit. But still, I savor their slow degradation. The pain is still sensation. I live.

My heroic impulse, as you might have witnessed when I drove my maker from the bullet bound from his brain that instead shattered his testicle, was the best I could do. Years ago I might have been able to keep it from hitting him completely. Things have most certainly changed.

Change is not all a bad thing, however.

Invincibility is a concept my maker took for granted—which is what I tried to keep him from doing in the desert—but it was also that same determined idiocy that aided him through the direr times of his life. His father, for instance. Who would have ever expected that the amazing bastard Fearghas was still alive?

Though I have learned to perceive the actions of men as near-omniscient thoughts and urges, this one I could have never seen coming. Apparently, that day, before DiMaggio's Café, such a slight of hand was pulled that it altered the heavens, not in death, but deception. I can't even describe that which took place, but know it involved the reassembled carcasses of pigs.

As for the Dybbuk, however, it lived out its dark wishes in possession of poor Lily Zatkin. Over time, the one called H drove her to insanity, to the point where she fed off the living to strengthen his own selfish spirit.

What a rule to break. To take life, to give life.

The power provoked.

Abomination.

Near the end, before her arrest, her thoughts were only half her own. Imagine the tree of life, Etz HaChayim, or even better, the oak and linden tree of Baucis and Philemon, except uprooted and scrapped for the tafts of twenty magical spears. This is the tale of Lily Zatkin. An organism harvested for miracles. However, we must remember that, in the end, I may have not watched any of this occur, because I am still not sure if I exist, even as I die. As time has gone on, I have become convinced that my thoughts and actions are so controlled by the hand of a distant sadist, that I have no autonomous way to choose what I do, and when. But the boy, the Nemo, he has made me know some things. For example, he has given me identity.

What pureness resides in a child who thinks, and is, and doesn't care for the beliefs of others? If history is a snake that eats itself, than boys like he are meant to rip the head from the tail, milk venom from the teeth, sheer the scales, and braid them back together. This is how revolution takes place. By forgetting the sins of the father. I placed myself inside his dreams, and from them, a new Me was born. A new Denny. One that could inseminate his maker's child with what I can only refer to as seed. Even a Malach, then, can pass on its wisdom, as it waits for its maker to die.

There were no more miracles that fell to the earth on the night of T.H.E.Y.'s quietus. No shapes made by paper birds in the sky. Maybe it was because the heavens took pity, and wouldn't allow such awful disruptions in the fabric of right and wrong to manifest itself in my open skies. Or maybe it was because, over the time in which I have come to know myself, I have come to understand that, in the case of burdens, each side has something to bear. There is nothing magical about irony except for the fact that it negates itself, making, not only, for a lack of miracles, but a lack of fullness and truth. I feel sorry for death itself, that it has to be associated with the tragedy of life.

As my feathers fade from me, I see that I look like a fading peony, a dying, spectacular, silver thing shedding it's petals to a cold winter wind, but not too cold; a silver lake, warm and bio-logical, a reflection for me, as a Malach, a servant, a nonexistent reflection to cry for, as I take leave of my duty.

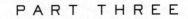

PART THREE

SUBMISSIVE MEMORY

When the stars threw down their spears,
And watered heaven with their tears,
Did he smile his work to see?
Did he who made the Lamb make thee?

—William Blake

CHAPTER THIRTY THREE

SUBMISSIVE MEMORY

It had been years since Neal saw his father. America had just elected Earnest Oswald—or 'Earnest Oz,' in line with the campaign slogan—the Republican incumbent from New York, to become its 46th president. This followed the almost terrifying economic reboot of 2016, and a few years of liberal growth, both in turn cancelled out by a terrorist attack at the Port of Oakland that the administration hadn't prevented. Earnest Oz ran on the perennial platform of aiding small businesses, lowering taxes, flexing muscles to ruthless outsiders, and shrinking an already-small government, while, at the same time, plotting to unleash an arsenal of conservative social ambitions dating back to the Reagan era, or even further. He won the 2024 election by a landslide, and immediately after repealed Kidfree, a children's healthcare program, before grandstanding in the face of the Saudis. But, then again, in times of economic prosperity, especially when combined with the threat of war, Americans always became conservative. It was if they were infected by centurial pathogens that made them near sighted, and encouraged them to fear for their comfort.

There were three wars being fought over seas in the Arab world and South East Asia (all begun during moderate-liberal Albert Liaw's first serving term, strangely enough), with U.S. forces spread thinner than they'd been, even during the early 2000s. The administration, despite all its good efforts, had been unable to bring them home. Today's news, however, was China's currency had taken a flaming nosedive due to the recent Han revolts, still in flux, which in turn made the dollar skyrocket, and Americans could expect to enjoy a particular boost of luxury spending in a select 19% of the population, and on the upper fringes of the middle class. Against some expectations of the far left and right, luxury, affordability, and success itself was actually boosting once-considered minority populations into fiscally secure partialities. It was becoming harder to see Republicans as good old white boys from Texas and Tennessee. America was becoming a country where the dollar ruled all, and money could be expected to trump skin. The leader of Exxon Mobile was a Samoan named Buster, and a Japanese/Nigerian woman, Sally Takamura, had taken control of Pfizer at the end of 2019. Neither of them would concede to the latest clean air initiatives to come out of Japan and Scandinavia. The United States were still united, anyway, and soil could keep people warm enough not to care if the air around them turned cold.

Most trends were consistently continuing along the same lines they'd been in the early turn of the century. In America, Europe, and parts of Asia—Thailand, India, Cambodia—the average life expectancy was rising, in other parts of the world, spinning so wildly downwards that even the scroogier western politicians, fearing the worst, became concerned for the future of business. What had been China for capitalism, and then India, was trying to winnow its way into Africa. The Savage, Neal's father, who had changed his name back to Lenard Sikophsky in lieu of T.H.E.Y.'s death, was long in retirement. And happily so. He'd spawned a whole load of admirers, fanboys, copycats, all of which were widely unsuccessful, for mortal reasons, and refused repeated attempts by the U.S. military to call him back into service against the threat of terrorism, which was currently needling its way up the Mexican border at the behest of ancient Middle East insurgents, paid in divinity to export the revolution.

His wife Lily's dealings pre-incarceration led to a government-led research initiative on longevity a decade ago, following the ending tenure of the Obama administration. It was now called The Immortality Impetus, and was carried out by nominalizing certain proteins from one human's cells and using them to keep another's healthy. There were two scientists, one in Osaka and another in Berkeley, California, and their four test subjects, who had lived past the age of one hundred and nineteen safely (without seriously harming the transfuser). The oldest of which, the oldest in the world, was still surviving with the ability to walk and talk to the age one hundred and forty nine. There were several violent occurrences associated with the research, mostly because of an unstable chemical compound referred to as Atom, but they were covered up soon after in the media, and denounced as rumors (who shot lighting from his hands, anyway?). Electric planes were the new big thing, utilizing a hydrogen engine to reduce the use of rocket fuel. There was talk of making science fiction a reality in space with a fair amount of certainty with the implementation of light sails and plasma shields, but not at least for another twenty-five years. The polar caps were still melting, quickly, and though much could be done to stop them, it was safe to say humans would have to deal with a wetter world.

Neal was tired from last week's project. Days and days of blurring his eyes so that other people's—wealthy people's—lives could be easier. He never knew why he decided to become a CPA. N.I.L. was the name of his firm and he sometimes forgot what it stood for. After all the time he spent drawing and painting during his college years it was a miracle he'd mustered the guts to leave it all behind. As his plane lifted out of New J.F.K. with the warm aquatic boom of twin Zanburn engines (as they were called), he thought about the changeless nature of his world, and the fact that it also seemed to change so much. Humans, as a species, were pretty much the same in their vices and vagrancies, just like he was in his, but the globe's collective mind had evolved like an unconscious tide—so tall, so fat, it couldn't see its bottom, but when it crashed, made itself known.

Going from New York City, where he now lived in a gentrified South Bronx apartment with his husband Greg and their daughter, May, to Colorado, to the sleepy cardboard myopia of Arapahoe Falls, was also a hazy form of magic. Manhattan left him like insanity, an unalterable pylon of creativity and stray human atoms, and, when he landed at D.I.A., was replaced with immediate dullness. He was reminded of brighter places as Greg, sitting in the aisle seat, chewed sleepily on a breadstick, which he broke off out of a waxy package and handed to May. She was in the middle of them with her head on a tourniquet, smiling back and forth, and then bouncing.

Family, Neal smiled to himself. A sturdy little nest.

The abandoned chrysalis of dustier minds cluttered the Colorado highways and streets. On their way out of the airport before the taxis and shuttles, Greg turned to him, kissed him on the cheek, and then asked, "Can we do that here?"

Neal kissed him back, this time on the lips. He had thick, full lips that loved like they swallowed.

"I don't care if it's okay or not."

"If what's okay?" asked May.

She held both their hands in a greedy fashion, as if she was the only way the two of them could exist. She had the perfect mix of his and Greg's features. And fortunately so. The decision to ask Greg's sister, Lynn, to be a surrogate for Neal's sperm was their final commitment to each other, their writ in stone, and even though it rubbed the nerves of their parents, who were born in the early 1970's and were still a little old fashioned, she eventually agreed and produced the little miracle that was May. She had Neal's nose and mouth, Greg's tabular, Taiwanese eyes, but this sense of joy that had come from neither of them. No one, and Neal meant no one, he'd ever met had ever possessed that sort of joy. But that could have also been because she was his daughter. The love he felt for her could fill craters on the moon.

"If what's okay?" she asked again, tugging the collar of Greg's jacket. She was almost six, and talking more and more every day.

"Nothing at all, Diamond Drop," Neal said, and Greg looked at him insistently.

"She'll have to know how things are out here. Away from home."

"Yea," said Neal, fingering the keys of the rent-a-car. A Dodge Fiat Magnus 3, the biggest piece of shit to hit the planet. "Someday."

Neal hadn't seen his father in years, but it wasn't because he didn't want to. More than that, Lenard was an immortally self-sufficient bastard of a man, and never insisted on anyone helping him do anything at all. "Take care of your own damn life," he'd say with a ruined smile through the six-centimeter oxi-glass screen of Neal or Greg's iPhone Zx718291495ssssG. Even after the cancer came back, and the lymphoma returned faster than modern medicine could pace. "Don't worry about your old man. I've fought harder battles than this. Fuck you. Lose my number."

And for the most part Neal obeyed. They had May, anyway, and Lenard didn't like to travel any further than the neighborhood market, which was still Broods, to stock up on weekly rations of the shit he called food. But now, the lymphoma had gotten worse. His nodes were unable to squeeze themselves clean. His doctor, a well-meaning woman named Anaheim Dahl, surmised that the inability for the anti-cancer biologics to combat the tumors were being walled up, in all possibility, by the plutonium compound he'd stored in his system. It gave him strength, yes, remarkable strength—Dahl was amazed by the effects.But at a certain point in his life, as opposed to sustaining him, it began to accelerate his death.

"What madman could have done this?" she'd say, angry with the fact that she couldn't get the cancer to budge, despite all the life-defying treatments that kept people from dying this slow, sad, death these days.

"He's buried in my back yard," Lenard would say, squinting his entire face."If you want to see him."

And then they'd both manage to laugh, though the doctor was not exactly sure why.

As Neal, Greg, and May pulled up through the still-unchanged Arapahoe Falls, they were all confronted with the fearful prospect that some places, and people, could be completely left behind. May shined through it as she indefinitely would, but Neal, and even Greg, who had carefully chosen artistry as a way to escape reality, were stirred by this abandoned ghoulscape. After the great recession, and the rising/falling stagnancy of the Teens, the boom captured only about one-third of the continent, and left the rest in impregnable stasis. Everything looked the same as it had when Neal was still Nemo. The stenciled lawns and their earnest upkeep. Suspicious suburbanites with eyes set to shunning both residents and outsiders.

"I admire you," Greg said. "For growing up in a world like this."

"Admire me?" Neal said, thinking of the tumult of his teens, the fact that, after his mother was incarcerated, there was nothing left of growing up. "You had it much tougher than I did."

"Oh please," said Greg. "My family was amongst the guilt-trip-you-conservative, I don't want my son to be a fag but I guess I'll accept if I have to variety. They bitched and moaned a lot, but I was raised in The Presidio."

"Bitched?" piped May.

Neal clucked his tongue at Greg.

"Sorry, Diamond Drop," said Greg, arching his neck around the seat. "Daddy said a bad word."

"And where do bad words belong?" asked Neal.

May thought for a second.

"In the compost," she said.

They both brimmed with a little bit of pretentious, eco-conscious warmth.

Pulling up the driveway, Neal could already notice his father hadn't done a thing to maintain the property since he'd last been there. And not because of money. The rights to The Immortality Impetus kept all their pockets filled. What hadn't gone to lawsuits, anyway. As long as the government could go through the blood and history of Lenard and his family without limit, the checks would keep coming.

"Oh, Dad," said Neal, as they drew their luggage from the trunk and looked upon the banditry that had become 24 Survival Drive.

May jumped up the driveway and then, looking around, said, with histrionic disgust, "it's dirty."

Greg took her hand. "I know," he said. "But when you meet Grandpa, try and keep that a secret."

Thankfully it was spring and the hoarfrost of winter had been cajoled by biannual flowers floating through the neighbor's lawns. Lenard's house was overgrown with tall weeds and grass and, in some dryer patches where the earth had been hit with herbicide, dog shit, rigor mortising in the dirt. There were a few shattered boards of plywood strewn along the driveway.

After inspection they seemed to have fallen from the rooftop. The driveway was sealed shut by dirt and leaves. Unspeakable things bunched in the gutters.

They approached the front door, a gnawed down board of tobacco brown mahogany. Neal rang the doorbell, but it issued no sound, so May jumped up and knocked on the wood.

"We're going to see Grandpa," she said.

"Yea," said Greg. "But it won't be like on the Lomprompt."

"Grandpa's a little sick," said Neal. "Like we talked about at home."

A few moments later, the door cracked open, and there was Lenard. In a wheel chair.

"Well, hey there, you two," he said, scanning over his son and Greg. His eyebrows were like two pulled apart cotton balls stuck back on with bad glue. When the light swam to them, they turned yellow.

"And you," he said, looking down at the raven haired child dressed in acid washed overalls from some East Village boutique. "Who are you?"

"May," she said, nervously turning her head. She grasped at Greg's pant leg.

"Sorry, Dad," said Neal. "She's a little cranky."

"Long flight?" asked Lenard.

"Long flight."

"Come on, DD, give Grandpa a kiss."

They came in and made themselves what they could at home. There was a bad smell in the air, and the feeling that, though everything had been organized, beneath that organization was a self-breeding toxicity. There were pictures on the mantle in the living room, shoddily suspended over a nineties panoramic television that probably couldn't connect to Informational Cable. They'd never taken many pictures when Neal was young, but there were a couple—him, as an infant, for example, with a sailor's cap he looked oblivious to wearing. In elementary school, and at his college graduation at Penn State, with a beard. There was one of Steve Two, fat and sitting. And one vague printing of Lily, though it was hard to see her face.

While Greg was escorting May for a walk around the block, Neal began unpacking their bags. He'd resolved not to unload anything into the drawers and closets, fearing what he'd disturb. He looked out the window of what used to be his room and found, apart from the fact that it had been stripped of his mother's stars and repainted, the view was immaculate. Whoever had moved in across the street had repaved their walkway with flagstone. Besides that, nothing had changed.

"Don't get nostalgic," said Lenard. Neal turned to find him standing at the doorway out of his wheelchair. He could walk, though the doctors didn't recommend it. With each step he was probably in pain.

"Oh, I wasn't," said Neal, closing the blinds. "I see the neighbors re-paved their walkways."

"He's cheating on his wife," Lenard said.

"What?"

"The neighbor with the walkway. I've seen him screwing around with that fat flight attendant's wife next door."

"Dad," scolded Neal.

"Oh, give me a break," he grinned. "Like I give a damn."

Neal walked towards his father, gave him a hug. It seemed to shock him at first, but then he gripped him so fiercely Neal feared for the safety of his bones.

"Are you okay, Dad?" he asked, returning to his face. "I mean, with what just happened?"

"Oh, you know," he said, stepping around their baggage to the window, which he reopened. "Your mother was always an unhappy woman. If it didn't happen before she got out of the pen, than it would have soon after."

"So then. . . ."

"She hung herself, kiddo. Right before parole. What do you want me to say, that I processed it?"

"Jesus," said Neal. "You didn't have to say it like that."

"Well, that's how it happened. So that's what I'll say."

Lenard opened the window, letting the air rush in. Though parts of him, his face, eyes, his shiny bald dome of head looked old and haggard with disease, his frame was still strong. If Nemo had passed him without knowing him on the street, he could have mistaken him for a retired heavyweight.

"The doctors said her body, on autopsy, had the blood work of a sixteen year old girl," said Lenard, impressed. "Apparently she could have lived on for years."

"Amazing," said Neal.

"Something like that," said Lenard. "Or another Goddamn thing I never knew about her. And here I am, dying faster than a Ferrari. I suppose I was missing something along the way, wasn't I?"

"I know, Dad," said Neal. "Life isn't easy."

"Your damn right it's not easy," he said. "When I was young, I thought I knew a lot, but now I've realized I didn't know anything. And yes, I know that's been said before."

"You're right," said Neal. "That has been said before. By a lot of people."

"But a lot of things have been said before," Lenard said, rolling his eyes. "Like your mother, I always knew she didn't love me. Or at least I knew somewhere, deep inside. She loved an idea. She loved the freedom that came from fucking daydreams. And that's been said before, but it's nonetheless true: that you can't love someone who doesn't love you in return."

"She loved you Dad. She was just troubled."

"She hated me, kiddo. I wanted her to love me, and I think she wanted herself to love me too, so much so that she and I made you, and tried to raise you in what we thought was the right way. Or what I thought was the right way. It wasn't, though. She was always smarter than me. She was weaker, but smarter. I take responsibility for everything. Even her death."

As Lenard laughed at what seemed to be the absurdity of his own statement, Neal didn't try and correct him.

"People can try and do right for themselves, but when you're me, life has no sense of humor. I once thought: if only I could make her laugh, amuse her, make her see what I see in her, than we could experience the truest sort of happiness. . . ."

They heard laughter as May and Greg came around the corner and up the driveway.

Lenard smiled.

"But then I look at you, and your silly little boyfriend, and that dazzling creature that is your child, and, I know that I've done a little bit of good."

"You've done a lot of good, Dad," said Neal, putting his arm around his shoulder. He was oddly comforted by that deleterious sense of tough love people often talked about in the older generations. "Don't kid yourself. You've evolved."

"That's horseshit," said Lenard. "I still feel horrible things inside me. Prejudices, stupidities, all fostered in my youth. I've just learned to hate those things, now. Know they're wrong when I see them."

"That means you've become a good man."

"No," Lenard laughed. "It just means that I've learned how to exist without endangering others." He bent down to the bedside where he sat, trembling a little. He tried to smile the pain away, and failed. "Which I guess is a good thing. If you believe in right and wrong. You look just like her, you know. Your mother. Young beyond your years. Striking in the eyes. That immortal laughter. Ha—maybe you'll never grow up. Live twenty lifetimes, you know?"

The next couple of days were spent in a creaking attic of conversation, with the occasional, shrieking purity of May and her voice as she warmed up to Lenard and learned to call him Papa, and weeded her little arms around his neck to give him quick kisses on the cheek. He chased her around the house until his feet couldn't take it anymore, and then he used his wheelchair, until his arms couldn't take it anymore, and then he found himself confined to bed. Doctor Dahl called, said that he likely had little time left. Greg bought May a plastic toy, a lawnmower with bubbles that popped as she ran it across the lawn. She kissed Lenard once more on the cheek, and then went outside to play. Greg watched her from the doorstep. The sun approached noon. As she played, she looked up and thought she saw wings, a circle of them, crackling for an instant, before they seemed unable to bear their own weight, and fade into dust.

"Look, Daddy," she said. "A dying bird."

Greg squinted to the sun.

"I don't see anything."

Neal, upstairs in his father's room, stayed with his father for what could have been a couple of hours, but seemed like twenty minutes, looking out the window. Around high noon, when the sun was at its pinnacle, Lenard Sikophsky died.

He'd requested to be cremated and tossed anywhere air was present, but Neal, knowing what his father really meant, packed the urn of his remains into his bag. He packed his mother's as well—an even less pleasant experience being that he had to retrieve them from the coroner's office at Centennial Women's Correctional. He took them both down to the Smoky Hill creek. He tried to scatter them over the water—it flowed swift in the summer—but the ash slipped backwards beneath his feet and wandered off into the prairie.

With May and Greg standing beside him, he took a piece of paper from his pocket.

"The butterfly is of the order Lepidoptera," he read. "And that means, unlike many species, that birth, or rebirth, happens many, many times. Imagine that most creatures spark into being as smaller, often defenseless versions of their older selves. A newborn baby has tiny fingers that will one day develop into larger fingers, with wrinkled knuckles. A butterfly, however, is born as a caterpillar, a sluggish, naked-looking thing, and then, as opposed to growing into a larger caterpillar, cocoons itself in a state of rewind. Later, after a mystery of growth, emerges this beauty so uncanny that even higher minds feel shy. Is it because we, like the butterfly, long for many births? Is it because we only think we have one?

"It is true that, when I was a child, my mother gave me a present, a striking peablue butterfly with gossamer wings, along with another gift, one that is gone, or, if still skulking from hand to hand, has been used to do what captivity did to Pinocchio. A thread on a finger. A broken kite. My parents, they spent their lives in various stages of birth and rebirth. It is true that Lily, Laura, Lantana, Lenard, knew pain well. Ethereal pain. Bright, momentous pain. Symbols of broad, sweeping dreams."

From his pocket he took an envelope, the same one he'd placed below the gun years ago, with the pulverized body of Pinocchio inside. The river ate the insides quickly, since there was nothing but glitter and dust.

They flew back to New York the next day. May went back to school. Greg was working on a new installation at a private gallery in Midtown dealing with what America had left behind. Neal, however, found himself unable to return to work immediately, and spent the first day passing through the parts of Manhattan that had always made him feel sane. He had Cuban corn with queso blanco, lime, in SoHo, and sat at the hub of Union Square listening to a stringy Indian man in threadbare jeans sing out the edges of his angst. He went to the bank to open his safety deposit box. He took what was inside and held it to his chest, held it tight, and contemplated disposing of it many, many times before catching the 1 line, to the Village, to pick up May. She passed through the front doors at her teacher's heel, saw Neal and ran to embrace him. He held her in his arms as if he'd never held his child in his arms before. He thought she wasn't real.

She was mana.

In the year 2024, in Tompkins Square Park, he sat her down on a park bench and revealed what he'd taken from the safety deposit box.

"That's an old book, isn't it Daddy?" she said, running her fingers down *The Manaton's* bind.

"It's a very old book," he said, watching her tiny fingers. "And it's very special."

"Why is it special, Daddy?" she asked, before the low clouds of spring and their tendrils.

"Because," he said, watching his daughter's sinless eyes. "It's the type of book that can be rewritten."

SAMUEL SATTIN is a graduate of the Mills College MFA in creative writing and the recipient of NYS and SLS fellowships. His work has appeared in *Salon, io9, Kotaku, The Good Men Project, The Cobalt Review, Cent Magazine,* and *Generations*. He is currently a Contributing Editor at *The Weeklings* and lives in Oakland, California with his wife and beagle. *League of Somebodies* is his first novel. More at www.samuelsattin.net.